TUNNEL THROUGH THE VOID

A hideous darkness filled the wizard's study, like a wavering cloud. Caris could see through its edges to where the candles still burned. But they shed no illumination into the heart of that well of black space that stretched into a falling eternity of nowhere.

Far along that darkness, Caris thought he saw a dim figure fleeing, a stir of movement in those terrible depths. In those terrible depths, the blackness retreated, farther and farther in an endless plunge that never seemed to reach the opposite end.

Caris cried, "NO!"

His sword was in his hand as he plunged after that retreating shape into the darkness, and the cold abyss swallowed him up.

By Barbara Hambly
Published by Ballantine Books:

DRAGONSBANE

THE LADIES OF MANDRIGYN

THE SILENT TOWER

The Darwath Trilogy:
TIME OF THE DARK
THE WALLS OF AIR
THE ARMIES OF DAYLIGHT

The Silent Tower

Barbara Hambly

A Del Rey Book

BALLANTINE BOOKS • NEW YORK

A Del Rey Book
Published by Ballantine Books
Copyright © 1986 by Barbara Hambly

All rights reserved under International and Pan-American Copyright Conventions. Published in the United States of America by
Ballantine Books, a division of Random House, Inc., New York,
and simultaneously in Canada by Random House of Canada Limited, Toronto.

Library of Congress Catalog Card Number: 86-90956

ISBN 0-345-33764-6

Manufactured in the United States of America

First Edition: December 1986

Cover Art by Darrell K. Sweet

TO THE MEMORY OF
JUDY-LYNN

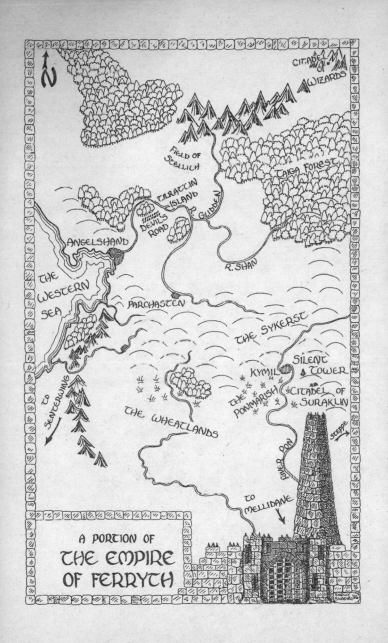

A PORTION OF
THE EMPIRE
OF FERRYTH

CHAPTER I

"HAS THE ARCHMAGE RETURNED?"

The wizard Thirle looked up sharply at Caris' question, strongly reminding the young man of a fat gray field rabbit at the crack of a twig. Then he relaxed a little. "Not yet." He picked up the garden trowel he'd dropped when Caris' shadow had fallen over him on the brick steps of his house, where he had been kneeling. He got to his feet with the awkward care of the very fat and dusted off his black robe. "Can I help you?"

Caris hesitated, his right hand resting loosely around the hilt of the sword thrust through his frayed silk sash. He cast a quick glance at the doorway of the house next door. Like all the houses on the Mages' Yard, it rose tall, narrow, and cramped-looking from the flagstones of the little court, dingy with age and factory soot. Two or three of the other sasenna, the archaic order of sworn warriors, lingered, waiting for him on the steps. Like him, they were clothed in the loose black garments of their order, crisscrossed with

1

sword sashes and weapons belts; and like him, they were sweaty, bruised, and exhausted from the afternoon's session with the swordmaster. He shook his head, and they passed into the shadows of the carved slot of the doorway.

"I don't know." He turned back to Thirle, noting automatically, as a sasennan must, the tiny details—the sweat on his brow, the twitch of his earth-stained fingers—and wondered what it was that troubled him. "That is . . ."

The look of preoccupied nervousness faded from the fat man's eyes, replaced by genuine concern. "What is it, lad?"

For a moment, Caris debated about simply shrugging the problem off, pushing it aside as he had pushed it aside last night, and returning to the only matters which should concern the sasennan—serving his masters the mages and bettering his own skills in the arts of war. "I don't know whether I should be asking this or not," he began diffidently. "I know it isn't the Way of the Sasenna to ask—a weapon asks no questions of the hand that wields it. But . . ."

Thirle smiled and shook his head. "My dear Caris, how do we know what the dagger thinks when it's sheathed, or what swords fear in the armory when the lights are out? You know I've never approved of this business of the sasenna being—being like those machines that weave cloth and spin thread in the mills, that do one job only and don't care what it is."

Under the warm twinkle in his eyes Caris relaxed a little and managed a grin at Thirle's heresy.

Of the dozen or more houses around that small cobblestoned court on the edge of the ghetto of the Old Believers, only eight actually belonged to the Council of Wizards; of those, three were rented out to those—mostly Old Believers—who were willing to live near wizards. Few mages cared to live in the city of Angelshand. Of those few, Caris had always liked Thirle.

The Archmage, Caris' grandfather, had been absent since Caris had come out of the morning's training. If he did not return before dinner, there was little chance Caris would be able to speak with him until tomorrow.

It was not the Way of the Sasenna to fear, and Caris did not think he could endure another unsleeping night with the secret of his fear gnawing his heart.

But having spent the last five years in rigorous training of muscle and nerves, he was uncertain how to speak of fear. Nervously, he ran his scarred fingers through his short-cropped blond hair, now stiff with the drying sweat of training. "I don't know whether I should speak of this," he said hesitantly. "It's just that—A weapon wasn't always what I was." He struggled with himself for a moment, then asked, "Is there any way that a mage can lose his magic?"

Thirle's reaction was as unexpected as it was violent. A flush of anger mottled the fat cheeks and layers of chin. "No!" He almost shouted the word. "We are born with powers, some greater, some lesser. They are like our flesh, like our souls."

Confused at this rage, Caris began, "Not even . . ."

"Be silent!" Thirle's face had gone yellow as tallow now with fury. "You might have been mageborn to begin with boy, but your powers never amounted to anything. There's no way you could know about power. You are forbidden to speak of it. Forbidden!" he added furiously, as Caris opened his mouth to explain.

To be sasenna is first to serve; when, after three years' grueling training in the arts of war and the sneakier deaths of peacetime, Caris had made the last decision of his life, he had sworn his warrior's vows to the Council of Wizards. The vows held good. He closed his mouth, willing himself not to feel the scathe of astonished hurt, and made himself incline his head.

His hands shaking, Thirle picked up his trowel and watering can and hurried through the door of the house, slamming it behind him. Standing on the step, Caris observed that the little mage had been so agitated that he'd left half his beloved pot-plants, which clustered the step and every windowsill within reach, unwatered. Across the city, the big clock on the St. Cyr fortress began striking five. Caris would have less than an hour for dinner before going on duty in the refectory when the mages ate.

Confused, Caris moved down the step with the sasennan's lithe walk. He felt shocked and stung, as if he had been unexpectedly bitten by a loved old dog; but then, he reflected a little bitterly, it was not the Way of the Sasenna to pat even a loved and toothless old dog without one hand on one's knife. He made his way to the house next door that was shared by the novice mages and the sasenna of the Council with the frightening chill that lay in his heart unassuaged.

It was years since Caris had even thought of himself as mageborn. He was nineteen, and for five years he had given himself, heart and soul, to the Way of Sasenna. But he had originally entered it, as many mageborn did, only as the gateway to greater learning which had never materialized.

His powers, he knew, had never been much—a sharpness of sight in the dark and a certain facility for finding lost objects. In his childhood he had desperately wanted to become a mage and to take the vows of the Council of Wizards in order to serve and be with his grandfather, who even then had been the Archmage. From studying the Way of Sasenna as a means to an end, it had become an end in itself; when he had realized, as he eventually had, that his powers were insufficient to permit him to become a wizard, he had remained as a sasennan. When it had come time to take his warrior's vows, it was to the Council that he had taken them.

Was that why Thirle had refused to reply? he wondered. Because Caris, having what he had, had turned from it?

It might have explained his refusal to answer, but, thought Caris uneasily, it did not explain the note of fear in his voice.

At dinner that night Thirle was absent—odd, for though the wizards in general ate plainly, the little botanist was still very fond of the pleasures of the table.

There were seven wizards and two novices who lived in the Court. The fourteen sasenna who served them regularly traded off dinner duty, some serving, some standing guard, as there were always sasenna standing guard somewhere in the Yard—a few still sleeping, or just waked and ready to go on night watch. Though few of the thieves and cut-purses that swarmed the dark slums of Angelshand would go near the Yard, the mageborn had long ago learned that it never paid to be completely unguarded.

A little uneasily, Caris noted that the Archmage had not yet returned. His place at the high table had been taken by the Lady Rosamund, a beautiful woman of about forty, who had been born Lady Rosamund Kentacre. Her father, the Earl Maritime, had disowned her when she had sworn the vows of the Council of Wizards—not, Caris had heard rumored, because in doing so she had revealed herself to be mageborn in the first place, but because the vows precluded using her powers to benefit the Kentacre family's political ambitions. Undoubtedly the Earl had known—his daughter had been nearly twenty when she had sought out the Council—and had probably arranged to have her secretly taught in the arts of magic by one of the quacks or dog wizards who abounded in such numbers in any major city of the Empire. But for Lady Rosamund, the half-understood jumble of piesog, hearsay, and garbled spells used for fees by the dog wizards had not been enough. To obtain true teaching, she must take the Council Vows, the first of which was that she must never use what she had learned either to harm or to help any living thing.

"He should never have gone without a guard," she was

saying, as Caris bore a tray of duck and braided breads up to the high table.

Beside her, the thin, tired-looking Whitwell Simm protested, "The Regent wouldn't dare..."

"Wouldn't he?" Cold fire sparked in her green glance. "The Prince Regent hates the mageborn, and always has hated us. I'm told that the other night, after a ball in the city, he was getting into his carriage when an old man, a shabby old dog wizard, accidentally brushed up against him on the flagway. Prince Pharos had two of his sasenna hold the old man while he almost beat the poor wretch to death with his cane. The rumors of what goes on in the dungeons of the old Summer Palace, which he has taken for his own, are a scandal. He is as mad as his father."

"The difference being," remarked Issay Bel-Caire on her other side, "that his father is not dangerous, except perhaps to himself."

At the foot of the table, the two novices—a short, red-haired girl of seventeen or so and a creamily dark, thin girl a few years older—said nothing, but listened with uneasy avidity, knowing that this was not merely gossip, but something which could easily affect their lives. Near them old Aunt Min, the most ancient of the mages who dwelt in the Yard, sat slumped like a little black bag of laundry in her chair, snoring softly. With a smile of affection for the old lady, Caris woke her gently up; she lifted her head with a start and fumbled at the tangle of her eternal knitting with hands as tiny and fragile as a finch's claws, muttering to herself all the while.

Whitwell Simm said, "Even if the Prince hates us, even if he believes our magic is nothing but charlatanry, like that of the dog wizards, you know he'd never dare to harm the Archmage. Neither the Council nor, as a matter of fact, the Church, would permit it. And we don't know that Salteris has gone to the Palace..."

"With the Regent's sasenna everywhere in the city," retorted Lady Rosamund coolly, "it scarcely matters where he goes. Prince Pharos is a madman and should have been barred from the succession long ago in favor of his cousin."

Issay laughed. "Cerdic? Maybe, if you want quacks and dog wizards like Magister Magus ruling the Empire."

Her ladyship's aristocratic lip curled at the mention of the most popular charlatan in Angelshand, but she turned her attention to her plate with her usual air of arctic self-righteousness, as if secure in the knowledge that all opposing arguments were specious and deliberately obstructive.

Caris, clearing up the plates afterwards and getting ready for the one last training session with the other sa-senna which the incredible length of the midsummer evenings permitted, felt none of the wizards' qualms for his grandfather's safety. This was not so much because he did not believe the mad Regent capable of anything—by all accounts he was—but because Caris did not truly think anyone or anything capable of trapping or harming his grandfather.

Since Caris was a child, he had known Salteris Solaris as his grandfather, a mysterious man who visited his grandmother's farm beyond the bounds of their Wheatlands village, sometimes twice in a summer, sometimes for the length of a winter's storm. He had known that afterwards his mother's mother would sing at her household tasks for weeks. The old man's hair had been dark then, like that of Caris' mother—Caris took after the striking blond beauty of his slow-moving, good-natured father. But Caris had the Archmage's eyes, deep brown, like the dark earth of the Wheatlands, the color of the very old leaves seen under clear water, tilted up slightly at their outer ends. For a time, it had seemed that he had inherited something else from him besides. When he had taken his vows as sasen-nan to the Council, it had been with the aim of serving the old man as a warrior, if he did not have the power to do so as a wizard. Only lately had it come to him that there would be a time when it would not be the old man who was its head.

Caris was too much a sasennan even to think about his grandfather, or the secret fear which he had carried within him, during that evening's training. With the endless, tepid twilight of midsummer filtering through the long windows of the training floor on the upper storey of the novices' house, the swordmaster put the small class through endless rounds of practice sparring with split bamboo training swords. Ducking, parrying, leaping, pressing, and retreating under the continuous raking of barked instruction and jeers, in spite of five years of hard training Caris was still sodden with sweat and bruised all over by the time he was done, convinced he'd never be able to pick up a sword again. He was familiar with the sensation. In that kind of training, there was no room for any other thought in the mind; indeed, that was part of the training—to inculcate the single-mindedness critical to a warrior, the hair-trigger watching for the flick of an opponent's eyelid, the twitch of the lip or the finger, that presaged a killing blow . . . or sometimes the sense of danger in the absence of any physical sign at all.

By the time it was too dark to see, it was past ten o'clock, and Caris, exhausted, stumbled with the other sasenna back downstairs to bathe and collapse into bed. It wasn't until he was awakened by he knew not what in the tar-black deeps of the night that he remembered his grandfather and what he had wanted to ask of him, and by then it was too late.

His magic was gone.

Long before, Caris had given up his belief in his magic. Only now, lying in the warm, gluey blackness, did he understand how deeply its roots had run and how magic had made the skeleton of his very soul. Without it, life was nothing, a hollow, gray world, not even bitter. It was as if all things had decayed to the color and texture of dust—as if the color had been bled even from his dreams.

He had heard the mages speak in whispers of those things by which a mage's power could be bound—spell-cord and the sigils made of iron, gold, or cut jewels, imbued with signs that crippled and drained a wizard's powers, leaving him helpless against his foes. But there was nothing of that in this terrible emptiness. His soul was a mold with the wax melted out, into which no bronze would ever be poured—only dust, filling all the spaces where the magic had been.

He would have wept, had the Way of the Sasenna not forbidden tears.

Unable to bear the hot, close darkness of the sasenna's dormitory another moment, he pulled on his breeches and shirt and stumbled downstairs to the door. The Way of the Sasenna whispered to him that he ought also to put on his boots and his sword belt; but with the loss of his magic, all things else seemed equally trivial and not worth the doing. The fresher air out on the brick steps revived him a little. Across the narrow, cobblestoned Yard, he could hear the sleepy twittering of birds under the eaves of the houses opposite. Among the squalid alleyways of the Old Believers' ghetto, a cock crowed.

Thirle had said that it could not happen—ever. But it had happened to him last night, a few moments' sickening waning that had wakened him, his heart pounding with cold terror. It was something he knew even then should not happen, as Thirle had said . . . And now magic was gone completely.

He leaned against the carved doorframe, hugging himself wretchedly, wondering why he could feel almost nothing, not even real grief—just a kind of hollowness that nothing, throughout the length of his life, would ever again fill. Looking across to the tall, narrow windows of his grandfather's little house, he wondered if the old man had

returned. The windows were dark, but that would not necessarily mean he was asleep—he often sat up reading
without light, as the mageborn could do. Perhaps he would
know something Thirle did not.

But at the same time, it seemed pointless to speak of it
now. Gone was gone. Like his long-departed virginity, it
was something, he told himself, that he would never recover. To the west, a drift of noise floated from the more
populous streets of Angelshand, from the bawdy theaters
on Angel's Island near the St. Cyr fortress, and from the
more elegant gaming halls near the Imperial Palace quarter.
Carriage wheels rattled distantly on granite pavement;
voices yelled in all-night taverns.

Almost without thinking of it, Caris found himself descending the brick steps, feeling for the purse in his
breeches pocket, knowing he was going to go over to the
Standing Stallion and get drunk.

Get drunk? He stopped, surprised and disgusted with
himself. There was no stricture against the sasenna drinking. If need arose, Caris could hold his own against most
of his mates when they went to the taverns; but on the
whole, he preferred to remain sober. It was the Way of the
Sasenna to be ready to fight at all times, and Caris had
never believed in blurring that edge.

But now none of it seemed to matter. He was dimly
aware that what he wanted was not the wine, but the
numbing of his awareness of grief, and he knew also that it
would do him more harm than good. But, after a moment's
hesitation, he sighed, not even caring that he was unarmed
and hadn't put on his boots, and continued down the stairs.

As his bare foot touched the uneven cobbles of the
court, he heard Thirle's voice cry desperately. "NO!"

Five years of training had inculcated into Caris the automatic reaction of drop and roll for cover until it was instinct. But now he stood, paralyzed like a stupid peasant,

in the waxy moonlight at the foot of the step as the fat black shape of the wizard came stumbling out of a nearby alley, aptly named Stinking Lane. He saw the man's round moonface clearly and the shocked panic in his eyes as Thirle began to run clumsily across the court, arms outspread like a bird's wings for balance.

From the darkness on the opposite side of the Yard, Caris heard the crack of a pistol.

Thirle rocked back sharply at the impact of the bullet, his feet flying out from under him as he flopped grotesquely on the stones. A dark shape broke cover from the shadows on the opposite side of the court, running toward Thirle, toward the mouth of Stinking Lane behind him, a black cloak covering him like a wing of shadows. All this Caris watched, but all of it, including the fact that he knew Thirle was dead, was less to him than his grief for the loss of his magic. None of it mattered—none of it had anything to do with him. But deep within him shock and horror stirred—at what was happening and at himself.

In a daze of anger, he forced himself to run, to intercept that fleeing black figure. He'd gone two steps when the digging bite of the cobbles on his bare feet reminded him belatedly that he had neither boots nor weapons. Cursing the carelessness and stupidity that seemed to be upon him tonight, he flung himself to one side into the black pocket of shadow between the novices' house and Thirle's. From across the court, he caught the flash of a pistol shot.

Splinters of brick exploded from the corner of the house, so close to his face that they tore his cheek. He knew it would take his man some moments to reload and knew he should dart out and take him then—but he hesitated, panic he had never known clutching at his belly. He heard feet pounding the cobbles and forced himself to stumble upright, to race in pursuit, but his legs dragged as if tangled in wet rope. It meant nothing to him. His soul had turned as sterile and cold as the magicless world around him. It would be easier to stop now, shrug, and go back to bed—Thirle's body would still be there in the morning. Dully angry at himself, he made himself run. For five years, in spite of exhaustion, occasional illness, and injuries, he had made himself pick up the sword for training, but forcing himself now was more difficult than it had ever been. In some oblique corner of his mind, he wondered if this were a spell of some kind, but it was unlike any spell he had ever known.

His steps slowed. The fugitive leaped over Thirle's body and vanished into the utter blackness of Stinking Lane. Caris dodged sideways, pressing against the house wall and slipping forward to the corner, knees flexed, ready to drop if that hand with its pistol appeared around the edge. The two shots had been so close together that the killer must have had two weapons—both empty now—and possibly he had a third. Through Caris' thin shirt, he felt the roughness of the coarse-plastered wall and the dampness that stuck the thin fabric to his ribs with sweat. He found he was exhausted, panting as if he had run miles.

He reached the mouth of the lane and looked around.

He saw nothing. No light—no walls—no sky. There was only a black and endless hollow, an abyss that seemed to swallow time itself, as if not only the world, but the universe, ended beyond the narrow band of pallid moonlight that lay on the cobbles beneath his feet.

Terror tightened like a garrote around his throat. He had not felt that hideous, nightmare fear since he had waked in the night as a small child to see the gleam of rats' eyes winking at him in the utter dark of the loft where he slept. Staring into that emptiness of endless nothing, he felt horror pressing upon him, horror of he knew not what—the whisper of the winds of eternity along his uncovered bones. He pressed his face to the stone of the wall, squeezing his eyes shut, unable to breathe. He felt in danger, but his training, like his magic, had deserted him; he wanted to run, but knew not in which direction safety would lie. It was not death he feared—he did not know what it was.

Then the feeling was gone. Like a man dreaming, who feels even in sleep the refreshing storm break the lour of summer heat, he felt the hideous weight of hopelessness lift from him. Still pressed to the chill stone of the wall, Caris felt as if he had waked suddenly, his heart pounding and his breathing erratic, but his mind clear. His magic— that trace of intense awareness that all his life had colored his perceptions—had returned. With it came a moment's blinding fury at himself for being so child-simple as to wander abroad unarmed and barefoot.

His knees felt weak at the thought of what he knew he must do. It took all his will to force himself to move forward again, crouching below eye level though he knew that the man with the pistols was gone. It was the Way of the Sasenna never to take chances.

Cautiously, he peered around the corner into the alley.

Filtered moonlight showed him the moss-furred cobbles, the battered walls of the houses, and the glitter of noisome gutter-water in the canyon of dark. There was a puddle right across the mouth of the lane, too wide to jump, but there were no prints on the other side.

Caris turned back to where Thirle lay like a beached and dying whale in the silver wash of the faint starlight. Lights were going up in the houses around the Yard, and voices and footsteps made a muffled clamor on the edges of the darkness. As he reached Thirle's side, Caris saw the dark glitter that covered all the breast of his robe. With a gut-teral gasp, the fat man's body twitched, lungs sucking air desperately. Caris fell to his knees beside him, and for one moment the dark, frantic eyes met his.

Then Thirle whispered, "Antryg," and died.

* * *

"The police must be fetched."

The Archmage Salteris Solaris, kneeling beside Thirle's body, made no reply to the words of the skinny old sword-master, who stood in the little cluster of men and women, Old Believers and novices, all clutching bedclothes about them and looking down at the body with the wild eyes of those startled by gunshots from sleep. Caris, kneeling beside him, looked from the corpse's eyes, staring blindly now at the faint pearliness of false dawn visible between the crowding black angles of the roofs, to the thin, aquiline features of his grandfather. The old man's white brows were pinched down over the bridge of his nose, and there was grief in his eyes for the loss of one he had known for so many years—grief and something else Caris could not understand. The old man glanced up at the crowd behind them and said "Yes—perhaps."

The Lady Rosamund, standing fully dressed even to the hyacinth stole of a Council member—a mark of rank that the Archmage seldom wore—sneered. As the scion of one of the noblest houses in the land, she had little use for such bourgeois institutions as the Metropolitan Police. "The constables will find some reason to wait until light to come."

Salteris' thin mouth twitched in a faint smile. "Very likely." He looked back down at the plump heap of black robes. In the soft glow of bluish witchlight that illuminated the scene, hanging like St. Elmo's fire above his high, balding forehead and flowing white hair, the muscles of his lean jaw tightened.

Something twisted inside Caris, and he put out a hand to touch the old man's square, slender shoulder in comfort, but he remembered that he was sasenna and stopped himself with the gesture unmade. He was used to death, as the sasenna must be. He had killed his first man at fifteen; the schools of the sasenna were given prisoners condemned to die by the Emperor or the Church, for even in peacetime, they said, the sword blade must learn the taste of flesh. As the sworn weapon of the Council of Wizards, he would have cut Thirle's throat himself, had they ordered it. But still, it had been many years since anyone he had known personally had died. A little to his shame, he found that the training had not changed that shocked grief of loss, and anger stirred in him that anyone would cause the Archmage pain.

Salteris stood up, his black robes falling straight and heavy around his thin form. For all his snow-white hair, for all the worn fragility that had begun to come over him in the last few years, he took no hand to help him. "We should get him inside," he said softly. He looked over at the two sasenna who had been on patrol duty that night. When they opened their mouths to protest that they had been in the alleys on the far side of the Yard, he waved them quiet. "It was no one's fault," he said gently. "I believe Thirle was killed only because he was in the man's way as he fled—perhaps because Thirle saw him and would give the alarm."

"No," a cracked, thin old voice said from the darkness of Stinking Lane. "You forgot about the Gate—the Gate into the Darkness—the Gate of the Void . . ."

Salteris' head turned sharply. Caris stepped forward in a half second of reflex, readying himself to defend his grandfather, then relaxed once more as he recognized the voice. "Aunt Min?"

From the shadows of Stinking Lane, the bent form of the old lady who had once been known throughout the Council as Minhyrdin the Fair hobbled determinedly, her black robes coming untucked from her belt and dragging in the puddles, her workbasket with its everlasting knitting dangling haphazardly at her side. Half-exasperated, half-concerned for the old lady, Caris hurried forward to take her fragile arm.

"You shouldn't be up and about, Aunt Min. Not to-night . . ."

She waved the remark fussily away and twisted her head on her bent spine to look up at Salteris and Lady Rosa-mund, who had also come to her side. "There is evil abroad," she piped. "Evil from other worlds than this. Only a curtain of gauze separates us from them. The Dark Mage knew . . ."

Salteris held up his hand quickly against that name, his silky white brows plunging together. Caris glanced quickly from him to Aunt Min, who had returned to fussing with the trailing strands of her knitting, and then back. "Other worlds?" he asked worriedly. His eyes went unwillingly to the dark maw of the alley, an uneven agglomerate of dim stone angles, with the gutter picking up the quicksilver light of the sky like a broken sword blade. "But—but this *is* the world. There is no other. The Sun and Moon go around us . . ."

Salteris shook his head. "No, my son," he said. "They've known for years now that it is we who go around the Sun, and not the Sun around us, though the Church hasn't admitted it yet. But that is not what Aunt Min means." He frowned unseeing for a moment into the dis-tance. "Yes, the Dark Mage knew." His voice sank to a whisper. "As do I." He put his arm around the old lady's stooped shoulders. "Come. Before all else, we must get him inside."

They sent one of the night-watch sasenna—the only two sasenna to be dressed—for a physician. Rather to Caris' surprise, it was less than a half-hour before he ar-rived. In the low-roofed closeness of the Archmage's nar-row study, Caris was telling Salteris, Lady Rosamund, and old Aunt Min of what he had seen—the pistol-shots, the chase, the terrible Gate of Darkness—when he heard the swift *tap-tap* of hooves in the Yard and the brisk rattle of what sounded like a gig. He was surprised that any citizen of Angelshand would come to the Mages' Yard during the dark hours, and even more so when the man entered the study. He had expected Salteris to send for a healer of the Old Believers, whose archaic faith was still more than a little mixed with wizardry. But the man who entered wore the dapper blue knee breeches and full-skirted coat of a professional of the city.

"Dr. Narwahl Skipfrag." Salteris rose from the carved ebony chair in which he had been sitting, extending a strong, slender hand. The physician took it and inclined his head, his bright blue eyes taking in every detail of that small room, with its dark ranks of books, its embryos bottled in honey or brandy, and its geometric models and crystal prisms.

"I came as quickly as I could."

"There was no need for haste." Salteris gestured him to the chair that Caris brought silently up. "The man was killed almost at once."

One of Skipfrag's sparse, sandy eyebrows tilted sharply up. He was a tall man, stoutish and snuff-colored, with his hair tied back in an old-fashioned queue. In spite of the fact that he must have been wakened by Salteris' messenger, his broad linen cravat was neatly tied and his shirt-ruffles unrumpled.

"Dr. Narwahl Skipfrag," Salteris introduced. "Lady Minhyrdin—Lady Rosamund—my grandson Caris, sasennan of the Council, who witnessed the shooting. Dr. Narwahl Skipfrag, Royal Physician to the Emperor and my good friend."

As a sasennan should, Caris concealed his surprise. Few professionals believed in the power of wizards anymore, and certainly no one associated with the Court would admit to the belief these days, much less to friendship with the Archmage. But Dr. Skipfrag smiled, and nodded to Lady Rosamund. "We have met, I think, in another life."

As if against her will a slight answering smile warmed her ladyship's mouth.

Slumped in her chair, without raising her eyes from her knitting, Aunt Min inquired, "And how does his Majesty?"

Skipfrag's face clouded a little. "His health is good." He spoke as one who remarks the salvage of an heirloom gravy boat from the wreck of a house.

Lady Rosamund's full mouth tightened. "A pity, in a way." Salteris gave her a questioning look, but Skipfrag merely gazed down at his own broad white hands. She shrugged. "Good health is no gift to him. Without a mind, the man is better dead. After four years, it is scarcely likely he will reawaken one morning sane."

"He may surprise us all one day," Skipfrag remarked. "I daresay his son thinks as you do."

At the mention of the Prince Regent, Lady Rosamund's chilly green eyes narrowed.

"It is about his son, in a way," Salteris cut in softly, "that I asked you here, Narwahl. The man who was killed was a mage."

The physician was silent. Salteris leaned back in his chair, the glow of the witchlight gleaming above his head and haloing the silver flow of his long hair. For a time he, too, said nothing, his folded hands propped before his mouth, forefingers extended and resting against his lips. "My grandson says that he heard Thirle cry 'No!' at the sight of a man standing in the shadows on this side of the court—the man who shot him, fleeing to the alley across the yard. Caris did not see which house the killer stood near, but I suspect it was this one."

The bright blue eyes turned grave. "Sent by the Regent Pharos, you mean?"

"Pharos has never made any secret of his hatred for the mageborn."

"No," Dr. Skipfrag agreed and thoughtfully stared into

the witchlight that hung above the tabletop for a moment. He reached out absentmindedly toward it and pinched it, like a man pinching out a candle—his forefinger and thumb went straight through the white seed of light in the glowing ball's heart, the black shadows of his fingers swinging in vast, dark bars across the low rafters of the ceiling and the book-lined walls. "Interesting," he murmured. "Not even a change in temperature." His blue eyes returned to Salteris. "And that's odd in itself, isn't it?"

Salteris nodded, understanding. Caris, standing quietly in a corner, as was the place of a sasennan, was very glad when Lady Rosamund demanded, "Why? Few believe in our powers these days." There was bitter contempt in her voice. "They work in their factories or their shops and they would rather believe that magic did not exist, if they can't use it to tamper with the workings of the universe for their personal convenience."

Softly, the Archmage murmured, "That is as it should be."

The deep lines around Skipfrag's eyes darkened and moved with his smile. "No," he said. "Most of them don't even believe in the dog wizards, you know. Or they half believe them, or go to them in secret—the dog wizards, the charlatans, the quacks, who never learned true magic because they would not take Council vows, so all they can do is brew love-philters and cast runes in some crowded shop that stinks of incense, or at most be like Magister Magus, hanging around the fringes of the Court and hoping to get funding to turn lead into gold. Why do you think the Church's Witchfinders don't arrest them for working magic outside the Council vows? They only serve to feed the people's disbelief, and that is what the Witchfinders want.

"But the Regent . . ." He shook his head.

Through the tall, narrow windows at the far end of the
room, standing open in the murky summer heat, the sounds
of the awakening city could now be heard. Caris identified
automatically the brisk tap of butchers' and poulterers'
wagons hastening to their early rounds, the dismal singsong of an itinerant noodle vendor, and the clatter of farm
carts coming to the city markets with the morning's produce. Dawn was coming, high and far off over the massive
granite city; the smell of the river and the salt scent of the
harbor came to him, with the distant mewing of the harbor
birds. At the other end of the table, Salteris was listening
in ophidian silence. Aunt Min had every appearance of
having fallen asleep.

Skipfrag sighed, and his oak chair creaked a little as he
stirred his bulk. "I was his Majesty's friend for many
years," he said quietly. "You know, Salteris, that he was
always a friend to the mages, for all he held them at an
arm's length for political reasons. He believed—else he
would never have raised the army that helped you defeat
the Dark Mage Suraklin."

Salteris did not move, but the witchlight flickered with
the movement of his dark eyes, and something of his attitude reminded Caris of a dozing hound waked at an unfamiliar footfall.

"Pharos' hatred of you is more than disbelief," Skipfrag
went on quietly. "He blames you for his father's madness."

Lady Rosamund waved a dismissive hand. "He was
hateful from his boyhood and suspicious of everything."

"Perhaps so," Salteris murmured. "But it is also true
that, of late, the Regent's antipathy toward us has grown to
a mania. He may fear me too much to move against me
openly—but it is possible that he would send an assassin."
His dark eyes went to Skipfrag. "Can you find out for me
at Court?"

The physician thought for a moment, then nodded. "I

think so. I still have Pharos' ear and many other friends there as well. I think I can learn something."

"Good." Salteris got to his feet and clapped Skipfrag lightly on the arm as the big man rose, dwarfing the Archmage's slenderness against his blue-coated bulk. Caris, hurrying before them to open the outer door, saw in the watery dawnlight outside that Thirle's blood had already been washed from the cobbles in front of Stinking Lane; the puddles of water left by it were slimy and dismal-looking. The swordmaster and the two novices still stood on the brick steps of the novices' house, talking quietly, all three wrapped in bedgowns, though, Caris noticed, the swordmaster had her scabbarded blade still in hand, ready for action.

It occurred to him suddenly to wonder, as he watched Salteris usher the physician over to his waiting gig, what Thirle had been doing abroad at that hour of the night at all? For that matter, what had Rosamund been doing up; she had been fully dressed, her hair not even crumpled from the pillow, so she must have been so for some time. He glanced back into the room behind him. Aunt Min, too, was dressed, though her thin, straggly white hair was mussed—but of course, reflected Caris, with rueful affection for the old lady, it always was.

Had they all, like himself, been restless with the damp warmth of the night?

Tepid dawn air stirred in his close-cropped, fair hair and stung the tender cuts on his cheek, where the assassin's bullet had driven brick-chips into his face. The day was beginning to blush color into the houses opposite, the black half-timbering of their shabby fronts taking on their daytime variation of browns and grays. The jungly riot of Thirle's pot plants was wakening to green in daylight their owner would never see.

Down in the Yard, Skipfrag was climbing into his gig, adjusting his voluminous coat skirts and gathering the reins of the smart bay hack that stood between the shafts. Salteris stood beside the horse's quarters, talking quietly to him. The physician's voice came clearly to Caris where he stood on the steps. "It's best I was gone. My reputation as a physician might carry off experiments with electricity, but it would never recover, if word got around I believed in magic. I'll learn for you what I can—do what I can, at Court. Until then, watch yourself, my friend."

Salteris stepped back as Skipfrag turned the gig. The iron wheels clattered sharply on the stones. Then the Emperor's physician was gone.

The Archmage stood still for some time after Skipfrag was gone. The brick steps were cool under Caris' bare feet, and the dawn air stirred his torn and muddied shirt. He looked down at his grandfather in the paling light of the Yard and noted again how the old man had aged in the eighteen months since Caris had taken his vows and come to live at the Mages' Yard. When he had last seen the Archmage before that time—before he had gone into training in the Way of the Sasenna—the old man had had a kind of wiry strength for all his age. Now he seemed like antique ivory worn to the snapping-point. With a sigh, the old man turned back, stopped, and looked up when he saw Caris on the steps.

"What did Aunt Min mean?" Caris asked softly. "About other worlds? About the Void and the Gate in the Void?" He came down the steps and offered the old man his steadying hand. "*Are* there worlds, besides this?"

This time Salteris took the hand. The cold, thin fingers felt delicate as bird bone. Not a big man, Caris was conscious as he had never been before that he stood slightly taller than the Archmage, this gentle old grandfather who had once lifted him up in childhood. Though it was not his way to think much about the passage of time, he felt its fleeting shadow brush his thoughts. He was silent as he helped the old man to the top of the steps.

As they stood there together, the Archmage was quiet, too, considering, as he often seemed to do, what he could say to one who did not have the training in magic ever to understand fully.

Then he nodded. "Yes," he said quietly. "And I very much fear that what you saw, my son, was a Gate such as Aunt Min described—a Gate through the Void that separates world from world."

Caris stammered, "I—I've never heard of such a thing."

A faint smile flicked those thin lips. "Few have," the Archmage said softly. "And fewer still have crossed that Void, as I have—once—and walked in a world on its other side." For a moment, the dark eyes seemed to gaze beyond him, as if they saw past the stones of the Yard, past the dawn sky, past the cosmos itself. "As far as I know, only two men in this world have ever had an understanding of what the Void itself is, how it works, and how to touch and feel it, to see across it to its other side. One of them is dead . . ." He hesitated, then sighed again. "The other one is Antryg Windrose."

"Antryg?" Caris murmured. "Thirle said that name . . ."

Salteris glanced at him quickly, and the long white eyebrows quirked up. "Did he?" A moment's doubt crossed the dark eyes, then he smiled. "He would have, if he thought—as I do—that some danger might be coming to us from across the Void. Antryg," he repeated, and Caris felt a stirring in his memory, like an old story overheard in childhood.

"Antryg," Lady Rosamund's derisive voice echoed behind them.

Caris turned. Darkly beautiful, she stood in the doorway of the house behind them, her slender white hands folded around the buckle of her belt, her dark curls lying thick on her shoulders like a careless glory of raven flowers.

Memory seemed to filter back to him of things spoken

across him, without his understanding, by the mages. "He was a wizard, wasn't he?"

"Is," the Archmage said. He shifted his dark robes up on his thin shoulders, and his eyes, again, seemed to look out across time.

"A dog wizard." Lady Rosamund's voice could have laid frost-flowers on glass. "Forsworn of his vows and no more than the dog wizards who peer into treacle and asses' dung for the secrets of gold and immortality at the bidding of any who'll pay."

"Maybe," Salteris said softly. "Except that he is, beyond a doubt, the most powerful mage now living. Thirteen years ago, he was the youngest member ever elected to the Council of Wizards—three years later he was expelled from the Council, stripped of his rank, and banished for meddling in the quarrel between the Lords of the Wheatlands and the Emperor. Since that time, he has been reinstated and banished again, and I and the other mages have had occasion to hunt him half across the face of the world."

Caris frowned. Half-recalled childhood memories ghosted into his mind, framed in amber hearthlight—the Archmage sitting beside the brick chimney oven of Caris' grandmother's house, and beside him the tall, thin young man he'd brought with him, gravely constructing a pinwheel by the light of the kitchen fire, or telling horrific ghost stories in a deep, extraordinary voice that was beautiful and flamboyant as embroidered brocade.

"Is he evil?" Caris did not remember evil.

Salteris thought for a moment, then shook his head. "I don't think so. But his motives have always been obscure. No one has ever, as far as I know, been able to tell what he would do, or why. He is, as I said, more powerful than any mage now living, including myself. But his mind is like a murky and bottomless well, into which all the wisdom of the ages and all the accumulated trivia of several universes have been indiscriminately dumped. He is both wise and innocent, incredibly devious and hopelessly scatterbrained, and by this time, I fear, quite mad."

Lady Rosamund shrugged with the grace that only years with a deportment master could impart. "He has always been mad."

"True. A smile flicked across the old man's face. "But the problem with Antryg is that no one has ever been able to tell just how mad." Then the lightness died from his eyes. "And for the past seven years he has been a prisoner in the Silent Tower, whose very stones are spelled against the working of magic. After that long, held prisoner by the Church and separated from the magic that is the core of any wizard's being, I can only hope that Antryg Windrose is still sane enough to help us. For I fear that, if we are dealing with some threat from another world than our own, we may need his help very badly."

CHAPTER II

```
**ERROR:  UNRECOGNIZED  CONDITION  IN  BINARY
TREE STRUCTURE
**CORRECT AND RE-TRY:
OK>
```

"Binary tree?" Joanna Sheraton groaned. "I just corrected the goddam binary tree."

Patiently, she typed:

```
>SEARCH: TREE. DATA.0
OK>
>EXECUTE TIGER.REV8
```

A moment later, green letters materialized on the gray
of the screen:

```
**ERROR: UNRECOGNIZED CONDITION IN BINARY TREE
STRUCTURE
**CORRECT AND RE-TRY:
OK>
```

"I'll give you an unrecognized condition," she muttered. She scanned up the screen, looking for anything else in the miles of data that could conceivably be preventing the running of the program. "Well, what's wrong with it? You didn't like my tone of voice? I didn't say 'Mother, may I'?" She tried again:

```
>SEARCH: TREE.DATA.0
OK>
>EXECUTE TIGER.REV8
**ERROR. UNRECOGNIZED CONDITION IN BINARY
TREE STRUCTURE
**CORRECT AND RE-TRY:
OK>
```

"You know, I'm getting very tired of your OK." She pushed the soft tangle of her shoulder-length, too-curly blond hair from her eyes and reached for the much-thumbed program that rested on top of the precarious stacks of printouts, manuals, schematic drawings of Tiger missiles, and scrawly handwritten ads for the in-plant newspaper, the *San Serano Spectrum*, that heaped the desk on all sides of the keyboard. "And I'm also getting very tired of you," she added, scanning the long, cryptic columns on the screen. "You're supposed to be the hottest mainframe west of Houston, you know. We shouldn't have to play Twenty Questions in binary every time I want to run a . . ."

Her hand froze in mid-gesture.

There was someone out in the hall.

But when she listened, she heard nothing but the faint hum of air conditioning. Even the massive radios of the janitorial staff, which generally drove her to take long walks to the coffee machines in the far corners of Building Six, had ceased, she realized, some time ago.

It occurred to her that it must be very late.

Security, she told herself and turned back to the monitor.

She didn't believe it.

She'd worked enough overtime, running analyses of missile test-flight results, to know well the sounds of the security staff as they patrolled the corridors. That swift, breathing rush of light footfalls outside her cubicle had nothing in common with the familiar hobnailed tread and jingle of keys.

With reflex reassurance, part of her said, *If it isn't Security, Security will take care of it.* Another part, with equally reflex dismissal, added, *Don't be silly.* It was probably some poor technician wandering around looking for the john or for a coffee machine that still had coffee—or what passed, at San Serano, for coffee—in it at this hour, whatever this hour was.

It was nothing to worry about.

Nevertheless, Joanna worried.

She was a small girl, with an air of compact sturdiness to her despite her rather delicate build. Ruth, the artist who lived downstairs from her, was of the often-expressed opinion that Joanna could be beautiful if she'd take the time, but Joanna had never seen the point of taking the time—or anyway not the hours a day Ruth put into it. Now she soundlessly hooked the toe of her sneaker under the pull of the desk drawer and slid the metal bin open far enough to allow her to dip into her mailsack of a purse and produce a hammer.

Then she sat still and listened again. This time she heard nothing.

It occurred to her that she had a throbbing headache. It

must be after ten, she thought—there had still been people around when she'd started working on the program for analyzing the Tiger missile test results for next week's Navy review. There was no telling how much longer she'd . . .

Her eyes sought the green luminosity of the clock.

2:00 A.M.

Two! She could have sworn it wasn't later than ten—well, eleven, since the janitors had gone home.

No wonder I have a headache, she thought, and ran her hands through the feathery tangle of her hair. She recalled vaguely that she'd been too busy to eat dinner; in any case, she'd long ago given up buying the overpriced slumgullion doled out by the junk machines in the break-room to those who worked on after regular hours. That was the tricky thing about the whole San Serano Aerospace Complex she had learned. The cool, even, white lights never varied; the unscented air never altered its temperature; and as a result no one ever had a very clear idea of what time it was.

But two in the morning . . .

Without warning, a wave of despair crept over her, fill ing the farthest corners of her tired soul like cold and greasy dishwater. The uselessness of it all suddenly overpowered her—not only getting the program to run, or the tedious documentation that would have to follow, or the fact that the data was going to have to be altered tomorrow in any case. Her whole life seemed suddenly to open before her in a vista of uselessness, an empty freeway leading nowhere.

It was strange to her, for she had, since she left her mother's house, been pretty content with her solitary life. Maybe that was one of the things wrong with her, she reflected. She knew herself to be far less good with people than she was with machines—no matter what you looked like, a computer would never laugh at you behind your back. Computers never expected you to be capable of things you had not been taught to do, or cared one way or the other what you did in your spare time.

She was familiar with the vague sense of an obligation to be other than she was—to be more like her bright and sociable co-workers—but she had never experienced this hollow, gray feeling of the futility of either staying as she was or changing to what she ought to be.

The image of Gary Fairchild returned to her mind— handsome, smiling, and enamored. Her loneliness seemed suddenly overwhelming, her vacillations over his constant request for her to move in with him suddenly petty and futile. *Why not?* she thought. *If this is all there is ever going to be . . . Maybe everybody's right about living with someone, and I'm wrong . . .*

Yet the thought of giving up what she had filled her with the dread of some inevitable doom.

Within her, a small voice struggled to insist, *In any case there isn't anything you can do about it at two in the morning. Tomorrow I'll see him. . . .*

As swiftly as it had come, the dull sense of hopeless grief ebbed away. Joanna blinked, rubbed her eyes, and wondered with the calm detachment that had gotten her into trouble in the past, *What the hell was that all about?*

The thought that she had, for one second, seriously been planning to accede to Gary's next demand that she live with him made her shudder. She might, she knew, be the sort of mousy little woman men never went out with, sealed like an anchoress in a chapel with a pile of books, computers, and cats, but it was preferable to the struggle between her conscientious efforts to please Gary, her boredom with watching TV in his enormous, gray-upholstered party room, and her sneaky sense that she'd rather be by herself, reading. It was not, she knew, the way she ought to act or feel about the man who loved her. But shame her though it did, it *was* how she felt, despite all her efforts to convince herself otherwise.

I must be hungrier than I thought, she reflected. *They say low blood sugar can make you depressed—they didn't mention it could make you suicidal.* With a sigh, she began backup procedures, to save what she'd done for tomorrow. At this point, she knew, she would make more errors through sheer exhaustion than she would correct. She chucked the floppies on top of the general heap. Her co-workers never believed her when she said that she located things in the heaps of printouts, programs, floppies, data, reports, management bulletins, journals, and ads on her desk by the oil company principle of geological stratification. They were all mystified by it—Joanna herself would scarcely have been surprised to find trilobites in the bottom layer.

It was only when she stood up that she remembered the stealthy footfalls outside her cubicle.

Don't be silly, she told herself again. *San Serano is a security installation. The idea that anyone could get in without being checked out by the guards is ridiculous.*

But somehow, she felt unconvinced.

She patted the pockets of her faded jeans for her car keys, dug her purse—an enormous accessory of Hopi-weave and rabbit skins bulging with rolled-up printouts, computer journals, and an incredible quantity of miscellaneous junk—out of the desk drawer, and made a move to slip the hammer back into it. Then she hesitated. She'd feel awfully silly if she met a guard or a co-worker—*what co-worker's going to be around at 2:00 a.m.?*—walking down the corridor with a hammer in her hand. But still . . .

You are twenty-six years old, she told herself sharply. *The odds against your meeting the boogieman in the corridors of the San Serano Bomb and Novelty Shop are astronomical.*

So were the odds against meeting a mocking and judgmental co-worker, but she compromised by sliding the hammer into her purse with the handle sticking out. Then, soundlessly, she pushed open the cubicle door and stepped into the corridor.

Somehow, the bright lighting of the corridors made her uneasiness worse. The doors of the other cubicles she passed and the typing bullpen were wells of eerie, charcoal half-light, the machines all sleeping in unearthy silence. Corridors leading to the test labs on the other side of the building made ominous echo tunnels which picked up the padded *swish-swish* of Joanna's sneakers on the dark-blue carpet, incredibly loud in that brilliantly lit silence. Once or twice she glimpsed the industrial-strength cockroaches who lived in such numbers in the warm mazes of the backs of the equipment in the test labs, but that was the only other life she saw.

Then light caught her eye.

She stopped. Not the even white illumination of the fluorescents . . . *Candlelight?* No more than a finger-smudge of gold reflection against the metal molding of the half-open door of the main computer room.

Fire? she thought, her pace quickening. The main computer room contained a lot of printout bins. The main-frame, a Cray the size of a Cadillac, the biggest defense computer west of Houston, could be tapped into by any of the desk stations, but there was a lot of work in the computer room itself. There was no smoking in the room, but one of the yobos on the janitorial staff might have dropped a cigarette into a trash bin, though the light looked too small and too steady for a fire.

It was, as she had thought, a candle. An old-fashioned tin candle holder, rested on a corner of the monitor desk. A gold edge of light danced over the dark edges of the three massive monoliths of the Cray, over the huge six-foot graphics projection monitor screens and the smaller CRTs and keyboards. As she came up the slight ramp which raised the level of the room above the subfloor wiring, the single red eye of the power-light regarded her somberly beside that seed of anachronistic brightness.

Now what the hell was a candle . . . ?

It was her natural nervous timidity which saved her. She knew she hadn't heard the man behind her, but it was as if, half-ready, she felt the dark shape loom up behind her a moment before hands closed around her throat. Certainly her hands were there, clutching at the long, cold fingers as they tightened; she cow-kicked back and up, half-conscious of her foot tangling with fabric.

The grip loosened and fumbled; the gray, buzzing roar which had filled her ears and the terrible clouded feeling in her head abated for one instant, and she whipped her right hand down to the hammer ready in her purse. There was breath, hot against her temple, and the smell of wood smoke, old wool, and herbs in her nostrils. She struck back over her left shoulder with all her strength.

Then she was falling. Her head struck the floor, hard under the thin, coarse nylon of the rug. She had a last, confused glimpse of the candle propped before the monitor, of a shadow bending over her—of something else on the wall . . .

She came to choking on ammonia. Her flailing fist was caught in a large, black hand, her scream was nothing more than a wheezing croak.

The face bending over hers focused—worried, black, and middle-aged. "You all right, miss?"

She blinked, her heart hammering and her whole body shaking with an adrenaline rush that nearly turned her sick. The upside-down beam of a flashlight at floor level gleamed brassily off a security badge and made dark lines along the regulation creases of the guard's light-blue shirt as he helped her to sit up.

"Did you get him?" she asked confusedly.

"Who?"

Her hands fumbled under the tangle of her blond hair, to

feel the bruises on her throat. She swallowed, and it hurt. Her head ached—she realized she was lucky she'd hit the slight give of the raised floor and not the cement subfloor beneath. "Somebody was in here. He grabbed me from behind . . ." She looked back at the desk. The candle was gone.

The guard removed a walkie-talkie from his belt. "Ken? Art here. We've got a report of an intruder in Building Six, near the main computer room." He turned back to her. "Did you get a look at him?"

She shook her head. "He was taller than me . . ." She stopped herself ruefully. Everyone was taller than she. "But I think I heard him walking in the hallways earlier."

"What time?" he asked.

"About two. I—I saw a light in here."

"And he attacked you with this?" The guard held up the hammer, protected from his hand by a handkerchief and gripped by the very end of the handle.

Joanna blushed. "No," she said, feeling very foolish. "I had that in my purse."

The guard cast a startled glance at her purse, then saw the size of it and nodded at least partial understanding.

"I sometimes carry one when I know I'm going to be working overtime," she hastened to fib, because she generally carried one as a matter of course. "For walking across the parking lot." This wasn't as odd as it sounded—San Serano was situated in the dr᠆ chaparral hills beyond Agoura, as deserted an area as you could get that close to L.A. Though parking lot crime was generally limited to the more ostentatious vehicles—'Vettes, Porsches, and four-wheelers—being looted or stolen outright, it was still a spooky walk across the enormous paved emptiness late at night.

The guard's walkie-talkie crackled. He listened, then said, "We've called on extra people. They'll be here to search the plant in about twenty minutes. He's not going to get away."

But that was, in point of fact, precisely what he did do. Joanna sat in the guard shack—actually a modest cement-block building near the plant's main gate on Lost Canyon Road—drinking tea and feeling conspicuous and hideously embarrassed, listening to the reports come in and answering questions put to her by the guard. Every door and entrance to Building Six was checked, and found to be inviolate. The building itself was methodically quartered by teams of security officers, and nothing was found.

At four, Joanna went home. She'd toyed with the notion of calling Gary, because the idea of returning to her apartment in Van Nuys alone tonight was somehow frightening, but she discarded it. This late, Gary would argue that she should come and spend the night with him, since his house was just over the hill, and she was in no mood for the "But *why* don't you want to?" argument that she knew would follow. Why she didn't want to was a question she'd never been able to answer to either Gary's satisfaction or her own—it was too often easier to consent than to explain.

In the end, the guards walked her out to her solitary old blue Pinto sitting in the parking lot, and she drove down the dark canyons to the freeway and the brighter lights of the Valley. She wasn't sure just why the thought of going home alone would frighten her. When she reached it, the place was quiet and normal as ever; but when she finally slept, toward six, it was not restful sleep.

No trace of an intruder was ever found.

CHAPTER III

THE SILENT TOWER STOOD TEN MILES FROM THE ANCIENT royal city of Kymil, separated from it by the sheet-steel curve of the River Pon, and by the silver-and-green patchwork of the Ponmarish, where sheep and pigs foraged among the boggy pools and town children hunted frogs in the long summer evenings. As Caris and his grandfather crossed the long causeway toward the old city gates of Kymil in the hush of the endless dusk, farmers and the river-trade merchants who made the money of the town drew aside from the sight of the old man's long black robes, making the sign against evil. The folk of Kymil had long memories and reason to fear the mageborn, even Salteris Solaris.

From the causeway, Caris could see the Tower, lonely on its hill; a finger raised in warning.

A warning, certainly, that no mage ever forgot.

A stage line ran between Angelshand and Kymil; though, like the Old Believers, the mages did not travel by stage, it meant that the roads were good. Two nights on the road, Caris and his grandfather had lodged in peasant huts, and once in the self-consciously rustic country villa of a wealthy merchant from Angelshand who had conversed with earnest condescension all through dinner about "the hidden strength of these ancient beliefs," and whose daughters had stolen downstairs after the household had gone to bed to ask Salteris to read their fortunes in the cards. Two nights they had slept under the stars. Caris worried that, in spite of the warmth of the fading summer, a chill might have settled into the old man's bones. Still, Salteris was tough. Like most sasenna, Caris slept only lightly, and when he had wakened in the night, it had always been to see Salteris sitting in silent meditation, gazing at the stars.

At the highest point of the causeway, Caris paused to shift his knapsack across his shoulders. Around the feet of the raised roadway and along the walls, just out of reach of the marshpools, were the hovels of the poor, built each spring when the waters went down and abandoned with their winter rising. Now children in rags were playing in between the sorry little huts, shouting and throwing pebbles at one another; a religious procession appeared, en route from one of the numerous shrines which dotted the marshes, and a whiff of incense and the sweetness of chanting rose to where he and his grandfather stood. People in the shantytown below paused to bend a knee to the gray-robed priests, as did half-naked boatmen from the river and a scarf vendor decorated like a Yule tree with his wares; a merchant crossing the causeway behind them, in his sober blue broadcloth coat and breeches, did likewise, and Caris felt the man's eyes on his back when neither he nor Salteris made this sign of subservience to the Church's will.

"We can stay at the House of the Mages in the city tonight," Salteris remarked, looking out past the marshes to the silence of the pale hills beyond. The hills marked the

edge of the Sykerst, the empty lands that stretched eastward two thousand miles, an eternal, rolling plain of grass.
"Nandiharrow runs it—the Old Faith has always been
strong in this city, and many of those who came here
twenty-five years ago for the trial of Suraklin found welcome enough among them to make it their home."

A touch of wind moved across the hills, murmuring
among the willows at the level of their feet and bringing
the wild scents of distance and hay. "Suraklin was tried
here?"

"Indeed, my son." The old man sighed. "Tried and executed." The breeze flicked at his white hair, he gazed into
those undefinable distances, with no elation for the memory of his ancient triumph.

"I didn't know," Caris said softly. "I thought, since the
Emperor presided over it—the Prince, then—it must have
taken place in Angelshand."

A wry expression pulled at the corner of the old man's
mouth. "It is difficult to try someone for the misuse of his
wizardry in a city where few believe in it," he said. "Suraklin was known in Kymil. Even those who did not think
that his powers stemmed from magic dared not cross him."
He nodded out towards the silent hills. "His Citadel stood
out there. They have thrown down the standing-stones that
marked the road that led there, at least those that were
visible from the city; the Citadel itself was razed, and its
very stones we calcined with fire. The Tower..."

In the blue-gray softness of the dusk, Caris saw the old
man's white brows draw down, bringing with them a whole
laddering of wrinkles along his high forehead.

"The Silent Tower had stood there of old, but we
strengthened its walls—I and the other members of the
Council. We put our spells into its stones, spells of nullifi-
cation, of void. We fashioned the Sigil of Darkness from
the signs of the stars and the Seal of the Dead God, which
binds and cripples a mage's power, and that we placed

upon the doors, so that no mage could pass. In the Silent Tower Suraklin awaited his trial. From it he was taken to his death."

He turned away. "Come," he said quietly. "It is not good to talk of such things." And he led the way along the dusty causeway toward the square, gray gates of the city.

They passed the night in the House of the Mages, a big, rambling structure in the heart of Kymil down near the river. Like most buildings in Kymil, it was built of wood; unlike most, it was fancifully decorated, with odd carvings and archways, small turrets and little stairways leading nowhere, balconies whose railings were carved into intricate openwork filigrees of flowers and leaves overlooking miniature gardens no larger than a single flowerbed, but so thick with vines that their small central fountains could scarcely be seen. Most of the buildings in Kymil, Caris noticed, were rather plainly built, and often garishly painted, pink or daffodil or a hard phthalo blue. One, near the gates as they entered the town, was illustrated in a wealth of architectural detail that the building itself did not possess—colonnades, friezes, facades, balconies, and marble statuary in niches, all painted in careful detail upon its flat wood sides. None of them appeared to be much more than twenty years old.

"That wasn't Suraklin's doing, was it?" he asked later that night of Le, second-in-command of the small troop of sasenna attached to the House of the Mages.

The dark, blade-slim woman nodded. "There was a deal of destruction wreaked in the town when the mages broke his power," she said. "Other houses were destroyed later and were found to have the Dark Mage's mark in them, drawn on a wall or a doorpost." She glanced across at him out of jet-bead eyes under her short crop of dark hair, then up at the head of the hall, where the mages of the house were talking quietly over their after-dinner wine. The four or five sasenna who had table service that night were moving quietly about in the dim candlelight, clearing up. There was rumored to be a poker game starting up in the barrack-quarters, but, like those they had sworn to serve, Caris and Le had lingered over a last cup of wine to talk before going to investigate.

"But what would it matter, after Suraklin was dead?" Caris was familiar with the principle of wizards' marks, though to make one was far beyond his rudimentary powers.

Le shook her head. "They say they weren't only to guide him there and let him enter where he'd been before. They say that, through the marks, he could influence the minds of those who were much near them; sway them to his thoughts from afar; sense things through them, even, in his dreams. It might be only stories, for folk feared him enough to believe anything of him, but then again . . ."

"Did you ever see him?"

The full mouth curved, but the expression could hardly be termed a smile. They were sitting at one of the long refectory tables in the lower part of the hall, the last of the sasenna to leave; at the other low table, parallel to theirs like the arms of a U below the main board where the mages sat, and nearer the vast, empty darkness of the fireplace, a couple of novices discussed spells with the earnestness of new explorers in some strange and wonderful world. The novices' table would be the more comfortable in the winter, but in the summer, with the diamond-paned casements that punctuated the length of the room thrown open to let in the milky warmth of the hay-smelling night, there was no comparison.

"I only saw him the once," Le said. "I was eight. I saw him die and saw what was left of his body strung up and burned. The Church's Witchfinders wanted to have him burned alive, but your friend the Archmage . . ." She nodded towards the head table, where Salteris sat, slender hands folded, fingers extended against his lips, nodding gravely to something the big, stout, graying mage Nandi-harrow was saying. ". . . wouldn't have it. The Church has no jurisdiction over those that have sworn their vows to the Council and, though they needed the Church's might to subdue him, the Church would not be given the right to kill a mage—any mage." She pushed the sleeves of her loose black jacket up on her arms, and Caris saw, with some envy, the scars of half a dozen fights in a white zigzag over the fine, hard muscle of her forearms. "But as for Suraklin, I doubt it made any difference to him by that time. I don't know what the Council and the Witchfinders and the Prince did to him, but I remember he came to the block broken, stumbling, and silent. He never so much as raised a hand against the headsman's sword."

Her words returned to Caris' mind the next morning as he and the Archmage left the city by the Stone Road Gate and took the track that wound toward the hills. In the marshes near the town, the road was well-repaired and used; down in the lowlands, all around them, men and women were cutting hay from the common lands of the city corporation, carting it in wheelbarrows or on their backs to the higher ground to dry, their voices and laughter rising from all around like the cries of unusually noisy marsh birds. But away from the town, the road quickly dwindled to a narrow track; though it saw some use, Caris could tell that it had been long since much traffic had passed over it. As they passed into the green, silent folds of those treeless hills, he saw where huge standing-stones had once lined its sides, but had been thrown down and were now half-buried in the long summer grass.

"This was the road to Suraklin's Citadel?" he asked softly, unwilling to break the hush of the hills.

The old man seemed to wake from some private meditation at the sound of Caris' voice. "Yes, it led to his fortress. But the road was older than he—these stones were cracked with a thousand winters before ever he made people curse them as his."

Caris frowned, looking at the fallen menhirs. Another such line ran near Angelshand, mile after mile of ancient stones, standing like sentries in the deep grass, guarding what had long been forgotten. The Devil's Road, they called it. "What were they?" he asked, but his grandfather, relapsing into thoughts of his own, only shook his head.

On the hill to their left, the Silent Tower rose, dark-gray against the wind-combed emerald silk of the grass that lapped against them on all sides.

Caris saw now that it was more than the single finger of stone he had seen from the causeway. A curtain wall surrounded it, pierced by a single gate; the portcullis was down, unusual for daytime; through it, he saw what looked like a small monastic barracks. People were moving about inside, some in the black uniforms of sasenna, others, with the shaven heads of priests, in white. Near the gate, he got a glimpse of someone robed like a monk, but in flame-red rather than gray, the staff of a wizard in his hand. One of the Church Wizards, the Red Dogs. For the first time he felt uneasy at the thought of entering those walls.

"It's all right," Salteris said softly. "They don't see us yet."

They stood within full view of the gate, but Caris knew better than to question the Archmage's statement. From his robes the old man drew a small wash-leather bag and, opening it, tipped a little ball of what looked like hard-baked dough onto his palm.

"This is a *lipa*," he said. Looking more closely, Caris saw that it was, in fact, made out of dough. Runes had been scratched into it with a pin or a fine stylus, covering its surface with an almost invisible net of tracery. "Keep it where you can get to it. Should any harm befall me, or should you and I be separated for more than three hours, burn it. The other mages will come." He pulled shut the strings of the bag again and handed it to Caris, never taking his eyes from the gates of the Silent Tower.

He started to move off again, but Caris held him back, troubled. "If Antryg's a prisoner, he can't work magic against you, surely?"

Salteris smiled. "Antryg is the least of my worries at the moment. No, he cannot work magic in the Silent Tower— but then, neither can I. Once within its walls, I will be only an old man, alone among people whose relations with the mageborn have always been at best a guarded truce. There has been no trouble between the Church and the Council of Wizards since Isar Challadin's time—but the Church is old. They watch and they wait." His dark eyes warmed with wry amusement. "I should not like to be the first one to hear of a surprise attack."

Caris looked back along the deserted, perfectly straight road and felt again how isolated the Silent Tower was in these empty hills. Le's words of last night returned to him —how the Church Witchfinders had wanted to burn the Dark Mage alive, and how Salteris had refused to give them the power of life and death over any mage, even the most evil. The Church might say that it forgave, but he knew that it never forgot.

He tucked the *lipa* into the purse at his belt, and they resumed their walk up the narrow track to the Tower compound. As they approached the gatehouse with its shut portcullis, Caris mentally reviewed the location of every weapon from his sword and the garrote in his sleeve to the hideout dagger in his boot. Glancing back, he saw that, beyond the turning where that track left the straight, ancient path, the old road was almost completely eradicated by grass. Where it passed over the crest of the next hill, he could see that the stones along its verges still stood.

His eyes went to the old man who walked at his side, trying to picture him as he had been twenty-five years ago, when he had led the Council against the Dark Mage. He

had been Archmage even then, for he had come young to
his power and to the leadership of the Council. His hair
would have been black, Caris thought, and the silence that
coiled like a serpent within him not so deep. The lightness
in him that Caris remembered from before his grandmother's death five years ago would still have been there;
the capacity for teasing and jokes that he had loved so well
had not yet been replaced by that glint of irony in his eye.

The Bishop of Kymil met them at the gate. She was a
tall woman in her fifties who had never been pretty. Her
head was shaved, after the fashion of the Church. Heaver
than she appeared at first glance, she was robed in velvet
of ecclesiastical gray with the many-handed Sun of the
Sole God like a splash of blood on her shoulder. As she
held out a hand in greeting to the Archmage, she looked
him over with a fishy, blue-gray eye. "My lord Archmage."

Looking past her into the court as the gates were
opened, Caris wondered how many of the Church's sworn
sasenna were stationed there. Le had said that five of the
sasenna from the House of Mages were on Tower duty at a
time—Caris guessed there were at least twenty sasenna in
and around the small, dreary yard now. The two Red Dogs
he had glimpsed stood quietly behind their ecclesiastical
mistress, observing him and Salteris with cool, fanatic
eyes. The Church called them hasu, the Bought Ones—
bought from Hell by the blood of the saints and the Sole
God. The less refined among the mages used the feminine
form of the word—hasur—which had its own connota-
tions.

"My lady Bishop." Salteris bowed. They touched
hands, a formal contact of two fingers quickly withdrawn.

"You wrote that you wished to see the man Antryg
Windrose?"

The warriors fell in around them as they crossed toward
the tower itself. The place stank of a trap, of the crosscur-

rents of formality covering the resentments and envy the Church held against the only group ever successfully to defy their law; Caris was conscious in his bones of the portcullis sliding shut behind them. A quick look around showed him that escape from the compound would be difficult; no building was close enough to the curtain wall to allow a jump from roof to battlement, and in any case the drop on the other side was far enough to make breaking a leg a virtual certainty. The air here felt hot and still between high walls of parched gray stone, a bleak and cheerless place in contrast to the hills beyond. The sasenna moved about with somber faces, like most Church sasenna only one step from becoming monks. It was not the Way of the Sasenna to feel pity, but Caris felt it now for anyone who would be held prisoner here for the rest of his life.

At a sign from the Bishop, the captain of the Tower unlocked the massive iron fastenings of the Tower door. It swung open to reveal a dense mouth of shadow, cold even in summer. On the door's inner side, just above the lock, Caris could see an iron plate fastened. Affixed to it was a round plaque of lead, about the size of an Imperial eagle coin and incised and inlaid in some design that lifted the hair from his neck. In spite of himself, he turned his head away, abhorrence clutching at his belly, as if a rat had crawled over his flesh. As his head turned, he saw his grandfather flinch from it also, averting his eyes. The two Church wizards did not even come near.

He did not need to be told what it was. It was the Sigil of Darkness of which his grandfather had spoken, the Seal of the Dear God, which bound a wizard's power like a chain of despair. As the guard carried it away from the door to allow the Archmage to enter, Caris felt for the first time the true power that lay in the walls of the Silent Tower. He knew in himself that not all the harsh discipline of the sasenna could have induced him to touch that Sigil or any door that it sealed, no matter what was at stake. His own powers of magic were small and, he suspected miserably, failing; but through them he felt its influence as they entered those cold blue shadows, with an oppressive sense of horror lurking in the smoke-stained, windowless stone walls. What they must be to his grandfather's greater powers he loathed to think. He understood then why his grandfather had said that he hoped that, after seven years of it, Antryg would still be sane.

At the end of a cold, bare passage was a large guardroom, smoky, dark, and close-feeling in the smoldering glare of torches. The tower was windowless, the air freshened by some hidden system of ventilation that did not work particularly efficiently. They ascended an enclosed stone stair, the treads worn into a long hollow runnel in their center, slippery and treacherous. The two Church sasenna who followed them bore torches. Looking up, his hands pressed to the walls for support on the age-slicked stone steps, Caris could see the low roof entirely crusted with soot.

Owing to the tapering of the Tower, the room above was smaller; but though cluttered and untidy, it was clean, lacking even the stench of the guardroom. All around the walls, boxes had been piled to form crude shelves for the books that filled the place; more books were heaped on the floor in the corners and along the back of the small table that stood against the wall. The tops of these barely cleared the disordered piles of papers burying most of the table's surface; among them Caris could see a pot of ink and a vast number of broken quills, magnifying glasses, yellowing scientific journals, an armillary sphere, two astrolabes and the pieces of three more mingled with the component parts of elaborate mechanical toys. About a dozen cups, scattered through the colossal litter, contained the moldering remains of cold tea. Among the papers, he saw scribbled mathematical formulae and the complicated patterns of the Magic Circles, drawn as if the artist had been memorizing them by rote, although he could use none of them; with them were sketches—a leaf, a bone, the Bishop, the stars at certain times of winter nights, or simply the single many-branched candlestick that reared itself amid the confusion with its long stalactites of guttered wax.

The Bishop stood for a moment in the doorway, looking around the appallingly untidy room with pinched disapproval on her flat, potatolike face. Then she said to her guards, "Fetch him down."

They turned towards a door that would lead, Caris guessed to another dark seam of stair and a yet smaller, windowless room above. Almost against his will, he felt a twinge of anger at this final violation of the prisoner's privacy. But before the guards could reach it, the door was flung open from the other side, and Antryg Windrose strode into the room in a tattered swirl of mismatched robes.

"My dear Herthe!" Passing between the startled guards as if they had been invisible, he seized and shook the Bishop's hand with old-fashioned cordiality and genuine delight. "How good of you to call! It's been—what? Six months? Seven months? How's your rheumatism? Did you take the herbs I prescribed?"

"No!" The Bishop pulled her hand away irritably. "And no, it's no better. I've brought . . ."

"You really ought to, before it comes on to rain tonight. Salteris!" He turned and checked his stride for a moment, looking into Salteris' face with startled gray eyes behind his thick-lensed spectacles. Then he stepped forward and clasped the Archmage's hand. "I haven't seen you in—oh, five years?"

Tall, thin, no longer young, Antryg Windrose had a beaky face in which all the individual features seemed slightly too large for the delicate bone structure, surrounded by a loose mane of graying brown hair and a straggly beard like frost-shot weeds that had been trailed in ink. Crystal earrings glinted in it like the snagged fragments of broken stars; half a dozen necklaces of cheap glass beads flashed tawdrily over the open collars of an assortment of ragged, scarecrow robes and a faded shirt. Behind the thick spectacle lenses, his wide gray eyes were bright, singularly gentle, and not sane. It must have been months, if not years, since he had seen anyone but the Tower guards, but there was neither reproach nor self-pity in the deep, extravagant voice Caris remembered so vividly. It was as if, for him, time had ceased to have meaning.

"Quite that," agreed Salteris with a gentle smile, though Caris, watching him, thought he glimpsed a kind of wary scrutiny as the Archmage met the mad wizard's eyes.

Antryg cocked his head to one side like a stork's as he returned the old man's gaze; then he turned away. For all his gawkiness, he moved with the light, random swiftness of a water strider on a hot day.

"And—Caris, isn't it? Stonne Caris, your daughter Thelida's boy? You probably won't remember me. You were only about six at the time."

Caris found himself saying, "No, as a matter of fact, I remember you very well."

The disconcerting gray eyes flared a little wider, suspicion and wariness that could have been real or feigned in their demented depths. "Indeed? The last time someone said that to me, I ended up having to leave Angelshand in a hurry." He glanced over at Salteris. "Will you stay to tea? and you, too, my dear Herthe . . ." The Bishop stiffened, evidently not liking being called so casually by her first name by a man who was her prisoner. ". . . and these gentlemen too, of course." He gestured toward the guards and moved over to the hearth where a kettle bubbled on the small fire. In spite of the fact that it was still summer, the fire was not uncomfortable. The tower was damp, and its shadows cold—little of the sun's warmth penetrated from the outside.

"Is this purely a social call, Salteris?" Steam rose in a mephitic veil around his face as he tipped the kettle into a chipped earthenware teapot on one corner of the raised brick hearth. "Or is there something I can do for you? Within the limits imposed by circumstances, that is." There wasn't a trace of sarcasm in his voice—he might have been speaking of a prior engagement rather than imprisonment for life. He stood up again, all his tawdry beads rattling. "I'm afraid all I can offer you is bread and butter. I keep ordering caviar, and it never comes."

The prelate looked affronted, but Caris saw the corners of his grandfather's mouth tuck up in an effort to suppress a smile; at the same time, he was aware that the Archmage had relaxed. "Bread and butter will be quite acceptable, Antryg."

Antryg turned to extend the invitation to the Bishop's guards; but, at a signal from her, they had stepped into the black slot of the doorway. With a shrug, he took a piece of paper at random from the mess on the table, lighted a corner of it in the fire, and proceeded to kindle the half-burned candles in their holder to augment the sooty torch-and firelight of the dim room.

"My lady," Salteris said quietly, "may I have your leave to speak to this man alone?"

The Bishop's pale, protuberant eyes grew hard. "I would rather not, my lord. Too often there has been collusion between the mageborn. And my predecessor told me that this man was once your pupil—that it was only through your intercession that he was placed here at all and not executed. As chief prelate of the Empire I cannot . . ."

"She doesn't trust you, Salteris." Antryg sighed, shaking his head. He blew out the half-burned paper and dropped it back onto the table. "Well, never mind."

The Archmage had already taken one of the two chairs

at the cluttered table; Antryg offered the other one first to the Bishop, who refused it indignantly, then to Caris, as if he had been a visitor in his own right and not merely the sasennan of the Archmage. Refused on both counts, he took it himself, setting his teacup precariously on top of a pile of papers. "What did you want to see me about?"

"The Void," Salteris said softly.

The candlelight flashed sharply across Antryg's spectacles with his sudden start, his hand arrested mid-motion. "What about the Void?"

"Can you sense it? Feel it?"

"No." Antryg set his cup down.

"You used to be able to."

"Outside, yes. In here, I can no more sense the Void than I can feel the weather. Why do you ask?"

Salteris folded his hands and rested his extended forefingers against his lips. "I have reason to believe that someone from another universe passed through it and killed Thirle in the Mages' Yard. Shot him," he went on, as Antryg's look of grieved shock reminded Caris that he, too, must have known and liked the little herbalist, "Though, when the ball was drawn, it was unlike any pistol ball any of us have seen."

Caris frowned suddenly in the reddish, springing shadows. "And there was no smell of powder," he said. "No smoke, though it was a still night."

"Curious," Antryg remarked softly.

"Caris here saw something that sounds like the Gates that Suraklin used to open in the Void," the Archmage went on. "Aunt Min thought so, too. Are there mages in other worlds beyond the Void, Antryg, who could open the Void and come here to work mischief?"

"Oh, I should think so." Antryg looked down into his tea. Salteris was watching that strange, expressive face as the steam laid a film over the thick rounds of the spectacle lenses; but Caris, watching the long fingers where they rested on the teacup's chipped pottery side, saw them shake. "It doesn't necessarily mean he—"

He broke off suddenly, and Salteris frowned, his white eyebrows plunging down sharply over his nose. "He what?"

"He what?" Antryg looked up at him inquiringly.

"The fact that the intruder came through the Void doesn't necessarily mean what?"

Antryg frowned back, gazing for a long moment into Salteris' eyes. Then he said, "I haven't the slightest idea. Did you know that all the wisdom in the cosmos can be found written in magical signs on the shells of tortoises? One has to collect and read an enormous number of tortoises in order to figure it out, of course, and they have to be read in the correct order, but somewhere here I have a collection of tortoise-rubbings . . ."

"Antryg," Salteris said reprovingly, as his erratic host made a move to search the jumble of shelves behind him. The madman turned back to regard him with unnerving intentness.

"They don't like to have rubbings taken, you know."

"Quite understandable," Salteris agreed soothingly. "You were saying about the Void?"

"I wasn't saying anything about the Void," Antryg protested. "Only that, yes, some of the worlds one can reach by passing through it are worlds wherein magic can exist. In others it does not. And there is continual drift, toward the centers of power or away from them. So, yes, a mage from another world could have opened a Gate in the Void last week and come through for purposes of his own."

"I thought you claimed you could not feel the Void." Caris stepped forward, into the circle of the candelabra's light. "How do you know it was last week?"

Antryg regarded him with the mild, startled aspect of a melancholy stork. "Obviously you came here as soon as you knew the problem involved the Void. It's a week's

walk from Angelshand to Kymil—unless you took the
stage?" He glanced inquiringly at Salteris, who sighed patiently and shook his head.

"Purposes of his own," the Bishop said suddenly. Like
Caris, she had remained in the denser shadows at the edges
of the room. Now she came forward, her thick face con-
gealing with suspicion. "What purposes?"

"What purposes did you have in mind?" Antryg dug a
long loop of string from beneath the general litter on the
table; the multiple shadows of the candle flame danced
over his long, bony fingers as he began constructing a cat's
cradle.

The Bishop's wary glance slid from him to the Archmage. "To bring abominations into this world?"

Salteris looked up sharply. "Abominations?"

"Had you not heard of them, my lord Archmage?" Her
gruff voice grew silky. "All this summer there has been a
murmuring among the villages of strange things seen and
heard and felt. In Voronwe in the south a man was seen to
go into his own house in daylight and was found there an
hour later, torn to pieces; in Skepcraw west of here there
has been something like a sickness, where the hay has been
left to rot in the fields while the people of the town huddle
weeping in the Church or else drink in the tavern, not
troubling to feed either themselves or their stock. We have
sent out the Witchfinders, but they have found nothing. . . ."

Salteris frowned. "I had heard rumor of this. But it has
nothing to do with Thirle's murder or the opening of the
Void."

"Hasn't it?" the Bishop asked.

"I scarcely find it surprising that you've found nothing,"
Antryg remarked, most of his attention still absorbed by
the patterns of the string between his hands. "Old Sergius
Peelbone, your Witchfinder Extraordinary, is looking for
some*one* rather than some*thing*—if he can't try it for

witchcraft and burn it, it doesn't exist. Besides, Nandiharrow and the others at the House of the Mages would have known if unauthorized power were being worked in the land—and in any case, there are sufficient evils and wonders in this world, without importing them from others. Could I trouble you . . . ?" He held out his entangled hands to her and waggled his thumb illustratively.

Irritated, she yanked the string from his fingers and hurled it to the floor. "You are frivolous!"

"Of course I'm frivolous," he replied mildly. "You yourself must know how boring gravity is to oneself and everyone else. And I really haven't much opportunity to be anything else, have I?" He bent to pick up the string, and the Bishop, goaded, seized him by the shoulder and thrust him back into his chair.

"I warn you," she said grimly. "I can have you . . ."

"You can not!" cut in Salteris sharply. "He is the Church's prisoner, but his person is under the jurisdiction of the Council of Wizards to which he made his vows."

"Vows that he foreswore!"

"Does a priest who sins pass from the governance and judgment of the Church?" Salteris demanded. For an instant their gazes locked. The wizard was like an old, white fox, slender and sharp as a knife blade against the Bishop's piglike bulk. But like a pig, Caris knew, the Bishop was more intelligent and more dangerous than she seemed; here in the Tower, Salteris, like Antryg, was at her mercy.

"A priest's sins concern a priest alone," the Bishop said softly. "A wizard who foreswears his vows not to meddle in the affairs of humankind endangers not only all those he touches, but all those he encourages to follow his example. He can not only be a danger, but he can teach others to be a danger, and if we cannot trust the mageborn to govern their own . . ."

"Can you not?" Salteris replied in a voice equally low. Deep amber glints shone catlike in his eyes as they bored into hers. "Were it not for the mageborn on the Council, it would be Suraklin who rules this city, and not yourself."

"Suraklin was defeated by the army led by the Prince."

"Without us, his precious army would not so much as have found the Citadel. Suraklin would have led them like sheep through the hills and, in the end, summoned the elemental forces of the earth to swallow them up. By our dead that day, by this . . ." With a swift move Salteris flung back the long sleeve of his robe. Age-whitened scars blotched his arms, beginning like a sleeve, four inches below his elbow and, Caris knew, covering half his chest. ". . . I have earned the right to say what shall be done with a man who has taken Council vows."

He turned suddenly back to where Antryg was calmly drinking his tea and taking no further interest in the discussion of those by whose whim he would live or die. "Antryg," he said. "Has there been movement through the Void in these last weeks?"

"There must have been, mustn't there, if you've seen an intruder," Antryg said reasonably. He swirled his cup in his hand and gazed down into its dregs. "Do you realize the spells on this tower affect even the tea-leaves?"

"I think you're lying," the Archmage said softly.

Antryg raised his head, startled. "I swear to you I haven't gotten a decent reading in seven years."

Salteris rested his slender hands among the junk on the table and looked for a long moment down into the madman's wide, bespectacled, gray eyes. "I think you're lying, Antryg," he repeated. "I don't know why . . ."

"Don't you?" Their gazes held, Salteris' wary and speculative, Antryg's, suddenly stripped of the mask of amiable lunacy, vulnerable and very frightened. The Archmage's glance slid to the Bishop, then away, and something relaxed in the set of his mouth. He straightened up and stood for a moment looking down at the seated man. Light from the candles in their holder, clotted with stalactites of years'

worth of dribbled wax, glinted on the round lenses of Antryg's spectacles and caught like droplets of yellow sunlight in the crystal of his earrings.

Then abruptly Antryg got to his feet. "Well, it's been very pleasant chatting with you, but I'm sure we all have things to do." With manic briskness he collected teapot and cups, stacked them neatly in one corner of the table, and piled papers on top of them. "Herthe, why don't you put a division of your guards at the Archmage's disposal? I'm sure they'll come in handy. Salteris . . ." He looked away from the Bishop's goggling indignation to his former master, and the madness died again from his eyes. In a sober voice he said, "I think the first place you should look should be Suraklin's Citadel. You know as well as I do that it was built on a node of the lines. If there is some sort of power abroad in the land, signs of it will show up there."

Salteris nodded. "I think so, too."

For a moment the two wizards faced one another; in the silence between them, Caris was again made conscious of how quiet the Tower was. No sound penetrated from the outside, save a soft, plaintive moaning of wind in the complex ventilation; no light, no warmth, no change. Antryg was not a young man, but he was not old, and Caris was aware that mages could live to fantastic ages. Was this room and the one above it all the world he could look forward to for the next fifty years? In spite of himself, in spite of what he now knew about Antryg, he felt again a stab of pity for that tall scarecrow, with his mad, mild eyes.

Salteris said, "Thank you, Antryg. I shall be back to see you, before I leave Kymil."

Antryg smiled like a mad elf. "I shall see what I can do about getting us caviar by then. Come any day—I'm generally at home between two and four." He thought about it for a moment, then added, "And at any other time, of course."

"Are you?" asked Salteris, in a voice so low that Caris, startled, was barely sure he heard the words. Then the old man turned and, followed by the Bishop and his sasennan, descended the blackness of the narrow stair to the guard-room below.

It wasn't until they were again on the ancient road, shadowed now by the gray, unseasonable clouds that were riding up from the river to cover the town with the soft smell of coming rain, that Caris said, "He was lying."

The Archmage glanced over at him and raised one white brow.

Caris jerked his head upward, toward the clouds. "He said that he could no more sense the Void than he could the weather. But the first thing he said to the Bishop was that it would rain tonight."

With a brisk jingling of harness, shockingly loud in the wind-murmuring quiet, the Bishop's carriage passed them by, returning to her palace in Kymil. Counting her out-riders, Caris noticed that Herthe had left the two Red Dogs back at the Tower. Through the thick glass of the windows, he caught a glimpse of the lady herself, fretfully rubbing her aching joints as the badly sprung vehicle jolted over the unpaved way. The Bishop did not even spare a glance to the old mage and his sasennan walking in the long grass at the road's verge.

Salteris sighed and nodded. "Yes. I feared it was so. He's hiding something, Caris; he knows something, or there is something he will not speak." The wind made its soft, thrumming thunder in their ears and lifted the long white hair from his shoulders. The waning daylight glinted in the sepia depths of his eyes.

Caris was silent for a time as they walked on through the dusk. He thought about the practiced ease with which the mad wizard had sparked the tensions between Bishop and Archmage, to make them turn upon one another and cease questioning him. Antryg had said it had been five years since they'd met—Caris wondered how he had known the suspicion would be so easy to arouse, for that touchiness of temper was something which had grown in the old man more recently, he thought, than that. But then, Antryg had known Salteris well.

He glanced back at the windowless tower, its surrounding buildings hidden again by the hills, a single warning finger lifted against the twilight milkiness of the sky. Then he dug in his purse for the *lipa* and returned it to the Archmage. He was plagued by the odd sixth sense that the sasenna develop, the feeling that there was coming a time when the old man was going to need it badly.

CHAPTER IV

THE SILENCE AFTER THE PRINT-RUN FINISHED WAS LIKE THE drop of a cleaver. Joanna looked up, startled as if by a noise.

But the only noise in the cubicle now was the faint, self-satisfied hum of the air conditioner.

Around her, Systems felt suddenly, terribly empty.

In something like panic her eyes jerked to the clock.

6:45.

Her breath leaked away in a small sigh. Not so very late.

You can't keep doing this, she told herself, shoving off with one sneakered foot against the filing cabinet and coasting in her wheeled swivel chair to the printer to tear off the long accordion of green-and-white paper. *The data's going to come in from the SPECTER tests this week, and everybody in the plant is going to be working insane overtime. You can't refuse to do the same on the grounds that you're afraid of the boogieman.*

She didn't even look at the graph as she folded it and stashed it on top of the stratified layers of junk on her desk. Her small hands were perfectly steady as she punched through backup and shut down, but she was wryly conscious that she performed the activity in record time.

You can't keep doing this, she repeated to herself. *It's been almost two weeks. Even if they didn't find him, nobody could live in hiding in this building for that long. And they've been over it a dozen times.*

But as she stashed her copy of *Byte* and the massive roll of printout from one of her own programs that she'd sneaked in to run on the Cray, her fingers touched the smooth handle of the hammer that she always carried with her these days. Once or twice in the last ten days, particularly when she was working late, she had had the feeling of being watched, and it came unbidden to her mind that there were a vast number of places in Building Six where someone could hide. The Analysis and Testing building was two stories high, but in most places it had only one floor. Above the labs and test bays loomed a vast loft of space crossed by catwalks where someone could lurk for hours unseen. Joanna knew it well—she had been tempted, over and over, to go there during the periods of gray and causeless depression that had come to her in the last few days, and only her fear of what she might meet there had kept her away. But Digby Clayton, the Programming Department's resident crazy, frequently went there to meditate—and have visions, so he said—and a number of people in the Art Department claimed to have gone up there and made love at ten-thirty on a Tuesday morning unnoticed.

It wasn't the only place, either, she thought, stepping resolutely into the well-lit blankness of the empty hall. The garage where they kept the fork lifts and electric trucks was accessible from a door near the supply offices. With a pocketful of change, you could live indefinitely from the junk machines—until malnutrition caught up with you, anyway, she added with an inner grin, in spite of her fears. And in the teeth of the much-vaunted security system, thefts had, as the guard said, proceeded regularly—everything from paper clips to computer components to telephone equipment by the metric ton. It would be easy to hide out there and wait. . . .

For what? Joanna demanded sensibly of herself and, with some effort, prevented her step from quickening. *If the man was a thief, he'd have gotten himself out the same way he got in—never mind what it was—and be long gone. Nobody in his right mind would hide out in San Serano for a week just to jump out and strangle people.*

But nobody in his right mind would climb to the top of a University bell tower to take potshots with a scope-sighted rifle at passers-by, either, her mind retorted, or murder perfectly innocent, semiretired rock'n'roll stars just to say they'd done it, or do any of the other gruesome things that had made the headlines within her memory.

You're paranoid, Joanna.

Who told you I was, and why? she retorted jokingly, and glanced once again over her shoulder.

It was like scratching a mosquito bite, she thought—something that didn't help, that you shouldn't do, but you couldn't stop.

Uneasiness stalked her, like the faint sound of her sneakers on the carpet. She found herself increasingly loath to pass the darkened openings of rooms and hallways on both sides of the lighted corridor, though she was not certain what it was that she feared to see.

At the junction of the main corridor she stopped, hiking her heavy purse up onto her shoulder and pushing her soft, unruly hair out of her face. Around her, the plain pastel walls were decorated with walnut-framed blowups of some of the more scenic photographs of the San Serano plant, dramatic in its barren backdrop of chaparral hills and clumps of twisted live oak, the grass either the white-champagne of summer or the exquisite emerald velvet of winter rains. The shots, Joanna was always amused to notice, were carefully set up to exclude the parking lots, the barbed wire, and the bluish blanket of Los Angeles smog in the background.

Down the dim hallway to her right was the main computer room.

The lights there were still on, though she could hear no voices. No shadow moved across them to blot the sheen of them on the metal of the doorframe. She'd been in the room almost daily since the assault, but there had always been people at the monitors and graphics printers connected to the enormous mainframe, and she had had deadlines prodding at her back. A half-memory from that night tugged at the back of her mind like a temptation she could not quite define—some unchecked incongruity that she had not spoken of to the guards because it was too absurd, and she had feared their laughter, but she wanted to verify it in her own mind.

It took more determination than she thought it would to make herself walk down the unlit hall toward the glow of the doorway. Knowing herself to be timid and passive by nature, her very reluctance made her go on.

The trouble is, she thought wryly, stepping up the slight ramp and into the clean-lit, cold vastness of the room, *you can't always tell what fears are irrational and what are only improbable. It would certainly help if this were a movie—I could listen for the creepy music on the soundtrack to warn me whether I'm making a stupid mistake or not.*

The computer was still up. In good lighting it was beautiful, its tricolored bulk looming like the Great Wall of China amid a tasteful selection of add-ons, which included four input desks, several banks of additional memory, and two six-by-six-foot color monitors capable of forming the most exacting of projections. Digby Clayton assured her that Pac-Man played on such a monitor was a truly visceral experience.

A blue-gray polyester blazer hung neatly over the back one of the chairs, and Joanna identified it, with a slight sinking of the stomach, as Gary Fairchild's. Better, she thought, to get this over quickly before he returned and asked her what she was doing here. She did not precisely know herself and she was never good at explaining things to people, particularly to Gary.

She walked a little ways into the room, and knelt on the floor in approximately the place she'd been thrown. Her memory of what she was seeking was a little clearer from down here, as if she'd left it like a contact lens on the carpet. She'd seen the candle in its anachronistic holder, the candle of which the guards had found no sign, sitting in front of the nearest monitor. A precaution, they'd said, against turning on the lights and possibly alerting a passing guard—but a flashlight would have served better, she thought, as she had thought then. There had been a black shadow descending upon her as her own mind darkened and, at the last moment, that glimpse of something on the wall.

From her angle near the floor she narrowed her eyes, finding the place.

Of course there was nothing there now.

She got to her feet again, feeling a bit silly. Brushing off the knees of her jeans, she walked to the spot. It had been a mark, she remembered, like a Japanese pictograph, but definitely not Japanese, about eight inches above her own eye-level and a foot to the left of the doorframe. It had been clear and sharply defined, but somehow unreal, like a spot of light thrown from a stray reflector rather than anything actually written there. She'd only had a glimpse of it, a sidelong flicker from the corner of her eye as she fell, and the memory of it was fogged by panic and terror. In any case, there was certainly no sign of it now.

She put the side of her face to the wall and peered side-long at the spot, hoping to see something from the different angle, as sometimes could be seen with glass.

Still nothing.

Mentally she shook herself. The janitors would have washed the wall since then, if nothing else, she told her-self, or—*did* the janitors wash the walls here? Probably—the computer room was a favorite showplace of the front-office boys. Or maybe there had never been anything in the first place.

Alfred Hitchcock's profile? she wondered frivolously. George Lucas' signature of THX1138? The footprint of a giant hound?

When someone yelled "Boo!" behind her, she nearly jumped out of her skin. A week of the jitters had, however, schooled her reflexes—her hand was in her purse and gripping the handle of the hammer before she had com-pletely swung around enough to recognize Gary Fairchild.

"Hey, calm down," he said, with his deprecating smile. "Did I scare you?"

She was trembling all over, but, rather to her surprise, her voice came out level and very angry. "Why? Wasn't that the idea?"

He looked confused and taken aback. "I—uh—Don't get mad. I mean—you know." That explained, he hastily changed the subject. "Were you looking for me?"

It was in her mind to say, *Why would I look for someone who'd play juvenile tricks like that?* but there was no point in getting into a fight with Gary. He'd only hang onto her, apologizing like hell for days, until she got tired enough to forgive him. Instead she said, "No, I came back in the hopes of catching the criminal when he returned to the scene of the crime."

Nonplussed, Gary said, "But that was days ago, babe. You don't think he's lurked around here all this time?"

"With a mental *Oi, veh,* Joanna said, "Joke, Gary."

Obediently, he gave a hearty laugh. Regarding him—white jeans, Hawaiian shirt bulging just slightly over conscientiously built-up muscles and an equally conscientious tan—Joanna wondered if she'd even like him, if she met him for the first time now.

In spite of two years of dating him, she had her own suspicions about that.

"Besides," she added, surreptitiously sliding the handle of her hammer back into her purse under the heavy wads of printouts, a brush, a mirror, pens, notebooks, screw-cap boxes, and a collapsible cup, "he might have come back. Whatever he was out to steal . . ."

"Babe," said Gary patiently, "what could he have stolen from here that he couldn't have gotten easier from the storage bays? Computer stuff is easier to rip off from there, before it's been dedicated—safer, too, because if it hasn't been logged in, nobody would even know it's gone."

This, Joanna knew, was true. She had her own theories about how Gary would know it. In her idle moments she had a habit of thumbing through the mainframe, breaking into files which the management of San Serano confidently assumed were hidden under their secret passwords; and she knew that, as a result of switching over to a new computerized system, the invoices were in a hopeless tangle. It was one of the things that had troubled her from the first about the guard's glib theory that she'd surprised and been surprised by a thief.

Her own alternative theories weren't particularly pleasant ones.

"I'll be done here in a few minutes, Joanna," Gary said after a few moments. "I can walk you out. Maybe we can stop someplace . . ."

She shook her head. "Thank you, but that's okay." She might be nervous about walking those empty corridors alone; but in her present uneasy mood, she knew Gary would be no improvement on imaginary maniacs. "I'll see you tomorrow, okay?"

He stepped forward and put his hands on her waist in the confident expectation of a kiss which, after a microsecond's hesitation for no particular reason other than that she simply didn't feel like kissing him, she gave him. As usual, he overdid it. "You are coming out to my place this weekend, aren't you?" he asked. "Everybody from the department will be there."

Reason enough to avoid it, she thought and vacillated, "I don't know, Gary..."

"I've got four new games for the computer, some good beer—even wine if you like that stuff—plus the new jet system in the jacuzzi, and some real nice..." He mimed blowing smoke in an elaborately silly euphemism for smoking pot.

Joanna sighed. So in addition to the boring middle-management types Gary hung around with, there would be drunk, stoned, boring middle-management types. On the other hand, she never went to parties, but she knew parties were the sort of thing people were supposed to enjoy. "It's a long drive," she began.

"Only ten minutes past here," he pointed out. "Most of the folks are coming up in the afternoon. We can sit by the pool, catch some rays, turn the speakers up full-blast.... What's the point of living clear the hell out here if you can't make a little noise now and then?" He repeated what Joanna had always guessed was the line fed to him by the real estate man who'd sold him the place. Since she knew Gary's taste in music ran to heavy-metal bands like Havoc and Fallen Angel, the prospect was getting less and less appealing all the time.

"The new graphics system I've got on the games computer is fabulous," he urged. "Please," he added, seeing her unmoved even by this. He flashed her a nervous grin that she had never liked and that had increasingly begun to irritate her. "Hey, you're my sweetheart, remember? The love of my life . . ." He drew her to him for another kiss. "I just wish we could be together. . . ."

"Gary." With sudden firmness that was less determination than simple weariness, she wriggled free of his indecisive embrace. "If you ask me to live with you one more time I really will quit speaking to you. I told you I don't know . . ."

"But why not, babe?" he asked, reproach in his big brown eyes and a suspicion of a whine creeping into his voice. "It isn't like your apartment is great or anything. You'd be closer to work here and not have to drive all that way; and you'd save on rent money. You know I'll always love you, babe . . ." She suspected he'd heard that line on TV. "Come Saturday, anyhow—see the place now that I've got the new computer stuff in. Are you doing anything else on Saturday?"

She wasn't, but hemmed, not sure how she should be reacting. "I don't know, Gary. I may be going out with some friends . . ."

"Invite 'em along," he offered. "Who are they? Anyone from here?"

Not feeling up to more flights of invention, Joanna sighed, "All right, I'll be there." His brown eyes warmed and his smile returned full-wattage.

"That's great, babe," he beamed. "Hey, are you doing anything else right now? I'll be done with this program in about fifteen minutes. . . ."

Joanna hesitated for a moment, wondering if she'd indulged in enough selfish behavior and ought to keep him company, even though it would probably involve dinner afterwards . . . and dinner at some coffee shop, at that. For all the money he made, Gary didn't believe in spending more than he had to on anyone but himself. But there was no guaranteeing how long any program would take to run —she was used to playing "Another five minutes" for up to an hour and a half at a time. "I don't think so," she said. "I'm going to go home, take a very long bath, and go to bed. I'll see you tomorrow." Ignoring his protesting, "Aw, babe . . ." she hiked her monstrous purse up over her shoulder and reciprocated his rather wet and amorous farewell kiss, more out of a sense of duty than enjoyment. Duty, she reflected later, walking down the dim hallway toward the bright rectangle of the main corridor ahead, not so much to Gary as to all those years of being pointed at as the School Nerd. She was conscious, as she walked, of a feeling of relief and wondered how she could ever have been in love with Gary Fairchild.

If it *had* been love, she thought, and not just the sexual glitter that surrounds the passage from virgin to nonvirgin. He had been, almost literally, the first man who had ever taken notice of her in her shy and bookish life. When she had first come to work at San Serano two years ago, Gary had asked her out, first to lunch and later to dinner, and had taken her home one night to the high tech Westwood apartment he'd been staying in that year.

He had always wanted her to live with him. Lately, he had begun to pester her about it, Joanna suspected, because he was thirty-four and reaching the age when he felt he ought to be living with somebody. He had bought the house in the expectation of it—or anyway, that was what he'd told her. But then, Gary was seldom completely honest, particularly if he thought he could drum up pity.

She sighed again, turning along the bright expanse of corridor. Twice in the last week, she had been plagued by the same queer, terrible feelings of hopeless depression which had come upon her on the night of the assault; at those times, she had found herself considering marriage to Gary, not because she loved him or even cared very much about him, but because she felt hopeless about her future to the extent that she did not much care what she did. Those depressions frightened her, chiefly because some small, sane part of herself realized that, in the grip of one, she had no real concern whether she lived or died—that if one came upon her while driving down the freeway, she would literally not bother to get out of the way of the other cars. The thought of living with Gary, she knew, was a little like that.

The rest of the time, she wondered what her life would be like now if she had moved in with him when first he had asked.

Well, for starters, she thought, you wouldn't be working here. And the reason you wouldn't be working here is because pool, jacuzzi, video room, an IBM-AT with 60 megabytes and $200,000 house in the hills notwithstanding, Gary would have driven you to leave him within two months by his assumption that he could interrupt whatever you were doing to keep him company, and you'd have quit your job and moved to another town.

Or else, she thought with a shiver, you'd be so chicken of change you'd still be with him.

And abruptly, the corridor lights went out.

Joanna stopped and swung around, feeling that the blood in her veins had turned to water. In brownish gloom, the corridor stretched empty behind her. Far back at the rear of the building, she could see the yellow glow of crossing hallway lights—ahead of her, the corridor stretched for another twenty yards or so, to the dim illumination around the corner that led toward the hall to the main lobby. *Just this section*, she thought. *Just a fuse . . .*

Terror breathed over her, like the wind from a half-open door that looked into the pits of eternity, unreasonable, shocking; she had to fight it to keep from breaking into a panic run. *It's just the lights going out*, she told herself, it's stupid to be afraid. . . .

Down some hallway to her left, she heard the stealthy slip of footfalls.

Gary, she thought, hoping against hope, but knew that

Gary never walked with that effort at silence. She hastened forward, her heart pounding, her hand sliding down to the handle of the hammer again, knowing it would do her no good. There was somethng else here, something past ordinary fear, a terrible knowledge that hummed over her screaming nerves.

Do I run? she wondered. *Or is this just what it's like to go insane? Were the depressions just a foreshadowing?*

But now the end of the corridor lay in darkness. The next section of cross-corridor must have gone out as well, she thought; but even as the idea went through her mind, she knew that no fuse failure could have produced a darkness like that. There was nothing beyond that darkness. She could not see the crossing wall with its bland photos of San Serano, only a shadow that seemed to have no end, as if she were looking into a starless night sky through a tube. Her reason told her it was a trick of the shadows, but her whole soul cried out against taking a further step toward that darkness.

Don't be silly, she told herself, sweat suddenly chilling her throat and clammy on her temples. *There's nothing to be afraid of in the dark.*

But there was. Was that movement, far off—farther off that could possibly be real, at the end of that corridor of darkness that could not actually exist? The glance of shadow along the fold of a robe, like a stirring of wind in the darkness—a breath of a smell she could not identify, but which shot her with an adrenaline injection of unthinking horror.

She turned right down a corridor, trying to remember how the other halls joined up to the one that would get her to the main lobby. . . . *This is silly,* she told herself, hastening her steps as much as she could while trying to keep them soundless. *Why am I having a nightmare when I don't remember falling asleep?*

The corridor plunged on, dim and uncrossed, to the far reaches of the test bays.

Without even questioning what she did or why, she opened the only door on that whole unbroken length, slipped inside and shut it behind her. It was a janitor's closet, smelling of ammonia and mildewing mopheads; as she shut herself in, the diffuse glow from the one-sixth-power lamps in the hall glanced briefly off a black, chitinous shape that retreated with offended haste beneath the baseboard. Even her old hysterical terror of roaches didn't trouble her now. She pulled the door shut and held fast to the inner knob in the darkness.

She could hear something in the hall.

It was hard to analyze, though she'd gotten good at identifying the minutest sounds from her months of living alone. Waking at night, she could track her way through her apartment with her ears—that was the refrigerator, that was the television antenna wire moving across the roof in the wind.

That soft, slurring sound outside now was like a stealthy footstep, but subtly different from those she knew. Fabric, she thought, remembering the heavy tangle of robe as she'd kicked at her assailant last week. . . . In the silence she wondered about the ears listening out there, and if they could hear the wild hammering of her heart.

Evil surrounded her, breathing and waiting, and she had backed herself into this corner in the stupid hope that it would pass. She heard the padding tread—walk, walk, halt. Walk, halt.

Does it know that I'm here?

There was a louvered grille in the lower part of the door to let in air and a feeble bit of light. Something blocked the louvers, some shadow. Under her hands, the doorknob moved testingly.

Her teeth and hands shut so tightly her bones ached. Terror jammed like a knot of unscreamed sounds in her throat, and she thought she could smell through the grille the faint, familiar odor of her earlier terror; the pungency of woodsmoke-permeated wool and the lingering cold scent or feeling that she could not define. The knob moved again, and she held tight to it, willing whatever was outside to think it was locked. Later she would find the gray plaid of her shirt soaked with sweat, but she had no consciousness of it now, nor of anything but a hideous dread. She knew if she had any courage at all, she should fling open the door, face what was outside, and see the intruder. What, after all, could he do to her in a public place like San Serano with help within easy call? But her resolve drained from her and a small, sane voice at the back of her mind whispered to her, *If you do that you will die.*

She wondered how she knew that, or if it was a common delusion. But her knowledge of it was so strong that she knew that nothing could have induced her willingly to open that door.

Filtered yellow light returned to the louvers. Whatever had blotted them was gone.

It is still in the hall, she thought—waiting for me. Waiting for me to think it's safe, to put my head out and look.

What?

What?

How long she stood in the smelly darkness she didn't know. Her legs began to shake, and dizziness swept over her. *There's a fifty-foot walk down this hall, around the corner to the next big corridor, and up along that to the lobby,* she thought. Her knees were trembling so badly she wondered if she'd be able to run.

Of course you won't run, the cool part of her mind said. *You've already made your reputation with the Man Who Wasn't There—not a fingerprint in sight and nothing but a few bruises which could have come from anywhere to prove there ever was such an intruder. They never found*

*the place where he got in. What are you going to tell them
if you go pelting into the lobby full-tilt and screaming?*

> *Yesterday upon the stair
> I met a man who wasn't there.
> He wasn't there again today.
> I wish that man would stay away. . . .*

It took all the courage she had to open the door. The
corridor was dim, innocuous, and totally empty. A few
yards away the main hall crossed it, brightly lit as always
and ordinary as only an aerospace building can be.

She managed to walk to the lobby. But she did it very
swiftly and drove down the hill toward Van Nuys at break-
neck speed through the darkness, to stare uncomprehend-
ingly at the television set until it was dawn and she finally
dared to turn out the bedroom lights.

CHAPTER V

STONNE CARIS REMAINED AMONG THE SASENNA AT THE House of the Mages for nearly a week. He trained with them, morning and afternoon, and enjoyed the chance to hone his skills with a new master's teaching and fresh opponents. One summer evening, all of the sasenna of the town, whether of the Mages, the Church, or the few nobles who kept permanent seats in the district and were wealthy enough to retain their own troops, went on a training hunt in the marshes. Caris had drawn to run with the wolves and dodged in and out among the boggy pools, accounting for four of his pursuers from ambush before Le struck him down from behind. They all returned to the city bruised, battered, and plastered with mud, to celebrate with much beer their joint funeral.

In that week he had a casual affair with a tavern girl, one of the few who did not open wide, kitten eyes at him and breathe, "You serve the *mages*? Is it true that . . ." and produce some fantastic piece of sexual practice rumor

ascribed to wizards. It was short-lived, though he was fond
of her; they quarreled during one of those strange, aching
episodes of depression, when his magic deserted him,
quarreled stupidly, as if they could not help it. Coming
down from her rooms, he heard her crying behind her shut
door; but in the strange colorlessness of the world, he saw
no reason to go back to comfort her. Afterward, ashamed
of the senselessly cruel way he had acted toward her, he
felt it was too late.

His grandfather he rarely saw. He knew the Archmage
was frequently at the episcopal palace, far grander than the
one attached to the St. Cyr fortress in Angelshand, for the
Bishop of Kymil was the chief prelate of the Empire. At
other times he knew the old man was simply abroad in the
countryside, tracing the stories of strange happenings and
abominations which seemed to haunt the surrounding villages like restless ghosts. One night by the fire in the small
sasenna barracks of the House, Le spoke of things seen,
heard, or rumored seen and heard—flopping white shapes
glimpsed between the birches of the woods by a home-
going farmer or the herd of sheep found slaughtered with
marks upon them no dog could have made or the three
people who went mad in the bright sunlight of an open
field near Poncross.

"Could that be connected with Suraklin's Citadel?"
Caris asked her the next morning, while they wandered
off-duty under the vast brick arches of the town's grimy
central market.

Around them a hundred stalls sent up a conflicting ca-
cophony of smell and noise, the heavy scents of violets and
roses vying with the half-spoiled meat and cheese of the
vianders and the overwhelming stink of fish. Chocolate
candy from Angelshand, fine cottons from the mills of Fel-
leringham and Kymil itself, daggers, shoebuckles, cheap
tin or porcelain pots of cosmetics, something advertised as
Electrical Hair Cream, clocks the size of a child's hand,

silk and delicately fragranced tea brought on caravans and ships at huge cost from distant Saarieque—anything could be had in that huge and gloomy emporium. They had bought rolls hot from the baker with primrose-yellow summer butter dripping from them and ate them as they roved among the stalls.

Le shrugged and took another bite of her roll. "Not that I ever heard," she said. With her short-cropped black hair and broken nose, she looked like a skinny teenage boy in her black jacket, trousers, and deadly, curving sword. "The fortress was razed by the wizards and the Emperor's Heir. All that's left are a few crumbled walls and a hole in the earth, far out in the hills."

"Will you ride out there with me?"

The lieutenant hesitated, as everyone, Caris had noticed, hesitated when it came to mention of the Dark Mage or anything he had touched. Then she nodded. "As long as we're back by four." They had duty that night, and Le, Caris knew, had a girlfriend of her own.

Once it passed the feet of the Silent Tower, the road to Suraklin's Citadel was lined once more with the standing-stones so hateful to the memories of those who dwelled in Kymil; it lacked even the pale traces of occasional commerce. Once or twice Caris, simply to test his own skills, tried to find signs that his grandfather had passed that way —as he knew that at some time in the last few days he had—but saw nothing. It took a powerful sasennan indeed to track a wizard. The road itself, overgrown to little more than a notch running through the round-backed green hills that crowded so close on all sides, ran perfectly straight, scaling the flanks of hills it could easily have gone around, or, on one occasion, climbing to the crest of a green tor from which Caris could see all the rolling, silent land beneath and the faint arrow of the road pointing inexorably away to vanish into the green wastes of the Sykerst, the empty lands to the east.

Wind thrummed in his ears and stirred his soft, fair hair and the mane of his horse; cloud shadows moved like torpid and amorphous ghosts across the land. The silence oppressed him. "It can't be this far, surely." For aside from the perfectly straight track of the old road, there was no sign that habitation had ever touched these bleak lands.

"It's a few hills over." Le, usually as calmly matter-of-fact as a pistol ball, did not raise her voice against that windswept hush. "You can't see it until you're nearly on top of it."

Caris shivered. He was conscious of how small he and the woman were in these hills, two black-clad forms in that empty silence. He looked around him for he knew not what. Old spells still clung to the land, the Dark Mage's might lingering in the stones. Squinting into the wind, he could see where another line of standing-stones crossed the far hills. Antryg had said to the Archmage that the Citadel was a node in the lines. The rudimentary stumps of Caris' own slight magic could sense the movement of power along this ancient road, and he realized that the Citadel had been built by some people far earlier than Suraklin along one of the energy-tracks that crisscrossed the earth.

The mages called them paths or lines or leys. Few understood what they were, and none knew why they existed. But exist they did—straight lines of energy along which magic could move, linked in some vast, unknowable grid. All magic—and all life, in some ways, the Archmage had told him once, back in the days when he had hoped to be a mage himself—was connected through them. The House of the Mages in Kymil lay in the line of this one—undoubtedly the Mages' Yard in Angelshand did the same with the line of stones called the Devil's Road. He felt, like a brush of wind, the touch of that moving power in his soul as he clucked to his horse and rode on.

The Citadel of Suraklin lay in the midst of a cup-shaped valley among the hills. Judging by the extent of the ruined walls, Caris could see that in its day it had been a great place indeed, yet he completely believed what Salteris had said—that without the help of the wizards, the troops of the Emperor's Heir, twenty-five years ago, would have wandered helplessly around the hills, unable to locate it, until the dark and nameless magic of that evil wizard had overtaken them. Though Suraklin had been dead these twenty-five years, some terrible spell of concealment clung about the place, and Caris literally was unaware that he was near it until Le called out, "Caris, watch out!" He woke from some momentary private daydream to find himself a yard from the vine-covered brink of an enormous pit, in the midst of a sprawling network of fallen stones that covered half a square mile of ground.

"It takes me that way sometimes, too." She rode up beside him as he cautiously kneed his horse to the very edge of the chasm. "Be careful—the ground isn't too good here." She glanced around her, her hand straying instinctively to the hilt of her sword.

The horses, knee-deep in the tangle of vines that cloaked much of the ruins of the Citadel like a rotting shroud, were clearly nervous as well. Caris felt a good deal of sympathy for the beasts' sentiments as he listened for some sound in the windless hush or scanned the skeleton outlines of stone walls still visible—hall, tower, workrooms outlined like the broken bones of a half-eaten carcass. Weeds forced apart broken paving-stones in what had been a vast court and lay in traceried circles of stringers. But mostly the ground had been torn open by the cumulative wrath of the wizards of the earth, and the pits which had underlain the Citadel gaped bare.

"They must have feared him," he said softly, "to leave no place where one course of stones stands upon another."

Le's curving mouth tightened. "You didn't live in these parts when his power covered the land," she said. "They said his ears were everywhere, and there was no telling who might be his agent; I know for a fact my uncle Welliger was involved in one of the attempts to contact the Archmage, with men he trusted—his own kinsfolk and his wife's, all men who'd had their goods taken or some member of whose family disappeared. But Welliger went blind before he could set out for Angelshand."

An odd gust belled in Caris' black jacket, flattened the thin shirt beneath against his ribs, then dropped to stillness again. Cloud shadows walked over the sun. Looking down into the pits, he could see down a number of levels, with shattered doorways with ivy and weeds. A tumble of white stones lay at the bottom like knocked-out teeth. It had been his grandfather's wrath that had called down the lightning to blast this pit—his might which had turned the tide against the cold evil that had so long festered here. It was hard to imagine it of the slender, quiet man who was his grandfather.

Like the final echo of the Dark Mage's decaying spells, wind sighed again in the nodding weeds. And without knowing quite how, Caris knew that someone was coming.

He glanced sideways at Le. She started to speak of something else, oblivious, and he signaled her silent. Though she was the elder and higher ranked, she obeyed his sign. They dismounted and led their horses down a crumbled ramp to what had been a shallow cellar, the only cover in that blasted ruin. After a few moments, Caris heard what had only whispered in his mind—the soft *swish-swish* of hooves in the tangling vines and voices which, in spite of their involuntary hush, sounded loud in the still air that hung over the Citadel.

A man's said, "Our men have followed him here thrice this week, my lord."

"So." That, too, was a man's, though higher and cold as the touch of metal on bare flesh. Caris was aware of Le's quick glance. Silent as a cat, he slipped forward, up the half-ruined ramp to the edge of the cellar pit. Lying flat in the wiry brambles, he could look along the ground to where the newcomers sat their horses at the edge of the ruins. "One may ask for what purposes. Abominations multiply in the lands . . ."

Somewhat diffidently, the first speaker, a middle-aged man in the plain gray breeches and narrow-cut gray coat that Caris recognized with sinking heart as the uniform of the Witchfinders, said, "The abominations have been seen for weeks, my lord; since long before the Archmage came to Kymil."

"He is a mage," the second man said. He turned his head. Against the summer sky, Caris recognized the ascetic profile and scant gray wisps of hair under the wide-brimmed shadow of the hat. It was Sergius Peelbone, Witchfinder Extraordinary to the Church. He felt something chill along his veins.

Peelbone went on, almost disinterestedly, "They say that the mages could move along the energy-lines at their will, traveling hundreds of miles in a day, to do a deed in Kymil when they had been seen that morning in Angelshand. And certainly it will be difficult for him to prove that he has not done so, particularly if it can be shown that he has been to this place." He scanned the desolation which lay about him. A scud of wind flicked the standing weed stalks by the broken stones, and his horse flung up its head with a nervous start. The Witchfinder's powerful hand twisted, dragging cruelly on the heavy bridle bit to force the beast to stillness. Even at that distance, Caris could see the smudge of blood that dripped to the grass.

"My lord," ventured the other Witchfinder, "it was the Archmage himself who brought about the ruin of this place and brought the Dark Mage down in defeat. It could be argued . . ."

"Anything can be argued," Peelbone said. "The old legends speak of the power of this place, before the Dark Mage raised his walls here; the old spells that linger are themselves enough to tempt in his dotage the mage who battled them in his youth. That, and the growing number of abominations in the land, should be enough to convince the Regent to give us the power we need, Tarolus—the power to put them all under arrest and to extirpate the heresy of witchcraft from the Empire."

The two horses moved off through the ruins. Caris said cautiously down to where Le waited, her hand over her mare's muzzle, her dark eyes hard. Caris found himself chilled all over with rage, both at the slandering of Salteris and at the calm deliberation with which Peelbone had spoken. As sasennan of the Council, he was powerless to do anything, for a weapon does not strike in anger, but he said softly, "Let's go. The Archmage should know about this."

They moved silently through the trenches of the broken cellars, leading their horses as far as the nearest ridge before mounting. Even so, as Caris glanced back at the silent ruins of the Dark Mage's Citadel, he could have sworn that the taller of the two mounted figures below turned to watch them as they disappeared over the hill.

"My lord! My lady! Please stop!"

Caris drew rein at the cries, looking down at the three or four men and women who came scrambling up the weedy, overgrown side of the marsh causeway from below. His horse, even before these people appeared, threw up its head with a snort, and Caris saw the white rim of fear around its eyeball. He cast a quick, semi-automatic glance down the other side of the raised roadbed, making sure it was not an ambush of some kind. There was no reason for it, but it was not the Way of the Sasenna to take chances. Then he and Le reined a step nearer to the panting farmers who came stumbling to their side.

"You are sasenna," the man gasped—little more than a boy of sixteen, stripped to his breeches for the haying, without stockings or shoes, his bare calves plastered in bog mud. "You must help us! Please! There's a thing—a thing in the marsh . . ."

"We can't stop," Le said coldly. "We are sasenna—we cannot strike without the command of our masters. . . ."

Caris held up his hand and leaned from the saddle. "What is it?"

"An evil—an abomination . . ." One of the women, stout and fortyish, with her voluminous skirts tucked up to reveal legs as muddy as the boy's, grabbed at the bridle of Caris' horse. The gesture made him nervous, even though he knew there was no ambush planned. "Oh, dear God, it's got Shebna!"

"Caris . . ." Le said warningly as Caris dropped from the saddle and pulled his sword sheath from his sash. "It is not for us . . ."

"My grandfather would command me to help them," Caris said. "I know it. He's the head of the Council. . . ."

Le's voice was sharp, "That decision is not yours to make!" Technically, he knew she was right; the anger in her voice stemmed from her own indecision "Your sword is not your own to draw."

One of the women sobbed, "Oh, please!"

An older man shouted, "Look, you heartless bitch . . ."

Caris caught that man by his bony shoulder. "No," he said. "She's right, but I'm coming anyway. Le—get the Archmage or Nandiharrow—or anyone." Hands were tugging at his sleeves, the faces all around him tallowy with terror and panic under the smearing of mud. He felt his own heart begin to pound with the rising lift toward battle. "Go on," he added as Le hesitated, her instincts to help warring with a lifetime of discipline in her sharp-boned face. He was turning back to the farmers before she had even lashed her horse to gallop away. "Where is it?"

It interested him to see how well his own training held. In spite of the cold excitement that surged through him, he found himself able to think clearly as they led him to the edge of the road and down the steep bank to the watery tangle of willows in the marshes below. For five years he had trained to become sasennan, yet now he was aware, with knife-blade clarity of thought, that, for all his training, he had never yet truly fought for his own life. The Empire was at peace; unlike many sasenna, he didn't seek brawls in taverns. Beside him, one of the women was sobbing, "It's the curse of the Dark Mage! He's left his curse upon the land! His devils are buried in the pools. . . ."

The smell of the marsh and the thick humming of the gnats that swarmed where the sunlight struck the scattered pools brought back to Caris his own childhood days of slogging after his parents at haying. His sword-sheath carried loose in his left hand, he cursed the head-high grasses that forced him to continually occupy his right hand in pushing a path—if there was an abomination here, the instants occupied in grabbing for his sword hilt might cost him or one of the people with him their lives.

"It's a devil," gasped the older man who had cursed at Le, his breath rasping with the effort of keeping up. "It's the Bishop we must be sending for, and the Witchfinders. . . ."

"Tell her to bring a sword, then," Caris snapped, still annoyed with him. "I may need . . ." His words ended in a gasp, as he stepped into the open shade of the willows.

The rank, standing sweet-hay had been cut for a little way along one side of a broad pool whose clouded brown waters showed how vast a thing had heaved itself up from their depths. The stubble, the felled hay—even the leaves of the willows above—were all dappled with the crimson brightness of splattered blood; it lay in little swirls in the water around the crushed skulls of the two men who sprawled on its verge. The thing on the far bank of the pool was holding a third person—a girl of thirteen or so—between its pad-fingered paws, her cracked skull still between its dripping mandibles. Blood overlay the reddish, tripy folds of its massive body like a glittering slime. At the sound of Caris' sword sliding from the sheath, it raised its crayfish head, rubbery, semitransparent pendules swinging his way for an instant; then, before Caris' shocked mind had a chance to do more than stare, it struck.

For all its size, it moved hideously fast. The water of the pool erupted in a surge of mud on both sides as it plowed through; Caris, used to the onrush of a man, had only time to gauge the paws and the stumpy, squamous, green-blotched tail before it was on him. Though his mind screamed to know what it was and from what obscene depth of insane horror it had risen, as sasennan his business and his training were simply to deal with it as an objective threat, a challenge like any other. That training saved him, letting him time the thing's incredible rush and spring aside, cutting down at the slender neck that connected that sagging, squidlike head to the rugose mass of body. The thing was turning even as he sprang, and the sword sliced through the dangling, stumpy tentacles that surrounded the mouth—or what might have been the mouth. Clear slime burst over him from the wounds, and the putrid fetor of the thing nearly made him gag as he twisted aside again and cut at the paddy, grasping, knotted paws.

His feet skidded in the mud. He was peripherally aware that, save for himself and the creature, whatever it was, the glade was deserted—the peasants had very sensibly fled. *They're unarmed*, he thought, desperately evading another lurching lunge, *and God knows, even armed and trained, how can I touch this thing?* Its long arms outreached him, and it moved with a horrible speed. His sword came down on the thin wrist and jarred on the bone—the blade that could cut off a man's leg with a single swipe. He felt the vibration of it through the bones of his arms to his shoulders, as if he had struck an iron bar; it crossed his mind to wonder if it had bones as he leaped aside. He splashed knee-deep in the muddy water and wondered, with sudden horror as the tepid liquid slopped over the tops of his boots, if there were more like this, buried in the immemorial black mud of the pool.

Something turned and rolled underfoot, and he staggered, hacking at the thing and trying to splash back to firmer ground. It was before him, churning in the shallows like an enormous cow, throwing filthy water up over his face, and he realized he was being driven. The water slowed his movements; his wet garments tangled stickily to his limbs. He cut at the grabbing paws again and opened one of them to the bone, but the sword jarred, unable to sever, and stinking, ochre slime leaked down the striated arm to pool like oil on top of the water. He sprang back and stumbled; something underfoot held for an instant, then shattered. His foot dropped into some cavity below and broken branches gouged his ankle through the boot leather. The next second, mud covered, slime-dripping paws closed bone-breakingly around his shoulders.

Waist-deep in water, pinned and nearly suffocated by the thing's stench, his hand fumbled for a dagger, even as he knew his own short life was over. He felt the massive strength of the thing tearing him free of the pool's bottom, lifting him toward the dripping beak, the slime running hotly down over his face as he tried to strike upward. . . . Then with a lurch the thing staggered, and the hideous vise of its grip slackened. Caris twisted and fell; mud half blinded him, but he saw the haft of one of the haymakers' pitchforks standing upright in the thing's back, flung at the last second by someone on the bank. As the creature tried to paw it loose, Caris rolled clear, scrambling desperately through the heaving waters that were now tobacco-colored with a mixture of blood and mud. There were people on the shore, many people. . . . He had a clouded impression of Le, of the Bishop Herthe standing in open-mouthed shock, and of the Archmage.

Salteris' voice cut like cold acid through his thickening senses. "Get out of the water!" The creature whirled and came slavering after him once more. Brown ooze streamed from it; the pitchfork bobbed and jerked in its back. Caris, still somehow clutching his sword, half crawled, half threw himself up on the bank among the damp, rank pads of the bloody hay. There was no time to get to his feet to run—he rolled over and over, inland, until he fetched up with a bruising wallop against the roots of a tree.

Thus he saw Salteris stride forward, his empty hand upraised. In the frame of silver hair, the thin features were very white, the dark eyes wide and somehow inhuman, calling down power as he had called it down against Sur-aklin. There was a leap and a crackle from the clear sky overhead, the harsh sizzle and stink of ozone, and thunder like a hand slamming Caris' ears. Blue in the daylight, lightning struck the brown waters of the pool. The creature was still knee-deep in them. For an instant, it seemed that the bolts crawled up over the whole of that hunched, hid-eous form. Then the thing convulsed, bending backwards, all the remaining, pendulous tentacles round its head stiff-ening out for an instant in a hideous corona around the flabby, desperately working mouth. The stench clutched Caris' throat and belly, even as the thing sprang and twisted, the pool waters heaving up around it in a brown and filthy wall.

Then it was rolling slightly, like a foundered boat, the muddy blobs of its feet sticking up above the slopping water and the tentacles of its head slowly relaxing in death. The pool was filled with crawling currents of nameless fluids and stank like a cesspit.

Caris buried his face in his arms, fighting the desperate sear of nausea in his throat. The frog-smelling hay scratched his face, and his wet clothes and dripping hair were suddenly cold on his clammy flesh as the battle-rush ebbed from him like blood from a severed artery. He was aware of the aching bruises on his shoulders, the sting of air through his torn shirt and jacket, and the excruciating ache of his right ankle. It was only gradually that it sank in upon him that he was still alive.

Footsteps approached. His every sinew protested as he did it, but as a sasennan must, he rolled over to meet what might be another attack with a drawn sword.

It was Le, as he had known it would be, and with her the boy who had guided him to the place and who, he suspected, had thrown the pitchfork which had distracted the monster's attention and saved his life. They helped him to his feet, Caris almost unable to stand with the violence of the reaction. He freed himself from their grip and picked up his sword, which was covered, like his clothes, with an unspeakable coating of mud and slime. Dripping like a halfdrowned sewer rat, he somehow walked by himself to the edge of the pool.

The Bishop Herthe stood there in the midst of her sasenna, still open-mouthed with horror. Against the gray of her velvet robes, her potato-like face looked pallid and boiled with shock.

On the churned and muddy brink, the Archmage Salteris gazed at the obscene thing still bobbing and wallowing in the pool. His white brows were drawn over his nose, his dark eyes not only baffled, but deeply troubled. Their expression changed to one of concern as Caris came near him. "Are you all right, my son?"

Caris nodded. He looked for some moments at the thing in the pool, thinking unbelievingly, *I fought that*, and wondering how he had dared. It was over twice the size of a horse. His whole body was one vast pain—his soul, too, with the shaken reaction to that single second when he had looked down the thing's pulsating throat and had known he would die. Shakily, he started to draw another deep breath.

But this close, the stench was enough to make him change his mind.

"What *was* it?"

The old man shook his head. "I don't know, my son," he said softly. And then, even more quietly, he added, "But I have a suspicion who might."

CHAPTER VI

THEY FOUND ANTRYG IN THE GUARDROOM ON THE LOWEST
level of the Tower, sparring with the captain of the Tower
guards with split bamboo training swords.

The journey to the Tower from the marsh had restored
the Bishop to her usual equilibrium—she had begun quarreling with Salteris before they were halfway there. As he
leaned against the stone arch that led into the guardroom
from the passage, Caris could hear them at it still. Before
him, in the jumpy light of a dozen torches, shadows looming huge on the fire-dyed wall, he could see the forms of
Antryg and the captain circling like cats. The captain's
loose black jacket and the shirt beneath and Antryg's trailing robes and beard were blotched with dark patches of
sweat; their wet faces caught the yellow glare of the light
as if they'd just doused themselves in a rain barrel.

The mad wizard, Caris was interested to note, didn't
wear his spectacles for the bout, but he moved unerringly
and with a dancer's grace. Caris had worked with the cap-

tain of the Tower once in the previous week; he was a huge Church sasennan, taller even than Antryg, fat and flexible and capable of crushing an opponent beneath the weight of his rush. Perhaps because of Antryg's madness, Caris had not expected the skill with which the wizard sidestepped and returned.

Looking at that odd face in its streaming tangle of hair, the gray eyes wide and intent with calm madness, Caris had the suspicion that, on the training floor, the mad wizard would be his master.

Behind him, he was aware of the Bishop's harsh whisper, "I cannot permit it," and the impatience in Salteris' voice.

"You needn't fear I will abet his escape."

"Needn't I?" Without turning his head, Caris could almost see the slitting of those shallow blue eyes. "He was your pupil, Salteris Solaris. It was only through your intercession that he was not killed, as he should have been, for meddling in the affairs of men at the time of the uprising in Mellidane. The Council of Wizards exist solely on the sufferance of the Church, a sufferance which depends upon our trust in you to regulate the teaching and practice of your arts and to keep those arts from ever touching the general life of humankind—*ever*. Look that you do not find the Church's might turned against you, as it turned five hundred years ago at the Field of Stellith."

"You *dare* . . ."

There was a note in his grandfather's voice Caris had never heard before. He swung around with such sharpness that every pulled muscle of his back twisted with a red stab of pain. The old man's eyes blazed with wrath and infuriated pride, looking amber as a wolf's in the firelight. His anger was like the molten core of a star sinking inward upon itself, swallowing both light and time. The Bishop fell back a pace before that sudden fury, her heavy face yellow with fear. In almost a whisper, the Archmage said, "You *dare* to threaten *me*?"

Her own anger kindling, the Bishop snapped, "I dare to threaten any who would break the vows that hold all things in order!"

Salteris opened his mouth in rage to reply, but Antryg's voice cut in reasonably, "In that case, we'll let you handle things the next time an abomination appears in the hay marsh." He had materialized without a sound at Caris' elbow, still holding his bamboo training sword. Sweat dripped from the end of his long nose and shone on his bare forearms as he drew the remains of a red Church wizard's cloak over his shabby robes.

The Bishop turned furiously on him. "What do you know of it?" she demanded, catching a tattered handful of his robe. Her face was scarlet with anger, as happened when one had been publicly driven to fear. Antryg shook back his sleek-matted hair and put on his spectacles, blinking at her from behind them in mild surprise.

"There must have been an abomination, mustn't there, for you to come in force like this to see me, and so urgently that Caris wasn't even able to change his clothes," he said. Caris, a little surprised, looked down at his dark clothes, still caked with the residue of mud and slime, though he had washed it from his face and hair and hands. "Whatever Caris did battle with, it was certainly in a marsh, and that marsh must be one of the hay marshes around the town. I'm surprised at you, Herthe—you're usually so good at the obvious."

He started to turn away. With angry violence, the Bishop seized his scarecrow robes and pulled him back to face her. The torchlight gleamed on her shaven skull and in her small, porcine eyes. "Beware, Antryg," she warned.

"Beware of what?" he asked reasonably. "I'm safe behind the walls of this Tower. It's you who have to deal with the things. Would you hold this?" He offered her the long hilt of the bamboo sword still in his hand. Surprised, she took it, releasing her hold on his robes to do so. He said, "Thank you," and vanished into the darkness of the narrow stair.

Her face flushed, the Bishop moved to follow, but Salteris laid a staying hand on her beefy shoulder. "No," he said softly. "It would do little good, with you there."

"We can compel him . . ."

The Archmage's voice was suddenly harsh. "No member of the Church—*none*—has the right to lay hands upon one who has sworn the vows to the Council of Wizards."

"The case is different!" the Bishop declared furiously. "The abominations . . ."

"The case is not different!"

For a long moment they stood, staring into one another's eyes. Caris felt the heat of the old man's pride and wrath again, as if he stood near the door of a stove, but hidden now, heat without light. The Bishop's heavy mouth set. Then, as if he realized where they were, without magic in the Church's power, the old man turned suddenly away. "Come, Caris. There is little to be learned here. But I tell you this, Herthe of Kymil. Should you or Peelbone and his Witchfinders or anyone else move against Antryg Windrose or any Council mage without my leave, I shall learn of it, and then . . ." His voice sank, and the dark brown of his eyes seemed to glint again with an amber flame, ". . . you will have to deal with me."

It was only when they were walking down the hill in the lingering blueness of the summer dusk that Caris dared to speak. The Archmage was walking very swiftly, his black robes billowing about him. Caris' hurt ankle jabbed him at every step; but, after five years of training, neither that nor the bone-weariness of stiffening muscles troubled him as much as that terrible silence that still hung about Salteris like the darkness of stormclouds.

As they reached the foot of the tower hill, Caris asked, "Why?"

The old man glanced testily at him. Then, seeming to see him for the first time, he slowed his steps. "Are you all right, my son? I'd forgotten—you were hurt. . . ."

Caris shook his head impatiently. "Why did you defend him? He knows more than he's telling. If they can compel him to speak . . ."

Salteris sighed. "No. For one thing, he's tougher than he looks, our madman, and far more clever. We could never be sure we were getting the truth, if in fact he is even aware of it himself. For another. . ." He paused, staring back at the darkness of the Tower against the milky twilight sky. "They are only waiting for that. The Bishop and Peelbone—it is their chance, to establish their jurisdiction over us, to gain a precedent. That is why, above all other things, I must be careful with Antryg."

As in another life, Caris remembered the sharp noon sunlight on the desolation of the Citadel and the Witchfinder Peelbone's thin cold voice in the silence. "*Could* Antryg be responsible for the abominations?" he asked.

Salteris walked on in silence for a few moments more, his white brows drawn together, and the look on his face was one of utter bafflement such as Caris had not seen him wear in years. "I don't know," he said at last. His soft boots scuffed the long grass that overgrew the edges of the broken pavement of the ancient road. "I don't see how he could, and I . . ." He hesitated, then shook his head. "But I am unfamiliar with these things. Though I have crossed the Void, I—I have not the sense of it that Antryg has—or had." His thin mouth hardened for a moment with something like annoyance. "It might be that they come through the Void—and then again, he could be creating them in some fashion. But in either case, he can neither work magic nor touch the Void from within the Tower. Else he would have escaped long ago."

"Would he?" Caris asked suddenly. He halted, hooking his hands through his sword belt, and looked at the old man doubtfully. "A room with an open door is not a cell."

There was a long silence. In the old man's face was the nearest thing Caris had ever seen to surprised enlightenment. Then he nodded slowly to himself. "Trust a sasennan," he said softly after a moment. "The best place to hide is in plain sight—I had almost forgotten that Antryg was always a genius at that. If he has found some way of working magic from within the Tower, its walls would prevent any other mage from knowing it." As if another thought crossed his mind, he frowned again and shook his head. "No—it is impossible."

"Is it?" Caris persisted. The discipline of the Way of the Sasenna made him unwilling to contradict the Archmage, but something about the dusk and his own stretched weariness lessened between them the barrier raised by years and his vows. As a child, he had trailed gamely after the old man while his grandfather searched for yarrow in the marshes, and had asked whatever he thought. In a curious way, he felt the echo of that old intimacy. "You said yourself there are things about the Void you don't understand. Perhaps he does. Could he be creating these things, instead of summoning them through?"

As they walked on, the old man said thoughtfully, "They say Suraklin could summon the elemental spirits and bend them to his bidding—could clothe them in flesh of his own devising, so that they could tear and hurt with their uncontrolled anger, instead of just knocking on walls or throwing pots as they usually do. But if that were the case," he continued, as Caris offered him his hand to help him down a stream cut which gouged the road, "I would not have been able to slay the thing as I did."

"How *did* you slay it?" His grandfather's scarred arm felt strangely light and fragile in his grip as he helped the old man up the broken stones and cracked hunks of old pavement. Now at the end of summer, the stream which had cut the road had long since dried—the mud at the bottom bore the marks of the constant trickle of feet, coming and going to the Tower.

The memory of the old man's dark, inhuman eyes as he summoned the lightning seemed as impossible to him as the white heat of his pride and anger against the Bishop had been—as, indeed, was the knowledge that it had been he who had led the assault on the Citadel.

The old man smiled. "With electricity."

"*Electricity*?" Caris' dark brows dove down over his nose.

His grandfather's smile widened. "This looks like a good place," he remarked, and led the way off the road, between two of the fallen menhirs, his robe slurring softly in the open grass beyond. Limping a little, Caris followed, as he used to follow in his childhood, not asking where they went or why. They passed along a little gully between the round backs of the hills. The dusk closed around them like veils of smoke-colored silk.

"Dr. Narwahl Skipfrag has been experimenting for some years with electricity," Salteris continued, as he picked his way along some unseen track in the deep grass. "It was his experiments, in fact, which first led him to speak with me —though of course we had met at the Imperial Palace in Angelshand. During the conflict with Suraklin, the Prince Hieraldus and I became friends. When he succeeded his father and became Emperor he patronized us as much as the Church and his reputation would allow, and I came to know a good many of the Court. Narwahl was the Emperor's physician, then as now, but he's also a scientist. At first, he thought magic might be some type of electricity, and it was thus that he and I came to speak."

They crossed the stream bed again—or perhaps a different one; this one had water in it, nearly choked in a brambly tangle of wild roses, around which the last bees of the evening swarmed drunkenly. As he helped the Archmage up the far bank, Caris reflected that he must have picked up his minute knowledge of the countryside around Kymil during the days of the war against Suraklin—he certainly seemed to know every dip and gully of these silent hills. Following along in the old man's tireless footsteps, Caris felt ashamed, not only of his stiff and aching muscles, but of the queer dread he felt in this haunted land. With the starry darkness, the memory of the abomination returned disturbingly to his mind. It had come from nowhere, and he was too aware that there was nothing to prevent the coming of another.

For five years, Caris had trained as a sasennan, a strenuous life, but uncomplicated. Now, moving through the dreamlike landscape of the summer dusk, he felt as if he trod the borders of a land he did not know, fighting unknown things with weapons which would have as little effect upon them as his sword had had upon the swamp thing's iron bones. Ashamed of his uneasiness he might be, but nevertheless he felt glad the Archmage was with him in the blue and trackless emptiness through which they passed.

Salteris moved his fingers, seeming to pluck a raveled thread of light from the air, and cast it before him to float like a glow worm along the ground a little ahead of their feet. "According to Narwahl, electricity can be conducted by water, in the same way that it is conducted by metal; and, moreover, metal or water will prevent the possibility of electricity grounding harmlessly away into the earth. Lightning, he says, is only electricity in its natural form." The same wry, astringent smile touched his lips. "I shall have to write to him and tell him of the successful demonstration. He will be pleased."

"And the abomination?" Caris asked.

The old man sighed, the smile fading from his face like the last fading of the daylight.

"Yes," he said softly. "The abomination."

For a time they walked in silence, Caris thinking again of that tall, gawky lunatic in his tattered robes and ink-stained beard and of the bright gray gaze behind those heavy lenses. Would a man who had been a prisoner for seven years retain that odd, buoyant calm? The scant experience of his own nineteen years gave him little help. Smelling now the late-summer headiness of the night, feeling the touch of straying breezes on his face, he doubted it. Like the breath of a ghost, the memory of the fading of his powers brushed him, the dust-colored uncaring and the terror he felt, knowing that those spells of fading would recur, as they were recurring more and more often. In the end, his powers would never return. Could one whom his grandfather had called the most powerful mage in the world have endured that loss?

Could that, in its turn, have driven him mad?

Or had he never suffered it?

Caris turned to look back over the hills, where the dark shape of the windowless Tower bulked against the sky.

"Here we are." Salteris gestured, and a clinging frost of light momentarily edged the deep blueness of a little hollow among the hills. A standing-stone had once been planted there, but had fallen long ago and now lay co-cooned in wild ivy and bramble. In the lee side of one crowding hill a thicket of laurel and hawthorn rustled with the quick nervousness of birds' wings; on the opposite hillslope, gentler and stretching off into a vague space of dusk that rose toward the deeper twilight of the sky, rabbits paused in their grazing to look down at the brief network of diamonds that the Archmage had cast. Then the swift glow faded, and with it the ravelly blue phosphorescence that had guided their feet. Caris made his way carefully to the fallen stone and sat on the bare place at its end.

"We will wait here," Salteris' voice said out of the shadows, "until full darkness covers the land."

His shape melted from the gloom; his face and the silky white mane of his hair were one large blur, his hands, two small ones at his dark sides. "And then, my son, we will return to the Silent Tower, and I will speak to Antryg Windrose myself."

He settled quietly at Caris' side. From somewhere about his person, he drew his worn black gloves, stitched with shabby bullion on their backs, a present from the Emperor, before imbecility had claimed the man. He began to put them on, then changed his mind and tucked them instead into his belt.

"Are you cold?" Caris asked, and the old man shook his head.

"Only tired." He undid the small satchel at his belt and took from it bread, cheese, and two small green apples, which he divided with his grandson. Though it was not the Way of the Sasenna to eat on duty—and Caris considered himself on duty—he accepted the food gratefully.

Ruefully, the Archmage went on, "And you must be in far worse case than I, my son. I apologize, but I must speak to Antryg alone, without the Bishop present, and it must be soon. If he knows something about the abominations, I must learn it, before the Witchfinders take it for their excuse to destroy us all. You heard them today. . . ."

Caris paused in wolfing down his supper to stare at him in surprise. "I did," he said, "but I had no idea *you* were there."

"I wasn't." The old man smiled. "But a mage can listen along the energy-trails—and I have been particularly watchful of Peelbone lately." He sighed and stroked the velvet-soft leather of the gloves at his belt. "It is an old trouble." He sighed. "And the reason, indeed, for the Council vows—the underpinning of the Church's whole attitude toward magic and toward the dog wizards. No society, they say, can exist with both magic and industry— technology—the use of tools and machines. It takes so little magic to ruin the balance of a machine, my son; and magic can be worked by so few. For thousands of years, power lay in the hands of those who were powerful mages themselves, or who could afford to hire them. It was in those years that the Silent Tower was built, and for that reason. It was then that all the binding-spells were wrought, great and small—from the Sigil of Darkness and other things like it which are utterly abominable to the mageborn, down to the little ones which make this or that thing na-aar—metaphysically dead and impervious to magic—like the pistols and crossbows of the Witchfinders, so that no mage can fox their aim or cause them to misfire, and such things as spell-cord and spancels. But it was all politics. The people were no better for it."

He sighed again. "The Sole God of the Church is not the god of the mageborn, Caris. As sasennan of the Council, you do not make the signs of obeisance in the presence of holy things. In time, the Church raised its own corps of wizards—the *hasu*—and used their magic to defeat the wizards in a long war which ended on the Field of Stellith, five hundred years ago. And they were aided by other mages, not of the Church, but who could see that, in that, the Church was right; the privileges of the few had to be curtailed for the rights of the many. That is the reason for the Council Vows.

"And since that time . . ." He shrugged. "I fear they were right. Humankind now has great new looms and gins to weave its cloth, in the factory towns of Kymil and Parchasten and Angelshand. They talk about making engines that will go from the power of steam to work them one day. There are new sorts of farm machines to sow the seed better than a man scattering it broad-cast from a sack, and engines to harvest and thrash the grain—who knows, one day they may find a way to power them by steam as well. They have ships built light and strong enough to race the wind that can make the voyage to Saarieque and the East in sixty days, to make men's fortunes in silk and tea and the emeralds of the Isles."

"But that isn't all!" Caris broke in, distressed at the sadness in the old man's voice. "There is more in the world than—than money in the pockets of the merchants and machines to make things to sell! Isn't there?"

And for a time, only the sweet hush of the long evening answered him—the sleepy twilight cry of whippoorwills from the boggy ground near the stream, the strange, half-hurtful stirring of the earth-magic whispering up out of the ground beneath the grass. He felt, even with his own small and, he suspected, fading resources, the magic all around him, alive and vibrant, and wondered how, even for the good of everyone in the world, it could be for a moment denied. The knowledge that one day soon he would lose it was like the knowledge that he would one day die.

"There is," the old man said finally. "The will—the fire—the striving. They deny it and claim that it does not exist, until all those who listen come to believe it and do not know how to name it once they feel it quicken in themselves, except by such names as 'foolishness,' and 'insanity,' and 'badness.'"

"And Suraklin?"

Caris spoke the name softly, within these hills that had been Suraklin's; within sight of the Tower where the Dark Mage had once been chained to await his death. Salteris, an almost invisible shape in the dusk, sighed again, and the last light caught one thread of silver in his hair. It was a long time before he replied.

"Suraklin was the last of the great ones," he said, "the last of the wizard-kings, born long after his time with the will and the strength to dominate. So much of his power came from the fact that most of those who obeyed him, through fear and, yes, through love, refused to believe that this magic truly existed. And his magic was the greatest— truly the greatest. I knew it. He would have been Archmage, were it not that the others in the Council distrusted the depthless darkness of his soul."

He turned and faced Caris in the intense, phthalo darkness of the summer night, his eyes nothing but shadows under the star-edged dome of his bald forehead. "That is why I fear now," he said softly. "Antryg Windrose was Suraklin's student."

For a time Caris could only stare at him, aghast and silent. For a week he had lived close to the legends that surrounded the Dark Mage; the memory of Suraklin clung to the land like a decaying ghost. It was hard enough to believe there were people alive who had known him, though Caris knew his grandfather must have. That the mad, oddly charming prisoner in the Silent Tower had been his pupil. . . . He stammered, "But—the Bishop said he was yours."

"I found him two years after the breaking of Suraklin's Citadel," Salteris said. "He was hiding in a monastery in the Sykerst. Nineteen years old; no older than you are now, my son, and already a little mad. I taught him, yes, though he had very little to learn. We traveled together for many years, both then and after he was elected to the Council, but always I had the sense in him of hidden pockets of darkness, buried so deep maybe he was unaware of them himself. There was a time when I loved him as a son. But I never underestimated him."

"Then don't do so now," Caris said, looking over at the old man's dim shape in the gloom with a sudden qualm of fear. "Don't meet him alone."

Salteris shook his haed. "In the Tower he is not dangerous."

"You can't know that."

"Caris . . ." The gentle voice was at once amused and reproving, as it had been when Caris was a child. "Are you now going to protect me? Even if Antryg is the cause of the abominations—even if it was he who shot Thirle as he fled back through the Void—I doubt he would harm me. In either case, I do need to speak to him alone."

"The guards won't let you in."

White teeth caught the gleam of the stars as Salteris grinned. "The guards won't see me. No magic is possible within the walls of the Tower itself, but I can still weave illusions in the court." He got to his feet and shook the bread crumbs from his robe. "Come and watch me."

Even two years of service to the Council of Mages had not quite prepared Caris for the Archmage's entry into the Silent Tower. The guards who raised the portcullis greeted them respectfully as they stepped from the darkness. Salteris apologized to the captain and said that he had discovered something while crossing the hills which made it imperative that he speak with Antryg Windrose once again. The captain twisted the spiked ends of his red mustache, his eyes glinting like agate in the uneasy saffron torchlight beneath the gate.

"I'm sorry, m'lord," he said at last. "It's forbidden to speak to him without the Bishop present, and those are my orders."

"Very well," said Salteris quietly. "Be so good as to send for her."

The captain opened his mouth to speak, but something about the frail old man before him made him close it again. He turned abruptly and bellowed into the watch chamber just within the portcullis, "Gorn! Get out and get a horse saddled." He turned back to Salteris. "It'll be a time— she's had a good hour's start."

"I understand," replied the old man, inclining his head. "Believe me, captain, if it were a matter which could wait until morning I would certainly not put her Grace to this inconvenience."

The captain grunted and scratched his huge paunch through his loose, dark jacket. For all his faintly sloven air,

Caris noted the polish of the captain's well-worn sword belt and the oiled gleam of the scabbard thrust through it. The blade within, he guessed, would not be one dulled with neglect. "Well, it's a nuisance all around. There's wine in the guardhouse . . ."

"Perhaps." Salteris favored him with a chilly smile. "But there is also tobacco smoke, for which I wouldn't trade the smell of the summer night. We shall do well here, until it gets too cool." He took his seat on a stone bench just within the heavy portcullis, where the watchroom door threw a luminous bar of shifting apricot torchlight across the intense blue gloom under the gatehouse.

"As you please," the big man said. "If there's anything you want—wine or food or tea or whatever—just give a shout for it. And you—" he added to the young man who appeared in the passage, leading a rat-tailed roan gelding, "—make it smart, hear? If you catch her Grace on the road, it'll be one thing; but if she's sat down to her dinner already, we're all of us going to be what she eats for dessert. Now off you go."

The hooves thudded on the road, and a faint whiff of dust blew back from the darkness. Then, with a rattle of weight, chain, and counterwheel, the portcullis rumbled slowly down. The gate was dragged shut behind it and the small bar put into its slots; the captain's huge back blotted the rosy watchroom light for a moment, and then was gone into the smoke and frowst within. In the resulting pocket of utter darkness under the gatehouse, Caris took a seat beside his grandfather on the bench. Through the lighted door, he could see the big man settle himself at one end of the rough wooden table and pull a quart tankard to him, grumbling as someone shoved him his cards.

He was changing his seat, Caris realized, to watch them unobtrusively through the door.

"Very good," Salteris' voice murmured, pitched for Caris' ears alone. "We should have over an hour until the

Bishop arrives." He folded his slender hands and settled his back against the stones of the wall behind him, like a man making himself comfortable for a long siege. In the guard-room, someone threw down his cards and cursed richly—there was laughter and profanity-sprinkled banter. The captain threw back his head to join in, but Caris was aware of the tiny glint of his sidelong glance.

He pulled a bit of chamois and an oilcloth wrapped in a rag from his belt purse and set to work getting the mud and dried slime out of the crannies of his sword hilt. Beside him, his grandfather murmured, "How are you at the courtly art of conversation, my son?"

Caris glanced over at him, startled, and again caught the quick glint of the old man's smile in the gloom.

"Do you think you could carry on half of a conversation, as if I were here?"

"You mean, just talk to the air?"

"That's right. It needn't be animated—just do as you are doing and, every now and again, address a remark my way or reply to one that I might make if I were here. Don't look into the guardroom," he added, sensing that the young man was about to cast a glance at the captain; Caris looked quickly down again, concentrating his attention upon the brasswork of the pommel instead.

"Will that serve?" Caris asked softly. "You're in the light . . ."

"And he shall see me in the light," Salteris replied, his voice equally low. "It's one of the dead giveaways of illusions, if the person next to one takes no notice of it. I shouldn't be long."

"But—"

"I'll be all right," he said softly. "I need you to cover my tracks while I'm gone. I should be able to handle Antryg, even if, as I suspect, he is not quite so powerless within the Tower as he would have us believe."

"But the Sigil? The Sign of Darkness?"

Salteris smiled. "I shall be able to deal with the Sigil of Darkness. Just stay here, my son, and talk—don't chatter, it looks unnatural—and I shall be back within half an hour. If I am not . . ." He hesitated.

"What?"

"If I am not," he went on, his voice suddenly deadly serious, "don't risk trying to deal with Antryg yourself. Get the other mages and *get them at once*." He moved to rise.

Caris had to prevent himself from calling attention to them by catching his sleeve. Instead he breathed, "Wait." The Archmage stood poised, like a dark ghost just beyond the edge of the light. "Will you leave me the *lipa*?"

Salteris thought about it for a moment, then shook his head. "I fear I cannot. For if my worst fears are realized, I may need it myself."

Then he was gone.

Caris sat in silence for a time, belatedly aware that, with his usual ease, Salteris had duped him into staying out of danger. Perhaps, for some reason, he really had wanted to meet Antryg with no witnesses present—perhaps it was only out of consideration for Caris' weariness and injuries, though, Caris told himself stubbornly, they weren't much. In any case there was no way he could follow now without giving the game away; he had to fight the impulse even to look, knowing the captain would be watching him from the door. In the soft twilight of the hills, the Archmage had made light of the peril into which he walked; it was only now that Caris understood that his grandfather, too, knew it for what it was.

But having seen the abomination in the marsh, the old man considered the knowledge Antryg might hold worth the risk of—what?

Caris did not know.

He realized he had been silent too long. No conversationalist even with someone who *was* present, he stammered, "Uh—did I ever tell you about the time cousin Tresta and I stole the town bull?" and turned with what he hoped was naturalness to the empty place at his side. Beyond, the small square of the yard lay under a thin wash of starlight, the cracks between the flagstones like a thin pattern of spiderweb shadow. He could see the door of the Tower clearly, with its two black-clothed sasenna side-by-side. His small magical powers permitted him to see in the dark after a fashion; he glimpsed a drift of shadow that must be Salteris near the wall. One of the guards at the Tower door sneezed violently as the old man's shadow passed before him; the other, startled, jumped. Caris was not sure, but thought he saw the heavy door open a crack. In the utter darkness of the slit, white hair gleamed like a slip of quicksilver—then nothing. He did not even see the door close, but when he blinked, he saw that it *was* closed.

He recalled the Sigil of Darkness and shivered. Evidently, he thought, there *was* some way of dealing with it—at least of getting in. If Salteris knew, there was the possibility that Antryg Windrose might, also.

Remembering what he was supposed to be about, he said quickly, "That's very interesting—uh—grandfather. How did Narwahl Skipfrag get interested in electricity?"

Yet his apprehension did not fade. It ebbed for a few moments, then grew again—not his own fear of detection, but something else, something he did not understand that prickled along his nerves, a sudden uneasy fear that brushed his neck like wind from a door which ought to be locked. It was something he had felt before, somewhere— some evil. . . . He was aware of an odd stirring in the back of his mind, neither nervousness nor fear, but akin to both, a sense of magic and a danger that could not be met with a sword. . . .

Something moved in the archway of lapis darkness that led into the court. Lines of shadow from the stretched ropes of the counterweights brushed blackly across the red robes of one of the hasu as he entered the dark gatehouse at a rapid walk.

Caris bit his tongue, forcing himself to remain still. Being mageborn, the hasu would see that he was alone on the bench; but then, the hasu did not know that there was supposed to be anyone else there. Caris knew he teetered on the edge of discovery—in his finger-ends he was ready to explain or to fight. Robes crimson in the gold glare of the watchroom torches, shaven head catching an edge of the sherry-colored light, the young hasu stood beside the captain's chair, speaking rapidly, worriedly, to the captain, glancing about him, as if he scented danger but knew not where to look for it.

He feels it, too, Caris thought suddenly. The foretaste of unknown fear blossomed within him. The darkness in the corners of the court seemed to ripple, like sunlight on the open plains in burning heat. He felt again the cold touch of the unreasoning terror that had come over him in the Mages' Yard, as he had gazed into the black eternities that lay beyond the threshold of the world as he knew it, as if those abysses lay suddenly within reach of his hand.

He realized, suddenly, what was happening within the Tower.

It was as if the ground had opened beneath him, plunging him into an ice stream. He was on his feet, rage and fury igniting in him. "*No!*"

The captain swung around, and in his eyes Caris saw the Archmage's carefully wrought illusion fail and crumble. The big man lunged to the door, brushing aside the slighter form of the hasu—"Where . . ."

Caris was already running across the court, his sword in his hand. "It's a trap! Antryg trapped him!"

Wolf-swift for all his great bulk, the captain of the Tower overtook him even as the guards seized him at the Tower door. Heedless, Caris twisted against their grasp.

"Let me in! The Archmage went in there, he tricked

you . . ." Close to the door the feeling was stronger, the cold breath of the Void like a death-spell whispering in his heart. The stupid, stubborn look on the guards' faces infuriated him. "Don't you understand? He thought Antryg was lying out of fear of the Bishop. Can't you feel it? Antryg wanted him alone!"

The hasu came panting up beside him, sweat glittering like a film of diamonds on his shaven forehead. "The strangeness in the air . . ." he began uncertainly, too young to trust in his own judgment.

"Let me into the Tower!"

For an instant the captain glared at him, gauging him with eyes like dark pebbles of onyx. Then abruptly he snapped at the guards, "Open it."

"But . . ."

"Open it, you fools!" he bellowed. "He's the Archmage —you wouldn't have seen him if he'd kicked you in passing!"

The breath of the Void seemed everywhere now, stirring and whispering in the night as one man removed the dark Sigil from the door and the other twisted the iron key in the lock. Looking back over his shoulder at the courtyard, Caris seemed to see flickering patches of darkness where no shadow should lie, swimming in the air of the court; the guards in the circular chamber at the Tower's base were clamoring with the edginess and anger of frightened men as Caris plunged impatiently through. Terror of the blackness of the Void and terror of what he would find pressed upon him, thicker than the darkness, as he plunged up the narrow, tenebrous spiral of the stair. He shouted, "Grandfather!" and his voice roared back at him in the strait of the walls. "Grandfather . . ."

A hideous darkness filled Antryg's study, like a wavering cloud. Like a cloud, Caris could see through its edges and make out, as if through moving gauze, the shapes of the book-littered table, the overturned chair, and his grandfather's bullion-embroidered glove lying on the corner of the small hearth. Through that darkness, the candles still burned, but the flame was a bleached and sickly white that shed no illumination into the heart of that well of black space that stretched into a falling eternity of nowhere. Far, far along the darkness, he thought he saw a dim figure fleeing, a stir of movement in those terrible depths. The darkness was already beginning to dissipate at its edges, clearing like smoke into the air; the black eye of its center retreated, farther and farther along that distance that never seemed, in all its endless plunge of miles, to reach the opposite wall.

Caris cried again, *"No!"*

His sword was in his hand as he plunged after that retreating shape into the darkness, and the cold abyss swallowed him up.

CHAPTER VII

THE NIGHT WAS SOFT AS SILK AND WARM AS BATH WATER.
The stars, Caris saw, were the ones he knew. The brilliant
Phoenix-star lay on the edge of the dark circle of hills,
calling to its mate a quarter of the way up the sky. The tip
of the Scythe still pointed to the inner and unmoving heart
of the heavens. The air was dry and sweet with the scent of
warm dust, underlain by some metallic tang that caught his
throat.

He, at least, was safe.

For a long time, his awareness consisted of only that.
Kneeling in the thin, dry grass, he fought the wave of
shakiness that threatened to wring his meager supper from
his guts. It was more than just the utter terror of that long,
half-falling run through cold and sightless chasms and that
terrible disorientation and the horror of knowing that he
could well be lost forever, without even hope of dying,
more than the sickening aftermath of fear-induced exertion
that had spurred his final, desperate run toward the retreat-

ing starlight at the end of the closing tunnel of eternity. He was more weary than he had ever been in his life. His exhaustion after fighting the abomination—had that only been this morning?—seemed petty and laughable now, for then he had been in a world he knew, surrounded by people of whose reactions he could be sure. Then the Archmage had been with him.

He wanted nothing more than to lie where he was and sleep for a week.

But it is the Way of the Sasenna to rise and go on.

He managed to raise his head.

The crest of the hill upon which he lay cast a black semicircle of shadow in the dell beneath. Beyond its edge, the smudgy light of a newly risen three-quarter moon lay upon the thin grass of the opposite hillslope, turning it the color of pewter, and illuminated the bizarre figure of Antryg Windrose, standing above the body of a young man sprawled at his feet.

Aware that he himself lay just below the crest of the hill, and therefore in its concealing shadow, Caris very slowly rolled a few turns down the hill to the cover of a prickly leaved bush whose scent told him it was a kind of sage. As his eyes grew accustomed to the denser shadows, he saw that the hill slope was dotted with such plants.

The climate was warm enough, he thought, for spices of this kind to grow wild, as they did in the deserts far to the south-east of Kymil, on the road to Saarieque. By the stars, they were further south from Kymil. The Archmage had spoken of other worlds lying beyond the Void. Would they have the same stars?

It didn't matter. The Way of the Sasenna was not to ask questions, but to perform one's task. His sword, miraculously, was still in his hand. Keeping his head down, he crawled downslope to the next sage bush, as Antryg knelt beside the young man's body and passed his hand gently over the dirty, twig-entangled mop of fair hair, feeling the temples and then the pulses of the throat. The young man was nearly naked, but for a pair of extremely short drawers—natural enough, in a climate as warm as this—and sandals on his feet.

The young man stirred and flailed with one hand, which Antryg caught by the wrist. The wizard's voice was clearly audible to Caris in the stillness of the night. "Are you all right?"

Are we in our own world after all? Caris wondered confusedly. *Surely the inhabitants of another would not speak our tongue?* But in his heart he knew they were no longer where they had been. Perhaps Antryg only expected a reply because he was mad. But when the young man spoke, it was not in the language of Ferr, but in some other whose meaning Caris heard in his mind, as one hears the voices of people in dreams; and he understood that Antryg was using some kind of spell of understanding, whose field extended far enough to touch him here.

The young man said, "Hunh? Sweet Holy Christ, who the hell are you?"

"Are you all right?" Antryg repeated.

"Jesus, no." The young man made an unsuccessful effort to sit up, and Antryg put a hand under his arm to assist him. The stranger's voice was slurred, as if with drink or drugs—small wonder, Caris thought, that he does not notice that Antryg is not speaking his tongue. "Somebody must have spiked hell out of that punch." He blinked dazedly up at the wizard, taking in the long, unruly mane and straggly beard, the ragged robes and crystal earrings. Then he giggled. "Hell, I must be stoneder than I thought. You come out of the punchbowl like all the rest of the stuff I been seeing?"

"No," admitted Antryg. "I'm a wizard from another universe, and I'm here to save your world—and mine, I hope—from a terrible fate. Can you sit up?"

The young man laughed again and shook his head. "Crazy."

"Yes, I am crazy, too." Antryg helped him to his unsteady feet, the young man hanging on the wizard's shoulder, still giggling vapidly.

"Man, you're about the solidest hallucination. . . . That must be some dope." He threw a friendly arm around Antryg's shoulders. "My name's Digby—Digby Clayton. C'mon back to the party, man, have a drink."

Silently, Caris followed them.

From the shadows of the higher ground, he watched them as they found a pale track of dust, which broadened quickly as it turned around the side of the hill to join a dark, smooth roadbed. At some distance along the road, he could see a house, an L-shaped building lying in a pool of brilliance in the darkness, illuminated with blazing light— far too bright and far too steady for firelight. It was like the brilliance of magic, but Caris sensed it could not be. Stunted and rudimentary as his own small powers were, he knew that there was no magic in this world. This sensation was not like the prickling weight of the spells that deadened the enclave of the Tower or the hollow, gnawing grief of those times in which his powers faded. Here it simply did not exist.

Yet magic would have been the only way to explain the house that lay before him in the island of yellow-white glare. In a courtyard behind it lay a huge pool of water, its turquoise reflections playing over the stone and glass of the house walls and the dark plants that grew around the low wall surrounding the court. People moved about on the sides of the water or swam in it like seals—men and women, naked save for bits of glaringly bright-colored cloth, drinking and eating and shouting at one another to be heard over the raucous, pounding music which seemed to ~e from no source, but which hung over the house and and hills around like the pall of carrion stench.

From the hillside, Caris calculated his cover as his quarry and his drunken host passed through a little iron gate in the low wall to the court. The wall was stone block to half its insignificant height, and iron spindles the rest. The unkempt juniper hedge surrounding it on the outside offered unpromising protection; but, by the look of it, most of the people in the court were far too drunk to pay much attention. The brightness of those lights would blind them to movement in the surrounding darkness.

He had sheathed his sword, but carried the sheath loose in his hand in preparation for battle. He now hooked it to the back strap of his harness and, flattening to his belly, crept down the hill.

Down near the house, the noise was incredible; the heavy, thumping rhythm of the music vibrated in his bones. The air was rank with the sickly odor of spilled beer and the queer, sweetish scent of burning marijuana, such as peasants in the villages smoked when they couldn't get gin. But there was gin—or liquor of some kind—in appalling abundance here; and by the way everyone laughingly accepted what Digby was saying, they had all evidently taken advantage of that fact to the fullest. "This is a hallucination, a genuine, *bona fide* hallucination," he was announcing over and over at the top of his voice to those few interested enough to come over and listen. Antryg, Caris could see, was looking about him in fascinated delight.

But for the lack of magic, Caris would have thought the mad wizard had somehow led him through into the Realms of Faërie. The courtyard was an unreal paradise of brilliant light and velvet shadow, of glaring colors, sparkling water, and smooth, bare, golden flesh. Clouds of steam rose from a smaller pool, which bubbled like a cauldron where a man and two women sat dreaming in its warmth. Now that he was closer, Caris could smell the odd, almost metallic tang of the waters, and see the clumps of clothing strewn at random all around the inside limits of the court. He could hear scraps of conversation as well; but, though Antryg's spell of languages gave him understanding of what he heard, it made no sense, even taking into account the thoroughgoing insobriety of the speakers—software and graphics, special effects and video, carburetors, micro-waves, and Republicans. Through an enormous wall of glass, Caris could see into the dimness of the house, where people sat clumped around square, dark screens upon which images moved, some of them the shadows of peo-ple, like living paintings, others mere collections of swiftly flowing colored dots. Abandoned drinks, bits of food, and the spilled ruin of liquor were everywhere, along with dis-carded shoes and boots and clothing; and over all was the sourceless, screaming throb of music.

A woman was hanging onto Antryg's arm, her billowy red robe falling open to reveal great amounts of seal-sleek charms. "So you're a friend of Digby's?" she giggled.

"No, actually, I'm a wizard from another universe." Antryg pushed his spectacles up a little more firmly on the bridge of his beaky nose and regarded her with polite inter-est.

"You mean like Middle Earth and all that?"

Caris had never heard of Middle Earth. By the look in his eyes, neither had Antryg, but he smiled widely, his teeth gleaming in the tangle of his beard, and agreed, "Yes."

She moved nearer to him, molding her ample form to his bony one. "Far out."

He considered the remark for a moment and informed her factually, "Well, in terms of the ultimate centers of power, less far out than this one."

"Is he friend of yours, Digby?" A woman's voice, speaking close to where Caris crouched, was so quiet it was only because of its nearness that he heard at all. It took his attention, because it was the only sober one he had so far heard. Moving his head a little, Caris could see the speaker standing in an opening formed by a sliding panel in the glass wall, next to Digby, who was supporting himself valiantly against it. A small girl with fair, brushy curls framing the thin bones of her face, she held a thick roll of greenish papers in one hand. Unlike anyone else in the court, she was watching Antryg with wary suspicion in her brown eyes.

"No, Joanna," Digby slurred happily. "Like I said, he's a hallucination. He just walked right out of this big hole in the air." He took a long swig from a glass in his hand, throwing his whole body into the gesture; the rippling reflections from the pool shone damply on the bulge of his soft little paunch. "You know Gary's looking for you."

"I know," the girl said tiredly. "That's why I'm down here talking to you. My program has an hour and a half to run yet, and he's gone to look for me in the computer room."

"Oh," Digby vaguely said, clearly not even hearing the sharp fragment of buried anger in the girl Joanna's voice. Across the court, the woman in red was leading the bemused looking Antryg into the darkness of the other wing of the house, laughing and saying, "Come show me some magic . . ."

Antryg paused in the doorway, looking around at that garish and noisy scene with his usual expression of pleased interest, like some mad saint with his ink-stained beard and tattered robes. Near him, Caris was aware of the girl Joanna watching Antryg with the same wariness that he himself felt, sensing, as none of the others seemed to, that something was amiss. But it was his own eyes, across the teeming chiaroscuro of the courtyard, that Antryg, for one instant, met. Then a hand reached out from the darkened room behind him and drew him inside.

Caris knew he had been seen.

Perhaps, he thought, Antryg had known all along that he had been followed; perhaps, in that chaotic darkness, he had heard Caris' stumbling steps at his heels. Perhaps this was the reason he had let himself be led to this strange place—so that going inside, he would leave his watchdog to guard the front entrance, while he glided out the back.

Lying in the heavy scents of the prickling juniper, with the dried slime that crusted his torn jacket scratching the wounds on his arms, Caris felt a sudden chill in spite of the evening's warmth. The nightmare run through darkness had terrified him; the echoing depths of nothingness had seemed populated by vast presences and by chaotic horrors, beside which the abomination in the swamp seemed friendly, solid, and familiar; but it came to him now that the dark figure of the wizard whom he had followed was, in fact, his only link with his own world. To lose him would not only mean losing all chance of finding his grandfather—it would mean being stranded in this insane, magicless, noisy world forever, with no way to return to that which he knew.

Cautiously, Caris moved to circle the house, counting exits.

Of these there were appallingly many. There were dozens of windows, some of which he tested and found impossible to open sufficiently to pass a body, while others would have admitted a horse. There were outbuildings, smelling of strange things, and a vast number of big, metal machines which were obviously conveyances and whose wheels had left tracks on the soft dust of the drive, though there was neither sign nor smell of a horse anywhere. *More magic?* thought Caris, puzzled, *in this magicless world?* To the south, over the hills, there was a glare in the sky, filling the whole southeastern quarter of the horizon with its reddish reflection, like a mechanical dawn.

Silent as the drift of shadow, he returned to the house, testing, checking. Garden doors led out onto a path that trailed through the straggly dust of the hills toward the dim shape of a shed, far up the nearest rise; pausing beside them, Caris heard voices raised in argument, the blond-haired woman Joanna's and a man's, slurred with liquor and self-pity.

"I'm sorry about what I said, Joanna, okay? I didn't mean it. . . ."

"Didn't you? You may be the only man who's ever wanted me and you may very well be the only man who ever will, but I don't really care to have that pointed out in front of people that I work with."

"I mean—you know. . ." Although, looking through the half-open doors, at the young woman's rather plain face, with its awkward nose and the first fine scratches of crow's-feet around the brown eyes, Caris could believe that was true, still he felt a stab of the uncomfortable feeling that he was seeing injustice done. It didn't help to recall his own stupid and meaningless cruelty to the girl from the tavern, earlier in the week.

"Hey, I'm sorry, babe. How many times do I got to say it?"

The dim lights of the room picked out the man's shape, nearly nude, like most of the people there, his muscular body speckled with droplets of water from the courtyard pool. The woman, as he had seen in the courtyard earlier, was one of the few people clothed—unbecomingly, Caris thought—in the faded blue trousers that seemed to be uniform for such men and women who wore anything beyond a few bright bits of cloth and a close-fitting white upper garment, which showed off the figure of a diminutive houri.

Her voice was cool and precise, "You can say it as many times as you need to in order to feel that you've made some kind of amends. But it will all be entirely for your own benefit."

"What's that supposed to mean? You're my sweetheart, babe, I love you."

"If you didn't keep making fun of me to your other friends, I'd find that a whole lot more convincing."

It was strange, thought Caris as he moved soundlessly on through the dust-smelling night, that the quarrels and griefs of those who peopled this alien world should be so similar to those he knew in his own.

The house was two storeys tall in its main portion, one storey at the wing into which Antryg had gone. Most of its windows, Caris had ascertained, looked inward toward the court, and the doors leading outside could all, he estimated, be seen from the roof of the farthest eastward end —if the stars were right it was east, anyway—of the low wing. Judging by their reactions to Antryg's alien garments, none of the revelers should comment, even if they did see Caris sitting on the roof; in any case the projecting cornices of the house should hide him.

One of the metal vehicles stood near enough the wall to give him footing. Its springs gave slightly with his leap, and his back muscles and bruised ankle cried out against the jarring scramble for footing. The roof itself had only a shallow slope, like the houses in Mellidane that knew no snow. In the dark, he felt its surfaces to be some kind of granulose shingle, firm and silent beneath his boots. Crouching, he moved along the edge, where the walls would take his weight and keep the beams from creaking within. Just below the spine of the roof crest, he stretched himself out, achingly glad to be able to rest and chiding himself for that unsasennanlike gratitude. On one side lay the darkness of the hills, the few windows throwing small squares of yellow light to gleam on the shiny metal of the vehicles or pick threads of sherry-colored grass through the soft haze of the dust. On the other lay the court, the music rising up like the blaze of colored light to the watching stars, and drifts of conversation floating above it like isolated wafts of perfume:

"... so you could boot it warm, but every time you booted it cold you got a B—DOS error..."

"Hell, you think that's bad? They had the whole fiber-optic Cray mainframe disappear in pieces from Alta Clara..."

"I swear to God the guy swings both ways..."

"... working until two in the morning. You'll never get *her* to believe it, but she's the sharpest programmer San Serano."

"You expect *Gary* to know the difference between *auslese* and Thunderbird?"

"... superhero and a mercenary, but in his secret identity he writes children's books..."

"Digby might be right about there being a Bermuda Triangle in Building Six. Sometimes that place feels so *creepy.*"

"I never found it creepy, but there are times there when I get just about suicidal."

"If I worked for Eraserhead Brown, I'd be suicidal, too...."

Exhausted, Caris felt himself slipping into the trap of relaxing and knew he must not yield to the weariness of his body. He toyed with the idea of trying to steal some of the food that was in such abundance down there, but knew it was too dangerous. Antryg, he thought, might be waiting for just such a distraction.

Occasionally, the vehicles would arrive or depart, powered, it seemed, by some internal force. Growling with throaty violence, with their yellow headlamps blazing like eyes and a thin cloud of stinking smoke puffing from their tails, they reminded him of flatulent, metallic beasts. Several times he saw red lights moving in the starry darkness of the sky, accompanied by a far-off bass roar that shook his bones, but no one in the court paid the slightest heed. Such matters, then, must be commonplace in this universe. But he flinched every time such a creature passed.

And above the pain of his wounds, the ache of his muscles, the weary confusion held at bay only by the years of discipline in the Way of the Sasenna, and his growing fear, was the single thought: *I must not let him escape.*

A dim light appeared in the large window of the second-storey room in the main wing. It had been cast not by any light in the room, but by the reflection of a hallway light when the door was opened. Caris froze into stillness, for the window was directly opposite where he lay; with the room in darkness, he would be perfectly visible to anyone who came to the window.

But it was only one of the revelers, looking vaguely about him as he polished his spectacles—Caris was amused to see that with all their wonders, these people still wore spectacles, some of them no different than Antryg's —on the hem of the close-fitting, short-sleeved black shirt that he wore. The light from the door picked up strange silver runes written across the chest as he replaced the light frame of wire and metal on his long nose.

The man gazed around him for a moment at the darkened room, with its banks of metal boxes with tiny red eyes glowing in their blank faces; their small, dark screens looked like polished beryl. Then he turned back, not to the door itself, but to the doorframe. With a gesture that reminded Caris curiously of the mages, he brushed the narrow molding of wood with his fingertips. . . .

A woman's voice said softly, "It was you. . . ."

He swung sharply around as a second shadow in the doorway appeared, and Caris recognized the woman Joanna.

A glimpse of crimson down in the court drew Caris' eye. It was, he saw, the woman in the red robe again, but of Antryg there was no sign. Cursing his inattention, Caris waited until the two people in the semidarkness of the upper room were both turned from the window, then slid soundlessly down the rough shingles and dropped, catlike, to the nose of the metal vehicle below and thence to the ground.

There was no one, now, in any of the rooms of that low wing.

The uninitiated imputed to the sasenna fearsome powers of profanity when they are in their rage. But the sasenna did not curse in true rage—oaths, like complaints and tears, wasted time and only served to cloud the mind.

There was no time for them now, if he was not going to be left in this world forever.

That afternoon, he recalled, he had thought that he had never had to fight for his life before. He realized now, that he had never had to track, hunt, and watch for his life, and he stood in danger of failing, with consequences beyond his power to imagine.

With painstaking care, he cast for sign all around the house. Even with his slight abilities to see in darkness, it was not easy, and he found nothing—no track, no sign, beyond the circle of the house-lights' glow, to mark the mad wizard's passing. Antryg was a mage and had, like all those who took Council vows, been trained as sasenna. Having watched him fight, Caris knew that, unlike many mages, he had not let that training sleep.

Caris moved as close to the house as he dared and began a second cast. The track of Antryg's soft boots would be distinctive among the sharp, bizarre patterns of the shoes of this world; all around the hard black pavement where the vehicles stood was a belt of dust and weeds. A long drive ran out toward the main road, but Caris had watched it from the roof and had seen nothing on it but the coming and going of vehicles.

There was a path, leading out into the hills, toward what looked like a deserted stable or shed, nearly a mile away. Surrounded by the moldering remains of fallen fences, it stood dark and untenanted at the crest of a hill overlooking the house itself. But by the dust at the head of the path, he saw that it was regularly used by a single type of footprint —someone ran there and back, wearing cleated shoes, almost daily. But there was no mark in the starlit dust of the wizard's boots, nor of the faint slurring that the hem of a robe would cause.

Caris was beginning to feel frightened.

Once, close to the road, a vehicle leaving the house in a great jerking roar of wheels and smoke nearly ran him over, its yellow headlights sweeping him as he ducked into the coarse sagebrush for cover. Casting for sign on the hillslope near the iron courtyard gate through which Digby Clayton and Antryg had originally passed, he heard the stifled giggles of a courting couple in the weeds, and a girl's voice called out, "Is somebody there?" After that Caris moved back farther from the house again, his unease increasing with the latening movement of the stars. Detection now would mean questions and delay, and delay was what he could not afford. Weariness was closing in on him, the ache in his body exacerbated by a longing for sleep; soon it would begin to impair his survival instincts. If Antryg passed through the Void again before he found him . . .

And suddenly, he felt it again—the queer terror, the sense, almost the smell, of worlds beyond worlds, the vibration of abyssal winds in his bones. The Void had been opened.

Panic touched him, with the knowledge that this was his last chance and he hadn't the slightest clue what to do. . . .

Where? he thought desperately, his frantic gaze sweeping the hills in the thin moonlight.

There was a man, walking swiftly along the path to that distant shed.

It was the bespectacled reveler from the upper room— the one who had been speaking to Joanna in the half-dark. The moonlight caught faintly on the strange metallic runes that marked his garment and on his spectacle lenses as he paused and looked back at the house with an attitude of bemused delight.

And as he moved on, with that gawky walk that was somehow light and graceful as a dancer's, Caris realized who he was.

What had Salteris said? The sasenna knew that the best place to hide was in plain sight, and Antryg had always been a genius at it. There had been enough stray clothing lying around the house for him to find garments that fitted his tall, skinny frame; without the beard and with his long hair cut, Caris had not recognized him among the others, and had gone off searching the hills, as Antryg had intended.

Anger surged through him, fed by fears, by his shame at feeling fear, and by his rage at having been duped. It drowned his weariness and his dread of passing through the Void once more, drowned everything but his determination for revenge.

Starlight flashed on glass as Antryg turned his head. He quickened his long stride, and Caris, knowing he had been seen, threw caution to the winds and flung himself forward, summoning the reserves of his strength. The wrenched and stiffened muscles of his ankle screamed at him as he crashed through the dry sage and dust of the unfamiliar ground.

Antryg, instead of running away, turned and headed for the shed. Caris knew it then—the shed itself contained the gate into the Void. Antryg was closer to it than he, with longer legs and fresher strength. Battle rage flooded Caris as he ran. With a sweep he drew his sword from where it hung upon his back. . . .

The inside of the shed was an echoing well of darkness. The night was too deep for him to see even a little of the place as it should have been—broken partitions, fallen beams, the dismantled metal bones of the strange self-moving machines, and the stinks of oil and dust. But the crumbling lintels framed a hollow, a chasm in which there was neither light nor time—only the endless, amorphous stirrings of the winds that drifted between universes.

With a yell of rage that did not quite succeed in purging the terror from his heart, Caris flung himself once again into the dark.

CHAPTER VIII

JOANNA WOKE UP IN DARKNESS.

For an instant she remembered nothing, except that she was cold, sore, and terrified of something she could not recall. The surface she lay upon was unfamiliar, narrow, and hard; under her bare arms she felt tight-stretched, satiny upholstery. She drew a breath and choked with the bruised ache in her throat.

Terror returned with an almost physical nausea.

She thought illogically, *The marks on the wall!*

There had been one in the computer room in Building Six, when she'd been assaulted by the Man Who Wasn't There.

He wasn't there again today.... The tall, thin, bespectacled form, the brush of long fingers over the doorframe of the upstairs room at Gary's—the sign that had appeared beneath that butterfly touch, like light shining onto the wood rather than any mark—

She had known him, of course—Digby's mysterious_

hallucination, defrocked and debearded. It had been the robe that had touched her memory at the party. Was that why he'd changed his clothes?

Joanna didn't know what was going on, but she wanted no part of it.

Had he left, after she'd spoken to him in Gary's upstairs room? She had the impression that he had, but her memory was clouded, events telescoping and confused. She'd come up to collect her program and leave, not wanting to put up with Gary whining at her heels for the rest of the evening, resolving even to unplug her phone when she got home, as Gary made up in persistence what he lacked in tact. . . .

He'd been there when she'd come in, she remembered, and she had known him then as Digby's hallucination. *Stepped out of a hole in the air.* . . .

The same black hole of darkness she had seen in San Serano?

She thought that he'd left, that she'd been sitting alone in front of Gary's big IBM, waiting for the modem buffers to spit the last information out from the Cray at San Serano. Had he come back later, or . . . ? She couldn't remember. Only the sudden, terrible grip of hands around her throat, the hideous gray roaring in her ears, the drowning terror . . .

And here.

Cautiously, she moved her legs. She was still dressed as she had been at Gary's, in jeans, a white tank-top, and sneakers. The idea that she had been unconscious in someone else's power made her shudder with loathing, but she could detect no bruises anywhere other than on her neck. Shrinking with inner dread, she put her hand carefully down over the edge of the narrow cot upon which she lay—like a child, she realized ruefully, who *knows* the boogieman waits under the bed. . . .

But she only encountered the floor—stone, and very cold.

Stone? she thought. She sat up, fighting a slight qualm of sickness as she did so, and groped at the sides of what she thought was a cot and which turned out to be a daybed, the eighteenth-century ancestor of the chaise lounge. At one end was a chairlike back, heavily carved; there was more carving on the tops of the thing's cabriole legs. Feeling along the floor beside it, she reached the familiar, enormous lumpiness of her purse and breathed a sigh of relief.

Although whoever had brought her here could have gone through it. . . .

Her digging fingers came in contact with her miniature flashlight. She switched it on, and the yellow light wavered wildly over the room with the shaking of her hand.

She thought, *Oh, Christ,* in a kind of frightened despair. The room was stone, small and windowless, like the turret chamber of a castle—or like somebody's idea of one. The daybed with its frivolous gilded scrollwork and rose-colored cushions struck her as a sinister incongruity, and she muttered, "Kinky," to herself as she got to her feet. She sat down again, quickly, a little surprised at the weakness and nausea that the heroines of movies never seemed to suffer after a violent assault.

The room had one door. It was only a few steps away and, not very surprisingly, bolted from the outside.

Joanna went back to the daybed and sat down again. Her knees felt weak.

Don't panic, she told herself. *Whatever you do, if you panic, you won't be able to do anything.* But her mind kept screaming at her, *Why me?*

Figure that out later, she told herself firmly, fighting not to think about the implications that she had been stalked. She dug through the contents of her purse, and her hand closed around the reassuring smoothness of her hammer. She set it beside her and checked out the rest—Swiss Army knife, several tin and plastic boxes, a measuring tape, scissors, calculator, wallet, checkbook, keys, note-

book, mirror, spare toothbrush, tube of sunscreen, collapsible drinking cup, Granola bars, rubber bands, safety pins,
a lipstick that she'd never used, a package of Kleenex, a
sewing kit, a bundle of plastic-coated wires she'd gotten
from plant maintenance, three and a half pairs of earrings,
and two floppy disks.

She selected the hammer and the Swiss Army knife,
opened the screwdriver blade, and returned once more to
the door.

It was designed to open inward. The hinges were the pin
type, though massive and, by the look of them, forged of
iron rather than steel. Joanna frowned as she shined the
beam of the flashlight over them, recognizing the anachro-
nism but unable to account for it. She knew the recre-
ational medievalists of her acquaintance made their own
chain mail, but their own door hinges?

Doubtfully, she cast the light around the room once
more. Of course, Southern California was rife with old
stone buildings, if you knew where to look for them,
but . . .

Later, she told herself again. *Right now the object is to
get the hell out of here*. Carefully, she began to work the
knife's screwdriver blade in beneath the hinge pin . . .

And stopped, at the soft snick of the door bolt being slid
back.

She had heard no footfall; but then, she had no idea how
thick the walls or door might be. Thick, she thought, for
she had heard nothing at all—no traffic sound, not even
the subsonic vibration of trucks, no airplane roar, and no
tread of footfalls elsewhere in the building. Adrenaline
surging through her like fire, she stepped back to where the
door would hide her, hammer in hand, heart pounding, but
feeling queerly calm. Her last thought was, *He's very tall,
I'll have to strike high*.

The door opened.

He was ready for her, catching her wrist on the downswing and ducking aside, though she heard him gasp as the hammer glanced off his bony shoulder. Like most women who have had little to do with men, she was shocked at the strength of his hands. He knew the tricks too; his arms moved and twisted with hers as she tried to drive her wrist against the weak joint of the thumb to break his hold, and he turned his body to block the knee she drove at his groin. The struggle lasted only seconds. Then something drove into his back from the dark door like a striking puma. A slamming foot behind his knee made his legs buckle. She heard him gasp again and looked up as the newcomer to the fray seized a handful of his hair, pulled his head back, and laid the edge of a knife to his throat.

Joanna pulled away from the suddenly opened grip.

"Are you all right?" The young man barely glanced at her as he spoke. In the skewed glare of the flashlight, his startlingly handsome face looked drawn with strain and exhaustion, lead-colored smudges of weariness around the tip-tilted dark eyes.

"I think so," gasped Joanna.

He jerked the knife roughly against the thin skin above his prisoner's jugular. His voice was thick with rage. "What have you done with the Archmage?"

The kneeling man remained immobile between them, sweat shining on his face and trickling along his exposed throat. "Nothing," he whispered. "Caris, listen..." His breath stopped with a quick, faint draw; a thread of blood started from under the blade.

"I've listened to you enough, Antryg Windrose." To Joanna, the young man said, "There's a silk cord tied around under my belt. Take it and bind his hands."

"Caris, no." The older man's lips barely moved as he spoke. "You have to get out of here. There's danger..."

Joanna's hands were moving quickly, picking apart the knots of the cord. The young man's clothing was black, oddly reminiscent, like the curved sword stuck through his sash, of samurai or martial arts gear, though creased, torn in places, and stained with caked mud and slime. Her first thought that she had somehow been caught up in some kind of role-playing event faded when she saw that, under the torn jacket and shirt, Caris' biceps and pectorals bore a collection of really shocking abrasions and bruises.

She pulled the silk cord free from the crossed sword sash and leather dagger belt. "Look," she said shakily, "thank you and all that—really, thank you very much— but could you please tell me what the hell is going on?"

Caris' knee dug viciously into Antryg's back. "This man is a renegade wizard," he said. "He has caused evils and abominations to appear; for what he has done I should kill him here and now."

Joanna, pausing in the act of tying Antryg's hands, said, "HUNH?"

"Caris, I had nothing to do with your grandfather's disappearance."

"Then how do you know he disappeared?"

"Look," Antryg said, turning his head a little against the grip on his hair to meet his captor's eyes. "There isn't time for this. There is danger coming, an abomination beside which the thing you fought in the swamp is as nothing."

"How do you . . ."

"*I know it!*" he insisted furiously. Then, more quietly, "Please believe me." His long hands caught Joanna's as she tried to put the cord around them, staying her, but without force. "I surrender to you, I'll be your prisoner, do with me whatever you want to—but *get out of here!*"

Joanna could feel his hands, where they touched hers, shaking. It didn't prove anything; hers were still trembling from the exertion of the fight, and she didn't currently have a knife at her throat. But in the silence that followed his words, she could feel a strange, louring threat, a dread that she had known before in the too-silent corridors of Building Six—a sense of evil, beyond anything she had encountered or could imagine. Beside that amorphous darkness, more human kinkiness and even quasi-medieval murder cults seemed oddly petty.

She said softly, "Look, I don't know what's going on but—I think he's right."

Caris glanced sharply at her, but only said, "Draw my sword."

Joanna obeyed. Whatever the scenario was, it was pretty clearly being played for keeps. There was something living and hateful in the silence that kept her from simply saying, "Count me out of this dungeon thanks," and walking out the door. As she had at San Serano, she felt again that outside the room lay, not death, but something worse whose nature she could scarcely even conceive.

Caris made sure the sword was ready to hand before he took the knife from his prisoner's throat. "Get up. If you try any tricks, I swear I will feed you your own heart."

Antryg got to his feet, wiping the trickle of blood from his neck. The tension in him was palpable; fear, thought Joanna, yet she had no sense that he was afraid of Caris, in spite of the fact that the younger man had come within a millimeter of slitting his throat. He whispered, "Stay here," and made a move towards the door, as if to check the corridor. Caris' swift, small gesture with the sword halted him again, and he regarded the young warrior in irritated frustration.

Knowing there was only one way out of this fox-goose-corn conundrum, Joanna said, "I'll look," though her stomach curled with dread at the thought of facing whatever might be in the corridor. Part of her insisted that this was absurd, but some deeper part, the part that had cowered in fear in the janitor's closet at San Serano, knew that Antryg was right and that Caris was a stubborn fool not to flee from the darkness that she could sense was gathering somewhere nearby.

Hefting the hammer that she knew would be utterly useless, she peeked around the doorframe.

The corridor stretched away in darkness to her right, unbroken, impenetrable, and hideously ominous. To her left, she thought there were doors, and beyond them, some sense of openness, of moving air. The fear was to her right —abomination, Antryg had said. There was no sound, and she felt she would have preferred anything to that unspeakable, waiting silence.

She ducked swiftly back into what had become a haven of safety. By the flashlight-glare, Antryg looked deathly white and Caris, his fair hair falling into his eyes, like a man grimly fighting his instinct to flee. She swallowed hard. "There's nothing moving out there."

"Good," Antryg murmured. In spite of the fact that he was officially a prisoner, he seemed to have effortlessly taken over the expedition. "Joanna, I'm going to have to ask you to douse that light, if you can."

Joanna, who had picked up her flashlight from where it lay on the floor behind the door, looked up at him, startled, and met only grave inquiry in his gray eyes.

"There is a way of putting it out, isn't there?"

Verisimilitude? she wondered. But he was frightened— she knew it, could feel it—frightened beyond the point where any role player would forget the bounds of a non-industrial persona and simply say, *Shut off the flashlight*.

Seeing the doubt in her eyes, he added, "I can see in the dark—so can Caris a little, can't you?"

Caris nodded—it was clearly not something that he even thought much about.

For the first time in that bizarre sequence of events, Joanna felt that she had just stepped off an edge somewhere, into waters deeper than she knew. Up until that moment, she had been sure, not of what was happening, but of the *kind* of thing it must be. Now for the first time, she doubted, and the doubts opened an abyss of possibilities whose mere existence would have been terrifying, had she believed in them. *Later*, she told herself again. Shouldering her heavy purse, she took a hesitant grip on the belt loop of Antryg's jeans and switched off the light.

Darkness swooped down upon her like a terror-bird. Her instinct was to shrink against someone for the reassurance that she was not alone, but Antryg had twice tried to strangle her, had kidnapped her from Gary's house, and brought her to this place. She knew she could not afford to tie up Caris' sword arm, even if he'd be chivalrous enough to let her, which she was pretty sure he wouldn't. So she only tightened her hold on the narrow loop of denim and tried to keep her breathing steady.

Antryg's hand touched hers and gave it a quick, comforting pat in the darkness, as if he sensed her fear; then he led the way forward, out into the haunted hall.

To Joanna's infinite relief, they turned left, moving swiftly and surely. Once, putting out her left hand, she felt the cold, uneven stone of a wall and guessed that, see-in-the-dark or not, Antryg was probably using the wall as a guide. Caris' shoulder brushed her bare arm, and the coarse, quilted, black cotton of the jacket was warm against her skin; she could hear the soft rustle of cloth and the creak of leather as that gorgeous young man turned periodically to look back. Once she herself risked such a glance and wished she hadn't.

It's only darkness, she told herself, *the same as the darkness in front of you. Nothing is nothing.* But it wasn't. Why it should seem so dense and terrifying she did not know, nor why, seeing nothing, she should have the sense that it stirred, as if with some passing form that even light would not have unmasked. *When I get out of this*, she thought, *wherever the hell I am, I'm taking the first bus back to Van Nuys, I am finding a new apartment, changing my telephone number, and looking for another job, if necessary. . . .*

But Antryg knew her now. And Antryg was one of them, whoever *they* were. Was this, she wondered suddenly, just a put-up part of the game? Was he leading her through darkness to something worse, phase two of some elaborately choreographed nightmare?

It was more logical than what she feared, in some far-back corner of her heart, might be going on.

Something stirred in the darkness. A wind touched her hair, blowing from behind them—a queer, cold smell that she vaguely recognized and which filled her with unnamed terror. She glanced back over her shoulder again and thought she saw, far back in the black depths behind them, some blur of luminosity which illuminated nothing. At the same moment Caris whispered, "Antryg . . ."

Antryg's bare, sinewy arm went around her shoulders, drawing her against him, and she felt by the movement of his body that he had shoved Caris ahead of them. He whispered, *"Run!"* There was a frantic fear in his voice that could not have been counterfeited; she felt, rather than saw, Caris start to run.

She had no idea how long they ran, nor when the ground beneath her feet changed from stone to earth, and from earth to the silky drag of grass. She stumbled and was hauled forward by main force, gasping for breath and exhausted, her mind blurred by panic of whatever it was that lay behind them. Sometime in that darkness, she was aware that the graveyard fetor that had so unreasonably terrified her had changed to wind and the thick headiness of cut hay; she stumbled repeatedly on the uneven slopes of the ground, trying to match her stride with the much longer one of the man whose powerful arm pushed her inexorably on. Through her terror, she became dimly aware of a dividing horizon between dark earth and dark sky. Then she stumbled, and fell into a final and deeper darkness.

* * *

It was just before dawn when she woke. She stirred, and sneezed. The air was thick with the fragrance of hay, with the smell of water and cows, with the twitter of whippoorwills, and with the incessant, peeping chorus of small frogs. For a blank moment, she wondered where she was. Her throat ached with bruises, and her body was stiff with the last, desperate run of the night. She was starvingly hungry.

Looking up, she could see Antryg sitting with his back to a haystack—an object which Joanna had never seen in her life outside of pictures, but which was indubitably a haystack. His long legs were drawn up, his arms rested across his bony knees, and he contemplated the glowing eastward sky with a look of meditative calm. Beyond him, Caris lay asleep, like an exhausted god, his sword still under his limp hand.

All around them, the world was bathed in the unearthly blue glow of predawn. Joanna sat up, scratching the straw from her hair. She felt a little cold, shaken, and very unreal. The hills behind them were still shrouded with the clear, purple darkness of the last of the night, but the waters of the marsh that lay in a series of crisscrossed hollows below them and to their left were already picking up the quicksilver brightness of the sky. There was no freeway roar, no growl of jets, not even the far-off moan of a train whistle. The sky was uncrossed by powerlines and, though it was late August, untainted by smog.

"Are you cold?" Antryg asked her, and she shook her head.

"Not very."

He smiled and touched the t-shirt he wore—black, with the silver-foil logo of last year's Havoc concert inscribed blazing across the chest. She recognized it as belonging to Tom Bentley, the department's would-be heavy-metal rocker. "If I'd known I might have to share, I'd have picked up something more substantial," he apologized. Then, following her glance to the sleeping Caris, he added, "It hardly seemed fair to escape while he was asleep, at least this time. He would have stayed awake to stand over me if he could; the last twenty-four hours haven't been his fault. In any case I wanted to see the sun rise. I haven't seen that in a long time."

Without the beard that had hidden most of his face when she'd first seen him at the party, he looked, not precisely younger, but more ageless. Joanna guessed his age at about forty, though his hair—an unruly mop, even when whacked off to less than half of its former length—was faded and streaked with gray, like frost-killed weeds. Behind the spectacles, his gray eyes were intelligent, a little daft, and at the same time very gentle. In spite of the bruises on her wrists left by his grip in last night's struggle and the crushed ache of her windpipe, Joanna felt her fear of him subside.

"Look," she said, sitting up cross-legged and shaking the last of the hay out of her hair. "Would it be too much to ask what the hell is going on?"

He regarded her for a moment with wary suspicion in those wide, oddly intent eyes. "Don't you know?"

She sighed. "If I knew, I wouldn't have been scared as spitless as I was last night."

He folded his long hands and looked down at the twined fingers for a moment—mottled with ink, she saw, and, in the slowly growing dawnlight, very white, as if he had spent years without seeing sun. "I suspect you would have been even more so," he said gently. "But it doesn't matter."

"Where are we?" She looked around her at the silent fields and dove-colored pools. "And why have you been stalking me? What kind of crazy game was all that supposed to be last night?"

He tilted his head to one side. "Have you been stalked?"

"I don't know what else to call your—your hunting me in the halls at San Serano."

"It is no game." Stiffly, Caris sat up and threw a quick, resentful glance at Antryg. Sullenly, he wiped his sword on his jacket and then sheathed it with a vicious snick. Pushing his blond, rumpled hair out of his eyes, he looked over at Joanna. "It is hard for you to understand, since there is no magic in your world. But you have been brought over into our world, into the Empire of Ferryth, for what purposes I don't know, by this man. He is Antryg Windrose, a renegade wizard, and I am sworn by my vows to the Council of Wizards to bring him to justice for the evil he has done."

Joanna stared at him for a long moment. "You're crazy," she said.

"No, I'm crazy," Antryg disagreed mildly. "Caris is only confused. And I'm afraid he's right about your not being any longer in your own world. Doesn't the mere smell of the air convince you?"

Joanna hesitated. There were plenty of places in the San Joaquin Valley, for instance, or up north, where smog was seldom smelled—but not, she had to admit, in the summer. And in any case, if she'd been out long enough to be taken there . . . She dug in her purse and found her watch. The readout flashed to the touch of a button—August 30, the day after Gary's party. She dropped it back into the general confusion of the purse and tried to make the times fit. Unless it was like one of those *Mission Impossible* stories in which dates had been meticulously rejiggered to convince someone it was last week or next week . . .

The countryside might have been somewhere in California's Central Valley, from what she could see of it— marshy hayfields before them, silent green hills behind, and the long brown curve of a river in the distance—except there were no mountains, not even as a far-off blue line against the sky.

Beside her, her kidnapper and her rescuer were talking softly. The younger, in spite of his dark and battle-shabby warrior's outfit, was handsome with the Nordic gorgeousness of a prince of fairy tales, save for a straight scar about an inch and a half long that marked a cheekbone straight out of a TV ad because it was the kind of thing that anyone could have had corrected by plastic surgery—and partly because, in spite of her guess at Caris' age as being less than twenty-one, it looked to be several years old. The jocks she had met had given Joanna a deep distrust of young men that good-looking, but Caris lacked the egocentricity she had so often encountered in the self-proclaimed hunks. It was as if his appearance was entirely peripheral to some greater force that dominated his life.

He was saying, "Why did you bring her to this world?"

Antryg, folding his long arms comfortably around his drawn-up knees, considered the matter gravely for some moments and replied, "I can't imagine. Perhaps Joanna could tell us? Joanna . . . ?"

Annoyed, Caris caught the wizard's shoulder as he started to turn toward her and pulled him back. "Don't play innocent. First you murder Thirle—then you kidnap the Archmage—now this woman. I want to know why."

"I must admit to some curiosity about that myself," Antryg remarked, disengaging his arm from the younger man's crushing grip with no apparent effort. "I should imagine poor Thirle was murdered simply because he had seen the Gate through the Void—or perhaps because he saw who it was who came out."

"Others saw the Gate," said Caris. "I, for one."

"You didn't know what it was, nor its implications."

"Aunt Min did. My grandfather did."

"But by that time, there were other witnesses. It was not simply a matter of silencing one. Joanna my dear, why

would someone—let's call it me for talking purposes—
have kidnapped you?" He turned those gentle, luminous
eyes upon her. "Who and what are you?"

"Be careful," Caris cautioned, as Joanna drew breath to
reply. "He's completely mad, but he's clever. He may have
brought you here to learn something from you."

"I don't know what," Joanna said, looking in puzzlement from the young man's onyx dark eyes to the inquir-
ing, bespectacled gray ones. "Even if he wanted a
computer programmer for some reason, the woods are full
of better ones than I am. But I've been stalked for a week
or more . . ." She turned back to Antryg. "What were the
marks you made on the walls? You made one at the house,
and there was one at San Serano, the night you tried to
strangle me there."

"I assure you, my dear," Antryg protested, "It wasn't
me."

"And it wasn't you who has been causing the abominations to appear?" Caris demanded sarcastically. "Or who
spirited my grandfather away?"

"Of course not."

"His glove was in your room. I saw it there."

"He left it when he visited me earlier in the week."

"He had them with him that evening! I saw them!"

"Both of them?"

"You are lying," Caris said, and his dark-brown eyes
were narrow with suspicion and anger. "As you have been
lying all along."

"Well, of course I've been lying all along," the wizard
argued reasonably. "If the Bishop or anyone else had suspected what happens when the Void is breached . . ."

"What happens?"

Antryg sighed. "It is where the abominations come
from," he said. "When a gap is opened in the Void, the
whole fabric of it weakens, sometimes for miles around.
Yes, I knew that someone was moving back and forth

across the Void for months before Thirle was killed. Not every time, but sometimes, when it was breached, a hole would open through to some other world, neither yours nor mine, and something would—wander through. Sometimes to die, without its proper food or protection against unfamiliar enemies, sometimes to find what food it could. I was aware of it, but could do nothing about it, since I could not touch the Void from within the Tower."

"Ha!" Caris said scornfully.

Unperturbed, Antryg went on. "I knew that eventually such a weakening had to take place within the walls of the Tower itself. I could only wait. . . . I suppose, if I hadn't been mad already, the waiting would have driven me so."

"You knew this," Caris said softly. "You knew where the abominations came from and yet you did not tell the Archmage of it?"

"What could he have done about it?" Antryg demanded with a sudden, desperate sweep of his arm. "He couldn't have stopped it. And they would only have chained me, to prevent my escape. I'd been in that Tower seven years, Caris. I haven't seen sunlight since before you were sasennan."

Joanna looked up sharply, hearing it then. The word *sasennan* came to her mind as *weapon*, but with a suffix connoting humanness. She understood, for the first time, that the words that she had heard in her mind were not the words that they spoke. She knew, then, that she had passed into some other world, alien to her own.

The brightness of the sunlight of which he had spoken diffused the sky and all the lands around them with pastel glory, flashing like sheet glass on the waters of the meres below. Gray and black geese rose from the rushes in a wimmering flurry of wings. Joanna wasn't sure, but they looked an awful lot like the pictures she'd seen of the extinct Canada goose.

For a long moment she wanted to do nothing except curl

up in a fetal position and hide. She felt bleak, sick, and frightened, as hopeless as she had felt when, as a child, she had walked for the first time into a new classroom filled with strangers. She cried, "Why did you bring me here?"

Caris and Antryg fell silent, hearing in her words the frantic demand, not for information, but for comfort.

It was Antryg who spoke, gently, without the indignant protest with which he had answered the sasennan. "I'm sorry, my dear. But truly, it was someone else."

"Can you take me back?"

He was silent for a long time. Then he said, "I'm afraid not. Even as Caris knows that I can't work magic here, because the other mages will know I've escaped and be listening for me, feeling for me along the lines of power that cover the whole of the earth in their net, so I cannot touch the Void now. The—the one who did kidnap you knows you're gone. That one will be waiting for me to touch the Void again, to find me—to destroy me and you and all of us."

Joanna looked up miserably into the odd, beaky face in its mane of graying hair and noticed for the first time how deep the lines were that webbed around the enormous gray eyes, running down onto the delicate cheekbones like careless chisel scratches and back into the tangled hair.

Sarcastically, Caris said, "Very plausible. Except that, if you did not kidnap her, who did? Even my grandfather, the Archmage, knew little about the Void and its workings; according to him, there *was* no one else." He got to his feet, and walked around to where Joanna huddled in the hay, feeling empty and suddenly chilled. His hand was warm on her bare shoulder. "Don't worry. We'll take him to the House of Mages in Kymil. If necessary Nandiharrow, the Head of the House, will send for the Witchfinders. What he has done has put him outside all protection of the Council. We'll make him tell what he has done with the Archmage—and when we find him, the Archmage will send you home."

CHAPTER IX

IT TOOK THEM UNTIL AFTER DARK TO REACH THE CITY OF Kymil.

It was one of the longest days Joanna had ever spent—literally; she guessed that Kymil lay well to the north of Los Angeles, but, even though the summer solstice was passed, the days were still very long. Well before the sun was in the sky, they began walking through the luminous world of predawn to which Joanna had always preferred another two hours' communion with her pillow. It had been considerably longer than seven years, she realized somewhat shamefacedly, since she had seen the sun rise.

Antryg was like a child taken into the country for the first time, stopping to contemplate cattails in the marshes below the road or to watch the men and women at work cutting hay. If nothing else could have convinced her that she had truly fallen through a hole in the space-time continuum, Joanna thought with a strange sense of despair, the sight of those peasants at work did. No role player, no matter how dedicated, was going to get out of bed at the crack of dawn and do hard labor in the coarse, awkward, bundly clothes they wore.

But in her heart she needed no convincing. She knew where she was.

"Do you want some sunscreen?" she asked Antryg as they stopped on a wooden bridge over the shining counterpane of marsh and hay meadow to watch the first hard lances of sunlight smite the water beneath them like a sounding of trumpets. "Something to keep you from sunburn?" She dug in the capacious depths of her bottomless bag.

"Thank you." He studied the crumpled tube gravely. "After seven years of living in the dark like a mushroom, right now I'd welcome any kind of natural sensation, but I'm sure I won't feel that way at the end of the day."

Oddly enough, Joanna felt more at ease and able to talk to Antryg, her kidnapper, than to her rescuer. Part of this stemmed from her distrust of extremely good-looking men, part from the fact that Antryg was sublimely relaxed about being a prisoner, far more so than Caris was about having one. Possibly, she thought frivolously, that was simply because he'd had years of practice at it. As she replaced the tube in her bag, Joanna found several Granola bars and offered them to her companions. Caris devoured his like a wolf, but Antryg divided his with the sasennan. "After yesterday, I'm sure he needs it more than I do," he said, as Caris suspiciously took the solidified mass of nuts and raisins from his hand.

"Why?" Joanna asked, glancing curiously from the wizard to the warrior. "What happened yesterday?"

"There was an abomination in the marsh," Caris replied, almost grudgingly. He touched the rip in the shoulder of his jacket and shirt, under which the bruised flesh had turned almost as black as the torn fabric. He glanced across at

Antryg as they resumed their walking, the bridge sounding hollowly with their footfalls. "He knew it was there."

"Of course I knew it was there," Antryg responded. "I'd felt the opening of the Void, and you could hardly have gotten bruised that way brawling in a pothouse."

Caris' dark eyes narrowed. "You have an explanation for everything."

Antryg shrugged. "It's been my misfortune to be a good guesser. Would it alleviate your suspicions any if I didn't have an explanation?" He gravely handed the crumpled Granola wrapper back to Joanna. "Tell me one thing, Caris. Who were the other mages abroad the night Thirle was killed?"

The young warrior shifted the scabbard that he held loose and ready in his left hand. "How do you know there were any, if it wasn't you who . . . ?"

"Another guess. Was your grandfather one of them?"

"No." Caris glanced sidelong at the wizard, his eyes filled with suspicion. After a moment, he said, "Lady Rosamund . . ." and paused, with a sudden frown.

"What is it?"

He hesitated a moment, then shook his head. "Nothing. Just that . . . She was up and dressed, literally moments after the shots were fired. Aunt Min's hair was flattened and mussed, as if she'd just risen from her bed. It was as if Lady Rosamund had been up some time before."

"Even as you were," Antryg remarked softly, and Joanna saw the young man look swiftly away. "What wakened you?"

"Nothing," Caris said, his voice curt. "Dreams. Nothing that has to do with Thirle's death."

"Oh, everything has to do with everything." Antryg smiled, shoving his big hands into the pockets of his jeans and kicking at a pebble with one booted foot. "It's one of the first principles of magic."

Joanna looked doubtfully up at him. "By magic, do you mean like pouf-you're-gone magic?"

He grinned. "Yes—in fact, pouf-you're-gone is precisely the question of the moment."

"Then why..." She hesitated, then went on. "This is going to sound really stupid, but why don't you use magic to escape?"

Caris looked indignant at the question and started to gesture with his sword; Antryg's grin, like that of a slightly deranged elf, widened.

"Well, two reasons. I believe I can convince Nandiharrow and some of the other mages of the Council to believe my side of the story and, at the moment, I feel I'd be safer as a prisoner of the Council than a fugitive from the Church, which has its own mages. At least the Council will listen to me. And then," he added, more gravely, "if I used magic to escape, the other mages, be they Church or Council, would be able to track me through it eventually."

"You're forgetting the third reason," Caris said grimly. "If you try to escape I will kill you."

"No," Antryg said mildly, "I wasn't forgetting," and Joanna had to turn away to smother a grin.

In contrast to the silent and preoccupied Caris, Antryg had a voracious interest in everything and anything and was, for all his talkativeness, a good listener. Joanna had never been at ease with men; but as they walked along the highroad that ran above the marsh, she found herself telling him, not only about computers and soap operas and the Los Angeles freeway system, but about her mother, Ruth, the cats, and Gary.

"Ah, Gary," he said. "The one with the cruel streak."

She shrugged, guessing he'd been one of the large number of people who'd overheard Gary's remarks about her. "He probably just thought he was being funny."

"I'm sure he did," the wizard said, polishing the spectacles on the hem of his t-shirt. "And that is the worst thing which can be said about him."

It was, but it surprised her a little that anyone, particularly any man, would see it as she did.

The sun rose to noon, and Caris negotiated with some of the hay cutters to buy a portion of their bread and ale, which the three ate sitting on a half-rotted willow log beside one of the gnat-swarming meres. Joanna found the bread harsh and strong-tasting and sprinkled through with grain hulls and specks of dirt. *So much*, she thought, picking a morsel of grit from between her teeth, *for the good old days of the old mill by the stream.* "Can't you do anything about this?" she inquired, glancing up at Antryg, who was contentedly downing his share of the ale. "I mean, you're a wizard—you should be able to turn this into quiche lorraine."

"It doesn't work that way." Antryg half turned to offer the flask to Caris, who, even when eating, stood behind him, one hand never far from the hilt of his sword. Caris shook his head, and the wizard passed it to Joanna. The ale was sweeter than the beer she was used to and considerably above the California limitations on alcohol content. "I could use magic to convince you that you were eating quiche; but when all was said and done, it would be bread in your stomach; and when the spell wore off, you'd still have sand in your teeth. There are wizards and spells which can convert one thing to another—real bread into actual quiche or into gold, for that matter—but they require so much power and take so much strength from the one who casts them that it's really simpler just to change millers."

"Not to mention," Caris said quietly from behind them, "that such meddling in even the smallest of human affairs is forbidden."

"Well," Antryg agreed blithely, "there is that."

Caris' face darkened with disapproval, and Joanna,

glancing sideways at Antryg, caught the flicker of his smile and wondered suddenly how much of what he said he believed—and how much was simply to get a rise out of his captor.

They had come, Caris said at one point during the long afternoon, from the far southeastern corner of the Ponmarish, where it touched the hills of the Sykerst. It was a long walk up the southward road to the gates of the city. There were few peasants in this portion of the marsh, and what few there were, Joanna noticed, worked hard and closer together than their tasks warranted. They appeared nervous, glancing over their shoulders. Poaching hay illegally? she wondered. On the lookout for the hay police? But by that time she was too exhausted and footsore to ask. The daylong walk, though it was not fast, was extremely tiring. She was a thin girl, but she had done no more strenuous walking in the last several years than was necessary to get from her car in the San Serano parking lot to her office, and by the end of the afternoon she felt a kind of wondering resentment about Caris' tireless, changeless stride. Antryg, she noticed, was more considerate—perhaps because it had been years since he, too, had done any great amount of travel. Caris only fretted and muttered that they would not reach the city before dark.

And it was, in fact, long after darkness had settled on the land that they walked through the sleeping streets of the warm, flat, mosquito-humming city, with its carved wooden balconies and brick-paved alleys that smelled of sewage and fish. The city was walled on its land side, though, in the flickering red torchlight of the enormous gateway, Joanna had gotten the impression that the gates themselves hadn't been closed in years. Caris roused a sleepy gatekeeper and rented a torch, which illuminated the tepid darkness of the narrow streets along which they passed. Down a side lane Joanna glimpsed the bent form of an old man, whose elaborately braided hair and beard would have trailed to his knees had the complicated loops of braid been undone, pushing a cart while he shoveled up the copious by-products of what was obviously a horse-dependent civilization. For the rest, the streets were quiet at this hour—Kymil, thought Joanna, scarcely qualifying as the Las Vegas of the Empire of Ferryth.

The House of the Mages lay a moonlit chiaroscuro of ice-gray and velvet black, gargoyle-decorated balconies and windows unlighted and silent, like an anesthetized dragon. Under the carved wooden turrets of the main door, a bonfire had been kindled on the flagway, and four sasenna sat around it, muttering amongst themselves and glancing worriedly about them at the dark.

In the mouth of the narrow lane, Caris stopped and swiftly doused his torch in a convenient rain barrel. Antryg, too, had flattened into the shadows along the wall. For a long moment, they looked out into the dim and mingled glows of moonlight and firelight in the square. Then Caris said softly, "Those are Church sasenna."

Antryg nodded, his spectacles gleaming dimly with the reflected brightness. With a slight gesture, he signaled them back into the alley; Joanna, mystified, followed him and Caris as they wove through a noisome alley where pigs grunted down below the cellar gratings of the narrow houses and around to another side of the square.

There was a smaller side door there. In that, too, armed men sat waiting, huddled more closely about the brazier of coals than the balmy night demanded. Caris glanced up at the tall wizard, his eyes suddenly filled with concern. In an undervoice softer than the murmur of the winds from the marshes, he breathed, "There are no lights in the house."

"Not even in the sasenna's quarters," Antryg murmured in reply. Moonlight touched the tip of his long nose and made a fragile halo of the ends of his hair as he put his head a little beyond the dense shadows in which they stood, then drew it back. Beside them, Joanna could feel, as if she touched the two men, the tension that went through them as they found their common enemy guarding the doors of the house.

Caris said, "It's a good guess there aren't guards inside, then." He glanced around at the black cutouts of oddly shaped roofs against the velvet sky. "No wonder the neighborhood's so silent. They can't have . . ." He hesitated.

"You yourself said that the danger of the abominations abrogated my right to protection by the Council," Antryg murmured, leaning one hand against the coarse, dirty plaster of the nearest wall and looking out into the silent square. "Perhaps the Church came to the same conclusion?"

"Come on," the sasennan said quietly. "We can get over the wall of the garden court—it backs onto the next alley."

That, Joanna thought wryly a few moments later, had to be one of the Great Traditions of literature and cinema: "We can get in over the wall." Staring up, appalled, at the seven-foot paling of reinforced cedar and pine, she felt the sensation of having been cheated by three generations of fictional heroes and heroines who could effortlessly scramble up and over eight-foot, barbed wire fences without breaking sweat or scraping off their shirt buttons as they bellied over the top.

And more than that, she felt weak and stupid, as she had all the way through high school, laboring wretchedly along in the distant wake of the class jocks and wishing she were dead.

"There's a footing shelf on the inside where the beam holds the palings," Antryg whispered. "Caris, you go up first and I'll lift her to you."

Caris, no more than an indistinct shape in the revolting darkness of the alley, turned his head sharply, and Joanna saw the silvery glint of narrowed eyes.

"I'm not going to run from you the minute you're occupied going up the wall," the mage added impatiently. "As much as you do, I've got to find out what's happened."

Caris started to make a reply to this, then let out his breath unused. Without a word, he turned, took a running start at the wall, and used it as a momentum to spring for the top and carry himself over.

"How did you know there was a footing on the beam?" Joanna asked as she approached the base of the wall and saw the sasennan's catlike silhouette crouched against the slightly paler darkness of trees and roofs. "Another lucky guess?"

"No. Up until seven years ago I was a—well, not perfectly respected—member of the community of wizards." The moonlight checkered through the trees beyond the garden wall and silvered the lenses of his specs and the foil HAVOC on his t-shirt. His hands on her waist were large and warm and, as she recalled them on her wrists when they'd struggled, surprisingly strong for his rather gawky appearance. "Up you get."

Joanna had always hated heights, hated exercise, and hated having to do things she couldn't do. Her hands scraped and riven through with splinters, she hauled herself gasping to the top of the wall, half-expecting Caris' mockery, even as the young man steadied her over. But he simply helped her down, following like a stalking cat into the pungent, laurel-scented darkness of the tiny garden. A moment later, the wall vibrated softly under Antryg's weight, and he dropped like a spider at their side.

"Can we risk a light?" he breathed as they entered the dark arches of a very short wooden colonnade that bounded the garden. "The nearest door's around the corner. That should be the barracks in through there."

Caris nodded. Joanna was about to dig into her purse to proffer a match when Antryg made a slight movement with his hand and opened it, releasing a tiny ball of bluish light which rose from his palm and floated a few feet in front of him, about the level of his chest. His grin at the look on her face in the faint phosphorescence was like that of a pleased imp.

Joanna said softly, "I'm not even going to ask." She had, she realized, just seen magic.

"That's just as well. Nobody's ever come up with a satisfactory answer, except the obvious one."

"In here," Caris murmured from the blackness of a small, half open door.

Through an open archway to her right, Joanna had a glimpse of a vast room, with moonlight flooding through long windows to lie like sheets of white silk over a disorder of upended trestle tables and fallen branches. In the room to which Caris beckoned them the disorder was worse. All along its narrow length, furniture had been tipped over, books pulled from the shelves that lined one wall, and strange brass instruments—sextants, astrolabes, celestial globes—had been hurled to the floor and lay like twisted skeletons, glinting faintly in the moonlight. The line of wooden pillars that bisected the narrow room and supported an even narrower gallery above it threw bizarre shadows on the intricate inlay of the cabinets that shared with the bookcases the long inner wall.

"It's the Church, all right," Caris muttered soundlessly as he tiptoed the length of the disordered room, opening and closing cabinets as he went. "Only they would have destroyed like this."

The ball of witchlight drifting along before his feet, Antryg picked his way after the sasennan through the mess, turning over the torn and scattered volumes. "They were in a hurry," he murmured. He paused to stoop, and Joanna saw, by the dim pallor of the witchlight, the black stains of tacky-dry blood on his fingers. "Nandiharrow," he whispered. "Now I wonder why . . . ?"

Caris turned from one of the cabinets, a pistol in his hand pointed at Antryg's chest. "Come over here," he said.

Antryg stood perfectly still for one moment, and Joanna prudently moved to Caris's side to be out of any possible line of fire.

"And don't think you can fix the aim on it, or cause it to misfire," the sasennan went on. "It's na-aar. Joanna, there are chains in the cabinet behind me—get them out."

Joanna's liking for the mad wizard caused her to hesitate for only a moment before obeying. The chains were light, iron rather than steel, and equipped with bracelets and locks.

"Look," Antryg argued, "this isn't necessary."

"Put your arms around the pillar there. Joanna . . ."

Keeping warily out of firing line, she fitted the heavy manacles around Antryg's wrists and pushed them shut. They locked with a cold click. Caris came over and checked them briefly, then nodded to himself, satisfied.

"Caris, don't be a fool. . . ."

"I'm not being a fool." The sasennan stepped quietly away from him, his pistol still trained on Antryg's chest. "And I am not sure whether my duty does not lie in killing you here and now. I don't know what happened, but the mages in Angelshand and other places have to be warned. . . ."

"You are being a fool if you think that, even traveling by fast horse, you could warn them in time," Antryg retorted. "The Church has mages who may swear they don't communicate by scrying-stones, but we all know they do. If the Bishop has gotten permission from the Regent to order the arrest of the mages, it's because she has convinced him that your grandfather somehow spirited me away from the Tower for sinister plots of his own. That order will apply everywhere in Ferryth. You know Herthe. You know she'll have no compunction about violating every Church rule about the use of magic for what she considers a righteous cause."

"Little suspecting," Caris said softly, "that it is the other way around." He stepped forward and put the pistol barrel to Antryg's temple. "Was that your intention all along? To use the Bishop as cat's-paw to dispose of the other wizards, once you had made sure my grandfather wouldn't be there to stop her? Or was that only fortuitous circumstance? Was that why you were so unconcerned about being my prisoner? Why you wanted so desperately to get us away from where I found Joanna—from where you were holding the Archmage . . . ?"

Antryg, his head trapped between the gun muzzle and the turned wood of the pillar to which he was chained, gazed straight ahead of him; but in the faint witchlight Joanna could see the sweat that suddenly beaded his face. "I had nothing to do with it."

The gun lock clicked, loud in the darkness, as Caris thumbed back the hammer. "Where is my grandfather?"

"They'll be in here in a minute asking you that," the wizard said calmly, "if you pull that trigger. And I'm certainly not going to be able to tell them "

For a long, frozen second Joanna held her breath, knowing that, frustrated, furious, and at sea in a wholly unprecedented situation, Caris would have liked nothing better than simply to pull the trigger in revenge for Antryg's having put him in such a position. Under the film of sweat, moonlight, and travel grime, she saw the young sasennan's jaw muscles harden and heard the deep rasping draw of his breath. Then he lowered the pistol, still breathing hard, and looked uncertainly towards the window, where the reflected firelight from the gates outside stained the bull's-eye glass.

Only Joanna saw Antryg briefly close his eyes with relief.

"Look, Caris," she said diffidently. "I don't know whether I get a vote in this or not, but if all the wizards have been arrested, and if your grandfather's gone, he *is* my only way of getting back home." Caris turned towards her, his agate-brown eyes glinting with the intolerant impatience of a strong man listening to the specious arguments of the weak, but Joanna took a deep breath and went on, "I don't know too much about the Church here, but I think, if the Church gets its hands on him, you may never locate your grandfather, either. I mean, if I were the Church and I'd just busted every wizard in the country, I wouldn't try too hard to get the Archmage back into action."

There was a long silence while Caris thought about that, and then something changed in his eyes. "No," he said quietly. "You're right, Joanna—however it came about, it's an opportunity the Church won't let pass by." He was quiet for a moment more. Joanna guessed that, for all his skill as a line fighter, he had never been required to think out the larger strategies for himself. He sighed and rubbed the inner corners of his eyes with his free hand, and some of the desperate tension relaxed from his broad shoulders.

"I'm sorry," he added quietly. "This world must be almost as bad for you to be stranded in as yours was for me."

Almost! thought Joanna, with indignant astonishment. *It isn't* my *world that has the Inquisition and ankledeep horse manure in the streets! Of course*, she added ruefully, *we do have the bomb and the 405 Freeway. . . .*

"It's just that . . ." he began—and stopped himself abruptly from admitting to an exhaustion that it was not the Way of the Sasenna to take into consideration and a love for the old Archmage that it was not the Way of the Sasenna to feel. After a moment he said, "I think the best thing we can do now is to go to Angelshand. The other members of the Council . . ."

"Have either been arrested or are hiding in the deepest holes they can find," Antryg finished. The hammered iron of the chainlinks made a soft clinking against the wood of the pillar as he clasped his big hands around it, almost encircling it with the span of his fingers. "The Bishop will have sent word to the Bishop of Angelshand. They'll have the Regent's consent to the arrests by the first post."

"Then we shall go to the Regent," Caris said stubbornly. "Narwahl Skipfrag is a friend of Grandfather's. He can get the Regent's ear long enough for me to explain the truth of what happened. And after that, the Witchfinders may have you, for all of me."

"Ah," murmured the mage, leaning against the pillar. "But what is the truth?"

Caris' face hardened in the zebra moonlight. "The truth," he returned, equally quietly, "is what the Witchfinders will have out of you." He turned to Joanna and handed her the pistol. "Watch him," he said. "I'm going to have a look around before we leave." Turning, he strode away down the long moonlit room and out into the darkness of the refectory beyond.

Antryg sighed and rested his forehead against the pillar, rubbing his long fingers, as if to banish the ghost of some old pain.

As well as she could, keeping the pistol in hand, Joanna righted one of the chairs, heavy black oak with waffle-crossed straps of leather nailed for a seat, and found a cushion in a corner to put on it to sit down. Her legs were immediately enveloped in a vast rush of pins and needles, and she felt she never wanted to stand up again. After a moment, she asked curiously, "If you're a wizard, can't you just break the locks?"

He looked up at her with a tired smile. "I could," he said. "That is, I could open them—they aren't na-aar, metaphysically dead, like the pistol. But the Church has its wizards, too. By this time, they will know I am free and they will be listening, smelling the air for magic, like the terwed-weeds beneath the sea that scent the tiniest ripple of the passing fish that are their prey. They would know and they would come. And then, too . . ." He paused, thought about it, and let the sentence go unfinished.

Very gingerly, Joanna folded her legs up under her—at five-feet-almost tall, no chair was particularly comfortable without an accompanying footstool. "But weren't you their prisoner before?"

"I was the Council's prisoner, in the custodianship of the Church. The Archmage . . ." He hesitated on the title, then went on, "The Archmage fought for my life."

"Caris' grandfather?"

He nodded. "Salteris Solaris, yes."

She frowned a little, her dark, feathery brows pulling together over her nose. "The one you made away with?"

"*I did not make away with him,*" Antryg insisted doggedly. "I never saw him. He never came there." But he looked away from her as he spoke.

There followed a long silence. In the balmy warmth of the night, she wasn't cold, but all the cumulative aches of the day were beginning to stiffen her unaccustomed muscles, and she had a headache from hunger—bread, cheese, and beer ten hours ago didn't, she reflected, have a great deal of staying power. It was Sunday night. *Well,* she sighed inwardly, *you didn't want to go to work on Monday and here you are.* But even as she smiled to herself, she shivered.

She hadn't wanted to go to work Monday because she had known that she was being stalked. And here she was, with the stalker—where? And more than that . . .

"Why?" she asked softly. "Why me? I've asked you that before. . . ."

Antryg looked over at her again and smiled gently. "My dear Joanna," he said, "if I knew that, I would feel a good deal happier."

Then suddenly he raised his head, listening to the silence of that hushed and darkened house. "What . . ." Joanna began, and he raised his fingers for silence. Strain her ears as she would, she could hear nothing but the faint sough of the leaves of the courtyard trees beyond the arched door and, from somewhere far-off over the wall, the dismal singsong of a kindling-seller's cry. The faint, bluish gleam of Antryg's witchlight died, and, like nocturnal hunters encouraged by the death of the light, the shadows seemed to creep forward around them.

In a voice no louder than the brush of a scrap of silk over footworn stone, Antryg whispered, "The Witchfinders."

Joanna knew better than to try projecting a sound that soft—she slid from her chair as noiselessly as she could and stood near enough to him that she could smell the lingering scents of hay and last night's cigarette smoke in his clothes. "I don't hear anything." She did not even vocalize the sounds, but he breathed a reply.

"At the far side of the house. They have Caris. There will be a key in the top drawer of the desk—Nandiharrow always kept it there."

Joanna hesitated. She had, after all, heard nothing herself. Caris would kill her if she let herself be tricked, particularly by something this simple. Presumably, someone like Sam Spade could just narrow his eyes and snarl confidently, "You're lying, Merlin," but Joanna had never figured out how to intuit that accurately. Trying to pitch her voice as soundlessly as she could, she asked, "Why would the Witchfinders want Caris?"

He closed his eyes and rested his forehead against the wooden pillar, listening to sounds that, try as she would, she could not hear. "They want the Archmage. They think he knows . . . Get the key!" he urged, with soundless urgency, his gray eyes opening wide, and added, when Joanna wavered, "I swear it isn't a trick! Caris . . ."

She held up her hand for silence, as he had done, and whispered, "I'll see."

He opened his mouth protestingly, but she had already turned away, and he knew better than to make any further sound.

It was perhaps that which half convinced her, even before she slipped into the darkness of the refectory across the court and heard the soft voices there. An inveterate reader of spy novels, she followed every half-remembered precept, moving along the wall so that floorboards would not creak, not to mention there being less chance of tripping over miscellaneous furniture along the wall. A nervous, orange reflection of firelight outlined a door behind what must have been the high table and picked out the shining lip of a turned-wood bowl and the metal edge of a tankard, fallen amid a great red stain of dried wine. She caught an indistinct murmur of sound, fought back her instincts to hurry and tested every step. By the time she reached the doorway she could make out the voices.

"My grandfather had nothing to do with his escape! He would have prevented it if he could!"

"Either the Sigil of Darkness works or it doesn't, boy," a thin, cold voice said, chill and poisonous as crimes committed for righteousness' sake. "If Antryg Windrose had the ability to spirit the Archmage away, the Archmage would have been able to prevent him from doing so."

Very cautiously, Joanna lowered herself to her hands and knees, so as to be below eye level, carefully keeping the pistol she held from knocking against the floor, and peeked around the edge of the door. After the soft, moony radiance in the refectory, the low redness of the hearth fire seemed bright. The room had clearly been the library; its half-emptied shelves were littered with torn and fallen books, and others lay thrown in the corners or had been heaped in the fireplace to provide such dim illumination as the room had. Caris was tied to a high-backed chair of spindled wood before the low blaze. Even in the wickering light, Joanna could see the fresh bruise livid on his cheek and the blood on his lip. His sword and three daggers glinted on the table behind them. Beyond, in the shadows, stood three sasenna in somber variations of Caris' torn and stained black uniform. Like a shadow himself against the firelight, a thin man stood in a narrow-cut gray suit, his lank gray hair falling down over a turned-over collar of white linen. His hands were behind his back—small, hard, lean hands, white as the bands of his cuffs and, like them, dyed red with the gory light of the flame. When he turned his face sidelong to the fire, Joanna caught a glimpse of lean, regular features that indicated he had probably been handsome in his youth, before the habit of self-righteousness had bracketed the thin lips with lines of perpetual disapproval. Another man in a similar suit of close-fitting gray stood beside him; it was to him that first one said softly, "When he tells us where the man Antryg is, take two of the sasenna and kill him. We can't afford these waters muddied."

The other man nodded, as if agreeing that, yes, mad dogs ought to be killed; an agreement that was self-evident. "And him?"

The Witchfinder glanced casually back at Caris. "Oh, him too, of course—but after we've learned where Salteris might be. We have most of the great ones, save that one alone—if this boy is his grandson, we may be able to use him as bait."

It was not so much the words he said that affected Joanna, but the way they were spoken, the soft, insidious voice calmly matter-of-fact, as if it were not people at all of whom he spoke. As soundlessly as she could, she backed away, more afraid of being detected and of having that voice speak to her than she had been of anything, even of waking up in the darkness with the print of the strangler's hands on her throat.

Antryg was watching the door with concern in his eyes when she glided back in. The tension relaxed from his shoulders when he saw it was she, but he neither sighed nor, she noticed, moved his hands from where they had been, lest the links of the chain make even the slightest noise. If he, a wizard, could hear the voices on the other side of the refectory, it stood to reason he feared that there were Church wizards there, too, listening for any untoward sounds. After a moment's debate, she shoved the heavy pistol into her purse and slung the unwieldy bag up onto her shoulder again. As she gentled the drawer from the desk, she wondered whether Caris would tell them—or would he realize that, once that soft-voiced man got his hands on Antryg, Caris would never have the chance to find out where the Archmage was or what, if anything, Antryg had done with him?

She came back, key in hand, and touched her finger to her lips for silence. Then she pulled Antryg's t-shirt up over his head and down his arms, to muffle the iron of the lock as she twisted the key. She gestured toward the door and looked a question.

"Peelbone," he breathed, with almost telepathic quiet. "Witchfinder Extraordinary—special branch of the Church." His hands freed, he pulled the t-shirt into place and shook his hair back, crystal earrings glinting in the moonlight, and straightened his specs. "An ideal man for his job but gets invited to very few dinner parties—not that he would ever accept, mind you. I wonder why it is that dyspepsia and righteousness go so often hand-in-hand?"

"Perhaps it's what they mean when they say that virtue is its own punishment?" returned Joanna, equally soundlessly, following Antryg through a small door partially shielded by a torn curtain and into a ransacked workroom.

The room faced opposite the direction of the moon and was almost completely lightless; a droplet of luminescence no bigger than an apple seed floated like a firefly behind Antryg's shoulder, edging his long, nervous hands and preposterous nose in a thin slip of silver as he moved from cupboard to cupboard.

"As I thought," he whispered. "The Bishop's guards came through and sacked the place but didn't take anything away. Afraid to, probably. I wonder the Witchfinders had the nerve to enter the place when they heard Caris moving about." As he spoke, he was drawing things from cupboards—two packets of powders, a mechanical implement that looked like a wind-up toy, and a small box tied tightly shut. Joanna, nervously aware that the small room constituted a cul-de-sac and the one window was far too narrow to admit even her, kept glancing over her shoulder into the barred and dappled shadows of the study beyond.

"We have to help him," she whispered, forgetting entirely that Antryg had every reason not to do so.

"If he's in the hands of the Witchfinders that goes without saying," he replied, the seed of light warming infinitesimally as he bent over the clockwork mechanism, disconnecting a gear and rod arrangement.

Joanna peered worriedly past his shoulder at it. "What is it? It looks like the innards of a clock."

"It is. Like most mages, Nandiharrow was interested in other things besides pure magic—whatever that may be. This is actually a musicbox mechanism run by a clock spring. . . . You didn't happen to bring along my chains, did you, my dear?"

Joanna shook her head, mystified; he *tch*ed under his breath as if she'd forgotten to bring money on a shopping trip and handed her a rag from a corner of the bench. She paused for a moment, hating the silent checkerwork of moonlight and shadow in the room outside and sensing through her skin the shortness of time. Having come in and found Caris, the Witchfinders would be fanning out through the building; it was only a matter of time until she and Antryg were discovered. Moving as quickly as she could without making any noise, she stepped over to the chair where she'd been sitting and where she had put the chains, covered them with the rag, and brought them in, cushion and all. As she did so, she felt, more than heard, the muffled tread of approaching feet on the refectory floor, and it was all she could do to keep from breaking into a run back to the workroom.

"They're coming," she breathed.

He nodded and moved soundlessly to the far wall, passing his hand swiftly down it as she had seen him do in Gary's computer room when the wizard's mark swam into brief, silvery life under his sensitive fingers. This time it was no mark that appeared, but a slit of still deeper black in the shadows. He pushed gently, and a segment of the wall fell back; the tiny light that burned above his head drifted forward to illuminate a very narrow flight of worn and mended steps. He paused, then handed her the clock-work, packets, and box; and to her speechless horror, he turned swiftly and vanished back into the darkness of the study. A moment later he was back beside her, shoving a small wash-leather bag into the pocket of his jeans.

"What is it?" she whispered as he led her into the secret stair.

"Money," he breathed. "Nandiharrow always cached the House funds under the bottom shelf of the bookcase. We'll need it come morning."

"For what?" They were ascending the stairs—wood, like everything else in that rambling house, and so narrow there was not even enough slack to creak under their weight.

"Breakfast, of course. I'm starving. Do you have anything like thread or string about you, my dear?"

Silently, Joanna fished into her purse and produced her sewing kit; Antryg swiftly unraveled about five feet of thread and tied one end to the middle of the chain, the other to some projection of the clockwork mechanism he had taken. Very carefully he cranked it tight. Joanna could hear the swift firm stride somewhere below now; she shivered.

"Right," he whispered. "Would you take the chains down a few steps, my dear? Thank you. Just set them down on the step." He made an adjustment on the clock-work, stood up, and held out his hand to her. She came back to him, careful not to step on the taut thread, and picked up her purse where she'd left it beside him. The weight of it reminded her of the pistol — he could have easily taken it and used it against her, but the thought didn't seem to have crossed his mind. He pushed open another panel in the blackness, and then they were in a long upstairs colonnade, with moonlight slanting through a series of windows that barred the wall to their right in molten silver and lay like pearl stepping-stones along the worn oak of the pegged floor.

Antryg shut the panel behind them; Joanna thought it blended invisibly with the linenfold of the walls, but in the uncertain light, it was difficult to tell where even unhidden doors lay. Taking her hand, he led her with that same cat-footed tread along close to the wall. They were halfway down the hall when Joanna heard, faint but audible, the soft bump and clink of the chain.

"The secret stair's like a sound tunnel," Antryg whispered as they reached the far end of the gallery. "You can't tell where the noise is coming from. The music box pegs should pluck at the taut thread intermittently enough to keep them looking awhile yet."

"How do you know about all this?" Shifting the weight of her purse, always considerable and now aggravated by five pounds of metaphysically dead iron, Joanna followed him down a broad flight of steps at the end of the hall, toward a darkness like a velvet well beneath.

"I told you, I used to stay in this house all the time. There are few enough of the mageborn in the world these days—whatever we think of one another, we are all acquainted." He halted again, this time in the embrasure of one of the stairway windows; for a moment Joanna could see him, like a gangly black spider against the light that picked a steely line along his spectacle-frames and made the lenses gleam like opal when he turned his head. She saw the glint of something in his hands and realized it was the box he'd taken from the workroom.

"It's fortunate for us," he went on, still in that soft, subvocal whisper, "that since I cannot use my own magic, I can borrow someone else's. There." He pocketed something—Joanna could see that it was the string that had tied the lid shut. "Whatever you think is happening," he went on softly, "don't turn aside—just follow me. All right?"

She nodded and took a deep breath. "All right."

He smiled at her in the moonlight in a way that made her remind herself firmly that he was the villain of the piece. "Good girl." Turning, he hurled the box outside into the darkness of the garden. Then he caught her hand and started to hasten silently down the stairs.

They had gone three steps when Joanna heard it, and her heart caught and twisted within her. Shocking in the alien night, Gary's voice had a frantic note to it that would have brought her up short but for the insistent drag of that powerful hand on her wrist. "Joanna! *Joanna!*"

There was some kind of commotion below—she heard Caris' voice cry *"No!"* and the scuffling crash of something falling. Antryg halted short, forcing her to stop, as two men in the black uniforms of sasenna raced past the foot of the stairs. A second later, she heard the crashing of their feet in the garden outside; already Antryg was dragging her down the stairs, and she was stumbling to keep up with his longer stride.

In the ransacked library, Caris was struggling wildly against his bonds, desperation and fury in his face. "Grandfather's out there!" he shouted, as Antryg scooped one of the daggers from the table. "I have to . . . !"

"It's a Crier." Red light slipped along the blade as the wizard slashed the bonds; he caught Caris by his torn jacket and sword belt as the young man lunged for the garden doors. "An illusion of summoning—Come on!"

"But . . ." Shaken Caris might have been, but not so shaken that he forgot to snatch his weapons from the table as they passed.

"It's true, I heard Gary's voice," Joanna panted. They were already on the run for the window. Footfalls pounded behind them on the oak of the corridor floors. Antryg kicked open the leaded casement of the window and swung through; Joanna scrambled next, still hanging onto her purse, and dropping a surprising distance into a pair of strong hands.

Antryg was already hauling her back into the shiny, green-black thicket of a camellia bush as Caris dropped from the window; in the tepid night air, the scent of the waxy white blossoms hung thick around them. Caris ducked back to join them, still shoving a last dagger into his boot, the bruise on his face showing up horribly against the exhausted grayness of his skin. Joanna thought about going over the fence again, and her every stiff and aching muscle whined in protest, but the thought of the cool, self-righteous voice of the Witchfinder brought the cold sweat of fear to her face. Remembering it and those chilled and empty eyes, she no longer questioned how an animal could bite off a foot to escape a trap.

Caris whispered, "They're outside, waiting for us to come over." Indeed, beyond the garden wall, she could hear men shouting in the street. With his teeth, Antryg ripped a corner from one of the sacks of powder and dumped a little into his palm, then did the same with the other. Shoving the sacks into the pocket of his jeans, he pulled a camellia from the dark shrubs around them and ground the white blossom into the mixture.

With a quick glance back at the window above them, he threw the blossom over the fence. Just as it crested the top of the wood, it burst into violent flame. Shouting rose beyond the palings and from the room they had just left. As Antryg dragged her away Joanna could see the sasenna who had run past the base of the stairs leaning from the window, pointing excitedly at the fireball. Running feet pounded the pavement outside the fence.

Very calmly, Antryg opened a small door that led back into the house and led the way at a swift walk down a short, darkened hall, across the ghostly moonlight of a rather bare reception room, and out one of the great doors and into the street outside.

There were no guards. Their abandoned brazier still flickered on the pavement, but Joanna could see them pelting around the corner towards the smoldering glare, their huge, jumping shadows thrown on the tall primrose and blue fronts of the houses opposite. His arm protectively around Joanna's shoulders, Antryg walked unhurriedly across the cobbled square and on into the concealing darkness of the nearest lane, with Caris trailing silently at his heels.

CHAPTER X

"YOU'RE A FOOL." CARIS CAST A NERVOUS GLANCE around the eating-house of the Bashful Unicorn as a stout, red-faced serving-woman in a greasy apron brought a platter of stew and breads to the table. "We could have been long on the road by this time."

"No matter how quickly we'd gotten on the road, the patrols looking for us would have been mounted." Antryg gravely poured ale from the earthenware jug for the three of them, the grimy, orange glow of the solitary lamp overhead glancing along his spectacles. "Even the ones who remained behind to search the quarter of the Old Believers, under the impression that they'd be likelier to shelter fugitive mages, would never dare risk being caught in a tavern, should their captain ride by." He raised his dented tankard in a toast. "Confusion to our common foe."

Caris paused, tankard in hand. "Have we one?"

"I'm sure we do, if we look hard enough." The mage

smiled. "Or should we say, 'To the Emperor's good health'?"

Across the dining room, a well-heeled young man in a mint-green satin court coat slumped forward across the table amid empty bottles and glasses; the two painted strumpets with him instantly ceased their uproarious appreciation of his jokes and got down to the serious business of relieving him of his valuables. In the street outside, the first clattering of the market carts and the crowing of cocks in a thousand backyard hen coops could be heard.

Caris drained his mug in silent disapproval. Joanna, sitting between the two men on the hard, backless bench, mopped her bread in the stew. Worried as she was about remaining in Kymil after daybreak, she could not help being glad Antryg had vetoed immediate flight on the grounds that they wouldn't get any breakfast.

From their escape from the House of the Mages, Antryg had led them, illogically enough, to an all-night public bathhouse. "Who'd think of looking for fugitives from the Witchfinders in the public baths?"—an argument Joanna found cogent and Caris dismissed as utterly frivolous. Emerging clean, shampooed, and gasping from the cedar-lined sweatbox with its bubbling tub, Joanna found a bundle of secondhand petticoats, blue skirt, pink bodice, and shift that Antryg had acquired from an old clothes dealer next door. "There must be more old clothes dealers in the quarter of the Old Believers than in the rest of the city put together," Caris had told her, when they'd met Antryg in the tavern, the sasennan looking uncomfortable and not very convincing in a peasant's knee breeches, woolen stockings, and coarse smock. "They all go into the trade and stay open till all hours."

Antryg had been waiting for them, his graying hair close-curled with dampness, resplendent in a much-mended shirt of ruffled lawn that was far too big for him and a rusty black court coat whose silver bullion embroidery had long since been picked out. He'd retained the jeans and harness boots he'd picked up at the party and had added to his crystal earrings an assortment of gimcrack bead necklaces and a cracked quizzing glass. "You might be prepared to take the road like a wolf in winter," he added, gesturing with his tankard at Caris, "but I'm not, and Joanna certainly isn't. By daybreak, the men who have been out combing the roads will be tired, and there will be enough people about so that we won't draw too much attention to ourselves."

Caris glanced at Antryg's attire, sniffed, and said nothing. Joanna had the distinct impression that Caris knew very well he was no longer the leader of the expedition, but wasn't entirely sure either how this had come to pass or what to do about it. Antryg was, nominally at least, still his prisoner—only with the Council of Wizards gone or in hiding, there was nowhere Caris could take his prisoner for the moment. There was a good deal of dour frustration in his mien as he watched the wizard spooning honey onto bread.

"Very useful stuff, honey," Antryg was saying. "Did you know the Mellidane scholars make a decoction of it to preserve embryos for study, as well as use it as a base for poultices?" He cocked his head a little, considering the thick, liquid-amber stream dripping from the spoon. "The ancient Saariens said it was the tears of the goddess Helibitare and mixed it with myrrh and gold and offerings—and it has other uses as well. You're aware, of course, that the guards at the city gates will be looking for the Archmage's sasennan who slew the abomination in the swamp? And they'll certainly be looking for that."

Caris shied back from the touch of Antryg's finger as the mage flicked the purpling bruise on his cheek. "My cloak has a hood."

"And terribly convincing in midsummer it is, too." The

mage sighed, sliding a few spare rolls into the capacious pockets of his coat.

"Did you really?" Joanna looked a little shyly up at Caris, remembering the mottled, hideous bruises she had seen on his chest and arms through the torn cloth of his jacket. "Slay it?" It felt strange to say. Nobody she had ever known had ever killed anything larger than a cockroach—or admitted to doing so, anyway.

"Not really," the sasennan said, pausing in his rapid and efficient consumption of a hunk of beef. "My grandfather slew it. He caused lightning to strike the water of the swamp—lightning that is in truth electricity. . . . Do you have electricity, in your world?" he added.

"Sure." Joanna dished herself out a second platter of stew and picked the trailing ends of her bodice lacings out of the gravy. The food made her feel much better, as had the bath. She had been twenty-four hours without sleep, much of it on her feet, either running or walking. It occurred to her suddenly to wonder whether Antryg had taken that into account in his erratic choice of a hiding place. "Our whole world runs on electricity—everything's powered by it, just about. Lights, radio, television, computers, you name it."

"That music?" Caris asked, a little sourly.

"Particularly music—although, mind you, I think it's an insult to Johann Sebastian Bach to call that stuff music. But we won't go into that. The instruments are electric; they're electronically synthesized and electrically recorded and played back. The only human things involved are the group who plays and the guy who wrote it, and even those are being computerized these days."

Across the room the two sluts rose and departed, leaving their incapacitated Romeo amid the beer mugs. The moving gust of air from the opening door made the brownish shadows jump over Caris' elegant cheekbones and nose as he glanced automatically up to make sure no one else entered. It was gray dawn outside, lightening towards day. Though recking of garbage and horses, the air smelled fresher than the dark and beery frowst inside.

"Record . . ." He looked back at her dubiously. "So that it can be reproduced at any time, you mean?"

Joanna nodded. "But you have the same thing. The— Crier, did you call it?" She glanced across at Antryg in time to see him cache the squat black bottle of gin he'd ordered in one of his copious coat pockets.

"Not really," the wizard said. "The Crier doesn't record a sound, but an emotional reaction which you associate with sound, in much the same way the spell of tongues allows you to understand what I'm saying now. There are other spells which reproduce sound—Screamer and terror-spells—fairly simple, really. Have you a screw-cap jar with a wide mouth in that bag of yours, my dear?"

Joanna wordlessly produced one. Antryg cast a quick glance to make sure the proprietress wasn't looking, then began spooning honey into it. He went on, "Caris heard his grandfather's voice calling for help, didn't you, Caris? Whereas you, Joanna, heard—your lover's?"

The word took her by surprise; her reaction to it, even more so. She had always subconsciously thought of Gary as "boyfriend"—a somewhat childish word never adequately replaced in adult parlance. She wondered, a moment later, why her first impulse had been to shy away from the use of the word *lover*—in the physical sense, that was what he had been. But she understood for the first time that she did make the distinction, and the distinction was a critical one.

Gary, she thought, a little sadly, would never be anything but a "boyfriend."

He probably wouldn't even realize yet that she was gone, she reflected later, as they left the inn with the first brightness of the day dispersing the gloom in the lanes. Her car would still be at his place. Possibly he'd deduced—although privately she didn't consider Gary capable of deductive reasoning—that she'd gone home with someone else.

As she remembered his words about his being the only man who'd want her, the thought pleased some small, vindictive corner of her heart. Thus he might not find it odd she didn't answer her telephone all day yesterday, which was Sunday. It was only when he went to work today, smugly counting on meeting her at the office and offering her a ride to his place to pick up her car—with the obligatory *Let's have dinner* and *Why don't you spend the night* thrown in—would he realize she was, in fact, missing. He might spend another day or two trying to reach Ruth before that jet-propelled, stainless steel butterfly remembered to listen to her answering machine, called him back, and they figured out that nobody had seen Joanna since Saturday night.

It was a slightly unnerving thought.

The air outside was fresher, reviving her and chasing the insistent cobwebs of sleepiness from her brain. The night had never really cooled off; the morning, already sticky-warm, though the sun was not yet in the sky, promised hot. It was in her mind that now would be the ideal time to make her escape from Antryg—except that, in this world, there was nowhere for her to go. It was rather like trying to escape from a rowboat in the middle of an ocean—her options were limited. The best she could do, she thought, was stay with the wizard and his captor and hope they could locate the Council—or, at worst, talk Antryg into sending her back himself.

Once outside the inn, Antryg turned, not toward the lane upon which it stood, but into the smelly little alleyway which ran between it and the bathhouse. Caris followed, clearly uneasy, because, in his peasant clothes, he couldn't openly have a weapon in hand. The pistol was concealed under his smock, available, but awkward to get at. Joanna, holding up her skirts from the mud, brought up the rear, reflecting that all the swashbuckler films she'd seen had apparently forgotten to mention certain facts of life, like pig dung in the lanes and the general awkwardness of petticoats.

In the alley, Antryg unscrewed the cap from his jar of pilfered honey, tore pellets from the bread he'd pocketed, and, with the assistance of a little of the mud and offal liberally available underfoot, created half a dozen disgustingly convincing pustules to cover the bruise on Caris' face. "I don't suppose you could manage to drool and stagger a bit?" he asked judiciously, producing the gin bottle from another pocket. Its reeking contents, dumped over the sasennan's clothes, totally drowned the smell of the honey. Caris only looked indignant. "I didn't think so. Pity the rag shop didn't have sasennan's gear to fit Joanna—then she could have carried your sword openly instead of bundling it up as it is."

Joanna glanced at the big, sloppy bundle which contained her own clothes, sneakers, and bulging purse, Caris' torn and shabby black uniform and boots, and a couple of hooded cloaks which could double as light blankets, should the weather turn cool. It was tied loosely onto a pole, which concealed the long, hard-edged shape of Caris' sword, but it still didn't look particularly convincing. "We could always say they belonged to my brother," she pointed out. "The Witchfinders only think they're looking for one person, or at most two, or . . . Could *you* pass yourself off as a free sasennan?"

"A free sasennan is a contradiction," Caris said, turning away from trying to catch a glimpse of his reflection in a nearby rain barrel. "There are no free sasenna. The Way of the Sasenna is to serve. We are the weapons, no more, of those who hold our vows."

Joanna shouldered the long bundle and followed the two of them from the alley and into the lane once more. Flies were already beginning to buzz around the greenish scum in the gutters; Caris waved furiously at them as they hummed around the fake sores on his face.

"But what about you?" she asked.

His back stiffened. Momentarily he forgot that he was supposed to be a pox-ridden drunk. "My masters are and always will be the Council of Wizards," he said. Under the dirty slime, his face was cold and proud as Athenian marble. "My grandfather is not dead. . . ."

"Isn't he?" Antryg asked softly.

Caris halted and turned to face the wizard in the lead-colored shadows of the lane. "If he were," he said with equal quiet, "there is only one way that you could know it, Antryg Windrose."

"Is there?" The mage tipped his head on one side, his gray eyes suddenly very weary behind their heavy specs. "He was my master, Caris; we traveled together for many years. Don't you think I would know?"

The sasennan's voice had an edge to it like chipped flint. "He was not your master," he said softly. "Suraklin was your master."

"So he was." Antryg sighed, turning back to the lane. "So he was."

They moved out into the main street. Though it was fully light now, the sun had not yet risen above the roofs of the houses; the gold brilliance of it flashed from the slates of the roofs, but the lanes themselves were like canals of still, blue shade. Rather to Joanna's surprise, since it couldn't have been more than five in the morning, the lanes were crowded, men, women, and small children jostling along the herringbone brick cobbles between the wooden houses. Some, in the dark livery of servants, carried market-baskets; tiny children and old men in rags held out skinny hands to them and whined for alms. A few of the women were better dressed, strolling with their maids and looking about them, as Joanna was doing, savoring the glory of sun flashing from the wings of the pigeons that circled overhead and the sweet, wild scent of the hay marsh that blew in over the stinks of the waking town. But most of those abroad on the street, roughly dressed and still-faced, hurried drearily along with the stride of those whose sleep has been insufficient and who care nothing for the beauty of a day which will not be theirs.

They turned a corner into the main thoroughfare of Kymil. The clattering of wheels and hooves which Joanna had heard far-off grew louder, and the slanting sunlight sparkled on the broad street before her, the tepid air redolent with the smell of horses. Carts in incredible numbers clattered by, laden with produce or rickety coops of chickens; butchers' wagons darted between them, as if trying to outpace pursuing swarms of flies; drays of sand or beer barrels rumbled heavily on the cobbles. Just ahead of them, Joanna saw a little boy with a broom dart out into the street to sweep a path through the accumulated muck for a couple of well-dressed ladies. One of them flung the boy a coin, which he caught like a Cubs outfielder jumping for a pop fly.

Joanna stood still upon the flagway, the bundle forgotten on her shoulder, staring around her in a kind of amazement. Yesterday's walk through the countryside and last night's brush with Church authorities and magic had not prepared her for the thoroughly prosaic scene before her. Antryg paused beside her, causing Caris to turn back toward them suspiciously, but the wizard only asked, slightly amused, "What is it?"

She shook her head. The truth sounded silly, but she said, "I sort of expected it to be . . . more medieval."

Antryg grinned, comprehending her surprise and appreciating her rueful self-amusement at her assumptions. "Not the sort of place you expected to find wizards in, is it?"

Joanna looked around her again. Down the lane to their left, massive, dreary brick factories crouched against the shining gold of the sun-shot river; a group of little girls in patched dresses moved past like a school of fish and, with unwilling haste, joined the throng of men and women milling toward the factory gates. Beside her, Caris said, "It is why wizards are forbidden to touch human affairs—so that we can have such a world." He shrugged, clearly ill at ease in his peasant clothes without a weapon in his hand. "Come."

As they moved down the street, Joanna cast a last glance back at the tired-looking children shuffling toward the factory gates.

"Flax mills," Antryg said softly, falling into step at her side. "They'll work till seven or eight tonight, to take advantage of the daylight. At twopence a week, the owners find it cheaper than hiring men. And then, running a machine doesn't require strength."

Looking up, she saw in his face the tired bitterness of one who sees suffering which he cannot alleviate and from which he has, by fate, been exempted. Thinking of those hurrying, tiny forms, she knew exactly how he felt.

He went on, "This is their technology, their industry for the betterment of all. To have no magic in politics, in industry, or in trade, to make no exceptions for the few at the expense of the many . . . For this world, we have forfeited what we are and could be."

"What you could be," Caris cut in frostily, "is what your master was—a despot who ruled this town by fear for years and who instilled in you the power to do the same."

Antryg sighed, his hands buried in the pockets of his preposterous coat, the lines of his face settling into an expression that aged him—the weight of too great a knowledge of human sorrow. "Yes," he agreed, his voice quiet. "But I've never seen that technology or this progress they keep talking about has helped those who must feed its machines. Yours is a world of technology, Joanna; it lies on the other side of a night of time which our eyes can't pierce from here. It is worth it?"

Joanna was silent for a time, her skirt-entangled steps quick to keep pace with the longer strides of the men, fishing through the dim memories of a period in history which had always bored her. "If you mean, does it get better," she said slowly, "yes. But that's six, seven generations down the line. And it gets worse."

"Much worse?" His voice was the voice of a man asking after the fate of his own children, not the sons of men and women three generations away whom he would never know.

"I think so."

The long, sensitive mouth twisted; he walked along in silence, while the morning brightened and bells all over the city began to ring for the first church services of the day. A couple of country girls passed them, their skirts hiked up to reveal tattered petticoats underneath. One carried a bucket of milk on her head, the other a tray of fish that could be smelled across the street; neither girl looked particularly well-fed. At the end of the broad street, Joanna could see the glint of sunlight on the gray, bulky towers of the city gates and the flash of steel pikes and helmets in their deep arched shadow.

"I suppose there's a certain economy to it," said Antryg at last. "To sacrifice seven or eight generations for the betterment of ten, or twelve, or a hundred."

The children of the last generations of downtrodden factory fodder, Joanna thought, had invented the atomic bomb. She said quietly, "Maybe not even that."

His glance was puzzled and worried—not understanding how, she thought, but understanding what. They were entering the jostling crowds of the square, where half a dozen streets and alleys met before the gate. The din of hawkers, wagon wheels, crossing sweepers, and soldiers calling back and forth was tremendous and masked the soft, deep richness of his voice from any but her ears alone.

"Sometimes I think it would have been better had I not been born with the powers of a mage," he said quietly. "I see what is happening and I know I am neither intellectually nor thaumaturgically equipped to remedy it. I know that those great, awful laws should apply to all, without exception. And yet, in individual cases—it seems different then."

Without warning, the strange despair that Joanna had felt two or three times in the last weeks washed over her heart. He was right, she thought—not only about his world, but about her own. She felt suddenly isolated by the pointlessness of it all. This world, working to become what hers suddenly seemed to her to be—colorless, alienated, so impersonal that she herself could disappear and it would be days before her closest friend and her boyfriend—she shied again from thinking of him as her lover—knew she was even gone. . . .

Though the warm brilliance of the daylight did not fade, it seemed as if all color, all animation had been drained from it, turning it into a tawdry carnival of pointless despair. Ahead of them, the city gates reared up at the end of the street, a clumsy monolith of dingy stone surmounted by a tarnished clock and cones of moldering slate. All the weariness of the last twenty-four hours descended crushingly on her shoulders. She could see the sasenna standing in the gatehouse shadows now, their black uniforms bearing the red sun-seal of the Church; with them were men in the gray, straitlaced clothing of the Witchfinders. She remembered the man Peelbone, and sudden panic clutched her heart.

But before she could speak, Caris balked and drew back suddenly into the mouth of a narrow lane. Under the grime and faked sores, she saw his handsome face and turned pale. His voice was breathless, "I don't like it."

Joanna shook her head, glad her own terrors were vindicated by the instincts of the warrior.

"We can hide in the quarter of the Old Believers," Caris went on hoarsely. "They'll know who I am."

"Don't be silly." Antryg ducked into the lane at his side. Joanna could see his face, like the younger man's, suddenly clammy with moisture. "Not finding us on the roads, they'll concentrate on the ghetto now." There was something else in his voice, something that she didn't bother to identify through that queer feeling of panic.

Caris went on, his voice stumbling, "We can't escape. They have the Council; they're destroying all the wizards. We could have gotten out—I was going to use a spell to make them ignore us—it was one of the few magics I could do. But now. . ." He paused, his breath coming fast, as if he fought a panic of his own. "Let's go back." He started to move down the lane, and Antryg caught his arm in that surprising grip.

"No," the mage said.

Furious, Caris dragged at his smock for his pistol; Antryg caught his other hand.

"It's left you, hasn't it?" he said softly. "Your magic."

Caris' eyes shifted. "No. Now move or I'll . . ."

"You'll what? Shoot me? Fifty feet from the guards at the city gate?"

They stood nearly breast to breast, the warrior in his filthy smock staring into the mage's bespectacled eyes in baffled, unreasoning rage. Then his mouth twisted, and his hand plunged for the knife in his boot. Joanna, watching, felt queerly distant from both of them, as if it were all happening to strangers and there would be no consequences. She wondered if the stew at the inn had given her dysentery and these were its opening stages, wondered if she would die of it and, if she died, if she would care. But even as Antryg caught Caris's knife hand, a cry in the street behind them snagged at her attention, though it, like everything else, seemed unimportant now.

Looking out, she saw that a lady, in a spell of crooked humor, had flung a halfpenny for one of the little crossing sweepers under the hooves of an oncoming dray. The boy had made an ill-timed dive for the coin and was now sitting on the edge of the flagway, clutching his bleeding leg and screaming while the drayman shouted at him and passers-by turned aside unheeding.

Something within her told Joanna that she should feel something, do something, but it was as unreal as a scene on television. Her head felt strange, as if with hunger, though she had a weird sense that she could eat for hours without filling the gray emptiness of her soul.

At the gates, the sasenna had closed around a young man in the long black gown and braided hair of an Old Believer.

Caris, looking dully past Antryg's shoulder, said, "It's Treman. One of the mages . . . It'll never work! We'll be taken. . . ."

"We won't," said Antryg quietly, seizing the young sasennan by the shoulder and steering him out of the alleyway, "because we're not using magic to get by the guards. Don't you understand? *You're not the only one whose magic has left you.* You're not the only one who feels this despair."

Caris blinked at him, struggling in his mind. "What?"

Antryg hauled the young man's arm around his shoulder. "Lean on me," he said softly. "You're drunk."

"It'll never . . ."

"I'll knock you over the head and carry you if you don't do as I say."

Caris made one indignant move to struggle, then shook his head, as if he suddenly realized the perilous stupidity of such a display of temper. He slumped against the taller man's shoulder, his head lolling. "I—I don't know what's come over me," he whispered. Joanna, clutching the bundle that now looked more than ever unmistakably sword-shaped, fell into step on his other side. "It's as if . . ."

"I don't either," said the mage softly, "but whatever it is, it has come over the guards, too."

"It can't have." Caris managed a convincing stagger, and clutched at the mage's arm. "It's only because my magic is fading. It's been fading for weeks. It hasn't anything to do with anyone else."

As they approached the shadows of the gate, Joanna felt almost ill with despair, knowing they would be searched. Even if the Inquisition did not take her, it would certainly take her companions. She would be left stranded in this world, with its filth and peril, unable to make her living, unable to return home. . . . Tears of fright and misery blurred her vision. She felt an almost uncontrollable urge to break away and bolt back to the sheltering shadows of the alleyways, and only some small, illogical corner of her that trusted Antryg's judgment kept her moving toward the massed sasenna in the echoing, stony darkness of the gate.

They were still gathered around the man Treman, who was looking terrified and at the same time in the grip of listless apathy. With a sudden oath, one of the guards struck him across the face. The other guards, watching this scene, paid scant attention to the cart and foot traffic clattering in and out of the gates behind them. The shadows were cold; by contrast, the sun on the causeway beyond, when the three fugitives reached it, was oppressively hot. Gnats hummed drearily over the marshes; the sun was blinding on the water. Joanna, Antryg, and Caris were some hundred feet beyond the gates before Joanna even realized they had successfully escaped the town.

"You feel it, too, don't you, Joanna?" Antryg asked quietly, as they lost themselves among the shuffling crowd of the city's poor who came and went on the marsh road, to cut hay or fish for their food among the pools. "And have done so for the last several weeks."

Joanna nodded, puzzled that he should know. Caris, the gates safely past, removed his arm from his Antryg's shoulders and took the bundle of weapons from Joanna. He remained walking between them, looking baffled and strained.

Antryg went on, "I don't suppose that woman back there would ever have thrown a coin under the horses' feet that way—even if the thought had crossed her mind; either inherent decency or, at the very least, fear of what her friends would think of her would have stayed her hand. Ordinarily the boy would have had more sense than to go after it and more skill than to get trampled." He looked from one to the other of them, his head cocked to one side, like a gray stork's. "Don't you see?"

A passing troop of mounted sasenna kicked dust over them; it clung like flour to their sweaty faces. Joanna saw one tired-looking old farm woman who barely raised her head as the riders bore down on her; and the boy who was with her saw them coming for some moments before rousing himself to pull his mother out of the way. Joanna shook her head, feeling strangely isolated and uncaring.

"It eats life," the wizard said softly. "It eats magic. It leeches the life-force, the energy that holds all life together, from every living thing and leaves in its place only the weary wondering of where it has gone."

"What does?" Caris asked, a kind of fear struggling against the uncaring dullness in his eyes.

"That," Antryg said, "is what I mean to find out."

CHAPTER XI

THEY TRAVELED FOR THREE DAYS, THROUGH THE GREEN and empty hill country that Caris called the Sykerst, and into the farmlands beyond.

The queer, terrible sense of deadness did not pass off until sometime after noon of the first day. Joanna, asleep in the shelter of the last haystack of the lowlands before the high ground began, felt the fading in her confused dream of being married to Gary, of protesting, *But it was all a mistake! I don't want to be married to anybody*, and of Gary's smug expression as he said, *I'm sorry, babe, but you did marry me. . . .* As if a fever had been lifted from her, she wept. She felt a hand, large but very light of touch, brush her hair comfortingly as she sank into deeper sleep.

Later, as they resumed their walk through the stuffy, clinging heat of the last of the day, she asked Antryg, "Did it affect your magic, as it did that of Caris?"

"I felt it," he admitted, producing three apples from the

pockets of his trailing coat-skirts and tossing two of them to his companions as they walked. "It didn't bleed all the hope from me—madness has certain advantages."

Joanna frowned up at him. "You mean magic is—is predicated on hope? Because I felt, more than anything, that was what was taken from me—the hope of anything."

He regarded her with quirked eyebrows for a moment, surprised by her understanding. "Hope," he said, "and belief in life. We move blindly from second to second through time. Hope, and magic, both involve the casting forward of the soul. In a way, both magic and hope are a kind of madness."

"Madness also has the advantage," Caris said, shifting the set of the pistol belted under his faded peasant smock, "of cloaking things which you find it more convenient not to explain—like the fact that you knew of the coming of the abominations, and why you, of all wizards, don't lose your powers to this . . . whatever it is."

"Handy, isn't it?" Antryg grinned, pleased. He finished devouring the core of his apple and flicked the stem into the nodding weeds of the roadside ditch. "Couldn't have happened better if I'd caused it myself."

Caris' coffee-brown eyes narrowed, and Joanna had to look away and purse her lips tightly against an involuntary smile.

"The thing that worries me," the wizard went on after a moment, "or one of the things that worry me about that, is that it happens everywhere. What about the children in the factories? There are enough accidents without that—uncaringness."

Joanna, who had lived all her life in a world poised a button push away from destruction, shivered. "Come to think of it," she said after a moment, "where I work—if they don't can me for being absent without calling in—on the days this whatever-it-is happened, there would always be zillions of stupid errors in documentation and programs."

"Documentation?"

Joanna hesitated, wondering how she could best explain computers to a wizard, much less to one from a world that had only begun connecting electricity with lightning. But no one, she reasoned, who wasn't interested in everything would have become a wizard in the first place; so she launched ahead and for several miles expounded upon the intricacies of programming, languages, CP/M pixels, ROM, RAM, mainframes, micros, hard disks, and floppies, while the dove-colored summer evening darkened to ultramarine and the dry-grass sweetness of the hill winds tugged at her hair.

"You are saying, then, that these—these computers—think?" Caris asked doubtfully. He had abandoned his guarding position at Antryg's back and walked now at Joanna's side, the bundle of their possessions still over his shoulder and the butt of the pistol visible against his hard-muscled belly through the half-open smock. He sounded worried.

Joanna shook her head. "They can be programmed to reproduce many of the processes of linear thinking," she said, kicking aside an encumbering fold of her petticoat which persisted in tangling around her ankles. "That is, any chain of thought can be broken down into a hundred tiny yes-or-no decisions—if A, then go to B, if not A, then go to C, and C will tell you what to do from there."

Caris frowned, puzzled, but Antryg said, "Rather like a music box—either a key is struck or it's silent—or the punched cards they rig in automatic series to change the weft patterns in jacquard looms."

"Since computers work very fast—and we're talking a hundredth or thousandth of a second here—" She shied from explaining nanoseconds to people who, she was fairly sure, didn't work habitually in units smaller than hours.

"—it has the appearance of operating like thought. But for the most part, they'll do exactly what you tell them to. It's both the advantage and the disadvantage of computers. You always know where you are with a computer, unlike a person—but they don't care what they do. They'll sit there printing out gibberish for hours, if you make the wrong request, give away state secrets to anyone who asks, or help you steal, if you know the right entry code—and any good hacker can break an entry code."

"Steal?" The sasennan's frown deepened. As soon as it had begun to grow dark, he had paused by one of the thin streams that trickled down from the hills, had washed the counterfeit sores from his face, and had rid himself of the faint, pale stubble of his beard with a razor from his belt purse. In the lingering dusk, the dark circles around his eyes had deepened almost to bruises. Joanna wondered if he had slept when they had taken refuge in the haystack for a few hours' rest or if he thought it behooved him still to keep an eye on Antryg.

"I thought you said those things were only boxes that did not move."

She shrugged. "They don't have to. It's all done over the telephone. Everything in our civilization is. A friend of mine at San Serano broke the ordering and shipping codes on the San Serano mainframe; I suspect he also used telephone modems to break the shipping codes on some of the companies that use computerized ordering systems where we get our supplies. Now and then I'll be thumbing through the mainframe and find somebody's put through an order from San Serano for some kind of equipment—like extra disk drives—and then later find that the order has been pulled from the file. When an order's pulled from a computer file, it's gone; it's as if it never existed. It's only light, after all—and when light's gone it leaves no tracks. Presumably, using modems, the record of the transaction can be removed from the shipper's files as well. That way

Gary can walk off with an extra disk drive—or a whole computer, if he wanted to—and nobody's the wiser, because there's no record of the thing ever having existed."

The affronted morality of years of warrior discipline was in Caris' voice. "He is a thief without even the courage of a common burglar," he said.

Joanna nodded in agreement. They stepped down into the weed-grown roadside ditch to let a shepherd and his flock pass them, a bleating, jostling confusion of wool and dust. "Except that he'd say that the companies have a profit margin for theft included in their annual budgets, so nobody's really losing anything."

"Except Gary himself." Hands in his pockets, shift ruffles like a shabby flower in the evening gloom, Antryg turned away from his delighted contemplation of the interplay between sheep and dogs to regard his companions. "And what he loses is the part of himself that honors the rights of others and honors his own integrity."

"Gary," Joanna said after a moment, "wouldn't really understand that integrity—which is free, and therefore cheap—isn't worth a two-thousand-dollar disk drive." She stepped back into the smelly dust cloud that hung over the road, kilting up her skirts into her belt as she had seen the farm women do, and resumed her tired walk north.

Much later, when Joanna looked back on those few days, it was with a kind of mild surprise at herself for the ease with which she slipped into companionship with both captor and captive. Timid by nature, she had always harbored an uneasy distrust of men, regarding them as an alien species who dealt with women in the relationship of users and used. But neither of the two men seemed to regard her as anything other than a comrade on the road, Caris because he was too single-mindedly intent on watching Antryg, and Antryg because it would never have occurred to him to deal with anyone except on that person's own terms.

"I don't know what game he's playing," Caris said, as

he and Joanna shared a bucket of wash water drawn from the horse trough of the posting house stable where the three of them had slept the night. "He could perfectly well have escaped last night." He folded up his shaving razor and returned it to his belt purse, then doused the water angrily over his face and head and shook out his wet, fair hair. Joanna, at Caris' instructions, had gamely taken a shift at watch the previous night and had fallen asleep ten minutes into it; Caris, she knew, had waked, sat in the dark hayloft for half an hour in pistol-clutching surveillance on the sleeping Antryg, and had dropped off as well. Antryg had waked both of them at dawn.

Joanna tried but failed to stifle her grin. "But he would have missed breakfast," she said, providing what Antryg's explanation would surely be. All she got from the disgruntled Caris was a sour look.

"He has his own reasons for wanting to go to Angelshand." His glowering eyes sought the tall, loose-limbed form of the wizard as it emerged from the back door of the posting inn, half a loaf of rye bread and a hunk of cheese in hand. Then he wiped his hands on the coarse linsey-woolsey of his peasant smock, its sleeves turned up to reveal the old, white scars which criss-crossed his muscular forearms, and brushed away a stray bit of hay. Joanna had quickly discovered that hay was surprisingly persistent stuff. "It's easy to believe in his innocence," he said after a moment. "I did, myself, if for no other reason than that he seems too scatterbrained to be devious. But he brought you here for a reason, Joanna, and it may be that he only appears so docile because he hasn't had the opportunity to carry you off."

As Antryg came up to them, Joanna was obliged to press her hand over her mouth to keep from laughing at the mental picture of the bespectacled wizard in his billowing, too-large black coat dashing away on foot across the hills with her thrown like a movie heroine over his shoulder.

Caris, to judge by his expression, did not share her amusement.

In the dry warmth of the morning, the smell of the new-baked bread the wizard carried was almost painful and the drift of scent from the doors of the posting house kitchen like a glimpse of heaven. Caris had relieved him of what little money was left of Nandiharrow's small hoard, but it only amounted to a few coppers; Antryg had earned supper last night, breakfast this morning, and a bed in the hayloft of the stables by telling fortunes in the posting house, to Caris' considerable disgust.

"Lady Rosamund was right," he had said bitterly, watching the wizard bent over the fat palm of a merchant who had come in on the mailcoach. "A dog wizard!"

Dog wizard or not, Joanna thought the following evening, it did pay for supper, and she privately considered that it ill-behooved Caris to complain about it.

The day had been an exhausting one. Though she was gradually getting used to walking all day, she still felt stiff and tired and miserably footsore. Her face, arms, and shoulders were sunburned. The situation was not helped by sleeping in hay for the past two nights. Thank God, she thought, with a twinge of amusement at herself, I don't have allergies—that's probably something selected against in the evolution of heroines. Though the hills of the Sykerst were empty, tenanted only by sheep, the road was fairly well-traveled, with pack trains carrying clay down to the pottery works in Kymil and farm carts from the lowlands beyond. At long intervals, the mailcoach would clatter past in a huge cloud of choking dust, an enormous vehicle drawn by a six-horse hitch, rattling with brass and glass windows and crammed with passengers—farmers in serge, black-clothed clerks in wide-brimmed hats, or harrassed-looking women of the poorer classes in faded print gowns and bonnets. Sometimes a carriage would pass them, with a coachman on the box and a couple of footmen hanging on behind, or small, lightly slung chaises, with postillions riding the horses instead of driving them.

Only once had they left the road, when a company of sasenna had ridden by, clothed in smart black uniforms braided in gold and heavily armed. As they'd climbed back onto the road again, Caris said, "The Prince Regent's men."

"Are you surprised?" Antryg asked, dusting off his velvet coat skirts. They had taken refuge in the shadows of one of the spindly clumps of birches which were beginning to grow with greater and greater frequency beside the road as it came down off the bare backbone of the hills and wended its way toward the farming and woodland country closer to Angelshand. "He has always hated the mages; it shouldn't come as a shock that he's sent his private body-guard to join the hunt."

Caris' beautiful lips set into a grim line, and he felt for the reassurance of the pistol in his smock. Further down the road, a farmer and his young wife were trying to coax their donkey out of the ditch into which they'd scrambled for safety at the troop's approach. Joanna was interested to notice that others beside the mageborn had reason to fear the Regent's men.

Seated now with her back to the stone chimney breast of the posting house, she watched Antryg peer with his cracked old quizzing glass at the dregs of a dowager's tea. The smoky shadows of the lamplight played unsteadily over his features and put a flickering embroidery of shadow on the woman's round cheeks from the lace flaps of her cap. Behind them, the other passengers of the mail coach crowded in an interested knot, drinking their evening ale and listening with the surreptitious fascination that even nonbelievers have in the words of oracles. Joanna couldn't hear what Antryg was telling the woman, but a stout man in a suit of dark-blue superfine who seemed to be her husband laughed and said, "Mind, Emmie, you're not believing all that wizardy twiddle, are you?"

"'Tisn't twiddle." The woman took the teacup from Antryg and held it defensively to her pouter-pigeon bosom, as if the future itself, and not merely its reflection, were held within its leaves.

Another man in a farmer's rough smock laughed. "Pshaw!" Joanna had seen the word written in novels of the British variety but had never actually heard anyone say it. "I went to one of them wizard fellows once . . ."

"What?" a red-cheeked girl teased him. "For a love-drop?"

The man blushed. "As happens, yes," he admitted and then grinned, showing broken and yellow teeth. "And damned if the girl didn't throw her cap after some other fellow."

"Perhaps the other fellow'd been to a better wizard?" Antryg suggested.

"That's what they all say."

"Suraklin . . ." began a thin, middle-aged clerk.

The first man, Emmie's husband, snorted, his round jowls pouching out over a high muslin cravat. "Suraklin wasn't more than a clever businessman who poisoned where he couldn't bribe or scare. He made the most of a few pieces of luck that fell his way, that's all, and fools called it magic. If you'll look into all those cases of people going blind or falling down the stairs or whatever they were supposed to have done, you'll find that none of it could be proved."

"And that," Antryg said quietly, coming over to Joanna with a tankard of beer in each hand, "was his strength, you know. For the most part, people didn't believe in his powers—and it was never anything you could lay hand to."

"Like this whatever-it-is," Joanna agreed. She looked up at him in the sooty shadows outside the circle of lamplight around the table, her brow puckering with frustration. "There isn't even a *name* for it."

"Which makes it all the harder to believe that something is actually happening." He settled on the bench at her side. Caris had already retired to the stables to sleep.

The casement windows of the post house were open to the azure deeps of the night, and suicidal swarms of moths, millers, and gnats hovered around each of the room's dozen or so smoky and stinking lamps. Joanna added a few more notes to her mental list of items left out of swash-buckler movies. It crossed her mind to be glad, if she had to be kidnapped for reasons unknown and haled all over the countryside in a parallel universe, she was there in the summer when the windows could be open to let the smoke and the smells escape.

"Which is perhaps," Antryg went on, handing her the tankard, "precisely what someone is counting on."

"Hunh?"

"Both you and Caris assumed it was some problem of your own—doubtless each of these people did as well." He gestured towards the fat squire and his wife, the farmer couple, and the two or three laborers, like a Hogarth print in sepia and gold, laughing over some joke in the chiaro-scuro of the lamplight. "It's another dubious advantage of being mad," he added. "I understand that what is in my head *is* real, at least to me."

Joanna considered him for a moment, watching the jump of shadows over the extravagant curves of his lips, nose, and hair. "Are you mad?" she asked after a moment. "Everyone says so, but—I haven't seen it."

"Haven't you?" His gray eyes sparkled appreciatively. "All the experts have said so for the last twenty-five years —but I was always unbalanced. Light-minded, Suraklin used to say, as though gravity were some kind of virtue. And for years I believed it was. I did try to take it all seriously, to become what I thought he wanted me to be . . ."

It was the first time Joanna had heard the Dark Mage spoken of with something other than loathing and fear. Curious, she asked, "Did you love him?"

Antryg turned his head a little to regard her with something like surprise at her understanding. "Oh, yes. I was halfway between being his slave and his son, from the time I was nine and my powers began to come. They came early. I understand now that he would have taken me by force had seduction not served, but it did. There was nothing I would not have done for him, except give up what I was . . . and for a time I did my best to do even that." His eyes were not on her now, nor on the cavernous gloom of the big room, with its bumbling shadows and the half-seen glint of the copper pan bottoms on the walls. He seemed to be gazing into some private seeing-glass of memory and, she thought, observing the sudden dip of wrinkles across his brow, not much liking what he saw.

"What finally turned you against him?"

He shook his head, and there was distant sadness in his voice. "I never turned against him." He leaned back against the stone of the chimney breast behind them; the shadows obscured his odd, craggy-boned face, save for the spark on one corner of his spectacles and the star-glint of an earring. "I fled from him and hid, but there was not a night that I did not feel him seeking me through my dreams. Even after Salteris found me, years later, and told me he was dead . . ." He paused, then sighed heavily. "I'm told he had that effect on many people. But I did love him. I suppose that's what made it all the worse."

Joanna was silent. As if that brown-velvet voice, with its flamboyant richness, could weave for her the smoke-visions that he himself saw, she had a momentary glimpse of a skinny and overgrown boy moving hesitantly in the old man's terrible shadow, trying to kill what he was in order to be what he was told he ought to be. Like a glass silver caught in a garment, she felt the unexpected stab of her own years of torn striving to conform to the fashions and morals of a peer group she despised.

Not knowing quite why, she asked, "Was he good to you?"

The fulvid edge of the light outlined the arched nose as he turned to look at her and gleamed opaque on a circle of glass. "Not really. Obsessive people seldom are. And his obsessions grew with the years, until every instance in which I could not be what he wanted me to be, every mistake I made, every day I played truant to go running to the hills or read poetry, was an insult to him."

The squire and his lady were making their way up the creaky wooden stairs to bed, their shapes wobbling huge in the reflection of a bedroom candle. The little clerk called for a final round of beer. A beefy young laborer with curly hair looked up and waved to Antryg to come back to them. The mage smiled ruefully at Joanna.

"Funny," he said, "if you're a mage, they always ask you to read the future, as if knowing it will help. I think three-fourths of all prayers prayed are for two and two not to equal four." He set his empty tankard on the hearth and got to his feet. Joanna rose to stand beside him, her head, as usual, barely coming up to the topmost tarnished silver button on his threadbare coat.

She glanced up at him curiously, remembering her own fears, doubts, and half-conviction at San Serano that she was either insane or in terrible trouble. Why she felt concerned for him or felt this strange kinship with him, she wasn't sure; he was, she reminded herself, the storm center of terrible and inexplicable events, the man who had brought her to this place, who had twice tried to strangle her, and who wanted her for some strange purposes of his own—the only man, at the moment, who could return her to the world she knew. Yet she found herself asking, "Have you ever prayed that?"

"Oh, frequently," he murmured, half to himself, she thought, as much as to her. "Frequently. Would you like me to tell your fortune?"

Joanna hesitated, knowing she was already too taken in by the daft warmth of his charm. Then from the yard came the swift clatter of hooves and the jingle of accoutrements, and Antryg turned swiftly, gray eyes wary, as the first of the sasenna entered the posting house.

They wore the gold-trimmed black livery of the Prince Regent, the braid glittering in the darkness like ropes of fire. Joanna had already identified the sounds in the yard as that of a coach, and a fairly substantial one, and was fading as inconspicuously as she could toward the rear door of the posting house. It was only as she reached it that she realized that Antryg had moved back again to the shadows of the bench by the hearth, unable to call her back to him. She got a glimpse of his wide, warning eyes as her hand pressed the latch.

Gloved fingers closed like a metal clamp over her wrist. She whirled, fighting a gasp of shock as a big, iron-faced woman in the black clothes of the Prince's sasenna pushed her back into the room. She stumbled and spun around in time to see among the black-and-gold sasenna and the cluster of crimson-liveried servants at the post-house door a man who could only be the Prince.

"She was sneaking out the back," her captor said briefly.

The Prince's queer, pale-blue eyes glistened in the shadow. "Was she, indeed?" His voice was soft and rather shrill; none of those at the tables dared move or call to themselves that odd, flickering gaze. The silence that had fallen was absolute, save for the desperate burr of a moth's wings against the hot glass of the lamp.

"A guilty conscience, child?"

Joanna tried to back away and met the hard-muscled shape of the female guard. The ebony satin of the Prince's coat was so heavily laced with gold that it seemed to glitter like black flame as he minced forward over the dirty straw of the floor. For all his diminutive prettiness, as he came close and put one small, moist hand under her chin, Joanna could see that, beneath the layer of cosmetics, his skin was coarse, pale with the pallor of one who has been weeks without sunlight or change of air. The carefully curled golden hair was limp and thin; the skin around the sky-blue eyes was painted to cover not only the fact that he was on the wrong side of thirty, but the ravages of sleeplessness and debauchery. In spite of the rouge that coated them, she could see his lips were chapped with nervous biting.

Any other man so dressed and so affected would have appeared ridiculous, but for those eyes.

She became aware that she was trembling.

His thumb and crooked forefinger tightened on her chin. Beneath their curled lashes, his eyes never touched hers. "Answer me, sweetheart."

Sweat crawling down her back beneath her peasant bodice, Joanna said, "I wasn't trying to run away, your—" What was the proper title for a prince? "—your Grace. Not from you, anyway. I—I'd had a quarrel with someone here, that's all, and wanted to get out." Not a very good story, she knew, nor, she was afraid, very convincingly told, but it was the best she could do on the spur of the moment. One of the sasenna sniggered. The Prince smiled, and his hand stole like a slug down the side of her neck.

"A quarrel? With a pretty wench like you? How very tasteless of them."

Instinctively she stepped back, loathing his touch, and his small hand snatched with the nervous quickness of a child playing jacks, seizing a handful of her shift and bodice at the shoulder. Joanna wondered desperately how far she should let this go and how much trouble they'd all be in if she struck him; but at that instant Antryg rose from his seat in the corner and drawled, "Oh, come, Pharos, you know you haven't any use for a woman."

There was a half beat of shocked, utter silence, as if someone had switched off the sound. Then the Prince threw Joanna from him, his indrawn breath of rage like the hiss of a snake. In a swooping flurry of gold-laced coat skirts and a blazing galaxy of diamond buttons, he strode across the room to where two of his men had already sprung to seize the wizard by the arms. Completely forgotten, Joanna faded back at once into the shadows. But though she knew that Antryg had bought her escape-time at who knew what cost, she could not bring herself to flee.

Had it not been for the utter silence, the Prince's voice would not have been heard, a hoarse whisper that shook with rage. "You *dare* . . ."

His arms pinned by the Prince's guards, Antryg did not struggle, but Joanna saw in the firelight the gleam of sweat along his jaw. For an instant the Prince stood, speechless —then he reached out and, with a hideous, gentle deliberateness, removed the spectacles from Antryg's face. The glass and wire rattled sharply as he flung them to the stone of the hearth. Then he held out his hand, and a crimson-liveried servant put into it a leather riding-whip.

No one in the inn so much as breathed.

The Prince struck twice, with vicious deliberation, across his defenseless victim's face. On the second blow, Joanna heard the Prince make a little sound in his throat, a whimper of satisfaction or some private, inner pain which sickened her. His hand came back for a third blow. She glimpsed in his eyes the lusting flicker of madness and knew he would go on with the flogging until he lost his already-slipping hold over himself. The candlelight caught the dark ruby gleam of blood on the leather and pouring down Antryg's still face. She thought blindly, *I should run*

. . . he's doing this so I can run. . . . But when she did take a step, it was forward, not back. . . .

The third blow never fell. In the midst of his back-swing, the Prince gasped, and his body convulsed as if he had been kicked in the stomach. The whip clattered on the hearthstones as the slender black form doubled over, hands clutching at the barley-gold curls as if to root out an invisible axe blade sunk in his skull. One of the sasenna holding Antryg's arm released his grip to catch his master before he toppled. Chaos erupted as the others crowded forward. To the man on his other side, Antryg said sharply, "Fetch a basin! He's going to be sick in a minute!" and the man made a dash for the kitchen.

Antryg scooped up his cracked spectacles and was fitting them back to his nose as he crossed the room, unnoticed in the fearful hullabaloo. "Let's go," he said softly. Taking Joanna's arm, he led her through the unguarded back door and out into the moonlight of the yard.

"What did you *do*?"

"Migraine headache. Psychotics often suffer from them." The greenish eyes of the horses flashed at them in the darkness of the stables as Antryg scrambled halfway up the ladder to the loft. "Caris!"

"Here."

Joanna spun around, her heart in her throat—the sasennan faded from the blackness of a nearby stall. Antryg jumped from the ladder, landing with light springiness on the ground; the wan moonlight turned black the blood running down from the opened flesh of his face and caught in the fracture of his left spectacle lens like a skeleton star.

Caris, Joanna saw, was armed, not only with the pistol, but had his sheathed sword grasped lightly in his left hand, ready to draw and fight. The small bundle of their belongings was strapped to his back. He must have been ready, she realized, from the moment the Prince's sasenna rode into the inn yard.

"Was it the Regent?" he demanded softly, as Antryg led them down the nearly dry stream bed that ran behind the inn. Shouts and neighs and the rattle of gear were already rising into the dark stillness of the hills. Antryg nodded.

"He took a fancy to our Jo—he might have anyway, even had she not tried to slip out the back. She couldn't have known he'd have the place surrounded before going in. He's suspicious of everyone and sees plots in everything and, as Emperor in all but name, he can do pretty much as he pleases. My only fear was that he'd recognize me when he took my specs off." He paused and raised his head over the edge of the stream-bank, ridiculously like a lanky, nervous setter dog in long grass. "Ah, good."

Encouraged, Joanna stood up beside him. Down in its nook in the hills beside the road, the posting house was still visible, but the moving lights that had begun to circle away from it were returning, like indecisive fireflies.

"They're turning back?" Joanna whispered disbelievingly.

"For the moment. There, look . . ." A single horseman went streaking away down the road toward Kymil; a moment later, a second thundered westward toward where Parchasten lay in the fertile valley of the Glidden beyond. "Now what we've got to do is get as far away from this place as we can, as fast as we can, and keep away from the road."

"I don't understand." Caris scrambled after him up the stony bank of the stream, giving a hand to Joanna, who followed, cursing the custom of the country that decreed that all women should burden themselves with trailing masses of skirts. "Why aren't they pursuing tonight?"

"Because Pharos suspects a trap—some plot to lure his men away into the countryside while he's attacked at the post house. I suspect the Bishop summoned him with a claim that there's a plot of wizards afoot. He won't be terribly surprised to have stumbled into one."

"It's what I'd suspect," Joanna added thoughtfully, "from the way you deliberately baited him at the inn. But —*would* he have recognized you without your specs?"

"He might have." Joanna had retrieved her purse from Caris' pack, and Antryg accepted the handful of Kleenex she dug from it, mopping gingerly at the blood on his face. They were moving down through the dense shadows of the hills, where the starlight glittered faintly on stream water only deep enough to soak Joanna's cowhide peasant boots and make the hem of her skirts slap wetly against her ankles, no matter how much she tried to hold it clear. "Wizards don't wear specs—we work our healing spells on ourselves from a very early age. My eyes started to go within weeks of being put in the Tower. I have no doubt, if I hadn't been mageborn, I'd have been blind as a mole from the age of ten."

He paused, looking back. A fold of hillside hid them now from the inn, but faintly Joanna could hear the commotion that drifted on the darkness. "By morning he'll have reinforcements from Kymil and Angelshand both combing the countryside. I know these hills."

"As Suraklin's student," Caris said dryly, "you would."

"Perhaps," Antryg agreed equably. "But as with fortunetelling, it's just as well for all of us that I do. Be careful here, Joanna—the rock is slippery."

Balancing carefully, her purse heavy on her shoulder and her bunched skirts held in her hand, Joanna stepped forward, and the strong, light hand from the darkness steadied her. "By the way," she said softly, "thank you."

Behind her, Caris said, "He went to the trouble of bringing you to this world, Joanna—he wasn't about to risk losing you to the Prince Regent."

In the utter gloom of the hill shadows, Antryg's grin sparkled as brightly as the starlight on his earrings. "That's my Caris," he remarked affectionately and led the way once more into the darkness of the hills.

They fled like foxes in hunting country, through a nightmare of blind exhaustion deeper than anything Joanna had yet known. From the sheep pens and roadside ditches of the hills, Antryg led them, doubling on their tracks and changing direction frequently, down to the woodlands and thickly settled farms of the valley of the Glidden. Her body ached for sleep and her ankles and shins stabbed with pain at every step, but Joanna struggled to keep up with her two companions, miserable with the guilty conviction that she was slowing them down and terrified that, losing them, she would be stranded in this world forever. Having walked all day, they kept moving through the night hours and on into morning, dodging, hiding, and listening for the quick rattle of hooves or the thrashing of bodies through the hedgerows.

At mid-morning, that strange, bleak emptiness struck again, bleeding what little energy was left from Joanna's soul. In her despair, she toyed with the notion of leaving Caris and his mad prisoner and seeking some way home on her own, but her saner self knew it was folly. Fear of the Regent and the memory of the cold-voiced Peelbone kept her moving. They were in the farm country then, hiding among the hedgerows and fields of standing crops, and even Joanna was aware that, during that time of gray sickliness, the hay makers they glimpsed in the meadows slacked their efforts and fell to quarreling over the whetstones and tools, while the storm clouds gathered in louring masses in the sky. The spell lasted until noon. By that time, Joanna suspected, the damage had been done. She wondered about what the effects of such a spell would be in her own world, on trigger-happy street-punks, on politicians, or on the men responsible for the thousand dull and niggling safety regulations concerning nuclear power plants and chemical waste.

Late in the day, they rested, exhausted and oppressed by the breathless heat of the coming storm, on an islet in a sluggish stream that Caris identified as the Shan. Antryg had gathered herbs from the waterside to make a poultice for the whip cut on his face and had fallen asleep between the roots of a willow tree, his head on his rolled-up coat. Caris slumped against the tree trunk beside him, leaning his face in his hands; by the time Joanna came back from the edge of the water, where she'd gone to dash a handful of it on her face, the sasennan, too, was asleep.

For a moment she stood looking at the both of them, elder and younger. Caris had to be at the end of his rope physically, she thought, studying his drawn young face in the watered-silk dappling of the willow's green shade, to conquer his nervousness about sleeping in the open. Antryg...

Under the poultice, she could see that the whole side of Antryg's face was a swollen and gruesome bruise. Oddly enough, though she was normally squeamish, this didn't sicken her or make her look away. She felt only compassion for the pain he must be in, guilt that he'd taken it for her sake, and...

... And something, she told herself, that kidnapped damsels had no business feeling for the villain of the piece.

He knows more than he's telling, she reminded herself. He's going to Angelshand for some reason of his own. It had not escaped her that, for all his lightweight chatter, Antryg had never again mentioned the place in the hills near Kymil in which Caris had found her. He had, as Caris had pointed out, led them away from it as quickly as he could. Was that out of fear of what lurked there or simply fear of what Caris, if he investigated the place, would find?

With a sigh, Joanna walked to Caris and gently removed the pistol from his slack hand. He didn't stir; only his breathing and the warmth of his flushed face told her he was still alive at all. Weary as she was, she couldn't bring herself to break that sleep.

I can stay awake for a little while, anyway, she thought,

sitting down cross-legged in a tangle of skirts and feeling the now-familiar agony of pins and needles through her thighs and calves. Somewhere upstream, the moving water clucked a little against the overhanging weeds and cresses of the bank. Sunlight lay like scattered pennies over her tattered blue skirt and damp, rumpled hair. She looked down again at Antryg, curled up like a child beside her, his long, straggly, gray-brown hair hanging in his eyes.

Why had he said to Digby, . . . *to save my world, and yours, too, I hope, from a terrible fate*? What fate?

This emptiness, this vampiric draining of life?

The Industrial Revolution that was rapidly overtaking these people like a sooty and impersonal flood?

Some mad notion of his straying wits?

Or something else?

Upstream there was the sharp, startled flurry of a frightened bird, and a horse's indignant snort.

Joanna felt her insides shrivel.

As quietly as she could, she tightened her grip on the pistol and sank to her belly, to crawl under the tangle of vines along the top of the bank. Brambles scratched her elbows and snagged her skirts and hair, and she hoped to hell she hadn't just taken refuge in a giant thicket of poison ivy. Angling her eye to a break in the bushes, she saw him—a black-clothed sasennan bearing the crimson sunburst of the Church. He and his horse were nearly invisible in the sun-splattered shade of the opposite bank.

Behind her, she heard a man say softly, "That's them."

Turning her head slowly as little as she could for fear of rustling the vines which covered her, she looked back. A sasennan and another man in the close-cut gray coat of the Witchfinders emerged on foot from the green laurel thickets of the little island; the sasennan was leading two horses. As they stood for a moment looking down at the sleepers, the Witchfinder murmured, "It's the Archmage's sasennan. He escaped from Kymil by magic three days ago. Whatever plot is afoot, the Archmage is in it, all right. Peelbone will be pleased."

He took a pistol from the holster on his saddle tree.

Two thoughts chased one another very quickly through Joanna's mind: *This isn't any of my business! I was kidnapped and I don't want to play;* and immediately thereafter, cold and calm, *The man in gray has only a pistol.* His shoulders were broad over a slim waist. They made an ideal target as he turned to fetch something from his saddlebags. Joanna heard the jingle of chain.

You'll have to break cover a second before you pull the trigger, she thought, as if it were something she was only reading about. Another part of her was wailing in panic, *What if I miss?*

The adrenaline pumping in her veins almost made her sick. *Just lie here quiet and they might overlook you. . . .*

And they might not.

The sasennan walked to the bank of the stream, saying back over his shoulder, "So will his Grace." He signaled. Joanna heard the quick splash of hooves in the stony stream bed as the mounted sasennan on the other side began to cross.

"There was a girl with him, wasn't there?"

The heat in the thicket clung on her sweating face like glue, the green, musty smell of the brambles smothering. She felt queerly estranged from herself, aware of the five pounds of dead iron in her aching hand and ridiculously conscious that having it meant there was no excuse she could give herself later for not using it. *Why does it have to be me?*

She rose to her knees in the tangle of the vines, held the pistol in both hands, straightened her elbows and took long enough, as every Western she had ever read recommended, to be sure of her aim, and fired at a range of less than a dozen feet.

The kick of the gun jarred slammingly in her wrists and

shoulders; the huge cloud of black smoke coughed forth from the muzzle burned in her lungs and eyes. The coppery stink of new blood exploded over the still air as the man in the gray coat was flung forward against his horse, the beast plunging in wild panic. At the same instant, Caris rolled, swinging his sword free of the scabbard which had lain, even in sleep, under his hand, and was on the unmounted sasennan before Joanna could have sworn he was even awake.

The sasennan crossing the stream was down off his own terrified horse with trained and deadly speed. Joanna, her pistol discharged, saw him coming for her with drawn sword and knew his intent was to kill. As in a nightmare, she feinted a lunge for one tree and dove to the cover of another. The man pursued, sword upraised and bright. Her unaccustomed skirts tangled in her legs, and brambles caught her ankles as she plunged across the small clearing toward the slumped form of the Witchfinder, her heart hammering with frenzy. *I must succeed—I can't let him touch me—I must finish this* . . . . His grabbing hand pinched the flesh of her arm, then fell away. She threw herself on the sprawled body of her first victim, thrusting it aside to fumble the pistol with its blood-sticky butt from underneath, just as the sasennan's shadow covered her.

She swung around, rising to her knees, pistol in hands. Mottled sun seared along the downswinging arc of the sword. There wasn't time to duck—every second of time felt queerly compressed. . . .

She pulled the trigger. Blood spouted out onto her face as the ball plowed upwards through the man's body, only feet away. She flung herself aside to avoid the body as it collapsed on top of her, and fell over the Witchfinder's body. She raised herself on one numbed arm in time to see Caris pull his dripping blade from his dead assailant's still-standing corpse.

Start to finish, the whole fight couldn't have taken eight seconds.

The smell of blood was everywhere. Joanna wiped at the hot, thick stream of it on her chin and felt the sticky gouts of it in her hair. Both wrists felt numbed and broken; so did some part of her within.

As a gray wave of dimness blurred her sight, she wondered detachedly which she would do first—throw up or faint.

"Joanna?" A deep voice penetrated blurrily through the grayness; strong, light hands pulled her to her feet, lifting her with effortless strength. There was the scratching slash of a passing branch against her bare arm, then the sudden coolness of river water flowing all around her.

She started to say, "What . . . ?" A hand pinched her nose shut and she was thrust bodily under the water, then dragged up again, gasping and dripping, her head suddenly clear.

She shoved back her soaked hair and saw Antryg standing waist-deep in the water beside her. His soaked shirt was stuck to his body, his eyes worried behind the cracked lenses of his specs. "Are you all right?"

Joanna nodded. The water had rinsed away the blood on her face and hair. She felt breathless, as if she had been awakened suddenly from sleep. Shakily, she managed a reassuring grin and asked, "Does this mean I'm now a member of the Church?"

The worry dissolved into a sparkle of humor in his eyes. Solemnly, he dipped a handful of water and dumped it over her head. Not jesting, he said softly, "I'm afraid it does mean that you've been baptized, Joanna. Naturally, I can't say I'm sorry you did it—but I'm sorry that you had to."

"It's okay." Her voice sounded weak and thready to her own ear.

From the bank, she heard Caris say harshly, "Come on!"

Antryg laid a gentle hand against her dripping hair, anxiously studying her face. She would have liked to hold him—to hold someone—and cry with the sudden, sick confusion in her, but the calm part of her mind knew Caris was right. The shots would have roused the whole woods. So she only nodded in answer to Antryg's unspoken question and said, "Thank you."

He helped her to the bank. Caris, both reloaded pistols in his belt and his sword in his hand, stood scanning the woods around him, remote and beautiful and inscrutable as ever.

It was only that night, after a nightmare day of stumbling flight and of hiding from patrols that seemed suddenly everywhere, that what had happened on the island became truly real to her. For a long time she lay awake in the half-filled hayloft where they had taken refuge, listening to the approaching rumble of thunder and the restless, gusty unevenness of the rain. Her wrists ached, but it was nothing to the hideous memory of panic and the kinetic recollection of that first jet of blood dousing her face. On television, she had casually watched hundreds of people allegedly die. None of it was anything like this.

She thought, *I have killed a man*, and only belatedly remembered that she had killed two.

She knew Antryg was asleep. She cringed from waking him, partly because she knew he was exhausted, partly . . . She did not know why, save that she had never shared grief and fear with anyone, and didn't know how to go about it. Caris was awake, and she stifled her sobs as best she could, lest he hear.

But after a long time his voice said softly from the utter blackness, "Joanna?"

There was the crunch of hay, and its warm smell as it shifted. Then the warm, dry touch of the sasennan's hand on her shoulder.

"Are you all right?"

That Caris would have been concerned came as a surprise to her. She sniffled, swallowed, and hoped her tears wouldn't be apparent in her voice. "You probably think this is stupid," she began and cursed the betraying tremor of her vocal chords. "But—how old were you, the first time you killed somebody?"

There was a long silence, filled only with darkness, rain, and the green smell of the hay.

"Fifteen," Caris said at last. "It's the first thing you do in training, you know. The man's tied up. They don't start you on criminals free to fight back until your second or third year of training. But, they say, a weapon must know the taste of blood from the first."

"Oh," Joanna whispered soundlessly.

She thought it was all Caris would say. It was no wonder, she thought wretchedly, that her own inarticulate scruples sounded ridiculous to that beautiful young man. But when Caris spoke again, she realized the long delay had been because the sasennan was inept with words; not wanting to hurt her, he had paused long to choose what he would say with care.

"But I had never killed a man before in a true fight—a fight for my life, one that was not in training. We're trained to be ready for it, but . . . it really seldom happens." There was another long silence. Then he said, "Do you know what the Witchfinders would have done—to me and to Antryg, and probably to you as our accomplice?"

Joanna shook her head.

Caris told her, in a wealth of clinical detail that made her almost physically sick.

"A weapon that thinks is a flawed weapon, Joanna," he said softly. "You had to do what you did. You didn't take two lives, you saved two, probably three—probably a lot more. I have to get Antryg alive to the Regent, not as his accomplice in some plot the Witchfinders are accusing us of, but free and on my own terms, as proof of the truth. Sometimes you can't think too much. Only do what you need to do."

And in those words Joanna took a certain amount of comfort, at least for as long as she remained awake.

CHAPTER XII

THE LOWING OF A COW WOKE CARIS, TO THE CLINGING, tepid heat of morning. Last night's storm had cooled the air enough to permit sleep after the killing exhaustion of the last twenty-four hours; but with the new sun, the rain was evaporating in clammy dampness which made his rough peasant clothes and coarse stockings stick to his body like an evil fairy's garment of itches.

He lay in the hay for a few moments, looking at his two companions in flight.

He had never expected the girl Joanna to be still with them after four days. What he had seen of her world and what she had told him and Antryg during the first day's walk to Kymil had made him doubt her abilities to keep up with them. Caris had been raised in the Way of the Sasenna, and, from what he had seen and heard, hers was a world in which machines, like the cars and computers of which she had spoken, had taken over both the work that strengthened the body and the entertainment that sharpened the wits. She was shy and, he suspected, more used to speaking to these computers than to people; but it had surprised him that she had not panicked yesterday. If asked beforehand, he would have laid money against her having the nerve to pull the trigger.

And, he reflected ruefully, lost it.

Curled up on the hay, she looked thin and even smaller than usual. They had gotten rid of her bloodstained peasant clothing, and she looked like a little boy in her scruffy blue jeans and creased and filthy tank-top, with hay caught in her feathery blond curls. Her arms and shoulders were brown and sunburned, covered with scratches and insect bites. For all her small size, weariness had printed lines on her face that even sleep couldn't erase, and she looked older than her age, which she had said was twenty-six, and very alone.

A little ways from her, Antryg lay with his head on his rolled-up coat. His cracked spectacles rested in the hay nearby and the strings of cheap glass beads around his throat caught slivers of hurtfully bright gold sunlight that streamed through the cracks in the barn walls. Under the unruly tousle of his hay-flecked hair, the bruises on his face already looked less swollen than they had. They were turning black; Caris had spent the last five years of his life training to be sasennan and had an intimate acquaintance with bruises; he knew they must hurt like the devil. He'd taken a swordcut on the cheek in his first year of training and he remembered that the pain had dogged even his sleep.

And well served, too, he thought bitterly. He sat up and shook as much hay as he could out of his smock. Like the pain of a burn, his anger returned to fuel his strength. *For what he has done to my grandfather—for what that disappearance did to all the mages . . .*

Outside, the cow lowed again. Raised to the rhythms of farm and village life, Caris recognized the pain in the sound. The beast was stray, he thought, and needed to be milked. The gray deadness that had gripped the country-side yesterday morning had left its effects; not a cowman between here and Parchasten had remembered to close his gates. All afternoon and evening, they had been seeing strayed beasts in the half-cut hay meadows and standing corn. Now that he thought about it, Caris looked around the barn. The storm, he thought, would have ruined the best part of the haying. It was late enough in the summer that this barn should have been full-stocked. He frowned to himself at the recollection of something the Bishop of Kymil had said regarding farms let fall to rot.

But a cow in milk is a cow in milk, and the bread that he and Antryg had variously pocketed during the last, distant supper at the roadhouse had long since been eaten. Casting a glance behind him at the sleepers, Caris slipped his scabbarded sword into his sash, ready to draw and fight, and moved cautiously to the door.

His first glance around, as he opened it a crack, showed him that the woods onto which the barn faced were deserted. His trained mind toyed with the idea of a trap, with the cow as bait, then dismissed it. Anyone who knew they were there could simply have come in and overpowered them, exhausted as they were, or simply burned the barn over their heads.

It was only at his second glance that he truly saw the cow.

She was standing a few yards from the rickety doors of the barn, and Caris did not even need his farm background to know there was something terribly wrong with her. She stood broadside to him, weaving on her feet; her white and cream hide was sunk over her broad pelvis and barrel ribs as if with long sickness, but the green stains of grass smudged her legs. She had been out to pasture. Caris pushed the door gently open and walked toward her. There was no sign of ambush or threat from the woods, but the sixth sense of a sasennan screamed at him of danger. . . .

Then she turned her head and forequarters toward him. Caris felt the vomit rise to burn his throat and the sudden chill of sweat stick his coarse clothing to his back.

There was an abomination fastened leechlike to the cow.

It was unlike the one he had seen in the marsh, but he knew it for nothing that existed in this world. It dangled, swollen, from the beast's shoulder like a monstrous tick, mottled green-black and purple and longer than a man's forearm. By the swelling under the hide where it was attached, Caris knew there was at least four inches of head buried under the skin.

The cow lowed again and stared at him with sunken and pain-glazed eyes. Caris gritted his teeth—sick as the thought made him, he knew he could never leave an animal to suffer in that fashion.

He looked quickly about. It was broad daylight now— early, by the elongated indigo shadows. The patrols would be checking every building they found. In a little pile of rubbish by the door, he found some old tools, including a couple of broken scythe handles and half-rotted leather straps. With one of the straps, he tied a bunch of hay onto the end of a handle; with the flint and steel no sasennan is ever without, he lighted this makeshift torch and advanced, rather queasily, upon the cow and its horrible parasite. The poor beast flinched a little from the pale brightness of the fire, but was too exhausted to flee. Caris gingerly gripped her horn and brought the burning end of the torch to the parasite's slimy back.

Like a tick, it twitched revoltingly; then it backed slowly out of the wound and dropped to the ground with a horrible squishing sound.

Clotted with blood and flesh, its head was almost indistinguishable—equipped, Caris thought, with at least three mouths, mandibled like an ant's, but infinitely more hideous. For an instant, the mouths worked with an unspeakable chewing motion. Then the head swung around, and

Caris leaped back as the thing writhed like a snake on the trampled grass and launched itself, with incredible speed for something so puffed, at Caris' groin.

As with the thing in the marsh, Caris' body thought for him. He struck at the thing with all the force of his arm, using the side of the torch like a bat. The mandibled mouth clamped around the wood; the tiny, lobster like claws grappled, and the thing lunged up the handle toward his chest. Horror-sickened, Caris flung the torch from him and ran; he heard the thing's body thump soddenly against the door as he slammed it shut.

"Antryg!" Renegade, devious, and student of Suraklin he might be, but he had spoken of the abominations as if he knew them. At least he would know what to do.

The wizard sat up, blinking, already fumbling his spectacles onto his lacerated face. He took one look at Caris and asked, "Where?" without bothering to ask what. Like a gawky heron, he unfolded to his feet and strode past Caris to the door to peer through the cracks. After a long pause, he held up a cautionary hand and pushed open the door slightly. Through it, Caris could see the cow lying on her chest, too exhausted to flee or even to stand. The parasite had returned to her, now hanging from her throat. Flies were already swarming over the first gaping wound its exit had left.

Caris was aware that he was shaking.

Antryg's voice was deep and oddly comforting in the hot, umber gloom of the barn. "There's nothing we can do for her now, except put her out of her pain, and I'm not sure it would be safe to get close enough to do that silently."

Quietly, Joanna joined them at the door. She made a small noise of utter revulsion in her throat at the sight of the parasite, but nothing more. "It's an abomination," Antryg murmured to her, "a thing that has come through a weakening in the Void when a gateway was opened. Or, more likely, it was a parasite on something that came through."

She took another cautious look, around him at the cow. "The original host could have died almost immediately," she said thoughtfully. "Who knows—maybe its parasites started off small and something in this universe made them grow."

The remark baffled Caris, but Antryg nodded as if he understood. There was a fleeting appearance of kinship between them, with their blue jeans and white shirts, their tangled, curly hair, and their sunburned faces. After a moment, the wizard walked back into the darkness of the barn, his white shirt a blur in the gloom. Caris saw what had not been apparent last night; the building had two doors, one facing toward the woods, through which they had come the previous night, and the other facing out into a lowland hay meadow. Green sweetness and a sharp square of primrose light breathed into the dim barn in a rush as Antryg pushed open one leaf of the vast portal. The meadow had only been partly cut; cows stood in the long, lush grass that ran down to a stream deep in cresses and ferns. When the wind shifted, Caris could hear another cow groan in feeble agony.

Antryg murmured, "As I thought."

Past the stream, the dark tangle of a quickset hedge marked the road; Caris shivered. He had not thought it so close, and wondered how obvious the barn was from it. Quietly he joined the wizard by the door. "We haven't time for this," he said softly. "We have to leave this place."

"Don't be silly." Antryg drew him back into the protective shade of the barn. He pushed his specs a little further up the bridge of his long nose with one bony forefinger, wincing where the metal of the earpiece touched the bruised mess of his temple. "We have to know at least a little of how to deal with the things. Look at how those cows are moving. They're all infected. It's more than

likely the things are in the woods as well." He walked back
to the piled hay where he had slept, unrolled his coat, and
put it on, the worn velvet rumpled and covered with shreds
of hay.

Joanna had remained by the door to the meadow. She
was looking out with what might have been nauseated fascination or what might have been simple watchfulness, for
it was only by close scrutiny that someone might be seen
on the road on the other side of the hedgerow. Caris followed Antryg back toward the door to the woods, but
caught him by the sleeve when he made to go through it.
For once, he did not fear the wizard making a break for it.
Indeed, he suspected that, unless Antryg was playing a
very deep game, Antryg would not try to escape until they
reached Angelshand itself. But the thought of stepping outside, where the dying cow and her hideous vampire still lay
joined in the brightness of the morning sunlight, made his
nape crawl.

Gently, Antryg shook loose the grip. He slipped through
the open door, stepped quickly to where the torch lay guttered out in the dust, retrieved it, and returned. Neither
cow nor parasite moved. His hair shadowing his eyes in the
early light, Antryg undid the strap, shoved a little more hay
under it, and cinched it tight again. He looked up at Caris.
"Either come with me or lend me your sword."

The descent into the hay meadow was closer to the hell
of the Church's Sole God than anything Caris had yet experienced in his life. He had been trained in the Way of the
Sasenna, taught to face and fight and kill any man or
woman living. But in the last weeks, he had faced, not
man or woman, but things he had never prepared for: the
mewing abomination in the marsh; the hideous, icy fall
through the blowing darkness that lies between universes;
and the ghastly uncertainties of trying to operate by the
Way of the Sasenna without a master to command him. To
fight even a monster was one thing; to walk through a

plague of lethal and filthy parasites was something for which neither he nor his masters had ever thought to prepare him.

The meadow was full of the abominations.

What little wind there was set from the woods; it was only when he and Antryg were in the long grasses of the meadow itself that the smell of blood came to Caris' nostrils. With it came a foul, half-familiar pungency he did not know, but which nauseated him. There were half a dozen cows in the meadow, drawn there to drink at the spring. Every one bore at least one parasite; some poor beasts had two or three, hanging like swollen, slimily gleaming bolsters from their sides or throats or lying draped over them, if they lay in the grass. The parasites themselves were anywhere above a foot in length; one, twitching over the heaving side of a yearling calf, was nearly four feet long.

In his rough smock and coarse canvas breeches, Caris had never felt so unprotected in his life. Horror and revulsion made him queasy, but he heard Antryg, peering through the quizzing glass at that sunken body with its hideous burden, murmur, "Fascinating."

Around the stream, the long, rank grasses thrashed with their squirmings. Antryg raised his head, curious. "There seem to be a lot of them down there."

A sharp rustle in the meadow to their left made Caris swing around, his sword in his hand; his mouth felt dry with fear. "Let's go back. . . ."

Antryg, torch in hand, advanced, wading through the deep ferns toward the stream.

Caris had only an instant's glimpse of the abomination in the ferns before it struck. It was three feet long and launched itself at Antryg like a striking cobra; Caris' sword was whining through the fetid air while his mind was still identifying what it was that he struck. His blade caught the thing in the middle of its swollen body, checking the strike as it fell in two pieces; Antryg stepped lightly back as the head end struck at him again, bouncing short, like a hellish ball, its spined mouth snapping. Grayish slime from the split abdomen stank as it pooled in the grass; Caris whirled in horror as the whole meadow around them erupted suddenly into a sea of frantic thrashings.

It seemed as if every filthy creature in that abominable meadow was galvanized into abrupt and greedy life. From every point of the compass, there were wallowing and lunging toward the two humans. From the hay barn at the top of the meadow, Caris heard Joanna's entirely unnecessary warning scream.

The abomination feeding on the calf pulled its filthy, purpuric head from the wound and struck at Caris in a streaming splatter of blood and fluid from a distance of only feet. Caris moved his sword to strike but the thing caught the blade itself, wrapping tiny, hideous claws around it, dragging it down with its huge weight. Reflex made Caris drop the blade and spring back, remembering how its fellow had lunged up along the torch; an instant later he cursed himself for dropping the weapon. Antryg's powerful hand closed around his arm and the two of them fled through the long grass of the meadow, both knowing it was only a question of instants before that wallowing circle of creatures closed around them. . . .

But they did not. They fell to feeding, instead, on the split carcass of the dead parasite. Halfway back to the barn, Antryg and Caris stopped, panting, to look back and saw nothing of the dead abomination and the stinking pool of slime around it but a writhing, struggling mass of slimy purple backs.

Something brushed Caris' ankle, and he sprang aside with a shuddering gasp. It was a foot-long abomination, plowing through the grass like a determined maggot toward the others. Caris' whole body was shaking with something more terrible than cold, but Antryg stood, his head a little on one side, watching.

"Caris, I think we've been snubbed," he remarked. Swinging the burnt-out torch, he walked back up towards the barn.

It was only when they were very near it that Caris realized that Joanna was not alone.

There was a wagon and team tied up at one side of the barn. A man in the green livery of a coachman was on the box; a footman, carrying a long, old-fashioned pike, stood beside it, nervously watching the meadow. Caris stopped in his tracks, feeling for his missing sword and cursing himself again for dropping it. But in any case, fighting would be hopeless. From the shadows of the barn, he saw Joanna wave, beckoning. In the gloom behind her, steel flashed.

Antryg laughed suddenly, and said, "Well done!" He strode forward, leaving Caris either to abandon his captive or follow. He had to run to catch up.

The man standing beside Joanna in the dense shade of the barn was wearing armor of the sort not seen in centuries—a suit of plate that covered the wearer from head to foot. The steel was ornamented with scallop and millefleur, bright with gilding, and every inch overwritten with spells and proofs against the workings of the rival champion's wizard. It was, in fact, the product of the last days before the battle of the Field of Stellith—massive, proof against both crossbow and heat-spell, and weighing well over a hundred pounds.

Only the helm of this archaic marvel was missing. From the enormous shoulders, with their cresting and giltwork, rose a head of startling modernity. The young man's round cheeks and a slight double-chin gave an indication of what sort of form lay beneath all that ensorcelled steel. His hazel eyes were bright with interest and meticulously painted; the soft, dark-brown curls clustering around his face showed an expert's assiduous hand in their arrangement.

The emblem on the massive breastplate was that of the royal house of the Emperors of Ferryth.

It was not the Way of the Sasenna to acknowledge lordship, other than of one's own master, not even the highest, but Caris bent his head respectfully and said, "Lord Cerdic."

The young man waved away the gesture of respect with one massively mailed hand. "That was brave—incredibly brave." He looked from the desperately thrashing meadow to Caris and then to Antryg. "Do I guess correctly that you are the mage my cousin's men have been combing the countryside for?"

Caris frowned disapprovingly, but Antryg nodded. "At your humble service," he said, with a glint in his gray eyes. "If it please your Grace, I shall keep my name to myself."

"Of course," Prince Cerdic said hastily. "Of course. I would never dream of asking such a thing of the mageborn." His painted hazel eyes returned to the field again, and concern creased his open brow. "What have you decided about them, my lord? My peasants came to me begging my help. I put this thing on—it's been standing in a corner of Devilsgate Hall for centuries and came down to have a look at them, though deuce knows what I'd have done if I'd fallen over out there in it."

"When were they first seen?" Antryg asked.

Cerdic shook his head. "Three, four days ago one of my cowmen reported finding one—a little one, no bigger than a sausage—on a heifer up in the high pastures near the Devil's Road. He got it to back out with a torch, then it struck at him, and he ran away; fire didn't seem to bother it. When they started showing up on the herds, we tried poison, and that doesn't slow them down, either. Perhaps, if your lordship used magic . . ."

Caris glanced sidelong at his so-called prisoner, with spiteful satisfaction. Antryg pushed up his spectacles, like a man who is stalling for time to explain why he has appeared at an evening function in a morning coat. "Well,

there is a reason I can't use magic," he said apologetically.
"And in any case, it would take—"

Still leaning against the jamb of the barn door, Joanna
turned her head from the thrashing grasses of the meadow
to ask, "What kind of fire did you use?"

Cerdic raised his plucked brows. "What other kinds of
fire are there, my dear? Fire is fire."

"If fire was fire," Joanna pointed out, a little diffidently,
"you'd be able to temper sword steel in the kitchen stove.
Have you tried destroying them with condensed fire, as in
a kiln? The hottest kind of kiln you have . . ."

"That would be a limekiln," provided Antryg thoughtfully. "They have steel hearths hotter in Parchasten, where
they can get the coke. . . ."

"But we do have a limekiln," Cerdic said eagerly. Then
his face fell. "But as for getting them in it—we could only
bait one or two at a time, and then they mightn't respond,
if the bait was inside the kiln." He glanced hopefully at
Antryg. "Unless there were some kind of a summoning
spell?"

Antryg sighed. "I'm afraid the abominations wouldn't
be the only things such a spell would summon."

"And we wouldn't have time," Joanna put in and nodded toward the horrible movement in the meadow outside.
"The things seem to be multiplying pretty fast."

"We may have less time than we think." Antryg shoved
his hands in his jeans pockets and cocked his head to one
side. "It all depends on whether they're ticks or maggots,
you see."

The remark made no sense to Caris, but Joanna went
white with horror. Feeling a little as he did when talking to
his grandfather, Caris demanded, "What difference does it
make?"

The wizard shrugged. "The most attractive thing that
can be said for a tick," he responded, "is that it isn't going
to turn into anything else that might have wings."

Caris stared at him in shock; the idea that the abominations might metamorphose had never occurred to him. Cerdic whispered numbly, "Mother of God . . ." He swallowed hard. "But if you will not use magic—if poison won't work—"

Caris' eyes went to the wizard's face, reading the struggle obvious there as he tried to figure some way of using his powers without summoning down the Council or the Church dogs, as well. Cerdic was watching him intently, and Caris wondered if he could use this unwillingness to turn the Prince from Antryg's ally to his own.

Then Joanna asked, "What would you need for a spell?"

Antryg shook his head. "Something to draw them. They came like ants after sugar to the body of the dead one. I'd probably send out some kind of an illusion of its smell to draw them to the limekiln. Once they were inside it could be fired."

"We've tried using blood," Cerdic added, clanking forward and awkwardly folding his arms. "Two or three came to it, but the poison didn't stop them. We used plaguecroot —the most virulent poison there is—quarts of it. The smell alone should have killed them."

"Try mercury or arsenic," Joanna said. "They're metals. No matter what kind of organisms the things are, a heavy metal should at least slow them down. Whatever they smelled in the dead abomination must be a concentrate of something from the cow's blood, to bring them so fast that they ignored everything else."

Caris shook his head. "One of them attacked me within feet of the carcass."

"Did it?" Antryg inquired suddenly. "As I remember, it attacked your *sword*. Which, of course, was smeared with fluid from the thing's body. It didn't leap after you, once it had the sword. And I'll tell you something else. Whatever they look for in blood, I think they also look for it in earth.

At least the stream bank was all chewed with the things tunnelings."

"A trace mineral?" Joanna suggested thoughtfully. She scratched at a fragment of hay in her hair—very different, suddenly, Caris thought, from the painfully shy girl who had accompanied them up from Kymil. She was not, after all, merely a talker to machines, and he wondered suddenly if it was this quality, this knowledge, for which Antryg had kidnapped her. "Blood is mostly water, salt, proteins, and some trace minerals and it carries oxygen. Obviously it isn't water they want or they'd have been in the stream itself. It might be nitrogen. . . ."

"Cerdic." Antryg turned to the Prince, who had stood throughout this with a look of mystification on his round, perspiring face. "Did there used to be a salt lick down by the stream?"

The young man looked blank. "Dashed if I know. Does it matter?"

"A salt lick?" Joanna asked, puzzled.

"Yes—a natural outcropping of salt in the ground. There's a trampled patch on the bank that looks as if it's where the cattle regularly came down. . . ."

At the Prince's signal, the coachman jumped down from the wagon and approached, casting a wary look at Antryg and a disapproving one at Joanna's jeans-clad legs. "Oh, aye," he said, when asked. "That's what the cows were doing in the meadow in the first place, after that good-for-nothing Joe left the field gates open day before yesterday. The cowman drives 'em down there regular, and a job he has keeping 'em out of the hay."

"Well," said Antryg simply, "the lick's gone, now. The whole bank's tunneled in."

"That's probably when they started feeding on the cows," Joanna said. She turned back to the baffled-looking Cerdic. "I think that's your answer," she said, and abruptly, as if she heard and feared the quiet authority in her own voice, her old shyness returned. Diffident but resolute, she continued, "Heavily concentrated salt as much of it as you can get—with enough water to make it liquid and as much mercury and arsenic as you have. If it doesn't kill them, it should slow them down enough to be shoveled into the limekiln."

Cerdic caught her hand between his two massively mailed ones and said what no knight in gilded armor ever said to any lady of any legend. "My dear girl, you're a genius!"

Joanna blushed furiously and shook her head. "It just took breaking it down into subroutines," she explained self-deprecatingly. "I mean—that's how all programmers think."

The Prince frowned. "Programmer—is that a sort of wizard?"

Antryg, seeing Joanna's confusion overcoming her, put a comforting arm around her shoulders and said, "Yes. And now," he added gravely, "I hope you mean to arrest us, because that would mean we could stop running and have some breakfast."

With equally sober mien, the Prince began to bow, and Caris, the coachman, and Antryg all barely caught him in time, before he overbalanced in the weight of the armor. He substituted a graceful gesture of his arm. "My lord wizard," he said, "please consider yourself under arrest."

"So what happens now?"

Antryg turned from the long rectangle of the window's shadowy luminescence. Far off, a line of smoke marked the first of the limekilns firing up.

"It seems to have worked," he said and smiled a welcome as Joanna gathered up the handfuls of green sprig-muslin skirts and petticoats and rustled her way across the parquet of the drawing room floor. The rooms the Prince had given them at Devilsgate Manor looked east over a short stretch of informal garden to the woods; at this hour, though the greenery outside was still spangled with the last brightness of the evening sun, the rooms themselves were growing dim. "And he was quite right, my dear. It was a stroke of genius, subroutines or no subroutines."

Joanna shook her head again, as self-conscious over the praise as she was over the ribbon-edged flounces and low-cut neckline of her gown. She still wondered who the Prince was in the habit of keeping spare gowns around for. "It comes from breaking everything down for programming," she said. "Talking to a machine, you have to think like one—choose one alternative or the other, decide A on what grounds, decide B on what grounds, if not B, what's C...everything in a million little increments." She made a move to sit on the edge of a nearby chair back and gave it up as the unwary move earned her a poke under the ribcage from the boning in the gown's bodice. "It may be slower than talking to a person; but if you do everything right, you always know where you are."

His gray eyes were kind as he heard the years of buried uncertainties in her words, but he only said, "A little like magic, then. To weave a spell, one must know everything about the object of the spell. Thank you," he added softly, "for taking over there. Because you did keep me from having to make a very awkward choice."

Joanna blushed, confused and embarrassed by praise. Fed, washed, and rested, clothed in a gown far more elegant and twice as uncomfortable as her former peasant disguise, she still found herself aching from the hardships of flight. Her wrists still hurt from the kick of the pistol, reminding her of what she had done not forty-eight hours before. That, like the cumulative exhaustion, was something she knew already would take more than a few hours' rest to cure. In a sense it would never be cured—it would always remain something she had done.

Antryg, she was glad to see, looked better, also. He'd

acquired a clean ruffled shirt, though he still wore his long-skirted velvet coat and borrowed jeans. The wound on his face was visibly less raw than it had been.

"Any programmer could have figured it out," she protested again. "And you were right—we had no idea of what those things could or might turn into." She hesitated. "And we have no guarantee there won't be others, do we?"

He shook his head—there passed across the back of his eyes some haunted darkness of knowledge, as if he guessed unthinkable possibilities. His voice was very low. "No."

"What happens now?"

Antryg sighed and seemed to brush aside the half-contemplated horrors. "I suppose I could read the cards to find out," he said. "Though the cards are a bit dangerous in themselves."

"Because you can be traced by the Council?"

"No—they're no more magic than dreaming is, really. But the cards have a nasty habit of telling one things one doesn't really wish to know."

Joanna leaned against the opposite jamb of the tall windows and ran her hand down the smooth, gilded molding. "But then you can prepare for catastrophe, if one's coming up."

"Perhaps—unless, like war or jealousy, it's the preparation which triggers it. It's easier to let go and deal with things as they arise."

"Maybe," she said, with a rueful smile. "But letting go of things and letting events take their course has always been the hardest thing for me to do." She shook her head, the damp, trailing ends of her hair brushing against her bare shoulders, brown and then white with the changed neckline. "It probably sounds pretty stupid, because I know there's something terrible going on, something evil, but all I really want is out."

He smiled. "It isn't stupid," he said gently. "From time to time, I find myself wishing I were back in the Tower, not because it was comfortable—which it wasn't—but because it was peaceful, and all my things are there, and I was safe."

She remembered her thought on the island, just before she pulled the trigger—*If I didn't have a gun, I wouldn't have to do this.*

"Are we safe?" she asked.

He considered the matter. "I shouldn't think so," he replied judiciously after a moment. "I'm certainly not, and you . . ." There was a long pause, during which, looking up into those mild gray eyes, she noted that they were in truth a very gray blue, flecked with white and hazel-yellow which gave them their silvery cast. There was a triangular pucker of skin, like a small V, among the crisscrossed wrinkles below the left one.

He sighed and said, half to himself, "I wish I knew."

Joanna reflected that she was beginning to feel like the poor *schlemazl* in *North by Northwest*, kidnapped and haled all over the countryside, being shot at by strangers without any idea of what was happening, and on top of it all . . .

There was, she realized, another part to that analogy.

For a long time, their eyes held.

She thought, with a curious sense of shock that was not surprise, *I expected it to be different than this.* For a time it seemed to her that neither of them breathed—that it was impossible that the only point of contact between their two bodies was where her petticoats brushed against his booted ankle in a froth of voile. Part of her mind was saying in its usual cool and practical tones, *This is ridiculous. I don't do things like this*—while another part said, *I want him.*

For a time the sooty-gray shadows of the empty drawing room were like completely still water, fathoms deep and silent but for the distant chatter of the birds outside. The smell of the woods, of grass damp from last night's rain and of the far-off acrid smoke of the burning kilns, came to her through the open windows, mixed with the faint scent of soap from his flesh and hair. He stood so still that one facet of the crystal earring he wore held a gleam of the last light from outside like a tiny mirror, steely and unmoving in the deepening gloom; the only thing that stirred was the white rim of light on the ruffles of his shirt with the rise and fall of his breath.

Everything seemed incredibly clear to her, but without pattern. It had nothing in common with her encounters with Gary and her nervous weighing and reweighing of pro and con. She only knew that she wanted him and knew, looking up into the wide, black pupils of his eyes, that he wanted her.

He turned abruptly, almost angrily, away and walked from the windows into the twilight cavern of the room. "I will not do this," he said softly. She could hear the faint tremor of his deep voice. "You are dependent on me and under my protection in this world. I won't take advantage of that."

His back was to her, the diffuse whiteness of the fading day putting a sheen like pewter on the velvet of his shoulders. She knew well enough that he was conscious of her eyes upon his back. She was aware of her own feelings less clearly, shocked and appalled, not by them, but by their strength. Nothing she had ever experienced with Gary, not even sex, came anywhere near this need—not to have, but to give.

After a moment he turned and walked silently from the room.

"You can't pretend you don't know what he's done!" Caris swung around in his pacing to face the Prince behind his inlaid fruitwood desk. "It is he and not the Church or the Inquisition of your cousin who is the true enemy of the Council!"

Prince Cerdic was silent. His round, smooth, white

hands with their old-fashioned rings of gold and rose crystal were folded on the marquetry before him, his painted
mouth settled and still. His study, with its old fashioned
linenfold paneling and coffered ceiling, looked north;
through the tall windows, Caris could see in the distance
against the milky twilight sky the first tall outliers of the
Devil's Road itself, crowning the bare top of the hill—
standing-stones, such as had guarded the way from Kymil
to the Silent Tower long before either city or Tower had
been built. Yet the long, silent line of stone sentries led
from nowhere to nowhere, traversed only by the wind and
by the queer, traveling energies of the earth that only the
mages felt.

Caris was coming to see that it was no accident that
Prince Cerdic, out of all the manors available to the Imperial Family, had chosen this as his principal seat. Doggedly,
he went on, "It is Antryg who kidnapped the Archmage
and who gave the Church and the Witchfinders their
chance to announce that the mages were plotting against
the Empire—gave them their chance to arrest the mageborn without fear of reprisals! Maybe he did it for that
reason—maybe for others. He is responsible for the abominations—"

"There's nothing to show that," the Prince protested.

"Then how has he known where they would be? How
does he make guesses about what they are or could become?"

The Prince still said nothing, only sat, among his gold
and shellwork incense-burners, while the images of the
twenty-one Old Gods watched his round, pink satin back.
Like many converts, Prince Cerdic was more devout than
most Old Believers Caris had met; he was the only one the
young man had seen who had statues of the Old Gods,
instead of the elaborate calligraphy talismans of their
names pasted to the walls with which most Old Believers
contented themselves. As he had told the Prince about the

abomination in the swamp, about his grandfather's revelations on the fallen stone, and about seeing the old man's glove in Antryg's room as the mad wizard vanished through the Void into that other bizarre and terrible world, he felt the eyes of those small idols upon him—dog-headed Lancres, Tambet with the baby Signius at her breast, Kahieret the God of the Mages with his stork's head rising from the long black robes of a wizard, the horned Dead God wrapped in his burial shroud. . . .

"I need an introduction to the Court," Caris said quietly. "If I bring Antryg to your cousin the Regent openly before witnesses—if I am able to leave freely—the Witchfinders cannot deny either his capture or his confession. They are not interested in truth, but only in what story will best serve their ends; allow them simply to destroy Antryg, and we will never find the Archmage, nor restore the Council's power."

Cerdic rubbed his smooth chin with one lace-gloved hand. "But maybe he is telling you the truth," he said. "The mageborn understand so much more of what is going on than mere mortals like you and me. . . ."

"The fact that they do does not mean he speaks the truth!" Caris almost shouted. "He keeps claiming that the one who has done this evil, who steals the life from the souls of the land, who calls the abominations through the Void, and who kidnapped the Archmage and brought the woman Joanna here is not him, but someone else. But according to the Archmage, there *is* no one else with that understanding of the Void!"

The light of the dozen candles illuminating the opulent study flickered in a rim of fire over the embroidery that laced the Prince's carnation-colored coat. Behind him, on the shelves with the idols of the Old Gods, Caris could see old and crumbling tomes of magic. Some he recognized from his grandfather's study in the Mages' Yard; others he knew only by the sneers of the Council wizards, volumes of piesog and earth-magic and granny-lore, the compendia of every quack and dog wizard for five hundred years. The Prince moved uncomfortably in his velvet chair, his diamond earrings casting a sprinkle of brightness over his shoulders and his pink-and-white cravat.

"In the first place, I'm not sure either my introduction or my patronage would do your cause any good," he said. "My cousin has always been insanely suspicious of everyone. Of late, those suspicions have begun to turn against me as well. It's one reason I'm here and not at Court, doing what I can to help the mageborn. He has me watched in the capital. It's absurd, because technically I am his heir, but I was beginning to fear for my safety.

"But in any case . . ." He frowned and smoothed the lace of his glove. "It is not for us to judge the mageborn. They were our first priests, servants of the Old Gods. They still commune with their ancient powers, beyond the ken of you and me."

Impatiently, Caris began, "That's nonsense! There aren't more than a handful of mages who are Old Believers."

"No matter what they call them," Cerdic said gravely, "the powers they exercise are still the powers of the Old Ones. It is not for any mere mortal to disturb the great webs of destiny, not even for motives which they themselves deem laudable. They say my uncle, the Emperor, had a great deal of respect for Suraklin and went to his prison cell many times to visit him after he was taken; but still, he took it upon himself to destroy a mage, and great evil fell upon him after."

"Twenty years later?"

The Prince's soft mouth pursed, giving his otherwise open countenance a mulish appearance. Caris, though he knew this young man was the second heir to the Realm after the mad Regent, was conscious of an overwhelming desire to knock that pomaded head against the wall.

"He ought never to have meddled in the Dark Mage's affairs. Woe comes to them who hold the mageborn in light regard."

Caris was beginning to understand the viewpoint of those nobles who preferred the Regent Pharos' sadistic madness to this kind of blind obstinacy. Antryg, he realized, knew how to pick his friends.

Slowly, he said, "Woe certainly came to those who held Suraklin in light regard. But that didn't mean that he should not have been stopped. And Antryg is his student, his heir, and privy to all his black arts."

Cerdic leaned across the variegated inlay of the desk surface, to catch Caris' hand. There was that maddening, ethereal kindness in his eyes as he said earnestly, "That is only what you believe, as an outsider looking in."

"I am not . . ." began Caris indignantly, pulling his hand away, but Cerdic's soft, rather high voice rode right over his words.

"It is not ours to judge—not yours, as a sasennan sworn to serve, and not mine, though I am of high rank in the things of this world. Ours is only to serve the mageborn in whatever way we can. I have put a light carriage, a phaeton, at Lord Antryg's disposal, with letters of credit for changing horses from here to Angelshand."

"WHAT?!"

For one instant, behind the gentle and eager convert to the ways of the mages with whom Caris had lived for the past two years, he saw in the Prince's face the stubborn pique of one who has never been crossed in his life.

"Whether he takes you with him is up to him, not you," the Prince said stiffly, and something in his voice reminded Caris suddenly that at Devilsgate, he was entirely in this young man's power. "So I suggest that if you have no respect for your betters in the affairs of air and darkness, you had better cultivate it."

Caris left the study, furious with the Prince's blind stubborn faith and with his own lack of finesse in not sounding out the ground before putting Cerdic on his guard. As he crossed the tall ceilinged hall and ascended the graceful oval of the stair to the higher floor, it occurred to him that he had put himself into a dangerous position indeed. There was nothing to prevent Cerdic from imprisoning him somewhere in the house until after Antryg was long gone—or, for that matter, turning him over to the Witchfinders, though he was unlikely to do that, simply because Caris might then help them to locate Antryg.

The upper part of the house was in darkness. The thought crossed his mind that Cerdic need not have imprisoned him—he need only have delayed him in that stupid interview while Antryg drove the Prince's phaeton off into the night.

Swiftly, he ducked into the room allotted him. His peasant clothes were still there—he had exchanged them for the plain, brown suit of a servant or upper-class tradesman provided for him by the Prince's staff—and his weapons were where he had hidden them in the canopy of the old-fashioned bed, including the sword which he had retrieved from the meadow after the abominations had, as Joanna predicted, been lured away. He checked the pistol—it was still loaded. Though it was forbidden to bear weapons into the presence of a member of the Imperial Family, he had kept a hideout knife in his boot. He checked it, shoved the pistol into the pocket of his short coat and, sheathed sword in hand, strode soundlessly from the room.

He found Antryg sitting in the darkness of the drawing room of the suite allotted to their use. His own mageborn sight picked out the tall, gawky form, sitting in a chair near the window, dealing cards from one of the Prince's tarot decks in silence onto a small ormolu table before him.

There was something in the tired angle of those bony shoulders that made Caris think he had been there some time.

Though the sasennan made no sound and there was only darkness in the hall behind him, Antryg said, without turning his head, "Come in, Caris. Are you prepared to leave tonight?"

Caris tipped his head to one side, suspicious. "You're deigning to grant me a place? Or do you just need someone to look after the horses?"

"Well, yes." A stray flick of the last daylight winked from spectacle lenses and what might have been the glint of his half-malicious grin. The long hands moved palely in the dark; the soft pat of cards on marquetry was clearly audible in the still blueness of the room. "And then, I doubt I could persuade Joanna to—er—fly with me unless you were there."

"And her feelings concern you?"

"Oddly enough, yes." The wizard's voice was carefully uninflected. "It's very difficult to carry off a young lady by violence and manage a team of horses, too—at least, I suppose an experienced person could do it, but we should probably attract a good deal of attention. The Regent is on his way here, you know."

Caris frowned and strode forward a step, then paused. "How do you know? He was on his way to Kymil."

"I expect he turned back at the roadhouse, or perhaps the Bishop and the Witchfinders met him halfway." Antryg tapped the spread of the cards. Caris could see over his shoulder the king of pentacles reversed, the eight of wands, the five of swords, the lovers. . . . "And he's going to be married," he added thoughtfully. "Strange sort of thing for Pharos to do, considering, but it does explain a good deal." Puzzled, Caris was about to ask, *Like what?* when, with a flick of his fingers, the mage tossed a seventh card down on the reading—death reversed. "Interesting."

Caris looked down at the cards in silence. As with the vision of wizards in darkness, he saw them without color, shadowless and strange. The Council mages, the academic mages, seldom used the cards, considering them the type of low-class cantrip dealt in by gypsies and dog wizards, but in the darkness he found their arcane shapes disturbing. He asked hesitantly, "Death reversed is . . . life?"

Antryg shook his head, and said softly, "No. It is stagnation."

His long, light fingers gathered the cards and shuffled them restlessly; Caris could see that his eyes were shut. He laid the six cards with the deftness of a faro dealer in their ancient shape and sat for a long time gazing down at them in the darkness. Looking over his shoulder, Caris saw in the center the hermit crossed by the Dead God, whose sign marked the Sigil of Darkness, flanked by emperor and priest, the knight of swords, and the queen of wands. The signs meant nothing to Caris, but he felt the flinch of Antryg's body through the chair back upon which his arm rested; after a moment, he heard the wizard's breath go out in a sigh.

Then the wizard flicked a seventh card from the deck and sat looking at it for some time. From the open windows, Caris heard the voices of the grooms in the stable yard below, calling to one another as they harnessed the horses.

At last Antryg whispered, "So," and got to his feet. Even in the darkness, his face looked strained and more tired than Caris had ever seen him. "It's time we went." Quietly, he left the room.

Caris looked back at the cards, their queer forms as troubling as the voices of things supposed to be dead. The seventh card lay among them—a dead man pierced with ten swords, lying alone in the cold darkness of coming night.

CHAPTER XIII

MOONLIGHT STREAMED BETWEEN THE STANDING-STONES of the Devil's Road, bleaching them where it struck or pitting them with inky shadow, like an endless row of broken and rotting teeth. Antryg drew rein beside a fallen one to whose lower extremity earth still clung. The pit where it had until recently been planted was a torn, black hole in the long grass. Looking back along the line of them, Joanna saw how straight they ran, to the top of a distant hill, and down into the unknown night beyond.

The mage said softly, "Hold the horses, would you, Caris." The sasennan, after a moment's hesitation, leaped down from the groom's perch on the back of the phaeton and obeyed.

For all Antryg was still officially Caris' prisoner, Joanna reflected, smiling a little to herself as the mage sprang down from the high-wheeled carriage, at the moment he was the nearest thing to a master the young warrior had.

After a few seconds' hesitation, Joanna gathered up her voluminous skirts and the shawl the Prince had lent her and clambered carefully down after him. Her interview with Antryg in the dimness of the drawing room at Devilsgate had left her shaken, not only by the violence of her own feelings, but by their inappropriateness to everything she had liked to think about herself. She had the sensation of being suddenly in deeper than she had thought, part of her wanting to unfeel what she felt for him and, more, to un-know what it was like to feel. It was that part, perhaps, which in Antryg wanted the safety of the Tower. Down to the taproots of her intellect, she knew that both her friend-ship and her desire for him were alike utterly stupid—not to mention, she added, that none of this was really any of her business. When she went back to her own world it wouldn't matter. . . .

Except that it did.

He was moving along the double line of the stones, his spectacles and the strings of cheap glass beads around his neck winking palely in the ghostly light.

As when she had killed the two sasenna on the island, she had the feeling of having crossed some line which could not be recrossed. Having seen color, she thought, she would never again be content with black and white.

No wind stirred the long grasses in the shallow dip of ground through which the Road ran; the moon, waxing toward full, outlined not only the stones, but every silken length of grass-blade in sharply contrasting edges of silver and ink. There was a chill on the air, and Joanna hugged her shawl about her; the Prince, a chivalrous young man, had also provided half a dozen dresses for her to wear on the road. Antryg turned at the sound of her step and waited for her, the moonlight picking up a queer, silvery sheen on his outsize black coat. Most of her life, she thought, as she came to his side, she had felt uncertain of her welcome. That, too, had changed.

"What are you looking for?" she asked.

He pointed to the ground. In a week, the resilience of the grass had nearly covered them, but the weight and size of the tracks had left their mark in the soft earth. She frowned, studying them, trying to decide what animal could have made them, and looked at last, puzzled, back at Antryg's beaky face in the moonlight.

He shook his head. "I don't know, either," he said. "But you can see they start here, as if they walked out of a door, then pass close to that fallen stone. The thing must have been massive, whatever it was. Cerdic tells me these high woods are not much frequented, having a bad name in the district. It's very probable its carcass is still rotting up there, while the parasites that lived on it or in it crawled away looking for better fare."

Joanna shivered. A stray touch of wind stirred the thick, fair tangle of her hair; she jumped as if at the brush of a hand. "A week ago," she said after a moment. "That was when . . ." She hesitated. "How far away does the Void weaken when it's opened?"

"Generally only a few hundred yards," Antryg replied softly. "But it was open on one of the energy-lines. All things travel along the lines, resonating forward and back; in the old times mages could speak along them or travel down them from node to node, covering hundreds of miles in a day." He turned his head, looking out along the silent Road with its waving, undisturbed grass. The pale light touched the dark blotch of the bruise on his face and glinted in his crystal earrings. "On certain nights of the year, the peasants still drive their herds along them, you know, in commemoration of the Dead God, though they've forgotten why he died. But for the most part they are shunned, as the mages are shunned. No man will summon the voices of the air, if they do not speak personally to him."

He reached out and took her hand with a half-unthinking

intimacy; she was conscious of the bigness of the bones beneath the flesh, and the deft lightness of his touch. After a pace or two, she stopped, and he halted and looked at her, his eyes colorless in the moonlight.

"Antryg," she said, "why are you going to Angelshand?"

He hesitated for a long time before replying, his face, which could be so dissimulating, tense with an expression of struggle, as if he debated within himself what he might safely say. Then, bringing out the words with care, he said, "I need to speak to certain members of the Council of Wizards."

Joanna stood for a moment, not certain what to say. It was the first time he had answered her, she thought, without evasion, but it was not what she had expected him to say. "But most—or all—of them are under arrest."

He nodded. "There is that," he agreed, as if she had said, *Most of those telephone calls are toll numbers.*

"About this—this fading? Or what really happened to the Archmage?" After a long moment, she collected enough nerve to add, "About whatever it is you—or someone else—needs or wants me for?"

In the long silence that followed, Joanna could hear one of the carriage team blow softly through its nostrils and heard the faint, bell-like jingle of harness brasses as it tossed its head. The long, odd curves of Antryg's mouth tightened; for a time, she thought he would not answer her or would turn away, as he so often did, with some bit of informational persiflage about ancient cults or botanical lore. But he finally said, "About something which happened twenty-five years ago."

"What?"

"Ah," he whispered, and the old warm, half-demented grin flicked suddenly at the corner of his lips again. "If I knew that, I wouldn't have to ask them."

He started to move back to the carriage, but Joanna

tightened her hand around his to hold him still. The bones of his fingers felt large and clumsy entwined with hers and only thinly covered with flesh; through them she was aware of him, blood and sinew and bone.

She said, "I don't understand."

"Don't you?" he asked gently. The ghost of his smile warmed a little. "That's good."

He was not, she sensed, jesting. It came to her again that she was a fool to trust him and an even bigger fool to care for him; for good or ill, she would return to her own world, and it would be as if he were dead and all of this had never happened. Still, when he hesitated to put his arm around her shoulders against the thin chill of the evening, too clearly remembering the interview at Devilsgate, she stepped into the circle of his warmth and slid her own arm around his waist. There was a good deal of comfort in the feel of the ribs beneath the worn velvet and the slight, steady movement of his breathing.

They walked back along the Road to where Caris stood beside the carriage in the brown livery of a groom. Even in the distance, he looked disapproving, his arms folded and tension radiant in his stance.

"Joanna," Antryg said quietly as they neared the spiky shadows of the carriage and the dark horses cropping the long grass in the moonlight. Even pitched low, for her ears alone, his voice was startlingly beautiful, at odd variance with his eccentric appearance. The fractured lens of his spectacles caught the light like a broken star as he looked down at her. "I have no right to ask you to trust me; in fact it would be an insult to your intelligence to do so, but . . . please believe that I won't let you come to harm."

"I've always believed that," she said. They stopped beside the tall conveyance, with Caris still keeping his distance beside the horses' heads. Antryg put his hands to her sides to help her up onto the high step; she shook back the thick masses of her blond hair and looked up into his face again. "Will you return me to my own world?"

His eyes evaded hers. After a long moment, he said, "When I can." He helped her up. She caught the high brass hand railings around the blue leather tuck-and-roll of the seats and stood for a time looking down on him in silence.

Then he said, "I can't tell you the truth, Joanna . . . and God knows I've lied to you enough. All my life I've trusted too easily. I can't risk doing so now."

He climbed up beside her and gathered the reins in his sure, strong grip. Caris, who had watched this tête à tête with deep suspicion, stepped back from the horses' heads and sprang up to his high perch behind as they started forward. For a long time, Joanna sat quietly, hanging onto the sides as the phaeton jarred over the rough ground toward the road. She wondered why she had the impression that Antryg was as appalled by his own reactions to that evening's interview as she was by hers—that, like her, he found himself trusting against his every better judgment. And she wondered, as the carriage rattled into the hay-thick warmth of the still night, what reason Antryg had to think he ought to fear her.

It took them a day and a night and part of the next day to reach Angelshand, a journey which left Joanna, unused to unsprung, horse-drawn conveyances, cursing the man who hadn't been born yet to invent shock absorbers and almost wishing they had walked. Angelshand was a far larger city than Kymil; from miles away that morning, she had seen the dirty pall of its factory smoke and, when the wind set off its harbor with the cool salt freshness of the sea, had smelled the fetor of its slums. They approached it through a sprawling network of outlying villages and graceful manor houses set in walled parks. Closer in, the phaeton mingled with a rattling press of citybound traffic, passing through dreary streets of crumbling tenements and the ugly brick edifices of the riverside factories. At Joanna's request, Antryg had taught her the rudiments of driving a team of horses on the country roads, but he took the reins back now; as Kymil's had been, the streets of Angelshand were deep in manure and crowded with drays and carts of all description, driven with a disregard for human safety which appalled even Joanna's Los Angelino soul.

They passed over the arches of a crowded bridge to cross the nose of an island that lay like an overcrowded houseboat in the middle of the Glidden River—like the Île de la Cité in Paris, Joanna guessed, the medieval heart of the town. All the buildings of Angelshand were built of the iron-gray local granite, giving an impression of darkness and weight absent in the largely wooden city of Kymil; on Angel's Island, the soot of ages added to the somber hue. The thick, stumpy towers of a fortress glowered above an assortment of crumbling gambrel roofs and gargoyle gutters, like an ogre's frowning brow; elsewhere, beyond, she thought she saw the spires of a church.

"St. Cyr fortress." Caris nodded towards those ancient walls. "The residence of the Bishop of Angelshand—and the prison of the Inquisition." He glanced up ahead of him at Antryg in the driving seat, unconcernedly steering the team around a mender of tin cups who'd set up shop in the middle of the lane and the elegant carriage whose owner had pulled up in the stream of traffic to watch him. In Caris' eye Joanna saw the speculation and wariness with which he'd regarded the mad wizard in the Ponmarish around Kymil and she felt a qualm of unease.

The truce was over. They had reached their goal. From here they would pursue their own purposes once again. At the thought of Caris turning Antryg over to the mad Regent, she shivered, though she knew that, for all his care of them both, Antryg had never proven his innocence of kidnapping both the Archmage and her. He had, beyond denying categorically that he'd had anything to do with any of it, offered no alternative account of his activities, and Joanna was uncomfortably aware that his protestations of complete ignorance were lies.

She glanced up at him now, as he guided the horses through the tight-packed traffic and indescribable clamor of the bridge from the island to the more stylish districts on the far bank. The din on the bridge was hellish, the clatter of iron-shod wheels on granite cobbles striving with the shrieks of ragged beggars, scarf sellers, match hawkers, flower girls and noodle vendors. The sidewalks were crowded with liveried servants and monks in gray, with Old Believers in their black robes and macramé braids, townsmen in coarse browns and blues, fierce-looking sasenna, and whores in bright chintz, painted to within an inch of their lives. The air was rank with the stink of horse droppings and the fetid odor of the murky river below. Beside her Antryg was rubbernecking like a delighted tourist.

He had, she remembered, been a prisoner for seven years.

It took them an hour and more, but eventually he managed to steer them away from the clotted slums and markets of the riverside and toward the more fashionable districts nearer the Imperial Palaces to the north. Knowing she wasn't likely to get an answer that meant anything to her, Joanna refrained from asking their destination. Caris kept silent as well, as much, she suspected, from a desire to remain quiet and have Antryg forget he was there until he was ready to take action as from the fact that, for the moment, there was absolutely no action he could take.

In any case, Antryg seemed to know where he was going; but then, Antryg generally did.

She was still a little surprised when he drew rein in an elegant square; she had been half expecting him to go to some shady acquaintance in the city's underworld for shelter. But this was clearly one of the best neighborhoods of the city. Tall townhouses of graceful, if narrow, proportion looked onto a central square of park, where little girls in miniature gowns and corsets walked under the eye of their governesses. Two other carriages were already drawn up, unmarked and with closed curtains, their coachmen wearing plain livery. Antryg grinned and shook his head as he helped Joanna down from the high step.

"Hasn't changed a bit, I see," he commented, as he led the way up the imposing flight of marble steps. To the footman in flamingo livery who opened the door he said, "Send someone down to hold our horses and tell Magister Magus that the greatest dog wizard in the world is here to see him."

Without batting an eye, the footman murmured, "Yes, sir," and stepped aside to let them in.

"Magister Magus?" Caris sounded scandalized as a second footman escorted them up a curving staircase with graceful iron balustrades and into a drawing room opulently furnished in rose, gold, and black. "That charlatan! That—that toadstone-peddler!"

"What, haven't you been here before?" There was a twinkle of deep mischief in Antryg's eyes. The only other occupant of the drawing room, a handsome if zaftig woman, brutally corsetted into yards of lilac faille, regarded them for a moment and then turned away with a sniff at the sight of Caris' plain livery and Antryg's shabby coat, crystal beads, and bruised face.

Looking around her, Joanna noticed that, for all its rather pseudo-oriental finery, its pink-and-black tufted carpets, and statues in rose agate and alabaster of the Old Gods, everything in the drawing room was of the highest quality and obviously expensive. Peddling toadstones, she surmised, was clearly something that paid extremely well.

"Certainly not!" Caris sounded as if Antryg had asked him that question about a leather bar. "This is . . ."

The word 'disgusting' was obviously on his lips, but Antryg finished the sentence with ". . . Far handsomer than your grandfather's, isn't it?"

The young man's eyes narrowed. His voice was very quiet as he said, "You should be the last one, wizard, to talk to me about my grandfather." But for just a moment, Joanna had the feeling that a good deal of Caris' annoyance stemmed from just that comparison.

After a few moments, the inner doors of the room opened to the sound of a softly tapped bronze gong. In a vast waft of fragipani incense, another woman emerged from them, also middle-aged and dressed in what Joanna guessed to be several thousand dollars worth of brocade and rose-point lace. She leaned on the arm of a slender, graceful man, whose black velvet robe bore as its sole adornment an emblem, rather like an ankh, of silver literally crusted with diamonds, which hung at his breast. This might have had a religious significance, but Joanna, studying the room, was rather more inclined to believe he'd chosen the combination to match his hair, which was black streaked through with silver, like frosted ebony. His voice, as he spoke to the lady, was low, trained, and extremely beautiful.

"So you see, there is nothing for you to trouble yourself about, Countess," he was saying. "I have seen in your future a young man to whom you were spiritually connected in a former life. Whether it is the young man who now troubles you, or one more fit than he, only time and the gods will reveal. As for your husband, do not worry. Only have faith, and these things will even themselves out, as ripples do upon the lake of time."

Raising one slender, white hand, adorned with a solitaire ruby the size of a man's thumbnail, he made a sign of benediction over the Countess' head. She sank gracefully to one knee, and kissed his hand; then, rising, she drew her veils over her face and at least a foot and a half of high-piled hair and was gone.

Turning to the other lady, Magister Magus said, "My dear Marquise." His eyes, Joanna saw, were the clear green of alexandrite or peridot, deep-set and penetrating under silver-shot black brows. "I can see that your heart is troubled, that you are faced by a situation in which you are caught between two alternatives. But a part of that trouble lies in the fact that today is the Day of Ill-Fortune for you, under the star of Antirbos. It is not a day upon which any advice would bring you good. Go home, then, and to your chamber. Eat only a light supper, drink a single glass of wine, and read and meditate, thinking pure thoughts to combat the leaden influence of the Black Star which weights your heart. If your grief is still with you on the morrow, return to me then."

Joanna privately considered this dismissal rather brusque—after all, there was no telling how long the poor Marquise had been waiting—but, like the Countess, she curtsied reverently and kissed the Magus' hand. "From you," she murmured—somewhat fatuously, Joanna thought—"even silence is good advice. It is all exactly as you say."

Soberly, he conducted her to the door. In a rustle of patchouli and petticoats, she descended the steps, while Magister Magus stood with his arms outspread to touch the sides of the doorway, still as a dark image of ebony and diamond, until the building vibrated softly with the closing of the outer doors.

Then, with a billowing sigh, he pushed the doors to and turned. White teeth flashed beneath his dark mustache. "Antryg, you old faker, where'd you spring from?" He caught the tall wizard in his arms, and the two hugged one another, laughing, like long-parted brothers. "Greatest dog wizard in the world indeed! A fine thing to say in the house of Magister Magus!"

"Well, you're the one who said I had it in me," Antryg retorted with a grin. Then, soberly, he laid one hand on Magister Magus' shoulder, gestured with his quizzing glass, and intoned, "As for your husband, fear not. I see in your future a man, handsome and well-favored, who will treat you with the kindness that a lady of your goodness and exalted destiny deserves. The River of Eternity flows past many shores, and fish of all descriptions glide in its waters. Sometimes its currents are rough, sometimes they are smooth. . . ."

The dog wizard laughed at the imitation with genuine delight. "It pays the bills, my friend—it pays the bills." He frowned suddenly. "But what are you doing here? Don't tell me it's *you* they've been looking for?"

"Well," Antryg admitted, "they *are* looking for me— the Council for getting out of the Tower, and the Regent for insulting him on the road, and the Church . . . Why?"

Magister Magus shook his head. "God only knows— and maybe the Prince Regent. But a week ago Sunday, every Council wizard in the town was dropped on by the Witchfinders, backed up with the Prince's men. They went through the Yard like reapers through corn. I was ready to run; but if I'd been caught running, they'd have asked why." He shuddered, then chuckled ruefully. "Too frightened to run. I'm told even Cerdic cleared out of town." He glanced at Caris, still in his rust-colored groom's livery, and back to Antryg with one brow raised. "A bodyguard? A sasennan?"

"In a manner of speaking." Antryg grinned. "I see trade hasn't been hurt."

"You call only two clients not hurt? Antryg, this place is generally full! They arrive as soon as they wake up— which is about three in the afternoon—and sit here until dark, just waiting to give me money for telling them what they want to hear. I'm almost as popular as a first-class hairdresser! This is the first day anyone's come in a week. The Court's like a bunch of children when someone's told nursie about the games behind the barn."

He sighed, and all the verve seemed to go out of him. leaving him just a thin little man in his elaborate robe and diamond chain, stressed, weary, and very frightened.

Quietly, Antryg asked, "And has your magic faded?"

Magister Magus' head came up with a snap.

"Oh, yes," Antryg said softly. "As I could have been a very good dog wizard, you could have been one of the finer Council mages, if you had had the teaching."

The dog wizard sniffed. "Much good my powers would have done me then," he muttered. "And my teaching was good enough. But for God's sake, Antryg, don't let that about! As I see it, my only defense against the Witch-finders is that they think I'm a complete fake. That's enough to make a cat laugh, isn't it?" he added bitterly. "I advertise powers they don't think I've got to make my living, and you . . ." He frowned again. "But you were always different, weren't you? How do you know. . ." His words caught a little, then he went on, ". . . about . . . about what's been happening to my powers?"

"What?" Antryg's voice was low in the incense-laden hush of the overdecorated room. "Three, four times in the last week and a half and twice or three times before that?"

Magister Magus was staring at him, as his own clients must stare when he revealed some private secret, deduced, as Joanna had seen Antryg deduce them when he was telling fortunes on the road, from the stain on a glove or the nervous shift of the eyes.

"It's happened to all the wizards, Magus—and to all people, hasn't it?"

The dapper little man shook his head disbelievingly, "Last week the Countess said . . . And the quarrels they've been having . . . Senseless, stupid! One woman said she seemed to wake out of a trance, with a knife in her hand, stealing toward her husband's room. Oh, she hates him, yes, but . . . she feared she was going out of her mind. . . ."

"Perhaps she was," Antryg murmured. "Perhaps it was only despair. It is sapping all life, all energy, drawing away both strength and hope for . . . what? I don't know what it is or how it's being done or why. But I know that it is being done. Do you know who's escaped the Church's net?"

"What?" Caught in the frightening vision of the fading of both life and magic, it took the Magus an instant to realize his friend had changed the subject again.

"Rosamund? Aunt Min? Old Whitewell Simm? It's an interesting thing," Antryg added, half to himself, "that they're making the distinction not of who has powers, but who can use them effectively—the Council mages, in fact. I wonder whose decision that was?"

The dog wizard shook his head. "God only knows," he repeated. "It must be all of them, mustn't it? Because if any one of the great ones escaped, it would stand to reason he'd rescue the others, wouldn't he?" He led the way through an impressively carved ebony door into a perfectly ordinary dining room and stripped off his velvet robe and pectoral as he went, to reveal beneath them the neat, dark-blue breeches, sober waistcoat, and white shirtsleeves and stockings of a city professional.

"Yes," Antryg agreed mildly, taking the soft velvet weight of the robe to hold for him, "so it would."

On his way to the sideboard for a glass of the wine that stood in the cooler there, the dog wizard paused and regarded Joanna curiously, then came back to her, his dark brows drawn down slightly over his aquiline nose.

"Please excuse me, my dear," he said after a moment's scrutiny. "I'm usually good at guessing someone's trade, if they have one. That so-called groom of yours is obviously a sasennan, for instance." Caris, in the doorway, stiffened a little, indignant. "Your demeanor clearly marks you as possessing a trade, my child, and an income of your own, but I cannot for the life of me determine what it is. Do you mind my asking?"

Confused and slightly embarrassed, Joanna admitted, "Computer systems designer."

"And upon that," Antryg took up, with a smile at Magus' baffled look as he took the wineglass from Magus' hand and gave it to Joanna, "hangs a tale indeed."

"Joanna."

Startled, she sat up in bed, her blond hair hanging in her eyes; the faint scratching noise she had attributed to rats came again from the door. She realized it was the more quiet alternative to knocking and scrambled through the gauzy white curtains which acted as an effective mosquito netting in a world whose wire-drawing technique did not yet extend to window screens. "Who is it?" Somewhere in the humid darkness beyond the tall windows, a clock chimed three; down in the street, a distant, dreary peddler's voice was singing a song about matches.

"Caris."

The moon had set long ago. In Angelshand there was no such thing as the reflected glow of streetlights from outside—there wasn't a streetlight in the whole city—and the only light in the room came from a tiny seed of fire in an amber glass night lamp on the washstand. By its minute glow, she located the nightrobe the Prince had included in her luggage, an amazing confection of gauze and lace, and went to unbrace the chair from the door.

He was standing in the hall outside. The tall, narrow house was silent, save for the soft, sonorous breathing of her host, which could be heard through the open door of his bedchamber next to hers. Caris was dressed, as usual, in the plain livery of a servant, but all of the costume he wore at the moment were the breeches, shirt, and stockings, all creased as if he had slept in them. His blond hair was ruffled from a pillow—she remembered how he had sat silently watching her and the two mages, as Antryg and Magus had exchanged stories and reminiscences until the small hours, and had then followed Antryg silently up to the attics to sleep.

"May I come in?"

She stepped aside. She knew that a month ago she would never have done so, even if he *had* rescued her from an evil wizard's clutches—but a month ago, she hadn't killed two men.

And oddly enough, in the last several days, a little to her own surprise, she had come to like the sasennan. She had formerly been slightly afraid of that silent, beautiful young man, distrustful of the scorn she was sure he felt for her plainness and inexperience. But like Antryg, Caris took people exactly as he found them; if he had not expected her to be able to climb walls and evade armed troops, neither had he assumed she would fail. It was she, she realized, who had held prejudiced expectations of him; but unlike Antryg, he wasn't the sort of man you could apologize to for it.

"Joanna," he said softly, "I need your help."

She said nothing. She knew—or hoped, anyway—that she wouldn't act like one of those whining and putty-willed movie heroines who took pot shots at the hero because of a desperate attachment they had formed for the villain, but she had hoped also that she wouldn't be asked to choose.

That, too, she thought, had been a stupid hope. Whether she wanted to or not, she was in a game for keeps; the riddles locked up behind Antryg's mad gray eyes and lunatic smile affected the fates of both worlds, hers, perhaps, more than Caris'. After a long moment, she found herself asking, "What do you want me to do?"

From his pocket, Caris brought out a creased scrap of paper. In the floating ochre light she saw it was a map. Though one house was marked, there was no number—

that was another modern innovation that Angelshand lacked.

"I suspect Antryg is going out soon as it's light," the warrior said softly. "He came to Angelshand for purposes of his own. I can't afford to lose him now. But I must get in contact with Dr. Narwahl Skipfrag. He's the only friend the Council has at Court, the only one to whom the Regent might listen. He's a friend of my grandfather's—a scientist, but one who believes there is something more to magic than hocus-pocus and dog wizardry."

He held out the paper to her. She took it, stiff and heavy-feeling in her cold fingers.

"Tell him what happened and where we are. Tell him that I need an introduction to the Court and that I have Antryg Windrose, if not my prisoner, at least in my sight. Telling him what happened to my grandfather."

She set the paper on the washstand. "I'll tell him your grandfather disappeared," she said slowly, "but to be literally truthful, I don't know what happened to your grandfather—and neither do you."

Caris' mouth tightened a little, and the brown eyes in their wells of shadow seemed to harden to agate.

Slowly, a little gropingly, Joanna went on, "I don't *know* anything, really—only what I've been told, either by you or by Antryg. All I want to do is get the hell out of this mess and go home. . . ." She broke off again, something strange stirring in her heart, because it wasn't, entirely, all she wanted. . . .

"And I tell you this," Caris said quietly. "That Antryg stalked you, and Antryg went to that house where he left his mark upon the wall to find you, and Antryg brought you here, for purposes of his own; and from that I collect that, unless we find my grandfather, unless we free the Council from persecution, you will never return to your home. Do you understand that?"

After a long moment Joanna sighed, and said softly, "Yes."

Caris stood for a time, looking down at his hands where they rested over the hilt of his scabbarded sword, thrust through the sash tied incongruously over his servant livery. Then, not so harshly, as if he, too, were fumbling for the right words, he said, "I am not asking you to do him harm. Whether harm comes to him . . . it could from any number of sources. But I must know what he plans in Angelshand and I must not let him out of my sight. You are only one I can count on. May I do so?"

Knowing he was right, wretchedly glad that it was no worse, Joanna nodded miserably. With a deep bow, Caris faded into the darkness of the hall. She stood still for a few moments with her hands resting on the satiny wood of the doorframe, wishing she knew, if not what to do, at least what to feel. Though the attic stairs ran close to her room, she did not hear his soundless tread as he ascended.

As Caris had guessed they might, both he and Antryg were gone from the house by the time Joanna woke. She had breakfast with Magister Magus, during which a solemn manservant in a truly startling livery of rose-hued plush announced that the Marquise of Inglestoke had arrived and awaited audience, and left him robing philosophically for the pursuit of his trade.

Although Antryg's spell of languages allowed her to understand and be understood, Joanna had no idea of the written word. Caris, aware of that, had drawn his map to Narwahl Skipfrag's house on Cheveley Street in careful detail, and she had no difficulty finding the place. It was about two miles from the square where Magister Magus had his lodgings, through crowded streets of shop fronts, offices, and squares of tenement lodgings where coster-mongers yelled their wares from handcarts and beggars whined to the passers-by; but having walked almost eighty miles in the last week, Joanna found the distance no concern.

It was only when she was within half a block of the place that she saw that two sasenna guarded its door.

She halted on the pavement, looking up the short flight of granite steps to the narrow frontage of the house. She shifted her purse on her shoulder, slipped the map from the pocket of her voluminous skirt and checked it, and counted doors from the corner—but in her heart, she knew the guarded door was Narwahl Skipfrag's. He was a friend of the wizards; the black livery of the sasenna was of the soft, samurailike cut of the Church sasenna, and she could see the sun emblem of the Sole God like gory flowers upon their shoulders.

For their benefit, she looked up and down the street again, sighed, and shook her head, then walked away down the flagway, still gravely studying her map.

At the corner, she turned and shoved the map into her purse. This was a larger street, bustling with foot and carriage traffic and redolent of horse droppings, garbage, and flies. Across the lane a furniture mender had moved most of his shop out onto the flagway to take advantage of the forenoon sun; a noodle shop run by a couple of braided-haired Old Believers released clouds of steam into the air and Joanna shuddered, thinking what the heat must be like inside. She walked along the pavement until she found the narrow mouth of the alley and, with a slight feeling of trepidation, picked up her skirts and turned into that blue and stinking canyon.

As she had suspected from the layout of Magister Magus' house, the houses of this row all had little yards behind them—by the smell of it, with the privy up against the back fence. Garbage choked the unpaved lane; nameless liquids reduced the dirt underfoot to nauseous slime. Against the faded boards of the fences, the red wax of the

Church's seal stood out brilliantly and saved her even the trouble of counting back gates.

She glanced up and down the alley and put her eye to a knothole in the rickety gate. There was no one in the narrow little yard, but, as on the gate, she could see the Church's seal had been affixed to the back door at the top of its little flight of steps. She tested the gate, pulled her Swiss Army knife from her purse, and slipped it under the seal, breaking it from the wood; then she pushed the gate softly open and went in.

The house stood silent. Empty, she thought—but in that case, why post guards?

The only friend the wizards had at Court, she thought. The Regent had turned back, returning to Angelshand, perhaps—going to visit Cerdic; certainly . . . Caris had said he was growing increasingly paranoid. . . .

She was aware of her heart beating achingly as she mounted the steps and leaned over to look through the window beside the door.

She saw a library, shadowy and barely visible giving an impression of comfortable, old-fashioned chairs and a heavy chimney breast with carving over it. No fire—but then in summer there wouldn't be.

Joanna took a deep breath, formulated her cover story about a dying sister who must see Dr. Skipfrag or perish, and thrust her knife under the wax of the seal. It cracked clear; she found her wallet, extracted a credit card, and used the thin, hard plastic to raise the latch.

The house was empty. She knew it, standing in the brown dimness of the hall. Carefully, she untied and removed her low-heeled shoes, cursed her yards of petticoat as she gathered them in hand to keep from knocking over furniture, and moved as soundlessly as she could along the wall toward the stairs.

In the bedroom on the second floor, she found a ruffled bed, the covers flung back but the creased sheets long cold.

A drawer was open in the top of the highboy; peering into it, Joanna could see that something had been taken hastily from it scattering cravats and gloves. On the marble top of the highboy a few grains of black powder were scattered, and the experience of the last week had taught Joanna the look and smell of old-fashioned black gunpowder.

Silently, she ascended the next flight of steps.

From uncurtained windows, a whitish light suffused the attic; the trapped heat of days made the room stuffy. The smell of old blood nearly turned her sick. It was splattered everywhere, turned dark brown now against the white paint of the walls and the pale plaster of the ceiling; little droplets of it had dripped back onto the pooled and rivuleted floor. For some reason, the sight of it brought back to her the memory of how hot the sasennan's blood had been, splattering against her face; she shut her teeth tightly against a clench of nausea.

The calm part of her that could analyze program glitches at three in the morning and that told her it was stupid to fall in love with a middle-aged wizard in another universe asked, *What the hell could have caused this?*

Curious, she took a step forward. She drew back her stockinged foot immediately as it touched something sharp. She saw it was a small shard of broken glass. When she bent to pick it up, she saw there were others, sparkling in the wan light on the bloodstained floor and, she noticed, embedded here and there in the walls, as well. She held the shard up to the light. It was edged with old blood.

With a nervous shake of her hand she threw it from her. She didn't know why, but there was something in the touch of it that filled her with loathing and with fear. There wasn't a great deal of glass—not more than one smashed beaker's worth—but it was widely scattered. Picking her way carefully, she crossed the room to the laboratory tables beneath the dormer windows on the other side.

It had been a long time since she'd taken her Fundamentals of Electricity course in college, but she recognized most of what she saw there—primitive cell-batteries with their lined-up dishes of water, a vacuum pump, and crudely insulated copper wire. An iron-and-copper sparking generator sat in the midst of a tangle of leads, and a glass Volta pistol gleamed faintly in the sunlight on a corner of the table. Other objects whose use she did not know lay among the familiar, archaic equipment—convoluted glass tubing and little dishes of colored salts. At the back of the litter sat a seamless glass ball, silvered over with what looked like mercury, gleaming evilly in the diffuse light. Joanna shrank from touching it, repelled without knowing why. Above the table, in the middle of the whitewashed wall, was the fresh scar of a bullet hole; beside her hand, the wooden table's edge was also freshly scarred, as if someone had smashed a glass vessel against it in a rage.

Her first thought was, *Antryg would know what happened*.

Her second, as she heard the soft jostle of an unwary step of booted feet somewhere in the house below her was, *I have no line of retreat*.

They'll have seen the broken-off seals, she thought, even as she scanned the low ceiling for a trap door to the roof. There was none. The windows might have been made to open once upon a time, but they had long since been barred to prevent the ingress of thieves. She thought, *There's a wardrobe in the bedroom—they might pass me by and I could get out behind them* . . . She had to fight with everything in her to walk, silently and carefully, instead of running to the stairs.

It cost her her escape. The two sasenna and the man in the gray garb of a Witchfinder had just reached the second floor as she came silently around the corner of the narrow stair.

CHAPTER XIV

"WHERE ARE YOUR FRIENDS, GIRL?"

Joanna did not look up. The Witchfinder Peelbone's eyes, like his voice, were thin, pale, and very cold and filled her with the panicky sensation that he knew everything about her; she kept her gaze down on her hands, which lay like two detached white things on the grime-impregnated table top before her. She could feel her heart hammering against her ribs beneath the blue striped cotton of her boned bodice and the crawl of panic-sweat down her back, but some small voice in her mind kept repeating, *Don't say anything. He can use anything that you say, but he can't use your silence.*

"We know you have them." She heard, rather than saw him rise from his big, carved chair on the opposite side of the table and heard the rustle of his clothes as he came around toward her. The room was windowless and lit by sconces backed by metal reflectors, one on either side of his chair; his shadow passed in front of one. When he stood beside her in the heat of the room, she could smell his body and the sweat in his clothes. She knew he was going to touch her; but even so, she flinched when he seized her hair and forced her to look up at him. "That's an expensive dress," he said quietly, and she hated the feel of his hand moving in her hair. "And your hair is clean. You spent last night somewhere. Answer me!"

His hand tightened, twisting at her hair unmercifully. She had forgotten from her grade school days how painful it was to have one's hair pulled. She forced herself to look up into that narrow, handsome face, with the eyes of colorless, austere brown under colorless brows, gritting her teeth against the wrenching pian.

If I don't say A, he can't say B, she thought desperately. She had always used silence as a weapon in arguments and had found it an effective one against everyone from her mother to Gary. There was a spy novel, she remembered, wherein someone had sat through hours of interrogation in silence. . . .

She remembered what Caris had told her about the Inquisition's methods and felt sick with fear at the thought.

The grip released suddenly, pushing her away with force enough to rock her on the backless wooden stool where she sat. She caught her balance and looked up at the Witchfinder again, trying desperately not to feel like a sulky, defiant child, trying not to think beyond the moment. The cold eyes stared into hers; she was reminded of a shark's eyes, with no more humanity in them than two round circles of metal.

"Such silence can't spring from innocence, I think," Peelbone said softly. "Very good—we know you are guilty of something. The only question is—what?"

She remembered him saying, *We can't afford these waters muddied*. She would ultimately be guilty, she knew, of whatever was convenient for them, even as they would sooner have killed Caris, back at Kymil, rather than risk him cluttering up their case with truth. When she said nothing, she saw the long, bracketing lines around his mouth move a little, like snakes, with irritation.

He raised one white forefinger. Joanna heard the guard behind her stool step forward and didn't resist when she was pulled to her feet; she was fighting a desperate terror, wondering how much they knew already and whether, if they searched her purse, they'd be able to backtrack to Magister Magus' house from Caris' map. She thanked the guardian god of wizards that she'd put the map in her purse instead of her pocket—there was so much other junk in there that it could easily be passed over.

The guard held her arms behind her, a hateful grip and terrifyingly strong. She expected Peelbone to strike her, as he had struck Caris back in Kymil. All her life she had managed to avoid physical violence of any kind, and the very unfamiliarity of being touched and handled added to her dread. But the Witchfinder studied her in silence for a few moments, then almost casually reached forward and ripped open her bodice, revealing the thin, sweat-soaked muslin of the shift beneath.

"Child," he said quietly, "if I had you stripped naked and thrown into the room where the rapists are kept chained, it would not in any way impair your ability to tell us about your friends an hour later." His disinterested eyes moved to the grinning guard. "Now take her away."

It took everything she had to bite back the desperate impulse to cry *Wait* . . . as the guard pushed her out of the room and into the torchlit hall. Her jaw set, she kept her eyes straight ahead of her, forcing herself not to see the leers of the two other guards out in the hall or hear their comments; she saw only the smokestains on the stone arches of the low ceiling and how the shadows of the torches jerked and quavered in the drafts that came down from the narrow stairways to the guardrooms above. The St. Cyr fortress, at the tip of the island which the city of

Angelshand had long since outgrown, was an ancient one, and its very walls stank of the lives that had rotted to their ends there.

The cell to which they took her was a dank and tiny stone closet that smelled like a privy. By the light of the torch that burned smokely in a holder near the low door, Joanna could see that it had only one other human occupant, not counting roaches of a size and arrogance to make the San Serano orthoptera blush with shame—an old woman, wearing the remains of the black robes of a mage or an Old Believer, who sat huddled in the corner as Joanna was pushed inside and the heavy wooden door closed behind her. The woman barely looked up as the heavy bolts were shot outside. Joanna, trembling, stood for a few moments at the top of the short flight of steps down into the room.

I can't cry now, she told herself desperately, her throat suddenly gripped by a surge of betraying pain and her eyes hot. It would weaken her, she knew; unless she kept keyed to this point, she could never face the Witchfinder in silence for the second interview she knew was coming. But neither Antryg nor Caris knew where she was—and even if they did, they would be unable to rescue her. *I never wanted this*, she thought, *I never asked for this*! *I was hauled here. . . .*

Antryg had said, *You are in this world under my protection. . . .*

Her legs felt weak as she descended the few steps. Raised in the protection of a technological society and under the enormous bulwark of Constitutional Law, flawed though it might be, she had never before found herself in the position of being so utterly without recourse. Her aloneness terrified her. Even if she told them everything they wanted to know and betrayed Antryg, Caris and poor, cowardly, charming Magister Magus to torture and death, she had the horrible certainty that it would not help her. She could not explain how she herself came to this world.

She was their accomplice against her will. She had done murder. . . .

You didn't panic then, she told herself grimly, *and it saved you. For God's sake don't panic now.*

A faint snore made her look down. The old woman, thin and fragile-looking, was curled up in the corner, sleeping with the light sleep of the very aged. As she watched, Joanna shuddered to see an enormous roach emerge from a crack in the stone wall and make its unconcerned way down the old woman's shoulder. Her hand cringing from the task, Joanna leaned down and swept the thing away with such violence that it shot across the tiny cell and hit the opposite wall with an audible crack.

The old woman's faded blue eyes opened and blinked up at her under lashes gone white as milk. "She was only walking, after all," she said in a reproving voice. And, when Joanna blinked, confused, the old lady shook her head and gestured with one trembling finger at the other wall, where the enormous insect was just disappearing through a crack. "Not doing harm."

Joanna swallowed queasily.

"They don't eat much," the old lady added, "and nor do I—so it's not that they're taking aught from me." She squinted up at Joanna's sickened face. "Were you raised in privies, likely you'd be loathly, too."

"Sorry," Joanna said and then, knowing what the old lady obviously expected, she turned toward the departed cockroach. "Sorry," she said, more loudly, and the old lady nodded her satisfaction.

For a long moment, those pale, ancient eyes looked up at her in silence; rather gingerly, Joanna gathered up her skirts and sat in the filthy straw beside her. "I'm Joanna Sheraton," she said, and the old woman nodded.

"Minhyrdin the Fair they call me. Are they arresting the dog wizards now, too? For you're none of the Council's."

Joanna shook her head. "No—at least, I don't know. I'm not a mage at all."

The old woman clucked to herself. "Never say so, child; they'll put you in with the street girls or the murderesses, instead of in those cells built to hold the mageborn. They took away my knitting. . . ." She looked fussily around her, as if half expecting to find it hidden under the straw. Joanna shivered and paranoically checked the straw around her skirts, hating the thought that one of the old lady's pet roaches might be crawling in her several layers of petticoat.

You are going to be raped, tortured, and killed, she thought, *and you're worrying about bugs in your skirts?* Tears of wretchedness and fear lay very close to the surface, but she couldn't keep from smiling with wry irony at her own capacity for the trivial.

"How did you come here, then?" the old lady asked, as if they'd met by chance at a Mendelssohn recital.

Joanna folded her arms around her knees, finding a curious easing of her fears in talking. "I was trying to see Dr. Narwahl Skipfrog," she said. "But I—I think he's dead, isn't he? Someone was killed there." She shivered, remembering that gruesome scene. "In the attic—there was blood splattered everywhere, even on the ceiling. That must have been the arteries. It must have happened days ago but the place still stank of it. The Witchfinder's men . . ." She swallowed. The bruises their grip had left were beginning to ache on her arms.

"It was—it was done by magic, wasn't it? There was broken glass scattered on the floor and embedded in the walls. . . ."

"Ah," Minhyrdin the Fair whispered. She folded her little hands and rocked back and forth; the few wisps of her thinning white hair swished against her sunken and withered cheeks. "So," she murmured to herself, "he's at his tricks again."

"Who?" asked Joanna shakily, looking over at her.

"Suraklin." She stopped rocking, but frowned off into the distance, as if trying to remember something. "Suraklin," she said again. "The Dark Mage. He'd call them up, spirits, elementals—hate and rage and destruction—and clothe them in what flesh he chose. He'd cast a handful of pebbles into the whirlwind; and like a whirlwind, they'd grow, till they ripped the flesh from the bone—or fling a handful of water into it, and those drops would multiply, whirling and tearing, till they drownded a man. . . ."

With horrible clarity, Joanna remembered the freshly chipped edge of the wooden table and the nearness to hand of the glass beakers. Easy enough, she thought, appalled, to seize and smash a vessel and fling the shards. . . .

Joanna whispered, "Suraklin is dead."

"Oh, yes." The woman began rocking again, her little hands folded on her knees and her tiny, pointed chin resting on the knotted fingers. "Dead . . . dead . . . for all that poor boy of his drove himself mad swearing he wasn't. But where's he been, eh? Just tell me that."

"Antryg?" asked Joanna, reflecting that Antryg wasn't the only one to be disordered in his wits.

"No!" The old woman looked at her impatiently. "We all know where he's been, meddling and wandering. Suraklin. He's been dead these twenty-five years, but where's he been, if he hasn't, eh?" And she resumed her rocking once more, like a lonely child. When she spoke, her voice had the curious, far-off note of a child's telling a story or a dream. "He wanted to live forever, Suraklin; he hated the thought that he'd die. He ruled all those around him, twisted them all to his will. But he knew he'd die, and it would all fall apart. All fall apart . . ."

Joanna frowned, remembering what Antryg had said in the moonlight of the Devil's road. "Is that what happened twenty-five years ago, then?"

"Twenty-five years ago it was," the old woman murmured, "And the Prince Hieraldus, that was so handsome, and the Archmage, and all the Council of Wizards riding south, with the Witchfinders in arms because they'd been claiming for years it never existed, and the Church lending its hand to us. . . . Ah, those were the days," she sighed. "Terrible days. The Church and the Witchfinders, they gave us help, but they never forgave us, they never forgave."

No, thought Joanna. *Now could they, after years of denying your existence and then having to ask your help?* She rested her forehead on her knees, her tired mind trying to fathom the strange whirlpool of darkness into which she had been drawn—kidnap, and flight; the agonizing kick of the pistol against her wrists and the spurt blood on her face; the crawling abominations in the meadow; Antryg's eyes in the wan gray afternoon light . . .

It had been on her lips a dozen times in the last week to ask him, as she had asked that first morning, *Why?*

I can't tell you the truth and I don't wish to lie to you. . . . God knows I've done that enough.

He had stalked her at San Serano—he had come to Gary's, knowing somehow that she was there.

How? She wondered. He had said, *I have always had the misfortune to be a good guesser.*

How had he known about the abominations? What had happened to Caris' grandfather the Archmage, who had vanished into the darkness of the Void with Antryg and who had not emerged from the other side? What did he know about that queer and terrible deadness, that sapping of the life of the world?

She wondered if it would be easier if the mere thought of him didn't shake the bones of her body.

You are in this world under my protection. . . .

As if a blanket of terror had been flung over her head, black darkness fell upon the cell, and the air outside in the corridor was split by a scream of such dreadful agony that

Joanna felt as if her liver and lights were trying to leap out her throat.

A second scream followed the first, footfalls thundered, and somewhere a man cried out in terror. The door shook as a running guard blundered into it with a rattle of weaponry; involuntarily, Joanna clutched at the dark bundle of rags beside her, clinging to the frail bones beneath, her heart pounding in her ears so that the hammer of the blood almost sickened her. As if in a nightmare, through a shimmering darkness, she thought she could dimly see the torch, still burning, though its flame was like a wan scrap of white silk, illuminating nothing. Other voices sounded in the corridor, shouts of terror and alarm; under the screaming, Joanna thought the whole St. Cyr fortress was up in arms, blundering in that terrible darkness.

Toward what?

"Joanna!"

Cumulative stress, terror, and weariness broke inside her; she flung herself to her feet with a sob and threw herself to the door. In blind darkness, she groped at the barred judas . . . "Antryg, get me out of here!"

"Get back from the window. I can't touch the door—it's spelled—put your hand up—gently. . . ."

Through the rusted iron of the peephole's crosspiece, she felt the prick of a sword against her fingers. Sliding her hand carefully up the blade, she felt a metal ring with a key on it. Fumblingly, she groped at the side of the door she thought she remembered the keyhole was on. It wasn't. Another scream rent the palpitating air, raising the hair on the back of her neck.

"What is it?" she gasped.

"It's a Screamer, a terror-spell—it's not going to last and neither is the darkness, so hurry!"

A splinter ran into her questing fingers—she disregarded it, guided the key into the lock, and wrenched the heavy mechanism over. Some how that deep, extraordinary voice defused the dread of the dark, reduced the cries of grief and anguish to what they were—noises—and made her expel her breath in a shaky laugh. "I thought you couldn't use magic . . ."

"I can't—this is courtesy of Magister Magus, and he's probably taken to his heels by this time."

She slipped through the half-opened door and felt the familiar strength of a bony arm in the worn velvet sleeve around her waist, dragging her along the corridor in the blackness. Already, shapes were coming faintly clear to her eyes—men running here and there, the torches burning like shreds of fluttering cloth. Another scream rent the air, horrifying with all the despairing pain of torture and grief.

"We can't . . ." she began, trying to stop, remembering old Minhyrdin the Fair.

"Yes we can. Now run!" Inexorably, he dragged her on. She could see him dimly now, the beaky face colorless in its tangled frame of graying brown hair, the spectacles beginning to catch the renewing light of the torches. He held a sword in his free hand, undoubtedly taken from one of the blinded guards. His longer strides made her stumble; he hauled her up a twisting spiral of stone stair and through a guardroom that seemed filled with men blundering about, weapons in their hands, not certain which way to go—shadows against a deeper darkness, their voices a clamor of terror and uncertainty.

"It's a curse!" "It's the mages!" "The Archmage . . ." "Where's it coming from?" "This way, you fools!"

Feeling as if she fled in a dream, Joanna gasped, "The others . . ."

"They'll have to do what they can!" They were in the open court, the darkness mingling into a raw and clammy fog that chilled her to the bone through her ripped dress. Parties of men were running everywhere, pikes and swords and crossbows in their hands; but with belated caution they were already running down toward the court.

The last scream died, and the darkness faded, just as they reached the gate.

Antryg dashed straight to the sentry in the gatehouse, pointed back across the court, and gasped, "In the guard-room . . ."

The man, involuntarily, turned his head to look, and the wizard's knobby fist, weighted with the pommel of his sword, smashed across his temple, even as the two guards who had been beside the gate came running toward him. Antryg caught the first man's descending halberd on the back of his blade, wrenching it up and stepping in under it to kick the man full, hard, and agonizingly in the groin; he was turning toward the second before the first man even hit the pavement. The courtyard behind them echoed with the clatter of boots—city guards, Church sasenna, and, Joanna saw, the Regent's men also, in their gold-braided black uniforms.

As if they'd rehearsed it, the instant the guard in the gatehouse had fallen, Joanna sprang to pull the pistol from his belt. It was double-barreled. She knew, if she tried to hit Antryg's current opponent, she would just as likely hit Antryg, so she swung around and fired at the closest of the black-clothed sasenna rushing toward them out of the fog in the court. Nobody fell, but the lead men flinched and ducked; Antryg was beside her, his blade bloodied to the hilt, shouting, "RUN!"

She gathered up her skirts and ran. She was aware that he was not with her, but couldn't look back—only at the gray arch of fog ahead of her, beyond the stone, shadow, and portcullis ropes. It was as if she ran in a dream, adrenaline scorching her veins and her heart hammering at her that she had to escape—that after this, the consequences of capture would be unthinkable. . . .

She smelled the stagnant little moat that blocked the landward side of St. Cyr from the rest of the old island part of the town; her stockinged feet thumped hollowly on the silly little wooden drawbridge. Ahead of her, buildings bulked in the fog, old-fashioned architecture and slanted roofs mingling with the squarer lines of building a century or more old and already fallen into decay. Looking back, she caught the flash of Antryg's descending sword blade in the gatehouse and saw him pelting toward her through the shadows, a last frantic run as the portcullis, its counter-weight ropes slashed, rumbled down-ward. . . .

Joanna felt as if her heart had stopped. Had it been a free drop, he could never have made it, but the geared wheels, even rolling loose, slowed the fall of those tons of iron just enough. He flung himself down and rolled, the weighted iron teeth of the grillwork gate grinding into their slots inches behind his body. Then he was on his feet and running toward her again, the ridiculous skirts of his too-big coat billowing behind him like a cloak. His face, she noticed in the fog, was as white as his shirt ruffle.

Men were crowding up against the portcullis, trying vainly to lift it without the counterweights. Pistols were thrust through the lowered grille; there was a deafening roar and a stench of black powder as Antryg reached her and caught her arm. Together they made a dash across the small, cobbled square. The rough paving-stones gouged her feet and the puddles soaked and chilled them through her thin stockings, but she scarely noticed. Three men started to run down the steps of a tavern toward them, waving sticks. From the portcullis behind them, Joanna heard the *whap* of a crossbow firing and from the corner of her eye saw the bolt of it bury itself with hideous force in the tavern's wall. The three men flung themselves flat, and Antryg dragged her into the noisome mouth of the nearest alley.

Voices were echoing behind them in the square, dimmed and muffled by the fog, which was growing thicker, drift-ing clammily between the somber buildings and limiting their visibility to a few feet. Holding up her skirts with one hand and thanking all the Fates that watch over heroines that she'd had, by this time, plenty of practice fleeing in petticoats, Joanna stumbled along after Antryg as he walked rapidly down the slimy mud of the lane. The first jet of strength that had carried her over the drawbridge was fading. She felt weak and suddenly cold.

He ducked through a back gate into a narrow yard which, by the smell of it, was used promiscuously as a toilet facility by the entire overcrowded tenement it served, led her across it, through a dark doorway into what had once been the lower hall of some great house and was now the black and gloomy bottom floor of tenement lodgings, and out again through the front door onto the street. The fog seemed, if anything, thicker there. Holding her arm, he led her across a narrow, cobbled street, dodging aside as the shape of a horse-drawn vehicle of some kind loomed suddenly out of the gray mists, and then into another alley beyond. She heard voices shouting from somewhere and the clash of weapons, and all she could think was, *We can't get caught. We can't get caught. . . .*

"Here." Antryg stopped. It seemed they were alone in a tiny bubble of solitude and the stink of rotting fish which permeated the mud underfoot. He seemed to see for the first time her torn bodice and disheveled hair, and a small, upright line that could have been pain or anger appeared between his brows. "Did they hurt you?"

Joanna shook her head. "Just threatened real good."

A corner of his mouth quirked at that, but his eyes remained grave, as if he guessed that, had she been hurt, she would have been too ashamed to admit it. "You're sure?"

Why this concern for her true feelings should make her throat hurt with the urge to cry again, she didn't know—possibly because he was the first not to take her brusque, "I'm fine," at face value, possibly simply because she was cold, frightened, and overwrought. She nodded, and he seemed to accept that. He pulled a tattered silk handkerchief from his pocket and wiped his swordblade with it, then sheathed it in the scabbard that was thrust, as Caris bore his when battle was at hand, through a sash at his waist. It made a sharp angle under the voluminous skirts of his coat. He took the pistol gently from her hand, checked it, and handed it back; then he stood for a moment looking down at her.

She thought he had been going to say something else, but he did not. It was coming to her that she was still alive and, at least for this second and possibly the next two, safe. It was against considerable odds that they both weren't lying dead in the shadows of the St. Cyr gatehouse. He put his hand up to touch her hair; then, as if half-doubtful of the wisdom of his action, bent and kissed her lips.

And he was right, she thought, to doubt. The kiss was probably intended to last much less time than it did. On the road their bantering had occasionally edged on flirtation, but he had been careful never to be alone with her, and for this she was, in a way, grateful. But now she was only aware of her own desperate need to hold him, all the terrors and dread of the last six hours swelling to bursting point within her, tightening her grip around his ribcage, the lock of the pistol she still held pressing awkwardly against his back, until she could feel every edge of shirt-ruffle and every button through her sweat-soaked shift and into her icy flesh. She was aware of his body against hers, holding her up as her knees shook, of the softness of the worn velvet under her hands, of the warmth of his breath on her cheek, and of her passionate desire to press her face to his shoulder and weep.

She tore her mouth free of his. She found she was breathing hard, trembling even as he was. She thought, *This is crazy!* But their eyes lingered, with a desperate knowledge that both of them were well aware verged on madness. Then he caught her hand and led her swiftly in the murk.

"Nothing quite so useful as a good fog," he said after a few moments. "They said that the Archmage Elsheiyin used to summon fog by combing her hair, but most people need water of some kind. Suraklin could do it with water dipped up in his hand. Mind you, it isn't easy to summon one this early in the year."

"Did Magister Magus do this?"

He shook his head. "No, this is mine. Tinkering with the weather is relatively safe because it's so difficult to detect. Magus is probably home under his bed by this time. No mage likes to get too close to St. Cyr, and he had to be almost up under the gatehouse to cast the darkness and the screams. To do him credit, he stayed much longer than I'd have thought."

"What would you have done, if he hadn't agreed to help you?" Joanna asked, as they dodged across what appeared, in the clammy mists, to be a small courtyard, where the ghostly forms of men and women crowded in house door-ways around mephitic braziers of coals amid a strong stench of smoke and gin.

"Given him a case of itches that would have worn out his fingernails for scratching," Antryg replied promptly, and Joanna, in spite of herself, the danger, and the fact that a moment ago she'd been perilously close to exhausted tears, was shaken with the giggles.

"We've got to get off the island," he added. "It's small enough that the Church's soldiers and the Regent's can quarter it between them. I was surprised to see the Regent's men; he must have returned to Angelshand. They'll know these alleys better than the Church sasenna will." He stopped, turning his head to listen in the fog, his hand tightening on Joanna's arm. She sensed shapes moving against the darker bulk of an almost unseen building and felt a sudden qualm of terror of being caught in the open, fog-cloaked though it might be. It was late afternoon, and the vapors were suffused with a thin gray light; shapes within them shifted, dark and indistinct. . . .

Silently, Antryg melted back into a doorway to let them pass. Like the faint drip of water, their footsteps tapped away into the distance. Above the stench of greasy cooking and stale urine in the doorway around them, Joanna could smell the murky river somewhere close by. She shivered, the pistol feeling suddenly heavy in her grip. The wizard's hand was very warm where he patted her back through the thin, sweat-damp muslin of her gown. Like a pair of ghosts, they stepped from the doorway again and drifted through the vaporous dimness toward the chuckle of the water. It occurred to Joanna that, whatever the reason Antryg had kidnapped her—if he had kidnapped her—she seemed to have thrown in her lot entirely with him now. There was no longer whatever alternative course Caris could offer. If she—

In the darkness of an alley to their right, a sword clanked on stone. Antryg whirled, his hand going to his sword hilt. At the same instant, Joanna saw in the black, eyeless socket of a doorway to their right the shadows solidify into the shapes of men with swords. She hadn't even the span of an intaken breath to cry a warning. Antryg, alerted by some sixth sense that he'd walked into crossfire, was already turning back as the weighted pommel of a sword cracked down on the back of his head.

In a telescoping instant of time, Joanna was perfectly well aware that she was unable to carry him as he crumpled down against her; she was also aware that she had only one shot in her pistol and that, if she fired it now into the thick of the half-dozen sasenna closing in on them from the mouth of the alley opposite, she might buy herself the time to flee. Instead, she swung around on the man in the doorway as he pointed his crossbow down at the wizard's

crumpled body on the wet cobblestones and cried,
"Don't!"

Iron hands seized her from behind, dragging her back
against an iron body as hard fingers wrenched the pistol
from her grip. She knew it was useless to struggle, so she
didn't. Looking up, she saw the red-haired sasennan who'd
caught her at the posthouse on the Kymil road, the captain
of the Regent's guards.

CHAPTER XV

"IT'S THEM, MY LORD." THE CAPTAIN OF THE PRINCE'S SA-
senna spoke softly in the black arch of the stone doorway.
"We brought them here as you said, instead of back to St.
Cyr."

"Very good, Joris," the Regent's shrill, edgy voice replied. "Keep the men within call." A ripple of gold flashed
in those inky shadows. Then the Prince stepped into the
room, into the dim circle of the charcoal brazier's softly
pulsing glow. "And I warn you, wizard," he added, his
words brittle as chipped glass, "at the first sign of trouble
from you, Kanner has orders to kill the girl."

Thanks, Joanna thought tiredly, fighting tears of sheer
exhaustion and fear. The guard who stood beside the chair
of ebony and ormolu where she had been tied didn't even
move his head at the sound of his own name; his dark eyes
wavered from her no more than did the barrel of his pistol.
His uniform was crimson, though he moved with the
quick-footed grace of the inevitably black-clothed sasenna.

His face was a mass of scars and old angers. Joanna looked away from him, shivering. She could not seem to stop shaking with cold, wretchedness, and fear. She felt, as Antryg had once said, a weak longing for the relative safety of the roach-infested cell in the St. Cyr fortress. At least, the Witchfinders were bounded by a sort of law—if nothing else, their self-deceptive righteousness might keep them from the baser forms of cruelty. Looking into the Prince's mad eyes, she knew that what he would do would be done without compunction, for his own pleasure.

Here—wherever this small stone chamber was, at the foot of its twisting stair—they were entirely in his power.

She had thought Antryg was still unconscious, chained by his wrists between the two pillars which supported the central groinings of the ceiling. But he raised his head groggily at the Prince's words, sweat shining along jaw muscles tense with pain. "The girl has nothing to do with this, Pharos," he said. "She's only my servant. She knows nothing of any of this. I forced her to accompany me."

"And took two cuts with my whip out of indifference to her fate?" The Prince walked slowly over to Joanna and caught her chin with one small, black-gloved hand as she tried to shrink away. His pale-blue gaze traveled over her throat and half-bared bosom; his mouth widened a little, but what was in his eyes could never have been called a smile. Terrified and loathing him, Joanna felt, as she had with the Witchfinder, that her best defense lay in silence. She met his eyes; it was the Prince who looked quickly away.

He turned back to Antryg. The wizard had gotten his feet under him, taking some of the strain of his unsupported weight from his stretched-out arms. His face was chalky with exhaustion and running with sweat in the hot closeness of the little room; Joanna could see the shift of his knuckles where he held the manacle chains, trying to ease the cut of the bracelets in his wrists. The chains were twisted through with thin red silk ribbon, incongruously gay—spell-cord, she recognized from Magister Magus' description. More of it was twined around the ropes that held her own wrists to the arms of the chair.

Though he was weaving a little on his feet, Antryg's gray eyes were calm. Through his open shirt, Joanna could see the steady rhythm of his breath. If he was even half as afraid as she was, he hid it well.

The Prince asked softly, "Who are you?"

Antryg sighed, and some of the tension seemed to drain from his body. "Antryg Windrose," he said.

The chill, pale-blue eyes narrowed. "So." For a long moment the Prince remained still, studying the form chained between the pillars in the ruddy, reflected glare of the brazier. Joanna could see the lines of sleeplessness on his face beneath a thick coating of rice powder and rouge; the dark rings of bister and fatigue made the queer eyes even paler. The Prince wet his lips, as if he feared the wizard, even chained and helpless, and had to nerve himself to approach. Then he stepped forward and, as he had before, reached up one gloved hand and carefully removed Antryg's spectacles from his face. Antryg flinched a little as the metal temple piece nicked the bruises, but his eyes never left Pharos' face.

The Prince folded up the spectacles and set them on the narrow ledge of the pillar's capital beside him. The fire-light slid along the soft black leather of the gloves as he put out his hands to frame the wizard's face between them, shoving back the loose lion's mane of graying hair to outline the delicate bones and wide, lunatic eyes.

"So," he said again. He stepped back. "Is what the Bishop of Kymil said about you true?"

Antryg tipped his head a little to one side. Without the cracked mask of the spectacles, his gray eyes looked even wider and strangely luminous in the dark smudges of fatigue. "Oh, probably not," he said mildly. "How much of what is said about you is true?"

The white gleam of teeth showed, very briefly, with the parting of the painted lips. "Everything," the Prince whispered. "I could flog you to death, you know, just to see how long it would take a wizard to die under it. No one would know. My palace—" He gestured to the dark room around them and the shadowy, convoluted vaults overhead "—stands in its own grounds, away from the main Palace and away from that stinking rabble of wizards my father used to surround himself with. Away from prying eyes, away from people spying on me, trying to kill me—yes, even my saintly cousin Cerdic!—whispering among themselves that I'm mad. Of course I'm mad! My father is, isn't he? And I am his true son . . ." His voice sank even lower, so that Joanna, watching that slender black figure, barely heard. "Aren't I?"

Antryg said, his tone quiet and conversational, "You would know more of that than I, Pharos. But being quite mad myself, I wouldn't hold madness against you; one sometimes does it in mere self-defense, you know."

The Prince's glance cut sharply up to Antryg's eyes for the first time. "What?"

"Goes mad."

The beauty of that deep voice seemed to calm the Prince; for some moments the blue eyes held the gray.

"Yes," Pharos said slowly. "Sometimes one must—go mad—or die. They said that you were mad." His glance shifted away again, as if he could not bear to show even that part of himself to another human being for more than a second or so.

Antryg nodded. Still low, still soothing, he said, "It was—the only thing that I could do at the time."

"Is it true that you've been a prisoner of the Church for seven years? That you were condemned to death?"

The harsh, metallic voice was uninflected, impossible to

second-guess. Antryg said, "Yes," and the Prince looked back at him again, suspicious, waiting for something. The wizard went on, "The rebels were my friends. The Emperor's dragoons had no right to do what they did. Not to the children. I thought that the Emperor..." He paused, for a long moment, then shook his head, weary, defeated by the old memories. "Yes, I was imprisoned under a commuted sentence of death."

"And the Archmage helped you escape?"

"No." Joanna saw Antryg's hands tighten again on the chains, holding himself upright against fatigue, shock, and the sick aftereffects of a really appalling crack on the head. In the dead-still, heated air, she could smell the musky stink of the Regent's perfume and the faint sourness of sweat from the guard Kanner, who stood beside her, silent as a statue, so close she could see the runes of na-aar written on the pistol barrel. Antryg moved his head a little, shaking aside the sweat-dampened ends of his long hair, where they clung in little circles to his temples and cheeks. "I escaped when the Archmage disappeared, but I had nothing to do with his disappearance, nor he with my escape. He had neither the intent nor the desire to set me free."

"No," the Prince murmured. "He knew our fat Bishop well—he knew the Witchfinders—he knew me. If he had helped you escape, it would have been far better done, wouldn't it? Not leaving you wandering the roads like a vagabond, nor leaving the other members of the Council to take the Church's wrath unaided. And you—you would have risked your life to rescue more than a chit of a girl. You can tell me nothing of them, can you?"

Antryg shook his head exhaustedly, the fatigue telling on him, sapping his strength. His voice remained calm, low and weary with memory and hopelessness. "I haven't seen any of them in seven years."

"Then why did you come to Angelshand?" the Prince

asked, his voice soft now, evil as the Witchfinder's and infinitely more deadly. "Surely, if you are a fugitive from the Council as you say, you would have run in the opposite direction?"

Antryg turned his face away. The gold light of the brazier shining through the damp, thin fabric of his shirt outlined his body as he drew a deep breath, then let it out, struggling, as Joanna had seen him on the road, between trust and silence. Then he looked back at the Prince, his deep voice still level but desperation in his eyes. "I have to reinstate myself somehow," he said quietly. "I can't go on like this. Not for the rest of my life. I'm a wizard, Pharos, and I haven't been able to touch that reservoir of power within myself for seven years. Even now I can't use it, for they would find me through it—the Witchfinders, the Church mages. I need to speak to them. . . ." He broke off, gazing into the Prince's face, the dark lines of strain suddenly cut deep in the discolored flesh around his eyes, hardening and aging them.

The Prince said nothing for a time, but stood with his gloved hands clasped together, an oily gleam of moisture glazing his maquillage and a sprinkle of reflected flame dancing over the bullion lace at his wrists as he shivered, as if with sudden chill. At last he whispered, "Is it real? This—this magic. This mumbo-jumbo—old women calling the weather among the fallen stones on the hills, things that mumble in the crypts, men who can summon storms by looking into a bowl of water—is it real? Not just stories with which to frighten us into obedience as children? Not just charlatans like those fakers my cousin fills his house with? Not just hags deluding themselves from their own helplessness?"

"No," Antryg murmured. "No, it's real."

The Prince stepped close to him, his voice hoarse with fear to believe. "Show me."

Antryg's fingers moved, brushing the spell-ribbon that

knotted through his chains. "You've taken care to see that I couldn't," he said softly. "Surprising care, for a man who believes it's all mumbo-jumbo and granny-rhymes. And, as I've said, I would not, even if you released me. They are seeking me—they would find me through it; and believe me, Pharos, I fear them more than I fear you."

"The Church dogs?" Pharos sniffed with scorn touched by the bravado of one half-afraid himself. "I gave the Church their mandate to act, when they said there was a plot by the Archmage and the Council. I can take it away again. I could protect you."

"Not from the Council." Antryg looked down at the Prince, the top of whose golden curls came barely to his lips. "I don't know how many of them managed to escape from St. Cyr this afternoon, but you never had them all, did you?"

Suspicion flared again in the Prince's mad eyes. "What do you know of it?"

The chains clinked faintly as Antryg shrugged. "If you had," he said simply, "you wouldn't still be afraid. And you are afraid."

The Regent stood for a moment, his face averted. In the absolute stillness, Joanna could hear how shaky was the draw of his breath. There was a cracked note to his shrill voice as he called out suddenly, "Joris!"

The captain of his sasenna, the tall, heavy-boned, red-haired woman who had captured them, emerged from the utter darkness of the hall.

"You haven't touched magic for seven years," the Prince said softly. "You couldn't have, not from the Tower, not as their prisoner." He signaled to the woman Joris.

Taking a key from the nail beside the door, she crossed into the dim circle of the firelight and unlocked the shackles from Antryg's wrists. For a moment, Joanna thought the wizard would collapse without the chains to hold him up, but he only leaned against one of the pillars, rubbing the flesh of his bony wrists where the metal had scraped the skin off it. At a nod from the Regent, Kanner stepped aside, though he did not put down his pistol. Joris came over to Joanna's chair and untied the ropes that held her. When the sasennan left, the big guard remained, his pistol still at the ready, silent as a sword.

During all this, Pharos stood with his hands folded in front of his breast, palms and fingers locked and pressed together so tightly that Joanna could see the knuckles bulge and work through the soft kid of the gloves. His eyes, when in their restless flickering Joanna could glimpse them, had lost their malice and were haunted and anxious; he caught Joris by the arm as she moved toward the door. "Be ready," he said softly, and the woman nodded briefly. She stepped back through the door into darkness, but in that darkness a shadow moved, and Joanna caught the gleam of pistol barrels, leveled at Antryg's heart.

After a long moment, the Prince began, "I need . . ." He stopped, standing close to Antryg, closer than Joanna would have found comfortable, the closeness of intimacy; but still he did not look at the wizard. It had undoubtedly been a long time, Joanna thought suddenly, since this dainty, evil little man had said, *I need* to anyone.

He swallowed hard and tried again. "Narwahl," he said quietly. His voice was very different now from the arrogant and perverted Prince who had held them at this mercy. Caris had said Skipfrag was the Regent's friend. There was a terrible tension in the Prince's words as he tried to speak calmly of that friend's death. "The neighbors heard a shot and then a shrieking like all the souls of the damned. They found . . ." He paused, unable to go on.

"I know what they found," Joanna said. "Broken and shattered glass. And blood all over everything—the floor, the walls, everywhere."

The Regent glanced to where she still sat in the carved ebony chair to which she had been tied. The corners of his mouth twitched. "Ah, yes. You were there, weren't you? At least, that's what Joris tells me the Church sasenna said." He took from one pocket a handkerchief—black, she noted. All his linen was black, an affectation that reminded her irresistably of a Hollywood pimp. With the care of one long used to working around makeup, he wiped his face, and she saw that his hand shook.

"I never knew he was associated with mages," he began again in a strained voice. "The Witchfinders said they found evil things and evidence of some horrible, angry spirit in his workroom. They asked me to order the house put under seal. I think they wanted to see who would come for them."

Joanna sniffed. "They would. All he was doing was experimenting with electricity. Peelbone would burn the inventor of the clock for daring to interfere with the Sole God's prerogative of determining time."

"Perhaps," Antryg said quietly. He took his spectacles from their ledge and seated himself carefully at the base of one of the pillars, wincing a little as he folded his long arms around his drawn-up knees. "But the fact remains that someone broke into his workroom. And I suspect, from what you two say, that it was someone who could summon and control elementals, give them body and form." He cocked his head up at the Regent. "Is that why you fear the Council?"

The Prince stood looking down at him for a moment, holding back that last surrender, that last admission. He drew a short, sharp breath that hissed through his nostrils and looked away. Joanna could see his mouth work for a moment. Then, as if he were aware of it, he pressed his hand to his lips, forcing it still. When he took his hand away, his fingers were shaking. "I don't know," he whispered wretchedly. "They are the ones who—who are supposed to have power. When the Bishop of Kymil said there was a plot and asked for my sanction to investigate it, I thought . . ." He took a deep breath, like a man fighting to steady himself against some terrible strain. "I do not know who it is I have to fear," he said at last. "I only know that, if you have been a prisoner these seven years, Antryg Windrose, it cannot be you."

Antryg said nothing, waiting in silence while the Prince considered what he could say. After a moment, Pharos went on, still in that hoarse, frightened whisper, "And you are a mage. It is why I ordered my men to bring you here when they caught you, instead of turning you back to the Witchfinders. Since Herthe told me you had been a prisoner in the Tower, unable to work magic, I knew that I had to find you. You are the only one I can speak to, the only one it is safe to speak to—if it *is* safe—of certain things."

The wizard's deep, beautiful voice was gentle and unalarming in the buried stillness of the firelit stone room. "What things?"

The Prince drew another deep breath and was quiet a moment, sorting his thoughts; even his restlessly twisting little hands grew still, clasped before him. "It was—balderdash," he said at last. "I was always told that. Magic. My father . . ." He swallowed. "He—he favored the wizards, but he kept them all at arm's distance. My tutor never approved. I thought his favor was excessive; certainly I never thought their powers were any more real than those cheapjack toadstone-peddlers or the granny-wives who claim they can put a bad word on someone's cow. They spoke of powers, but they never did anything at all. Even now, I don't know if I'm mad or sane, whether this is part of the old madness or some new twist."

Gently leading him, Antryg looked up at him and asked, "What?"

The Prince paced a few steps, then turned back again, some of the tension easing out of his body with a kind of hopeless inner surrender. When he spoke again, his voice was deliberately matter-of-fact. "About three months ago, I fell in love with a boy in the household of the Duke of Albrete—an enchanting youth, amber and alabaster, with skin so clear you could trace the path of a swallow of wine down his throat. Elfwith was his name—not that it matters, and I certainly didn't expect to remember it three months afterwards. I probably wouldn't, except for what happened to him." He stilled in his pacing and swallowed again, looking down at Antryg, who sat unmoving at the base of the pillar, the tawny light playing restlessly across his absurd, bespectacled face.

"He—died. I'd asked him to go up to my rooms and given orders for the guards in the secret staircase to let him pass—even the secret stair into the room is guarded. I was delayed by a matter of state—those wretched ambassadors from Senterwing about that brainless bitch I'm to marry. All very secret."

Antryg nodded. Joanna remembered, sometime on the carriage journey, Caris saying the wizard had read that marriage in a spread of cards. She felt very little surprise, even in the face of what she knew about the Prince's preferences, in hearing that it was true.

"Well, Elfwith came hurrying down to the guard on the secret stair, saying he thought there was someone in my rooms. They turned out and searched, they said—I heard all this later—but there was no sign of anyone having been there. So Elfwith went in to wait. And I found him, an hour and a half later, dying—dying horribly in my bed, his limbs covered with sores, eaten with them. If it was a sickness, it was nothing Narwahl had ever seen, but he claimed there was no poison that could do it, either. I swore him on his life to secrecy, because there was the boy's family to consider as well. Of course the bedding was all burned, but there was no other case of such a sickness ever reported anywhere, before or since. I know that, for Narwahl looked in every book and journal he possessed.

"Then—it might have been two weeks later—I was sleeping . . ."

"Alone?" Antryg inquired, and Pharos managed an ironic smirk.

"You don't think I ever let myself fall asleep in the presence of those stupid little creatures, do you? I send them away. Lately I've kept Kanner in my room when I sleep, though I didn't do so then. He's very loyal to me. He was sasennan until he lost his hearing through a fever. I know that, when sasenna become flawed, they're supposed to kill themselves, I suppose he's added the flaw of cowardice to that of deafness, but I've made it worth his while. I find having a deaf servant supremely useful. In any case, I woke up—I don't know why—it might have been a dream. I dream . . ."

He paused again, then visibly shied from the subject, like a nervous horse, and resumed his pacing. His gestures, repeated in vast, amorphous shadows on the wall at his back, moved as if they would shape the scene from air. "The bed curtains were open a little, and I could see part of the paneling of the wall by the light of the night lamp. There was a shadow on it, clearly thrown, but huge, distorted—the long robe of a mage. I saw him move his hand, doing something at the lamp table I thought. I cried out for the guards; but when they came in—nothing. There was no one there, nor was there a way he could have left; the corner he was in is near the outside wall, and there was no possibility of a secret passage, even if I had not had the room sounded a dozen times. I had the water in the pitcher that stood on that table given to one of the palace dogs. It seemed all right at the time, but the dog died four, five days later. Too long for poison, much too long. And yet . . ."

He pressed his hand to his mouth again, a nervous gesture, to still or to hide the unsteadiness of those too-full, painted lips. "I couldn't tell anyone after that, you see," he went on, a little thinly. "There was no proof. They would have mocked me if I'd said I thought it was magic, as they mocked me when . . ."

He caught himself up again, over some old memory, and went hastily on, "They would have said I was mad, as they did before. And I am mad. But not—not mad in that way. Not until now. Twice I've waked in the night and heard knocking somewhere in the room—it's vanished when I called the guards; and after the second time, I had Kanner in the room with me and at least one other guard. I don't even know whether I really heard it the second time or not—I was dreaming—I don't know."

He ran his hands through his barley-gold hair, twisting the careful furls awry; in the firelight, the muscles of his long, narrow jaw quivered with the violence of their compression.

"I fought against it for a long time," he said at length. "I did not believe in magic, but—I think someone is trying to kill me through its use. Is this possible?"

He turned back to look at Antryg, hungry desperation in his eyes.

After a long moment, the mage nodded. With a movement oddly graceful for one so gawky, he got to his feet, still steadying himself against the pillar, and put a gentling hand on the Prince's shoulder. "How long since the last attempt?"

"If it was an attempt," Pharos whispered. "It was only knocking. . . ."

"It was an attempt," Antryg said, and there was no doubt in his voice. "How long?"

"Two—three weeks. Shortly before—shortly before the Bishop of Kymil sent word that she had uncovered a plot of the Council of Mages against the Church and against the Realm. I issued jurisdiction for their arrest. Then, two days later, Narwahl . . ."

As if quieting the hysterics of a child, Antryg closed his

hands around the Prince's trembling fingers. It occurred to Joanna to wonder whether Pharos had seen that attic room, sprayed with fresh blood and glass.

"And you went to Kymil?" Antryg asked, and the Prince nodded. "To find out what Herthe knew?"

"Yes." The Prince nodded again, his voice a little stronger, a little steadier. "Herthe and her guards came and met me at the posthouse. She told me who you were. I knew then I had to find you, get to you before the Witchfinders did. I knew you were the only one who couldn't have done it, who couldn't possibly be in on it. She spoke of abominations in the land and said that it seemed likely you were coming to Angelshand. I made some excuse, turned back, and ordered my men to search for you, find you before the Church could have you killed. I thought you might have gone to Devilsgate, to take refuge with that stupid, saintly hypocrite Cerdic. . . ." A flash of vicious bitterness surfaced in his voice, like the glint of paranoia that suddenly gleamed in his narrowed eyes at the mention of his cousin's name. Antryg said nothing, and Joanna, who had been thoroughly charmed with the Regent's cousin, likewise refrained from adding her two cents to the conversation at this point.

After a moment, the madness faded from Pharos' eyes, and with it, his hard-held calm. He swallowed; his voice came out small and cracked with strain. "I came back here today. But it was as if—as if from the time I spoke to Herthe, the morning after I met you in the posthouse, I knew it was hopeless. It seemed to me then that I could see my whole future, and it was empty—that I was mad, like my father." He faltered, then went on, "And in time I would become an imbecile like him. Even though these things I feared had no existence, they would destroy me, and there was nothing to do, nowhere to come, except back here to my death. I tried having the Council mages imprisoned, but the Church has its mages, too. And there's still tonight to sleep through—"

His voice broke suddenly, as if weight had been put on a flawed beam; his breath hissed, and he stood for a moment, shivering in silence and, Joanna realized, shame at his fears.

Very gently, his hands still in the Prince's convulsive grip, Antryg said, "Here?"

When Pharos glanced sharply at him, Antryg went on, "I take it this is the dungeon under the original part of the old Summer Palace."

The Prince's lips moved in a quirk that might have been a smile; he glanced down at the big hands he still held and released them. As if aware of the wreck he'd made of his coiffure, he put up one gloved hand to straighten a snail-shell curl. "Yes. I've taken it over for my own. It's sufficiently isolated in the grounds to keep gossip mongers away when I want a little private sport."

"Is there anywhere else you could sleep?"

"Would it make a difference?"

"It might," Antryg said mildly. "If you were more superstitious, you'd probably have thought yourself of the possibility that there's a wizard's mark in your rooms."

There were seven of them.

Wearing a ruffled shirt and breeches fetched by Joris from the wardrobes of the Prince's pages ("I'm tired of walking around looking like I've just escaped from the cover of a historical romance!") Joanna followed Antryg and the Prince up several flights of stairs, passing from the ancient stonework of the dungeons to the renovated rococo grace of the Prince's palace above. It was now quite dark outside, but the Prince's private apartments blazed with the light of a thousand candles and lamps; as they moved from room to brilliantly lit room, followed by Joris, Kanner, and two other guards, it occurred to Joanna that the Regent was probably terrified of the dark.

The warm brilliance of the candles, so different from the hard and prosaic electricity Joanna had grown up with, lent a curiously dreamlike air to those rooms, with their shell-shaped curlicues of gold and scarlet, their delicate furniture, and their sinuous marbles. In his shabby black coat, spectacles, and quizzing glass, Antryg moved through them like some daft Victorian ghost hunter, tapping at the chinoiscrie of the panels and calling the marks, one by one, to faint and glowing life.

One mark, on the ancient stonework behind the paneling itself, was extremely old, readable only when Antryg pressed his hands to the painted wood. Another made him smile. "I wonder what the mage Nyellin was doing here? It's six hundred years old—nothing to do with you, Pharos—but she did have rather a reputation as a meddler herself."

His hand brushed the scarlet-lacquered wood between the bedroom windows. Under his fingers, another mark appeared, only to be seen from the corner of the eye—a chance glimmer of candlelight, floating, it seemed, above or below the actual surface of the panel, as if someone had scribbled with a finger on the air in light.

Joanna remembered, with an uneasy chill, the sign on the wall of the main computer room at San Serano, seen past the dark shadow of the strangler's shoulder; she remembered also the darkness of Gary's upstairs room and the red reflection of computer lights off Antryg's spectacles as he'd brushed his hand, just so, along the wall by the door.

I can't tell you the truth and I don't wish to lie to you. . . .

You are in this world under my protection. . . .

"A wizard's mark will call him to it," Antryg explained over his shoulder to the Prince, who followed, cautious as if the marks themselves could kill. "He can find it, wherever he is, and go to it. If the mark is strong enough, he can use it to influence things near it, even when he is not present, sometimes even work certain spells through it without being there."

He stood for a long time, staring at the paneling between the windows, where the mark had glimmered so briefly to life. Then he sighed and shut his eyes.

The Prince glanced nervously over his shoulder. "What is it?"

Antryg turned away and touched briefly the elaborate marquetry dressing table that stood beneath the mark. A branch of candles in the twining shapes of naked goddesses stood on it and beside them a pitcher of creamy, rose-colored porcelain, half-filled with water. "The mark is less than two months old," he said quietly. He looked suddenly very tired, his mouth taut and a little white, as if he had drunk some bitter and poisoned brew. "This one—" He crossed to the door of a dressing room and brushed a faint, brief shimmer of sign from its topmost panel, "—about ten years. Both by the same wizard."

"Who?" demanded the Prince, and Antryg shook his head.

"The second mark would reinforce the influence of the first," he went on, staring up at the place where the mark on the door had been. "But ten years ago . . ." He paused, his eyebrows drawn together over the absurd beak of his nose. "Ten years . . ."

"What is it?"

Antryg looked back at the Prince and shook his head. "I don't know," he said. "These have always been your rooms?"

"Yes. Since first I was given my own establishment when I was eighteen. I am thirty-five now and I assure you, my lord wizard, that no mage has been in here to make that first mark since they have been mine."

"Knowing how you've kept yourself guarded, I'd say I believed you," Antryg said, "except, of course, that one obviously was."

"They were always about the Court, of course," Pharos said. "My father..."

He hesitated.

"Exactly," Antryg said quietly. "Your father. And Cerdic later. I know your father had a good deal to do with Salteris, as Head of the Council." Listening, Joanna wondered if she detected the faintest of flaws in Antryg's voice when he spoke the Archmage's name. "Do you know who else?"

The little man shook his head. "I didn't want to know. I considered it—" He licked his lips, shying again from the subject, and then simply concluded, "I didn't want to know."

Antryg was silent for a long time, his arms folded, his head down, and his strange, wide, light-gray eyes distant with thought. From somewhere, Joanna heard a clock speak eleven silvery chimes and felt all the deathly weariness of the day closing in on her—flight, fear, and sudden, starving hunger.

Then the wizard sighed and pushed up his spectacles to rub his eyes. "It's very late now," he said, "and Joanna and I both are very tired. At least I am and, if she isn't, I suggest you hire her as your bodyguard. Unless you're going to lock us away for good, Pharos, there are two things that I'd like to ask of you in the morning. Three things, actually, counting breakfast. Can your cook make muffins?"

It was the first time Joanna had seen Prince Pharos laugh, the pale, pretty face and sinful eyes screwing up in genuine amusement. "My dearest Antryg," he said, laying what Joanna privately suspected of being an overly friendly hand on the Wizard's arm, "if the muffins are not to your satisfaction, I give you full permission to flog the cook. He won't quit, I assure you; he'd never relinquish his position as *my* cook. It's far more than his reputation would be worth."

"Excellent." Antryg smiled and pushed his spectacles up on the bridge of his nose with one bony forefinger. "The second is that I'd like you to send for the contents of Narwahl Skipfrag's laboratory, and the third . . . I'd like to look at your father's rooms."

"By the way," said Joanna quietly, "I never had a chance to say thank you."

Antryg, sitting in the dark window embrasure of the room the Prince had given him, up under the eaves of the Summer Palace's mansard roof, looked around at her and smiled. A flicker of bluish light appeared in the air of the room between him and the door where she stood; it floated, like a negligent firefly, over to the exquisite ormolu table in the room's center and came to rest on the wick of one of the unlit candles there. His voice was deep in the gloom. "I ought to say it was my pleasure, but diving under that portcullis—I can only think of two times I've been that frightened in my life. It is my pleasure," he added, "that we're both alive."

"I wouldn't say pleasure so much as stunned surprise." She crossed the room to him, and he drew up his feet on the window seat to make room for her. Through the open casement, she could smell the smoke from the lamps and torches of the guards in the courtyard three storeys below and, when the wind shifted, the thick green smells of the palace park. "Decent of the Prince to send us up supper."

"Considering what it took to get lobster patties at this hour," Antryg agreed. "No matter what the muffins are like for breakfast, I shall have to lie and say I like them. Such a cook ought never to be flogged more often than is necessary, as the Prince says, to keep him smart."

Joanna chuckled. "Not to mention the clothes," she

added, touching the high, pleated collar of the pageboy's shirt she wore. "He sent me up a gown for tomorrow. I'm wondering where the hell he got it."

"Possibly one of his boyfriends . . ."

She poked him reprovingly in the knee with her foot and laughed. "*Is* one of the mages trying to kill him?"

"Oh, yes."

"To put Cerdic on the throne?"

"If I were the sort of mage who routinely meddled in human affairs," the wizard said gravely, "it's what I'd do."

She remembered Cerdic's enthusiastic and unquestioning welcome of Antryg because he was a mage and the blind acceptance of the inherent rightness of wizards, started to speak, then was silent. For a moment, she contemplated that long, peculiar profile in the bluish glow of the witchlight, noticing how the reflections of the fires in the courtyard below touched hard little glimmers in the steel of his spectacle frames and the dreamy grayness of his eyes. He looked a little better than he had, less strained and gray, but the nervous energy that had gotten him through the last several hours was fading, even as it was for her. He looked tired and very vulnerable, sitting with his knees drawn up in the window seat, and she had to resist an overwhelming impulse to put out her hand and touch his arm.

Slowly, she said, "Are we dealing with several problems here or just one? The fading and the abominations—but you said you were coming to talk to some member of the Council? and there's the Archmage. . . . And poor Caris—whatever's happened to him?"

A smile tugged briefly at Antryg's lips in the wan lucence of the witchlight. "I imagine poor Caris is still waiting for me outside a vacant building on the south side of the river. He's very patient when he's on a trail."

"One of these days," Joanna said severely, "Caris is

going to murder you—and not because of his grandfather, either."

"Of course," Antryg said. "That's been the—" He stopped himself as Joanna's eyebrows came together, then went on quickly, "He's come very close to it twice. As for what we're dealing with here . . ." He shook his head. "There seem to be a lot of events unrelated to one another, except by juxtaposition in time—Narwahl's death, your kidnapping, the Prince's marriage . . ."

"Or things that happened twenty-five years ago," she said, remembering the old woman in the prison. *At his tricks again*, that one had said, rocking back and forth, and for the dozenth time Joanna found herself reminded that what Suraklin had known, Antryg undoubtedly knew. There was no way he could have murdered Narwahl—on the night of the physician's death, as far as Joanna could calculate, they had all been sleeping in the hayloft of some posting inn on the Kymil road. . . . Or could he?

She wondered suddenly whether an examination would reveal wizards' marks in that stuffy, blood-smelling room.

She was aware that Antryg had fallen silent and was looking at her with wary uncertainty in his eyes.

"How did you know I was there, by the way? Thinking about it, I was desperately glad to see you, but I don't think I was surprised; and now I realize I should have been."

"Not really." His earring winked in the tangled mane of his hair as he turned his head. "I was looking for mages, remember. Considering the current situation, the logical place to look was St. Cyr. I was loitering around inconspicuously outside when they brought you in. I assume Caris sent you to Narwahl's."

"How did . . . ?" she began, and then remembered saying to the Prince that she knew what the neighbors had found in that hideous upper room.

"Will that screw you up?" she asked after a moment.

"All the mages getting away from St. Cyr—or did they all get away?"

He shook his head. "I imagine most of them did. I've spoken to Pharos about releasing the others. There will be time enough to find them and to speak to them, after I've seen the Emperor's rooms."

"Will having them loose increase your danger?" she asked, and he shook his head absently. "Then you know which one to be afraid of?"

He looked quickly at her, his eyes suddenly wide in the dim gleam from the court below, as if he had suddenly seen that he'd walked into a trap. But it wasn't a trap, she thought, baffled; she had sensed him holding her at arm's length, picking his way carefully over conversationally shifty ground. He was braced for something, she knew, but she only asked, "Why are you afraid of me?"

He started to say something, then checked himself; for some moments, the little room under the eaves was quiet, save for the noises that drifted up from the court below through the opened casements and the faroff creak of some servant's foot elsewhere in the palace. Then he changed his mind and said, "Like the Prince, I'm afraid of a good many things. I've spent most of my life terrified of a man who's been dead for years."

He got to his feet and helped her to hers. The vagrant foxfire drifted after them as he led her to the door. She paused in its darkness, looking up at him, knowing he was evading her and coming up with an uncomfortable number of reasons why. But none of them accounted for the care he'd taken of her, none of them accounted for risking his life that afternoon to save her from the Inquisition.

She said, "I get the feeling that there's a pattern here somewhere—as you said, some connection between the fading and the abominations and between Narwahl's death and the Archmage disappearing and my being kidnapped. It's all subroutines of a program I can't see. I understand the kind of thing you hope to learn from seeing Narwahl's experiments—though they looked to me like perfectly straightforward let's-make-electricity stuff—but what do you hope to learn from seeing the Emperor's rooms?"

He shook his head. "Confirmation, perhaps, of a theory I have." He leaned against the doorframe, the will-o'-the-wisp light edging hair and spectacles and the curlicue line of shirt-ruffles with their snagged tangle of quizzing glass and beads. "And maybe the answer to something that's puzzling me very much."

She didn't really expect an answer, but asked, "What?"

After a long moment's hesitation, Antryg seemed to come to some decision within himself. "Why they would send him mad, instead of killing him."

At two in the morning the terrible, draining deadness began again and tortured Joanna's exhausted dreams with visions of old Minhyrdin until dawn.

CHAPTER XVI

"THEY SAID IT WAS A JUDGMENT, YOU KNOW." THE PRINCE Regent's pale, shifty eyes flicked from the parklike vistas of topiaried garden visible to both sides of the open coach back to the man and woman opposite him on the white velvet carriage seat. The deadness that had lasted until almost dawn had left its marks on him, adding to the keyed-up, exhausted nervousness of the previous night. His full-lipped red mouth twitched as he explained, "for his sympathy to the mages."

"I wouldn't say sympathy was your father's outstanding characteristic at my trial," Antryg mused. "Hanged, drawn, sliced, and broken—it was *years* before I could contemplate chicken marinara, not that I was given the chance to, mind you. But then, he never did like me. How did it happen?"

Pharos shook his head. "Would to God we knew," he said, quite simply. "He woke that way one morning four years ago. He . . ." He swallowed, wiped his moist hands on a black silk handkerchief, and tucked it back up among the sable festoons of his sleeve lace. "We didn't know whether it would go as suddenly as it had come—we still don't, but back then we hoped more than we do now. He used to try and talk then, or at least it looked like talking. In the first day or so, I sometimes thought he knew me. Now..." He looked away again, over the sun-splashed morning beauty of those manicured lawns and carefully pruned groves. Then his glance, half-embarrassed and half-warning, returned unwillingly to Joanna. "When you see him," he said carefully, "you must remember that he is a very sick man."

Joanna guessed what he meant and suppressed a qualm of apprehensive disgust. It interested her that he would feel enough concern for his father—who couldn't possibly have cared one way or the other—to warn her against showing repugnance. And afraid as she had once been of him, she now felt oddly sorry for this bejeweled little pervert.

Antryg asked, "Who were the mages who were habitually admitted to his rooms? Who would have had access to his bedroom, for instance?"

"No one," Pharos said promptly. "Well, they might have entered there from the rest of the suite. Rosamund Kentacre—her father dragged her there for him to convince her not to take the Council vows. Thirle, I believe..."

"Minhyrdin?"

Pharos sniffed. "That senile crone? My father's interests were in magic, not particularly in those who worked it or who were at one time able to work it. The members of the Council were admitted—Salteris, of course, Lady Rosamund, Nandiharrow, Idrix of Thray, and Whitwell Simm, and you."

"Not me," Antryg said. "Well, once, after I'd been elected to the Council, I had to be presented formally to him. But as I said, he never liked me." He frowned a little.

"During the Mellidane Revolts, I had the impression I was not precisely entrapped, but certainly maneuvered. He *can't* have been that ignorant of what was going on. But I never understood why. From my little acquaintance with him, he was perfectly capable of it, of course. . . ."

"Did you know him before . . . ?" began Pharos, then stopped himself. "No, you couldn't. You were Suraklin's student. Perhaps that was the reason." The dappling sunlight passed like a school of shining fish over his bright hair as the carriage moved through a grove of maples whose leaves were already edging with blood-red autumn flame. It was difficult to believe that beyond the park walls in three directions stretched the sprawling gray city, the dingy factories, and the crowded wharves of Angelshand.

The strain and tiredness were apparent in the Prince's voice as well as his face. Joanna heard the harsh, shaky shrillness of last night still there, held rigidly in check, as it had been, she thought, for weeks—perhaps for years. After a moment, he went on, "He never would have handed down a judgment like that before—before he rode with the Archmage to Kymil, you know. He—changed afterwards."

"If he saw anything of Suraklin's Citadel," Antryg murmured, "it would be surprising if he hadn't."

"No." The Prince's voice sank. "Sometimes he spoke of it—of the things Suraklin kept in darkness, things that he bred or called up, things that he fed on the blood from his own veins. . . ."

Beside her, Joanna felt Antryg flinch at some memory, but he said nothing. Back in Kymil, she'd noticed the old, tiny scars that marked the veins of his arms like a junkie's tracks.

"But I hated him for it," Pharos continued, "as much as I had loved him before. And I did love him. It's strange to say, but since he has—since he has become an imbecile, oddly enough, I love him now." He swallowed and passed his hand over his mouth, a nervous gesture. He spoke from behind the white, delicate fingers with their bitten nails, as if from behind a barrier. "They said of Suraklin that he had a terrible, almost unbelievable influence over the minds of all who had to do with him. They said he could break anyone's mind to his bidding, if given his chance. . . . But looking back, I realize it was only the things that he'd seen . . ."

His voice faltered. Feeling Antryg's eyes on her, Joanna turned her head and caught again the wariness and fear that lurked in the water-gray depths. After a moment, Pharos went on, his words coming rapidly to cover old guilts. "But I was only a child and a fanciful one—I understand that now. It must have been only that I was ten . . ."

"You were ten?" Joanna had been watching Pharos, but the note in Antryg's voice drew her eyes, as if he had shouted the words instead of whispering them almost inaudibly. There was shock on his face, as if he had been physically struck—shock and a terrible intentness that Joanna was at a loss to understand.

Pharos nodded, too sunk in private nightmares to notice the wizard's reaction to his words, the presence of the coachman on the box, Kanner on the footman's stand, the scrunch of the horses' hooves and the carriage wheels on the gravel path, or Joanna. Hands pressed to his mouth, he stared out ahead of him with the glittering gaze of madness.

"What happened?" Antryg whispered, leaning gently forward to take the Prince's hands. He drew them down, denying Pharos that hiding place, and asked again, "What was it that happened twenty-five years ago when you were ten?"

"Nothing." The Prince shut his eyes, squeezing the painted lids together like a child hoping desperately to deny the reality of what he was helpless to fight. "That's it— nothing happened."

"Except that you went mad."

"I was a child." The words came out as if strained by main force from a throat so constricted it barely passed the air of life to his lungs. "There was nothing I could do, no one even that I could tell. I used to dream about him, after he came back, and in my dreams . . ." He broke off again, his hands trembling violently in Antryg's sure, light grip. The mage said nothing, but his wide eyes were filled with horror, grief, and enlightenment—not for the Prince's sake, but as if, looking into the younger man's madness, he had seen the terrifying reflection of his own.

Blurtingly, the Prince sobbed, "In my dreams he was not my father!" Tears tracked down through the heavy paste of makeup; he wrenched his hands from Antryg's and fumbled for his handkerchief again, his body racked by tremors of grief and horror he could not stop. "I was only ten," he repeated, "and there was no one I could tell; they wouldn't believe me. But for years, I believed that the wizards had somehow stolen my father and put someone else in his place. And afterwards, when I realized it couldn't possibly be true—when I realized it was all charlatanry and faking—I hated them for that! God, how I hated them!"

Bitterness scorched his voice. As if something had broken in him, and he could not stop, he continued to sob, thrusting Joanna's comforting hand roughly away and huddling in his corner of the carriage, fighting alone for control over himself, as he had always fought alone. Antryg, perhaps understanding that the Prince would take comfort from a man that could not be taken from a woman, moved over beside the Regent and put his hands on those quivering black satin shoulders; though the touch seemed to calm the Prince, the tears would not stop flowing—a reservoir of them, damned for years.

As for Antryg, his face was that of a man who has

spoken a spell-word in jest and seen hell open before his eyes.

"He changed," the Prince whispered wretchedly. "How could I ever trust? There were other things to it. . . ."

"I'm sure there were," Antryg murmured, as if he spoke to himself of some hideous vision that only he could see.

"But that was the source of it. I'd loved my father, and they took that from me forever. In dreams . . ." With a final sob, the Regent sat up and made a clumsy effort to mop his face. "Curse it, there's the Palace."

With some startlement, Joanna saw that they had almost reached the gilt-tipped gates of the Imperial Palace's marble forecourt. His hands shaking, Pharos wiped with his black silk handerchief at his smeared cheeks. "I must look like some sniveling girl."

Antryg managed to grin, the enlightenment and the horror alike gone from his eyes, except for their shadow lurking somewhere far down in the water-gray depths. "I'm sure your father won't care."

From the short flight of marble steps, guards in white and gold were descending to meet the carriage as the shadows of the Palace's vast wings enfolded them. Rows of eastward-facing windows blazed with the reflected sun, and the gilded spines of the roofs sparkled like a frieze of fire.

The bitter rictus of a smile pulled the Prince's mouth, "No—not that he cares about anything. But . . ." The expression softened. Joanna saw that the Regent had spoken the truth; whatever hatred and fear he had borne his father through his adolescence and early manhood, the love of his childhood had been able to reassert itself since their roles had been reversed, since he had now become the stronger, and since his father was dependent upon him for care.

"And if any of the servants comments," Antryg added cheerily, as the footmen stepped forward in matched unison to let down the carriage step, "you can have him flogged."

The Prince shot him a devil's grin as they descended.

"Ah, you know how to gladden a man's heart," he retorted. Joanna followed them, wizard and prince, up the palace steps.

From what he had said last night, Joanna had expected Antryg to make a careful investigation of the Emperor's rooms; but either he had misled her or something had caused him to change his mind. The Emperor Hieraldus occupied a suite of rooms on the third floor of the north wing, reached by a small stairway from the State Rooms on the second. "One of my less creditable ancestors furnished them to house his mistress," the Regent explained sotto voce as he opened a painted panel in the gilded oak wainscoting by the fireplace of what was referred to as the Emperor's withdrawing room—a chamber the size of some barns Joanna had slept in during the course of the last two weeks. "He had the stair built—it's overlooked by the guard outside the door there. Father and Grandfather both used the rooms as their private living quarters, since they're more comfortable than the State Rooms."

Antryg looked around the huge withdrawing room, with its stately dark furniture and elaborate tapestries. "In the wintertime, I should imagine it would be difficult to find anything *less* comfortable. Your father always lived upstairs, then?"

The Prince nodded. Since his breakdown in the carriage, much of his suave deadliness had deserted him; Joanna, though she knew he was perverted, mad, and cruel—though the bruises of his whip had not yet faded from Antryg's face—found herself almost liking as well as pitying him. As she followed mage and Regent up the narrow stair, holding up the inevitable voluminous ecru petticoats, she shook her head at herself. *First you fall in love with Antryg,* she thought, *and now you like the Regent. I see you're batting a thousand on this trip.*

"He is looked after constantly," she heard Pharos say as

he turned the gold knob of the door at the top of the flight. It was typical of the Palace, Joanna thought, that even the doorknob was a minor work of art, with gilded scrollwork and a tiny cloisonné painting of mythical gods disporting themselves among giggling nymphs. "None of his attendants have reported anything amiss."

"No," Antryg said, almost absently. "No, they wouldn't."

His examination of the rooms was almost cursory. Chamber after delicate chamber was crammed with all the beautiful things a man with unlimited wealth and good taste could accumulate, from delicate clocks to exquisite paintings, oppressive with the trapped, unventilated heat of early autumn, and pervaded with the sick, musty odor of a body that had ceased to look after itself.

The Emperor himself, led out by a careful and cheery attendant, did not shock Joanna nearly so much as she had been afraid he would. He was only a man of about her father's age, his scanty white hair clean and combed, his tidy clothes, apart from fresh food smears down his plain, dark waistcoat, speaking worlds of diligent and never-ending care on the part of his guardians. His mouth hung slightly open, and he stared straight ahead of him with blank eyes that barely tracked movement, but Joanna, who usually felt unease bordering on revulsion in the presence of the crippled or retarded, was a little surprised to find in herself nothing but an overwhelming sense of pity.

"Were the rooms marked?" she asked as they descended the steps once more, with courtiers bowing to them when they passed through the State Rooms and headed once more toward the courtyard where the carriage waited.

Antryg glanced at her, as if startled from a reverie of his own. "Oh, yes."

"Did it confirm your hunch?"

He hesitated, and she sensed he was trying to decide whether to tell the truth or to formulate some other evasion, and suppressed a strong desire to shake him. At length he said, rather carefully, "No, it didn't. I'd thought that the rooms would have been marked to—to do that to him by means of a spell. I don't think that was the case."

"Then what did happen?"

With his usual care, he helped her up into the carriage again and swung up to settle himself beside her; the Prince, looking rather pensive, was handed in by his footmen, and the carriage started off again. "I'm not sure," Antryg replied, a trifle too airily.

"Look," Joanna began, exasperated, but Pharos cut her off.

"Is he in danger?"

"I don't think so," Antryg said. "Not as long as you're alive, at any rate. Whoever wants you out of the way doesn't want to contest the issue of the succession yet. The Regency will do."

"Of course," Pharos said thinly. "There would be civil war before the nobles would assent to dear Cousin Cerdic being crowned, unless he had a nice, long Regency to get them used to the idea. I take it that is the plot?"

"Something of the kind, yes." Antryg's long fingers steepled over his chest. He had, she noticed, acquired a chain of sapphires and gold, a gift from the Prince that stood out like Fabergé work against dime store finery among his other tawdry necklaces. His voice was light, but his eyes, Joanna saw, were still deeply troubled, as if the information the Prince had supplied him, which had meant so little to her, had given him an answer to questions he did not want to understand. Typically, he pursued another subject. "Who knew of your marriage?"

Pharos sniffed. "Few enough."

"Did Narwahl?"

"He was my physician." The blue eyes narrowed within their discolored sockets. "Of course he knew. You're not saying it was because of that knowledge that—that he was killed?"

Antryg was silent for a moment, studying the prince's face, as if calculating what would be best to say. Then he said gently, "I doubt it. I think he was killed because of what he was doing in his experiments. The intruder was standing beside his worktable when Narwahl surprised him. . . ."

Pharos, who had been looking out across the park toward a miniature pavilion beside a toy lake, whirled with the suddenness of a mad dog, suspicion and rage blazing in his eyes. Before he could speak, Joanna, familiar by now with Antryg's Holmesian reasoning, said hastily, "He'd have to have been. The pistol ball was lodged in the wall just above the worktable."

"Of course," Antryg said, a little surprised the point would need further elucidation and blithely oblivious to how close he'd come to a quick trip back to St. Cyr. "At fifteen feet in the dark, Narwahl's shot could have gone wide, even if he wasn't shooting at a mage—and even in broad daylight at half the distance, the mageborn are notoriously hard to hit."

"So he could have told any one of the mages about the marriage," Pharos said, after a moment, his mouth suddenly wry with distaste. A mad flicker of suspicion danced like flame in the back of his eyes for a moment, and he added, "He could have been in a string with them too, couldn't he? All of them—Cerdic, the Council. . . ."

"In that case, it's hardly likely they'd have killed him."

The carriage drew to a stop before the old Summer Palace, on the far side of the grounds from the vast Imperial edifice. In the daylight, Joanna could see no sign of its greater age, except perhaps in the somewhat irregular lines of its facade. Like the greater Imperial Palace, this smaller building was faced with mellow, red-gold stone and trimmed with white marble. The statues of its niches were made of several particolored stones which reflected the Regent's more outré tastes.

Only inside, as they left the classical symmetry of the entrance rooms, did the building's age become evident. Though no architect, Joanna sensed that the lower ceilings and rambling, irregular layout of the inner rooms bespoke tastes less self-consciously elegant than those which had renovated the older palace in the classical style. As they moved down a long, narrow gallery, her eye was arrested by an occasional pointed arch or deeply coffered ceiling.

They ascended two or three steps to another hall and from there climbed an old-fashioned, enclosed staircase to the attics in the original wing of the building. "My men brought Narwahl's equipment here, just as it was," the Prince said as they paused before a thick nine-panel door into one of the attic rooms. "I also obtained your reticule, my dear Joanna—though the Witchfinder wasn't pleased to give it up. It contained devilish things, he said."

"Floppy disks?" Joanna asked, puzzled at this construction of the diabolical.

"To the pure, all things are pure," Antryg remarked, in Magister Magus' best soothsayer voice, "and to the unimaginative, all things are devilish."

The Regent sniffed. "Evidently most of the wizards in Peelbone's custody escaped in the confusion you caused. He suspects deep plots."

Antryg's hand moved for the door handle, and the Prince's small, white fingers touched his frayed sleeve ruffle. The blue eyes gleamed strangely in the gray-white light of the outer attic's small, round windows.

"And so help me, if by some chance he is right," Pharos added softly, "you will long for the death my father ordered for you as a man in the desert longs for water. Do you understand?"

Antryg was silent for a moment, like a man standing with one foot in a trap not yet sprung. Afraid of the

Prince's suspicions? wondered Joanna, prey to the now—
familiar sensation of being torn between her affection for
him and her better judgment. Or of something else?

In the end he said nothing, but silently turned, opened
the door, and ducked under its low lintel to enter the attic
beyond.

Dust sparkled faintly in the still air of that long, low-
ceilinged room. The place reminded Joanna uncomfortably
of the other attic from which they had taken these things,
with ceiling and walls splattered with their creator's blood.
This room was over twice as long, its far end heaped up
with a vast tangle of heavy furniture in dark wood, with
closed chests and occasional bolts of thick cloth whose nap
and weave were unsuited to the stiff lines of current fashion. The inner walls and ceiling were plastered coarsely;
the outer one, in which the three square, high windows
were set, was the raw stone of the old Summer Palace.
Against this wall stood a table, jammed with the gleaming,
Frankensteinian coils of Narwahl's experiments, the archaic workmanship of the components making wonderful
the prosaic collection of resistors and connectors. On one
corner, her purse lay like a dead and lumpy dog.

Walking over to the table, Joanna began to check the
equipment over. It was, as far as she could tell, as it had
been in Narwahl's laboratory. She traced the leads and
grounding wires, set up the tall sparking rods and the
hand-crank generator. Amid the chaos, the queer, shining
sphere that had caught her attention before seemed to
gleam with a baleful half-luminescence that made her uneasy.

Beside her, she was aware of Antryg's silence. She
glanced back and saw that his eyes had been drawn to the
sphere; there was recognition in them and an uncomfortable enlightenment, but no surprise.

"What is it?" She pushed aside her pink silk sleeve

flounce, whose laces had become entangled in a switch. "All the rest of this I recognize. . . ."

"Do you?"

She nodded. "My whole world runs on electricity." Her fingers traced the sinuous glass curve of a Volta pistol and brushed the awkward brass vacuum pump, but she found herself shying from the evil refulgence of that quicksilver sphere. "Hardware was never my field, but I know enough about it not to electrocute myself changing the chips on a breadboard—and Gary *is* a hardware man. So I know what Narwahl was doing. But that—that thing . . ."

As with her bizarre depressions, before she had realized they were something thrust upon her by an outside force, she found herself unwilling to speak of the loathing she felt for it. *What has no name isn't real,* she thought. She looked for confirmation of her repulsion in the wizard's eyes.

"Yes," Antryg said softly. He pushed up his spectacles and came forward to where she stood beside the table. "Yes, it is evil. An implement of forbidden magic. Making such spheres is forbidden; passing on to others the knowledge of their making is punishable by the Council by death."

"Why?" Even as she asked, she wondered why she wasn't startled to hear it.

"It is called a teles." Antryg's long, light fingers brushed the gleaming surface of the ball. "They have many uses. Suraklin used them. . . ." He hesitated on his ancient master's name, and an expression flickered through his eyes of some old horror, as if he had unexpectedly touched an unhealed wound in his mind. He recovered quickly and went on, "Suraklin linked them into the energy-lines and used them to extend his power over territory beyond his line of sight. He could control . . ." He hesitated again, frowning, and then glanced at the prince who stood in silence, framed in the attic doorway. Kanner, as always, loomed like a crimson shadow in the half-light of the hall beyond. "By the way, Pharos, what is the longitudinal coordinate of the palace?"

"What?" The Prince stared at him as if he had taken leave of his senses—which, of course, Joanna thought with irrelevant frivolity, he had, but that had been a long time ago.

"The longitudinal coordinate of the palace. Because, if I recall correctly, the energy-line marked by the Devil's Road runs through Angelshand, with a crossing-node of the Kymil line at the old stone circle on Tilrattin Island up the river. Suraklin . . . " He fell silent again, his hand resting on the side of the silvery teles ball. The high, sharp sunlight glinted on the fractured lense of his spectacles and touched Joanna's fingers on the table without warmth.

"Suraklin," Pharos echoed. "Always, we return to the Dark Mage."

Antryg's eyes flicked back to the prince. In them she saw again that braced look, as if he knew he walked among his foes. With a forced lightness he said, "Well, Suraklin wasn't the only one who knew how to make them, of course."

"Presumably," Pharos said softly, "he taught you."

"Oh, yes," Antryg agreed equably. "But it's a tedious and exhausting process. One's laid up for weeks afterward. Suraklin mostly used old ones that others had made centuries before. This one's very old." Joanna shivered as he picked it up, handling it with the tips of his fingers. "Suraklin had some that were thousands of years old and that had been absorbing power from the mages who touched them until they almost had voices of their own. No one really understands them well. Suraklin certainly didn't. But then, he used a lot of things he didn't understand properly. It was," he added, with a sudden hardness in his voice, "one of the things which made him so dangerous."

Pharos' voice was suspicious. "But how did Narwahl

come to have one? My father . . ." He stammered on the words lightly. "They should have been destroyed when Suraklin's power was broken."

"Indubitably." In a billow of coat skirts Antryg turned with swift, sudden lightness and hurled the teles at the stone wall like a volleyball center spiking down over the net. Joanna flinched with the involuntary reaction as one flinches in the quarter-second between the dropping of a light bulb and its explosion on a concrete floor, but the teles did not break. It hit the stone with a queer, terrible ringing noise and bounced sharply back into Antryg's hands. The ringing seemed to vibrate horribly on in Joanna's skull. "If you can figure out a way to destroy a teles, the Council will be delighted to hear about it. And in any case, this one may not have been one of Suraklin's. My guess is that Narwahl got it from Salteris. According to Caris, they were friends. Obviously, if Narwahl told Salteris enough for him to use electricity against the abomination at Kymil, Narwahl was using Salteris' help and advice for—what?"

"Experiments with the effects of electricity on magic?" Joanna guessed. She touched the concave metal bed in which the teles had rested. Copper wires led out of it, their ends twisted, showing they had been joined to other leads. *"Does* electricity have an effect on magic?"

"I haven't the faintest idea." Antryg set the teles back in its bed and looked over the tangle of wires and resistors with interested eyes. "I shouldn't think so. I've worked magic during lightning storms; and, according to the scientific journals I've read, not only is lightning electricity, but the air is charged with it at such times." He tracked a pair of wires to the generator and experimentally turned the crank.

"Hold on," Joanna said. "That's not connected to anything yet." She found the leads to the sparking rods and twisted the wires in pairs. Pharos, who had remained warily in the doorway, stepped forward, but drew back again as Antryg started turning the small generator crank. She saw the fear and suspicion on the Regent's face, as thin trails of purplish lightning began to crawl up the rods, and said, "It isn't magic, your Grace. If I turned the crank, or if you did, it would act the same. Here." She pushed up her sleeve flounces and took over in mid-turn from Antryg, feeling the stiffness of the crank as more and more power built up. Ghostly in the diffuse sunlight of the attic, the lightning continued to spark. "Don't touch it," she added quickly, as Antryg advanced a cautious finger towards the rods. "You'll get a hell of a shock."

She let the crank go. The iron-wrapped wheel whirled itself to a halt.

"So what was he trying to do?" Pharos advanced warily into the room once more. "Use electricity in some way to contain magic or protect against it? Make a shield of this tame lightning through which magic could not pass?"

Antryg, his hands in his jeans pockets, shook his head. "Salteris would have been the first one to tell him it wouldn't work as a protection," he said. "In fact, if you stood in a field like that and I was a mage who wished you dead, Pharos, it would be the simplest thing in the world to turn that tame lightning inward on you. Joanna . . ."

She paused in the act of tracking the compression on the vacuum-pump.

"What does it look as if he was doing?"

She shook her head, puzzled. "I don't know, but it sure as hell appears that he was running electricity either into or out of the teles. Look." She held up the wires from the teles' dish. "That means the teles is either conductive or is itself the source of electricity. Is it?"

"Not that I've ever heard," Antryg said, studying the wires emerging from the generator, then looking thoughtfully back at the teles.

Her fingers shrinking a little from touching the thing,

Joanna lifted the teles from its metal bed. Aside from feeling slick and queerly cold, there was nothing untoward about it. She set it aside and examined the connections. "That's funny. The ground wire here's a closed loop—as if it was grounding into itself." Frowning, she replaced the ball, then untwisted the generator wires from the sparking rods and connected the teles to the rods.

Not much to her surprise, nothing happened.

"Closed system," she said simply. "Read only. Nothing going in, so nothing's coming out. Electricity isn't created out of nothing—all power has to come from somewhere."

"A sound metaphysical and magical surmise as well," Antryg agreed quietly. "But on the other hand . . ." He reached forward and brushed his fingers along the oily-looking, slightly phosphorescent surface of the ball.

Joanna felt it as clearly as a sudden drop in temperature —like the heroine of *The Wizard of Oz*, as if she had wakened after the magic and color into a gray world of black-and-white. She felt sick and utterly weary, uncaring about what they were doing, hating Antryg for his lies to her, for his evasions, and for what he had done to her. He had brought her here and taken advantage of her dependence on him. He would keep her there, stranded in this filthy, dreary world in which she had no place. . . .

The rods began to spark. Lightning crawled up them, faster and stronger than before, bright enough to illuminate Antryg's strange, angular face as he stood looking down on them, his earrings flashing like diamonds in the suddenly sickened light of the gray sun.

"Stop it!" Joanna said, suddenly furious at him for doing this to her to satisfy some stupid academic curiosity of his own. "Turn it off. . . ." Some part of her was screaming, *This is important! This is the key to it all!* But smothered in the effects of the experiment, she scarcely cared.

Pharos pressed his hands to his eyes. "So this was it!"

His voice shook. "In these past weeks—the morning I spoke to Herthe at the posthouse—and last night—I thought it was only me! Only some new phase of my madness!"

"No." Antryg jerked free the ground wire, which ran so oddly from the teles back into itself. The lightning died on the rods; and like a cloud from the face of the sun, the cold grief lifted from the room. "The life-energy was being drained from you, Pharos—as it was being drained from everyone. Not enough to kill, but only enough to maim in a way for which there is no word."

Eerily, phosphorescent light continued to gleam for a time from the teles itself, shining wanly up through Antryg's fingers where he rested them on the silvery ball. His eyes were focused on some endless distance. Though Joanna could not understand what it was that he saw, she shivered at the reflection of dread, grief, and a knowledge that he did not want that she saw in his eyes.

"It was the whole course of Narwahl's experiments, I think," he went on after a moment, speaking as if to himself, his voice nearly unheard in the stillness of that sunwashed, enormous room. "It was for this that he killed—not because he'd discovered how electricity might affect magic, but because he had discovered how to use magic to draw off the life-energy which fills all the earth and use it to create electricity."

CHAPTER XVII

"BUT WHY?" JOANNA TUCKED HER FEET UP UNDER THE VO-luminous masses of her rose and cream petticoats to sit cross-legged on the thronelike oak chair Antryg had fetched for her out of the tangle at the far end of the attic. "Why electricity?" Her eyes went from the enigmatic snarl of glass, copper, and iron on the table to the ridiculous and equally enigmatic face of the man perched on the corner of the worktable beside her.

The Prince had gone, though his guards remained inevitably within call outside the door. A footman in the Prince's ruby livery had brought them lunch, which lay in a picked-at ruin on the tray on the floor at Joanna's side. Antryg had barely touched it or spoken.

Twice while she was eating the honeyed ham and comfits, Joanna had been aware of him watching her, as he had watched her in the silvery moonlight of the Devil's Road and again that morning in the Prince's carriage. Evasive he had always been, but the closer they had come to

Angelshand the closer they had drawn to the dark heart of the tangle of riddles surrounding them, the more pronounced that wariness, that fear, had become.

Studying his preposterous profile against the flat brightness of the windows, she wondered for the thousandth time why.

Was it because he knew her expertise lay in matters technological and he knew she would eventually scent through his lies and evasions to the mystery's real heart? But though she had a sense of pattern, a feeling that events connected, she had no idea what the heart of it all was.

The Prince's upcoming marriage, the attempts on his life, and Cerdic's stubborn attachment to the mages seemed to form one subset; the abominations, the original murder of the mage Thirle, and the fact that someone was going back and forth across the Void formed another. Her own kidnapping and that of the Archmage seemed linked in time, but not in any other way. The recurrent theme of madness—the prince's, Antryg's, the Emperor's—seemed broken by a hiatus of over twenty years. Like Ariadne's thread, the glittering trail of wizards' marks ran through the dark labyrinth, but it seemed to lead nowhere. As a programmer, used to breaking all situations down into manageable subsets, she found that this computerlike logic failed her when it came to working in the other direction.

Or was Antryg's fear of her, she wondered, simply because he feared to trust? He had trusted, he said, once too readily and once too often. Did he fear to care for her, as she feared her caring for him, because of the power such caring gives?

Maybe, she thought, if she were better with people than she was with programs and machines, she'd be able to tell whether he was lying or telling the truth. But in a sense, she felt that he had always done both.

Still he did not answer her, and she said quietly, "It would help if you'd trust me."

She saw the quick shiver that went through him, succeeded immediately by the wry flicker of his grin. "Believe me, Joanna, it would help if I could trust anyone. But I'm like Pharos—afraid the person I hire to protect me is the one who's been trying to kill me all along."

She frowned, hearing some note in his voice. "*Is* someone trying to kill you?"

He regarded her with surprised gray eyes. "Of course, my dear. Caris, for one . . ."

"He isn't the one you're thinking of, however," she said. Though he did not reply, he seemed to withdraw a little into himself again, not willing to give anything away. "You said you wanted to find out from the Council of Wizards what happened twenty-five years ago. Was whatever it was connected with why the Prince went mad? It happened at the same time. But if it was hereditary, from his father . . ."

He shook his head. "The Prince went mad because he could not accept the fact that two and two equal four," he said gently. "Even as I did. As for his father . . ." He looked away from her, his eyes suddenly shadowed again with horror and grief. "That is another matter."

"But it connects somewhere, doesn't it?" The pearl rosettes of her sleeve bows glimmered softly as she folded her arms. "And it connects with the fact that someone's been moving back and forth across the Void to get something from my world, something that needs electricity to operate. They heard about Narwahl's experiments with the teles . . ." She paused, frowning, and pushed at the corner of the tray at her feet with one slippered toe. "But why didn't they steal the teles when they killed him?"

"Obviously, because they had one of their own." He unfolded his thin legs and hopped lightly to the floor, pacing with his hands thrust deep in the pockets of his trailing black coat. "More than one, since the power seems to be drawn from such an enormous area. Suraklin used to link them in series to increase their power, and presumably that's what's being done here. What runs on electricity in your world?"

Joanna half-laughed, reminded absurdly of her mother's request that she "explain this computer stuff to me."

"God—What doesn't? Television . . ."

"It needs a transmitter as well as a receiver," the wizard objected. Joanna had explained to him some time ago the intricacies of television, though the ramifications of game shows and televised pro football had eluded him. "And no wizard with a good scrying-crystal would need one."

"Not unless he'd become secretly addicted to *Gilligan's Island* reruns," Joanna agreed. She started to lean back in the chair, then sat hastily up as the bodice boning poked her under the arm. "Same argument puts the kibosh on telephones. A factory, maybe? It would have a hell of an economic advantage over waterpower."

"With a supply of raw materials coming in, it would be a bit tricky to hide." Antryg paused in his pacing, toying thoughtfully with his gimcrack necklaces.

"Could they use magic to hide it?" Joanna suggested. "No," she answered herself almost at once, "because such generation of the electricity kills magic, doesn't it? Or could that be what they're trying to do? Cripple everyone's magic permanently? So whatever they're doing, they won't be found out?"

"It's a possibility." Antryg frowned. "And very like him, now that I think of it."

"Like who?"

He hesitated. "Whoever's doing this—whoever it is. He—or she—is very clever. . ." His frown suddenly deepened, and Joanna would have given much to know whether what he next said was his true thought or something to turn her from the subject. "Cripple everyone's power? Or drain it—and use it?"

She was silent for a moment, struck by the monstrousness of the implication. *"Could* they?" She remembered suddenly Caris' bitterness over losing his powers and Magister Magus' fears. It crossed her mind to wonder where Caris was now and what he'd been doing since . . . was it really only the night before last?

"I don't know." Antryg came over beside her and rested his long hands on the elaborate poppy-head finials of the tall chair back. "But power does move along the energy-lines. If it can be channeled into a central point . . ." Then he shook his head. "But I don't see why electricity."

"No?" Joanna turned in the chair to look up at him, and the boning of her bodice stabbed her sharply again. "Ever since we talked at Devilsgate and you said spells were similar to programming, I've been wondering. Would it be possible to program a computer to do magic? A big one, like a Cray, that reproduces all the functions of the human brain?"

"Reproduces the functions of the human brain," the mage echoed softly. He was silent for a long time then, his gray eyes staring off into some inner distance. What he saw there Joanna could not guess, but his eyes slowly widened, as if they looked upon some unimaginable nightmare. So he had looked, she realized, that morning in the Prince's coach, when he had learned or guessed what it was that had happened twenty-five years ago that had driven both himself and the Prince into the comforting refuge of madness. "Dear God . . ."

"What is it?" She half rose; her hand on his velvet sleeve seemed to pull him from some private hell-vision of that final revelation. His eyes returned to hers, like the eyes of a man newly come from some other world to find all things in this one not as he had left them. *"Tell me!"*

Their gazes locked; in his she saw the struggle of fear and trust, unwilling love, and the knowledge that he should not, must not, give to her more than he had. Then he looked away. "I—I don't know," he lied. "You've spoken of programs which can write, draw, and project events—which can lie, even, about their own existence!"

"That's not what I meant!" When he tried to turn away, she caught a handful of frayed lapel, the velvet soft as moleskin in her fist. "You've known something all along, something you've been lying about . . ."

"It's nothing," he said, his voice a little breathless. "It may not even be true—much of what I fear isn't, or so they keep telling me. What functions of thought can a computer reproduce?"

"Not a computer." Joanna released her hold on him and rose from the chair herself, standing separated from him by the width of its thickly carved, black oak back. "A program. A series of subroutines, done infinitely fast. A computer can't perceive patterns, but it can recognize them, if it breaks them down line by line. It's why programmers think the way they do. You say magic is predicated on visualization and hope. With a computer, that's graphics and statistical projection, since a computer doesn't care what should or shouldn't exist. But to write a series of programs that complex, you'd need a programmer who was also a wizard—or a programmer and a mage working together. Which you aren't likely to find in either of our worlds."

She stopped. They stood for a moment, looking at one another. In a hard-hearted and detached corner of her mind, she suddenly knew how Antryg had felt when he had seen whatever hideous realization had been reflected in the Prince's madness. Her own enlightenment beat upon her mind, as if she had walked from darkness into the agonizing glare of a magnesium flare.

Looking up into his face, she saw that he knew she'd guessed.

"You aren't likely to find it in either of our worlds," she repeated softly, "unless a mage came across the Void and kidnapped a programmer."

"Joanna . . ." There was neither surprise nor innocence in his face.

"And got her to trust him," she went on, and her voice suddenly shook. He had said, *I will not take advantage of you.* . . . She saw now that he had been like a cardsharp who passed the deal, using that, too, to gain her trust. Anger hit her—at him and at herself for falling for him, for caring. He had used her, played upon her sympathy for him and her dependence on him, as Gary had done years ago. He had seen her with Gary at the party. He must have known exactly what to do to gain first her trust and then her love. Her hand closed around the chair's carved finial until the edges of the wooden leaves dug painfully into her fingers. Her voice in her own ears sounded cold and distant, like someone else's.

"Or was there some other reason you brought me here?"

He said nothing, but there was despair in his eyes, the wreckage of all his hopes.

She turned and left the attic, each step that carried her through the old door and past the guard in the corridor seeming like a separate action, unconnected with any before or after. He neither called nor tried to follow as she walked down the stuffy enclosure of the stair and away through the quiet vistas of the palace rooms, her mind blank of thought and bitter confusion in her heart.

"Joanna!"

In contrast to the strength of the butter-colored sunlight on the lawn, the shade of the grotto where Joanna sat was like dark indigo. She wasn't sure how long she'd been sitting—not long, she thought. The shadows of the marble statues lining the lawn—heroes in archaic armor overwritten, as Cerdic's had been, with protective runes or the old, strange, animal-headed gods—hadn't lengthened much. She looked around at the whisper; but in the shade of the artificial bower's pink marble columns and twining roses, she saw nothing until Caris moved.

"Caris!" She untucked her feet from beneath her petticoats and sprang up. The sasennan had gone back to the matte, dark, flowing coat and trousers of his vocation, his long sword held ready in its scabbard in his left hand. Confused and shaken by her realization of what Antryg wanted of her and by the violence of her own feelings, she found herself suddenly weak with relief at knowing she was not, after all, utterly without options.

In the time she had been sitting here, it had dawned on her how absolutely in the wizard's power she was. She had always known she depended on him, but now it had come to her that she *could not* leave him, even if she were willing to risk being stranded forever in a world that was at best miserably filthy and inconvenient and at worst perilous even to those who knew what they were doing in it. There was nowhere in this world for her to go and certainly nowhere that Antryg couldn't talk the Prince into sending men to find her.

She felt ridiculously like bursting into tears, but Caris, she knew, wasn't the sort of young man who could cope with lachrymose females. Instead she took a deep breath and said, "You're all right."

He nodded. The smoke-colored shadows didn't hide the marks of strain and sleeplessness on his face. Some irreverant part of her came within an ace of asking him, *How long did you wait outside that vacant building?* but she pushed that thought away.

"We've been seeking you in a scrying-crystal," he said. "It wouldn't work while you were with Antryg, but when you were at a distance from him . . ."

"We?" she demanded. "The mages who escaped from St. Cyr . . ."

"The rest of them were released this morning," the sasennan said. "But I . . ."

"That was Antryg's doing," she said and frowned, puzzled. "Though I don't see why."

"He is closing in on his goal," a quiet voice said from the rose-hung shadows of the pillars. "And perhaps he fears what some of them might say of him, should his name arise."

In the fawn-spotted, green gloom a shadow emerged from the deeper shadows, a slender old man of medium height, his tall forehead laddered with wrinkles and his long white hair hanging to square, narrow shoulders clothed in the black of a wizard's robe. His eyes were the same dark coffee-brown as Caris', with the same slight tilt to the corners. Joanna knew at once who he had to be.

She stammered, "Your—I'm sorry, but I'm a stranger here, and this sounds really stupid, but I don't know whether I'm supposed to genuflect or kiss your ring, and I've *never* figured out how to curtsy in these damn skirts." She kicked aside the intrusive petticoats and stepped forward to take his strong, slender hand and to be greeted by the winter sunlight of his smile.

"Then we'll take your greeting as read," he said. "Caris told me of you. I must say I am both astounded and relieved beyond expression to see you alive, free, and—in possession of your own mind."

She stared at the Archmage in shock. *"What?"*

Dourly, Caris remarked, "I gather Antryg lost no time in getting on the good side of the Regent."

"The Regent needed his advice," Joanna said. "He needed a wizard who couldn't possibly have done magic in the last seven years."

"A convenient, if specious, argument," Salteris said drily. "Antryg has been coming and going from the Silent Tower as he pleases for some months now."

"I—I wondered about that." She stepped back and gestured the old man to the marble seat she had been occupying, a carved bench the size—and function, she suspected—of a love seat, embellished at both ends with cupids and wreaths of carved roses the size of cabbages. Neither it, nor the marble statues in the gardens, she had noticed, bore the usual festoons of bird droppings; the Prince's predilection for flogging his servants evidently had certain valuable side effects beyond his ability to get lobster patties for his guests in the middle of the night. "That is—Antryg always seems to know more than he should and he can't be *that* good a guesser."

"No." The old man gently shook off Caris' efforts to help him down and seated himself at Joanna's side. "He is in precisely the position of a doctor who doses a man's coffee with poison and then claims a miracle cure for producing the antidote—a favorite dog wizard trick. And Pharos, I fear, has placed his trust in him, to the exclusion of every mage who has been abroad in the world. In many ways, Pharos is as credulous as his cousin, though far more dangerous. I am only pleased, my child, to see you safe."

"Believe me, the feeling's more than mutual." She glanced up at Caris, who stood quietly at his grandfather's back. "I'm glad he found you safe."

"I did not find him," the sasennan corrected her. "He found me. No one finds the Archmage unless he wills it."

"But where *were* you?" She looked back at the old man. "Did . . ." But she found herself almost unable to speak Antryg's name.

He must have sensed it, for the dark, severe eyes softened with pity and understanding. "Lost," he said. "I don't know—the spell was one of confusion. I wandered for days, it felt like, but I had no way of telling how many, for there was neither day nor night where I was. Only darkness . . ." He shook his head. "I don't know. I escaped, but it has left me exhausted."

Quietly, Caris asked, "Could he have pushed you into the Void itself? To wander between worlds?"

Salteris passed a hand over his brow and shook his

head. "I don't know. Suraklin had a black crystal with a labyrinth inside. He could trap a soul within it, to wander forever in the lattices of a gem small enough to pick up in his hand."

"And Antryg was Suraklin's student," Joanna murmured, remembering the teles, the elementals that had slain Narwahl Skipfrag, and the abominations. . . .

The Archmage's dark eyes rested on her for a moment. Then he sighed. "No," he said softly. "No—it is worse than that. Antryg . . ." He hesitated, folding his hands with his forefingers extended against his lips, his deepset eyes gazing out into the sunlit vistas of the garden beyond the shadows. "My child, I fear that Antryg Windrose has not existed for a long time."

She didn't know why her eyes burned or her throat seemed to constrict with grief; it was grief, she understood, for someone she had never known. In the silence, she could hear the twitter of sparrows marking out their territories among the trees and the far-off clatter of carts beyond the walls of the palace parkland in Angelshand, a quarter-mile away. Words drifted through her mind:

> *He could break anyone's mind to his bidding . . .*
> *. . . He wanted to live forever . . .*
> *. . . Where's he been, if he hasn't?*
> *. . . I felt him in dreams . . .*

Even before the Archmage spoke again, she knew what he was going to say.

"Suraklin had worked for a long time on the notion of taking over the minds of others," the old man said. "With his slaves, of course, he controlled their minds with his own; those under his influence did as he bade them and were his eyes and ears, without thinking to ask why, and his influence was incredibly strong. That is why I said I am glad to see you still capable of leaving Antryg's side. But he wanted more than that." The old man sighed, his thin mouth taut and rather white, as if sickened by some unshared knowledge whose bare bones only he would reveal, not out of secretiveness, but out of mercy. "He took the boy Antryg, the most powerful child adept he could find. He taught him everything he himself knew, like a man furnishing a house with his own things. . . ."

"No!" Joanna pulled her mind from the hideous picture that swam there unbidden of a gawky, thin-faced, frightened boy staring with hypnotized gray eyes into the terrible yellow gaze of the old man. Intellectually she knew that she had never truly known Antryg. Why did it cross her mind that the nervous, gentle man, the man who had whispered, "I will not do this . . ." and turned away, rather than take her in his arms when she could not have afforded to say no, even had she not consented, had been in fact that boy and not the mage who had raped him of mind and body so that he could go on living in his stead. "Oh, Christ, no."

"I'm sorry," the wizard said softly.

She pressed her hands to her mouth, suddenly trembling, remembering the soft force of Antryg's lips on hers. It was Suraklin who had kissed her, an ancient intelligence in stolen flesh. She thought how close she'd come to lying with him on the road from Kymil to Angelshand and felt almost ill.

Slim and strong, the hand of the Archmage rested upon her arm. "When Caris told me you were with him, I was afraid. I know how strong a hold Suraklin could take, even over those he did not fully possess," He glanced back toward the irregular roof line of the Summer Palace, visible over the sun-spangled trees. "I fear he has the Prince's trust already; he will consolidate that hold in whatever way he can."

Sick with disgust, she recalled the mage's mock flirtation with Pharos; a game, she could have sworn at the time. But then, she could have sworn that Antryg's care for her was genuine and not simply the means to some other end.

"Antryg said . . ." She hesitated. It was not, she knew now, Antryg who had spoken. "He said he had loved Suraklin. Was that true?"

"That Antryg loved him?" Salteris nodded. "Yes, very probably. Suraklin had that talent of winning the hearts of those who came in contact with him. Their loyalty to him was unquestioning, almost fanatical, even in the face of evidence that he was not what he said he was."

Joanna blushed, not, she knew, because she had trusted Antryg, but because there was some large portion of her which cared for him still—or, she thought, confused, cared for the man who'd sat by her in the roadside inns and who'd talked with her on those long, weary afternoons on the road about television and computers and friends he'd met during the Mellidane Revolts, the man who'd stood so close to her in the dimness of the drawing room at Devilsgate. Why did she feel it was so absolutely impossible that that man was the Dark Mage?

His voice quiet in the gloom of the arbor, Salteris went on. "That was the thing I never understood, after I found Antryg in the monastery, years after the destruction of Suraklin's citadel—his story that he had fled shortly before the Imperial armies gathered. But I thought . . ." He sighed again and shook his head.

"Twenty-five years ago," Joanna said suddenly.

"What?" The Archmage raised his head sharply, an amber glint flickering in the onyx depths of his eyes.

"Antryg said he—he had to ask some member of the Council about something that happened twenty-five years ago."

"So." The old man nodded. "He feared someone else might have seen or known or guessed. And if he found them, if he learned that anyone had seen Antryg make a final visit to Suraklin before the execution . . ." The dark eyes narrowed. "And did he?"

Joanna shook her head. "He never found another member of the Council—or at least, not that I knew of. Pharos told him that his father had seen something or knew something after the taking of Kymil which changed him; and that seemed to horrify Antryg. But later . . ." She shook her head. "I don't understand."

"If I were trying to bring the mad Prince under my influence," Caris sniffed, "and learned his father knew anything, had any suspicion which he might have passed along, I'd be horrified, too."

"Maybe," Joanna said slowly. "He did say the Emperor never liked him. Somebody—I forget who—told me the Emperor visited Suraklin several times during his trial. Do you think he could have recognized him in Antryg? Or suspected, at least? Because he did sentence him to death seven years ago."

The old man sighed bitterly. "And I, to my sorrow, had the sentence commuted. But as Archmage of the Council, I could not permit the Emperor, the Church, or anyone else to hold the power of life and death over any Council mage, be he never so forsworn of his vows. At the time, I believed that that was all there was." He frowned into the distance again, all the parallel lines of that high forehead seeming to echo and re-echo his speculations and his grief. "Hieraldus was a brilliant man and a perceptive one. He would have felt the similarity. So did I, once or twice, at first. But I put it down to the fact that for many years the boy Antryg had been virtually Suraklin's slave. After that . . ." He shook his head, and a stray fragment of sunlight turned the edge of his long hair to blazing silver against the black of his robe. "Perhaps elements of Antryg's original personality survived—enough to keep those who knew him from suspecting the change. No one but

Suraklin had really known him well—and then, of course, he was always known to be mad."

"Useful," Caris sneered.

Joanna remembered the shadows of the roadhouse hearth and Antryg's lazy smile over the tankard of beer. *I never knew him,* she thought. *I only knew the lie. Why do I grieve for the lie?*

"Was he?" she asked. "Mad, I mean."

"The original Antryg?" Salteris shrugged. "Who knows? He may have become unbalanced by the struggle against Suraklin's will. Afterward, the reputation was Suraklin's shield and cloak, an armor fashioned to resemble vulnerability. I pitied him, but never suspected—until he struck." The old man's mouth tightened again, all the delicate muscle of cheek and jaw springing into prominence under the silky cloak of white hair. She understood then that hers had not been the only trust, the only love, betrayed.

"Where is he?" Caris' eyes sought the clustering turrets of the Summer Palace.

"I left him in the attics of the old wing." She looked down at her hands, folded among the silly profusion of ruffle and lace in her lap. "He—He and I looked over Narwahl Skipfrag's equipment. I don't suppose I told him anything he didn't already know. He's going to program a computer to do magic. With a big enough computer, the scope of the subroutines would be infinite. I think . . ."

She hesitated, then went on, ashamed at how nearly she'd fallen for something that now seemed so obvious. "I think the scenario he planned to use was that some other evil wizard—the one he said had kidnapped you and me and tried to murder the Regent and all the rest of it—was doing it, so why didn't I help him steal equipment and work out programs as a countermeasure. At least that would be the logical course of action. He was working up to it very gradually, winning my trust. . . ." She swallowed,

her throat hurting again at the loss of that gentle consideration with which he had, she now knew, baited his trap. "If I
hadn't guessed, I probably would have done it."

Cool and very strong, Salteris' thin hands closed over
hers. "It is perilously easy to come to care for one upon
whom one is utterly dependent," he said. "Particularly if he
has gotten you out of danger—which he did, didn't he?"

She remembered the vicious whine of Pharos' riding
whip in the darkness of the inn and the heartbreaking exhaustion of that last desperate run through the muddy lanes
around St. Cyr—remembered, too, Antryg's arms, surprisingly strong around her, and the desperate hunger of his
mouth on hers in the fog-bound isolation of the alley. She
felt hot all over with shame.

The old man's voice was like a gentle astringent. "He
miscalculated your strength, child, and your wits—but it is
as well you left him when you did. Because he would not
have stopped with simply winning your . . ."

He paused, and Joanna finished for him cynically,
"Heart?"

"Confidence, I was going to say. He could have gone
into your mind—you would have let him—and used your
knowledge of—computers?" He pronounced the alien
word hesitantly.

Joanna nodded. "Not only computers—systems and
program design. That's my job. It's what I do."

"He could have used your brain, your knowledge, like a
tool, even as he could have used your body."

She glanced up quickly at that, sensing different mean-
ings behind the phrase, but Salteris' dark gaze was already
fixed again on the distant vista of parterre and statues and
on the far-off glint of the roofs of the Imperial Palace,
which rose like a mellow sandstone cliff beyond the trees.

"As he used me," he murmured. "I was the one who
originally told him of Narwahl's experiments with the
teles, little suspecting that the dozen or so teles never

found of Suraklin's hoard had been hidden away by him."
He shut his eyes for a moment, bitter grief deepening the
lines already graven in the soft flesh of the lids. "Narwahl
was my friend," he added in a voice barely to be heard. "It
seems that in striving after justice, I have done naught but
ill." The narrow, sensitive mouth quirked, and he glanced
beside him at Joanna again, the bitterness of wormwood in
those deep eyes. "Like you, I have been victim to that
accursed charm."

She put her hand over his, feeling the warm flesh, thin
as silk over the knobby shapes of knuckles and tendon.
Archmage though he was, she felt in him suddenly only an
old man who knew himself responsible for his dear friend's
murder. She hoped he knew nothing of the blood-splattered
attic with its tiny shards of glass; but she also knew that the
hope was impossible, since he was the Archmage.

"I'm sorry," she said, and some of the bleak horror
faded from the old man's eyes.

"We have both been his dupes," he said gently.

Joanna shook her head. "All I've lost is some illusions,"
she replied. "Not—not anyone I know." *Only someone I
hoped to know. And the hope,* she reflected wryly, *was my
problem.*

His fingers tightened over hers, remarkably strong for
so old a man's. "Come," he said and rose to his feet, the
long, dark robe falling straight about him. "It's best we
find him, before he learns that I've escaped and am here."

The Summer Palace was curiously quiet as they approached it; the Regent's high, harsh voice was audible
from the terrace, but his words were indistinct with distance. Like three ghosts, they moved through the shrub-
bery, which, in accordance with the Prince's Gothic tastes
and desire for privacy, grew closer around the walls than
the formal vistas of topiary which surrounded the new Palace. Away from the graceful symmetry of its remodeled
facade, all pretense of the building's modernity faded. The

stable and kitchen courts were even to Joanna's untrained eye a jumble of styles and periods, mansard roofs crowding comfortably shoulder to shoulder with the oddly angled gambrels and projecting upper storeys of the Palace's earlier incarnations. "Won't someone ask us what we're doing here?" she inquired, glancing uncertainly at Caris' dark uniform and sword and at the old man's flowing dark robes.

They paused in the gloom of a grove of cypresses opposite the round, gray turret of the stable tower. Through the tower's broad gate the stable court was visible; grooms in the Prince's flame-colored livery were working with neat efficiency to harness a pair of coal-black horses to a light carriage of some kind. At Joanna's side, Salteris murmured, "I scarcely think so," and made a small gesture with one hand.

The nearer of the two horses, which had been standing quietly up until that instant; flung up its head in panic. A stableboy caught too late at the bridle, and the beast reared, frightening its harness-mate. Men began to run from all directions under the shouted orders of the gray-haired coachman in his gold-and-crimson braid. "Stay close to me," the wizard admonished. With Caris glancing watchfully in all directions and Joanna holding up the voluminous handfuls of her beruffled skirts, they calmly crossed the drive and passed unseen by the shouting confusion around the carriage.

"It's always easier to enter a house through the servants' quarters," the old man said softly, "provided you know what you're doing." The oppressive heat of steam and the damp smells of soap and linen enveloped them as they passed into the shadows of the brick laundries on the far side of the court. Salteris turned unerringly along a brick-paved corridor with a low, groined wooden ceiling, under which the day's heat collected with the mingled smells of smoke, cooking meat, and spices from the kitchens beyond. A man started to emerge from an archway of reflected daylight to their right. Joanna, startled, paused in her stride, but the old man beside her only flicked a finger; from the room beyond came a crashing noise that made the servant turn hastily back, yelling "Not that way, you stupid jolterhead!"

Something stirred in Joanna's consciousness. A dark, cold feeling of half-familiar strangeness, like an unheard sound, seemed to go through her, and she was aware of the sudden hiss of Caris' breath beside her. Salteris checked his steps in the narrow seam of the kitchen passage, his dark eyes narrowing and a flame seeming to spark suddenly in their depths. . . .

Joanna identified where she'd first felt that queer, haunted sense of terror a split-instant before Caris and his grandfather's glances met.

Then they all began to run.

There was a backstairs at the end of the corridor, leading to apartments in the old wing. Salteris, dark robe billowing about his thin limbs, led them unerringly to it, across an unused state chamber with its ancient linenfold and gilded coffer and up the stairs to the attic; Joanna followed in a sursurrus of silk taffeta. The memory of the blood-splattered attic in Narwahl's house and of Minhyrdin the Fair mumbling, *He'd call them up, spirits, elementals* leaped to her mind. Panic chilled her heart as she realized that Antryg had electrical equipment at his disposal.

But when they burst past the startled guard into that vast room, nothing met their eyes—nothing, hanging dark and shimmering where the sunlight had been, as if a hole had been opened in the fabric of the world and the night, momentarily, allowed to breathe through. It grew smaller and smaller, like a shrinking bubble of darkness, even as they watched, seeming to retreat without ever reaching the far wall. Along it, Joanna thought she could see something moving.

Salteris strode forward and Joanna reached involuntarily to catch the black fabric of his sleeve. The smells of woodsmoke and herbs came to her from it as he turned, as they had come from Antryg's—the smells of wizardry that had smothered her at San Serano, with the strangler's grip around her throat. She gasped, "Don't . . . !"

At the same moment, Caris shoved her roughly aside, his sword whining from its sheath. "We'll lose him!" The wind of the Void lifted his blond hair back from his forehead, and anger blazed in his eyes. For a terrifying instant, Joanna saw that her choice was either to fling herself willy-nilly after them into whatever second gap in the Void Salteris should open or to be trapped in this world, with neither good mages nor evil to help her, forever. . . .

She gritted her teeth and tightened her grip on her gathered-up petticoats, ready to run. But Salteris did not move. He only stood watching as the hideous black shimmer of the Void faded and vanished.

"No," he said. His voice echoed queerly in that enormous room, with its jumble of antique furniture and the sun glinting harshly on the glass tubes and copper wires coiled beneath the window. He turned back to consider them—Joanna in her ruffled and borrowed gown, and Caris with his sword half-drawn, his eyes the eyes of a hawk stooping to its prey. "No. I know where he has gone, my children. I read the marks of Suraklin that guide him like candles through the darkness." As if he guessed her fears from her grim eyes and braced chin, he smiled and, reaching out, gently touched Joanna's cheek. "I will not leave you alone here, child. Indeed," he added quietly, "when I cross the Void to trap him, I shall need you both."

CHAPTER XVIII

WHEN THEY REACHED GARY'S HOUSE IN AGOURA, THEY found it empty and silent. Just as well, thought Joanna, watching Caris make a rapid, wary circuit of the den, kitchen, and party room, naked sword blade in hand. The last thing she wanted at the moment was even to see Gary, let alone explain to him where she'd been for the last two weeks and who Caris and the Archmage were.

Letting herself in with the hideaway key, she had a strange sense of *déjà vu*, like the dreams she occasionally had of being in grade school again with her adult knowledge and experience. Some of it was simply aesthetic— her eye, used for weeks to rococo curves and molded plaster ceilings, found the high tech starkness of the place alien and strange, and her lungs gagged on the quality of the September air. But it was emotional as well—a sense of reality-poisoning that was increased by the impersonality of the house, the party room with its ugly, comfortless couches and prominent television set. Everything around her seemed almost audibly to speak Gary's name.

For no reason, she remember the ragged little mill girls in Kymil, hastening through the silent glory of late summer dawn, and the bitter, weary pity on Antryg's face as he'd asked, "Is it worth it?"

"It's all dead," Caris said softly. He came back from the big glass-and-chrome kitchen, sword still in hand, cautiously touching television, bar, and couches in passing. "I mean—it never was alive." He paused, his dark, beautifully shaped brows drawn down over his eyes with puzzlement as he looked at Joanna. "What is it all made of?"

"Plastic, mostly." She shoved her hands into her jeans pockets and looked around her at the house, realizing at last what it was that had chiefly bothered her about Gary. "It's cheap, and it'll do."

"But it isn't—it isn't *right*," the sasennan insisted.

Salteris, who had been standing by the patio doors, gazing thoughtfully out at the smog, let fall the drapes and turned back. "I doubt one person in ten notices, anymore," he remarked, almost casually. "People get used to things. In time, they cease to remember and don't miss what they've forgotten they had." He came back to where Joanna stood, once again in the well-worn comfort of jeans and t-shirt, and said, "The mark is upstairs, isn't it?"

The mark was at Salteris' own eye level. He brushed his hand along the wood, as Antryg had done on the white, curlicued paneling of the Emperor's suite. Like a glowing pixel, the scribble of light seemed to float up out of the depths of the grain. The wizard stood for a long time gazing at it; even when it faded again, as it did almost at once, he did not move, but remained, as if he could read it still.

"Was that the mark," he asked her at last, "that you saw in San Serano? In the great computer room there?"

"I think so," she said hesitantly. She pushed back her unruly blond hair from her face, trying to remember something beyond the terror, the queer, smoky smell of the robes, and the scorch of a man's breath on her temple.

"His influence can be incredibly strong upon the minds of those who know him," the old man murmured. Sharply through the curtains, a scissor edge of late sunlight rimmed his angular profile, so like Caris', and haloed the free—floating strands of his silver hair. "And even those who do not know him yet—the mark influences their minds, as if he spoke to them when their thoughts were elsewhere. The mark prepares the way. I see his influence in your eyes still."

She looked away, feeling her face go blotchy red with shame that he should guess.

"You do not want to believe entirely ill of him," Salteris continued gently. "You search for the reasons he did what he did, motives to make his use of you other than what it was. It says better of you than it does of him."

Her throat tight and aching as if she had screamed her heart out, she stood staring at the silent red eyes of the IBM in its bank of 20-megabyte disk drives.

"I know, Joanna." The slender, powerful hands rested on her shoulders. "Even now, even knowing what I know through the memory of the grip of his mind upon mine, even knowing I must meet him again, it is my instinct to trust him. That is the terror—and the strength—of his spell."

Caris turned sharply from examining the neat shelves of additional ROM and backup floppies, the sunlight slicing through the single chink of curtain bursting against the brass of dagger hilt and buckle. "Must you meet him?"

"He has not yet been here." The old man folded his hands in the sleeves of his robe. "He will come to this, his mark."

"Why?"

The dark gaze rested gently on her for a moment before the Archmage replied.

"Perhaps there is something here he wants," he said. "Perhaps—for very little, if any, magic operates here, and it is hard to say—perhaps because he will sense you near it. But he will come—he must. And I must meet him."

Caris asked softly, "Alone?" In the inflection of his voice, Joanna could hear that he already knew his grandfather's reply.

Salteris sighed and folded his hands before him, forefingers pressed to his lips. At length he said, "Caris, I am sure of myself. To introduce a second factor, even one that I trust implicitly, as I trust you, would be to increase the danger."

"But your magic doesn't operate here," Caris began protestingly.

"Neither does his."

"But he is twenty years younger than you and half a foot taller! He can . . ."

"My son," the old man said, with a smile, "do you think me that defenseless?"

Caris said nothing.

"And then, someone must stay with Joanna." The dark gaze moved thoughtfully to her in the close, hot gloom of the computer room. "I do not think he will pass me unseen, but he might. If he does, he *must not* be allowed to speak to her."

Neither Caris nor Joanna spoke; but judging by the sasennan's face, he wasn't any more thrilled with the idea than she was.

More gently, Salteris went on, "You stand in grave danger still, Joanna. Even knowing what you know, you want to trust."

She looked away again. Hating herself, she nodded. Dark and compelling, the old man's glance went to his grandson. "If you cannot prevent him from speaking to her in any other way, kill him." He turned and walked to the window, flinging back the curtain to admit a drench of harsh and smog-stained afternoon light. Beyond the window, the hills that hid San Serano bulked in the haze, and between them, like a gun sight, stood the dusty little shed in which they had stepped from the dark of the Void.

"I will wait for him there," he said. "He is sly. . . ." He lifted his thin, white fingers at the intake of Caris' protesting breath. "He will not speak with me, if you are near. He has reason to fear you, my son. Trust me." He looked back at them, the hot sunlight outlining the worn contours of his face, suddenly very fragile-looking in his faded black robe. "I know what it is that I do."

The light had shifted again to the sharp-edged champagne brilliance of the long Southern California afternoon when Antryg came walking over the hills.

Caris and Joanna were in the computer room, where they had been since Salteris left them, alternately speaking of what had passed since they'd parted at Magister Magus' and watching for movement in the parched ochre vastness of grass and dust.

Caris had turned from the window to regard Gary's monstrous new IBM among its red-eyed banks of monitors and surge suppressors, as he had done at intervals, all afternoon. After some moments, he said, "This is the thing that is your life and the life of all your world? The machine that thinks like a man?"

"Not like a man." Joanna folded up her legs to sit cross-legged on the corner of the computer table, the weary portion of her mind that was not trying desperately to avoid thinking of Antryg taking considerable comfort in the freedom of jeans. *He is walking into a trap,* part of her said, and she pushed the treacherous impulse to care aside. "Computers can arrive at the same conclusions a person can, with the same kind of logic people are capable of, when they aren't hoping that two and two won't equal four. . . ." She paused, then went on. "But not like a man."

She reached for the switch on the main terminal. "Would you care to try?"

He stepped back hastily and shook his head. Then, seeing her startled expression, he flushed a little and explained, "It is not the Way of the Sasennan. We are trained to be what we are, and to do what we do. All this——" He gestured around him at the high tech fixtures of the house, the soft hum of the air conditioner, and the alien richness of the world, "It is not supposed to matter to the sasennan. We are weapons, honed to a single end. That is all."

She remembered Kanner—remembered, also, Caris' uneasiness at operating without a master, or with only the dottily masterful Antryg to give him orders. In his own way, she realized, Caris was as bad with people as she.

Curious, she said, "But you were mageborn. You were going to be a wizard. Isn't that just the opposite?"

He hesitated, as if it were something he had never quite articulated to himself, let alone anyone else. As he always did when he was trying to say what he really meant, he spoke slowly. "It is, and it isn't. As a mage, one can't give oneself to any of it, either. They say neither the mage nor the sasennan drinks the world's wine, as street-warriors and dog wizards do. So it isn't——" He shook his head. "It isn't safe to sniff at the fumes. At least," he added more hesitantly, "it isn't safe for *me*. To be what we are, and only what we are, to put everything into that, is what hones us to a killing edge. Anything else is a softening."

"The more you do, the more you do." Joanna sighed. He had a point. It was a definite changing of mental gears to go from dealing with computers to dealing with people, particularly after she'd been programming for hours or days at a time. And indeed, most of the time she did feel more at ease dealing with her IBM than she did dealing with Gary or with any other human being . . . at least, until recently.

Antryg . . .

Not Antryg, she told herself wretchedly. *Suraklin. Suraklin.*

Caris turned suddenly. Though he did not speak, Joanna was on her feet and at his side, looking out toward the tiny, ragged outline of the shed.

In the fulvous sunlight, Salteris stood in front of the shed, unmoving save for the wind stirring his black robes and silky hair. After what seemed like a long moment, Antryg came into view above the tawny crest of the hill.

He had changed back into the jeans and scruffy t-shirt in which she had first seen him, here in this house. The slanted afternoon light caught the silver-foil HAVOC across his chest; though she knew it was only the name of a rock group, the word had a grim significance to her, knowing what she now knew. His cracked spectacles glinted as he held out his hand to the unmoving Archmage and took a step closer to him. Joanna thought he spoke; but at this distance, it was impossible to tell.

She could not see whether the old man replied. In her heart she knew her fears should be for Salteris' safety rather than Antryg's.

After a moment, the younger wizard stepped forward and bending his tall form, embraced the old man. After brief hesitation, Salteris' arms came up to return the embrace. Antryg led him gently into the shed.

Beside her, Joanna heard Caris whisper, "No . . ."

She caught him by the arm as he turned away. "He said he had to meet him alone." She was aware her hand shook.

"He also said that the one thing he feared was Antryg's charm." He stepped back from Joanna, the first true kinship she had ever seen for her in his face. "I know. I— when I first met him, I trusted him. And I've had to fight all this time to keep from trusting him again. I know." He nodded towards the silent shed in the puma-gold emptiness of the hills. "Are you coming?"

The air in the patio was hot, in spite of the cooling

proximity of the pool. From the iron gate that looked out into the hills, they saw Antryg emerge from the shed and stand for a time, his back leaned against the splintery wood, his head bowed in exhaustion. Caris glanced quickly at Joanna, fear in his eyes; when they looked again, the mad wizard was gone.

Caris, at a dead run, reached the hill long before Joanna did.

Parching and oppressive, the heat of the afternoon seemed to have imbued itself into the coarse wood of the shed, along with the stinks of dirt and old oil slowly baking in the summer silence. Pierced by splinters of blinding light from the chinks in the walls, the shed's darkness defeated Joanna's eyes as she stepped through the open door, but it seemed to her that she already knew what she would find inside.

The Archmage Salteris lay in a corner, behind a crazy pile of splintered plywood and the dismembered parts of a car. He had been laid out carefully, a small, frail form under his black robes. There was dust in his white hair. His eyes had been closed, and his mouth, also, though his face was still a hideous mottled gray-blue with strangulation. Even with the merciful masking of the shadows, Joanna could not deceive herself that he might be somehow revived. She had killed two men. She knew what death looked like now.

The unbearable brilliance of a crack of sunlight outlined Caris' face in gold as he knelt beside the corpse. He stared out straight ahead of him, his face blank with a kind of shock. He had relied on the old man, Joanna realized, as much as he had loved him. His rage at Antryg had come as much from fear of losing Salteris' support as it had been from his fanatical loyalty. He had been able to believe in his grandfather's disappearance, she remembered, but not in his death. He had made himself a weapon for those slender, blue-veined hands. It had always been inconceivable to him that they would one day fall slack.

His face inhumanly calm and still, Caris lifted one of those hands, limp now as a bundle of jointed sticks. He turned it over to look at the white fingers and palms, then laid it as it had been, back upon the breast. Tenderly, still with that odd, almost wondering numbness, he brushed aside the white silk of the hair and looked for a time at the bruises on the colorless, crepey flesh of the throat.

Joanna thought it was only some final seeking for contact with the old man he had loved, until she heard him whisper, "Why? Was your trust in him so great that you didn't even struggle when you felt his hands around your throat? Could he do even that to you?"

Then suddenly he doubled over, as if some poison, drunk unnoticed, had finally taken grip. The big, well-shaped hands pressed his face, and shudder after silent shudder of grief racked through his body. He twisted aside from the hand Joanna tried to lay on his back and knelt in the stifling dust, hands pressed to his face as if he could squeeze all tears, all sound, all feeling back inside of him, as it was the Way of the Sasennan to do. Barred with sunlight, Salteris' distorted face seemed strangely calm, as if he knew that none of this, nor any further machinations of the Dark Mage, concerned him any longer.

After a long time, Joanna asked, "What can we do?"

Joanna heard Antryg's light footfall in the party room an hour and a half later. Outside the kitchen windows, the afternoon light had slanted further, then taken on the curious crystal quality of evening, as the wind moved the smog further east. She had been sitting and staring out at the changes of the light since returning to the house. She felt empty and cold inside, as if some final illusion had collapsed; her thoughts seemed to have slipped into read-only mode, going round and round until they were exhausted, without producing anything except that, like Caris, she must do what she must do.

But when she heard the footfalls that she knew for Antryg's, it felt as if everything within her were passed suddenly through a wringer.

She heard him pause in the party room. Forcing a calm upon herself she had never known she possessed, she got to her feet, walked to the stove, and poured the water she had heated in the teakettle over the combination of instant coffee and crushed sleeping pills in the cup on the counter. She took a deep breath and conjured again for herself the vision of Salteris' dead, swollen face in the brown gloom of the shed. Then she picked up the cup and went into the party room.

He was standing near the curtained glass of the doors, looking sick unto death.

The naturalness of her own voice astounded her. "Did Salteris find you?"

He looked up at the sound of her voice, and some expression—shock, dismay, despair of a situation that was hopeless—superseded the misery and exhaustion on his face. He shut his eyes for a moment, fighting some terrible inner weight which seemed to have descended on his wide, bony shoulders, and whispered hopelessly, "You came with him?" Then, realizing that he should not even know of Salteris' presence in this world, he looked at her again and added, "Salteris?"

"He brought me back here," Joanna said. "He came to me in the garden—he said he had to speak to you. He didn't say why. We went up the attic but you had gone. So I asked him to bring me back, and he did."

He closed his eyes momentarily. The lines around them looked as if they'd been put in with a chisel in the discolored flesh. He said, "I wouldn't have left you."

"I didn't know that."

He looked so shaken, so drained of all his usual ebullience, that it was absolutely natural that she should hand him the coffee. She had to force her hand to it, force herself to look into his face as she did it, telling herself he was Suraklin. Suraklin! He drank it without a word, grateful for the warmth of it. After a moment he said, "Thank you." Going to the couch, he sat down as if he had only just recalled that it was possible to do so.

He ran his fingers through his graying hair and seemed to pull himself together. "I'm sorry," he said. "I didn't mean to leave you long—not even this long. I should have returned earlier than this." He swallowed, and she saw the muscles of his jaw harden for a moment. "And Pharos would have looked after you, kept you safe. But there was something here I had to find."

She remained standing in front of him, her arms folded and her heart hammering, but her whole body feeling strangly numb. "And did you?"

He shook his head, a small gesture, defeated. "No." He looked down, turning the remains of the drugged coffee in his big hands, staring down into the dregs as he had once studied tea-leaves in the posthouses to buy them supper. He asked carefully, "Did Salteris say where he had been?"

"No," Joanna said. "And frankly, I didn't care."

He looked up at her quickly, that look she had seen before, with the ruin of all that he had ever sought or hoped in his eyes.

"I don't want anything further to do with this," she said, fighting to keep the tremor out of her voice. "I only wanted to come home, to get out of whatever is going on. You said once . . ." Her voice faltered. "You said once you'd see I came to no harm. If you meant that, just leave me alone. All right?"

He said nothing for a time, but their eyes held, and for a long moment she had the impression that he wavered on the brink of telling her the truth, of stepping beyond that self-imposed wall and trusting her, as it was still her instinct, fight it though she might, to trust him. Then he sighed, and in an almost soundless voice, agreed. "All right."

She couldn't help herself. "Will you be all right?" *What a stupid question,* she told herself an instant later.

He managed the ghost of his old warm, half-demented smile. "Oh, yes." He set the cup down at his side. "As long as I stay a step ahead of the Council. As long as I can . . ." He paused and shook his head, as if trying to clear it. "I'm sorry, Joanna. But the mark on the wall . . . the mark on the wall . . ."

Then he slumped sideways and was asleep.

Chapter XIX

It was long after dark when he awoke. Joanna was still sitting on the curiously comfortless gray chair beside the couch, her mind blank, her body and bones cold with exhaustion. She almost literally could not believe that she had awakened that morning in the old Summer Palace at Angelshand or that it was only fourteen or fifteen hours ago that she had sat in the Regent's carriage, while he had wept as he'd spoken of his father. It was as if it had happened to someone else.

And in a way, she thought, it had.

The heat of the day had passed off. The party room was dim, illuminated only by the reflected yellow glare of the kitchen's lights. Through the open glass doors of the patio, the smell of chlorine came in off the pool with the warmth of the tepid night.

She saw Antryg stir, fighting his way to the surface of the dark well of his dreams, saw him try to move, and saw

347

how his breath stopped, then quickened when he realized that he could not.

His eyes opened, and he looked up into her face.

"I'm sorry, Antryg." Oddly enough, she meant it.

He made a quick motion and ceased at once. His wrists and ankles were knotted tight with the plastic-wrapped wire Joanna had carried in her purse and which she'd gotten, weeks ago, from the telephone man at San Serano. With weary irony, she remembered thinking at the time that it would come in handy. More than that, Joanna realized, recalling her own first experience with barbiturates, he must be prey to the grandmother of all headaches. The eyes that stared up into hers were dark with despair and terror, but showed no surprise.

"Caris is summoning the Council," she said quietly. "Salteris had something called a *lipa* in his robes."

His head dropped back onto the cushions of the couch. She saw the shudder that went through him; but curiously, as he closed his eyes, what was in his face was a kind of relief.

"Why?" she asked. "Who were you expecting?"

The bruised eyelids moved a little, but did not open. He whispered, "Salteris."

Bitter heat went through her as she remembered how the old man had embraced him, just before he'd led Salteris into the shed. Her voice shook. "You know as well as I do that Salteris is dead."

His eyes opened again and looked up into hers. "You saw?"

"I didn't actually see you strangle him, no—but we saw enough."

The breath went out of him in a sigh. Two and two, Joanna thought numbly, once again and inevitably equal four. She went on, "But he told us."

His head turned so sharply that he flinched, and the color drained from his face. In the sidelong light that came from the kitchen, she could see the sweat gleam clammily on his cheeks and the bridge of that absurd nose. "Told you what?"

"Who you are."

"Who I . . . ?" His eyes widened, as he understood. "No," he said softly. "Joanna, no."

"He had no reason to lie."

"He had every reason! Joanna, don't you understand? When Suraklin escaped for the last time from the body he was born in—the body that the Archmage and the Council slew and burned in Kymil twenty-five years ago —it was not my being, not my body, that he stole for his escape."

"Then why did he teach you everything he knew?"

"I was his chosen victim, yes," Antryg said quietly, and she could hear the desperation buried under the forced calm of his voice. "Although I didn't know what was intended for me, I suspected—I don't know what. It all became tangled with dreams and madness in the years I lived in hiding, knowing he was dead and feeling his mind seeking mine in my dreams. It's why I had to find a member of the Council in Angelshand to confirm what I feared, though I already knew it to be true—to find where he'd been, *who* he'd been, all those years. For I knew he was alive. In nightmares, I'd see someone I knew looking at me with Suraklin's eyes. . . . And then, in the Silent Tower, he came to me, and I knew him."

"Who?" Joanna demanded, closing her mind furiously against what she knew to be a trap.

"Suraklin," Antryg said softly. "Salteris."

"You expect me to believe that?" Panic made her hands tremble, and she closed them tightly on one another against the arm of the couch. "You expect me to trust your word, after you've lied and evaded me—"

"I had to!" Antryg cried desperately. He twisted against his bonds, then shuddered and went white again, to lie still, teeth clenched, until the nausea passed. "He had an accomplice in this world, Joanna. I knew that much from the marks on the walls here and at San Serano. None knows better than I the terrible strength of the hold he has on the minds of others. And I—I was afraid it was you."

She looked away from him, understanding suddenly why he had feared her; why he had feared even more the attraction that she knew he had felt toward her. Suraklin's gift was to win the trust of others, she thought. No wonder Antryg would mistrust even his love for her—if he was telling the truth.

"I wanted to trust you," he went on. "I couldn't. I didn't dare. If he even suspected I'd guessed he was still alive, he would have hidden, gone underground in some other body, as he did before. I'm only a man, Joanna—one of the very few left who knew him, who might be able to recognize him. And in this vampire state, going from body to body, he is deathless. He had to be stopped. . . ."

"And you're saying that's why you killed Salteris." She shifted her feet beneath her in the chair. Somewhere outside in the night, a warm stir of wind brought her the far-off sounds of the Ventura Freeway and the distant boom of a plane heading into Burbank. "Because Suraklin had taken over his body."

"No." The crumpled, weary lines around his eyes darkened with something deeper than horror or grief. "I killed Salteris because Suraklin had departed from his body. Don't you see? The body he first stole, the one in which he escaped from Kymil, was the Emperor's. As Emperor, he ruled Ferryth for twenty-one years. Only Pharos guessed, and Pharos was a child and could do nothing—could not even dare believe what his heart told him was true, that his father had ceased to be his father. As the Emperor, he tried to have me executed after the Mellidane Revolts—and maybe it was he who pushed me into aiding the rebels in the first place. I don't know.

But four years ago, he left the Emperor, left him mindless as he is now, to take over Salteris' mind and body, to become Salteris—and he left Salteris today, to go on to someone else. I killed Salteris . . ." He forced his voice steady, against the sudden stress of fatigue and grief. "I killed him because I had loved him, because he had been my master, and my friend. I could not bear to leave him as the Emperor is, a mindless, imbecile shell, cared for by others. And except for leaving Suraklin to begin with, it was the hardest thing I have ever done."

Like a litany, she whispered, "I don't believe you. They told me . . ."

"*Suraklin* told you," Antryg insisted desperately. "He had to discredit and kill me. He left one of his gloves in my room, the first time he visited me, and by sleight of hand got Caris to believe he had them both with him. He never came into my rooms the second time, never entered the Tower at all. He couldn't have touched the Void from within its walls; no one could, unless it was opened just outside. But he made Caris think he had by a spell of illusion, and if the Void had not weakened enough for me to escape then, Caris or the Bishop or the Witchfinders would have killed me that night, as he'd intended they should. He cannot afford to leave me alive. You must believe me, Joanna. Please believe me. . . ."

"Shut up!" She turned her face away, panic struggling to the surface of her heart. *If you cannot prevent him from speaking to her, kill him,* Salteris had said. Because she would hear the truth, she wondered, or because she would want to believe the lie?

She heard the rustle of his body as he tried to move again; then it stilled. His voice, when he spoke, was rapid, as if he knew his time were running out.

"He wanted to live forever. From a goal, it became an obsession with him. He had the magic by which he dominated the minds of others; he used spells to break down his own mind, his personality, into thousands of small cells—subroutines, you call them—as if he visualized and formed by magic a duplicate of his personality, which he put into the mind and body of another. I had to learn who it was he'd taken to flee Kymil the first time after his defeat. Until this morning, I didn't know who. And until this afternoon, when you said computers can reproduce the human brain, I didn't know what his ultimate intentions were."

"A computer," Joanna said quietly. She turned back and looked at the tall, gawky form in faded jeans and black-and-silver t-shirt, lying on the couch with his tawdry beads glinting in the reflected light. "Not program a computer to do magic—program a computer to be a mage. And use the teles to feed it electricity."

"At the cost of the life of your world and mine. At the cost of that dreadful pall of colorless grief, of unliving and uncaring, that will cover both our worlds when the computer is ready to run. And no one will understand quite what they are paying, or why. In a generation or two, they will not even remember what it was like before."

Something Salteris had said in this room caught at Joanna's mind. Past the open patio doors, she could see the dark shed against the black of the evening sky where Caris sat alone with the *lipa,* the summoning-spell, and with the Archmage's cold body. She felt a queer stirring along her nerves, the half-sensation of fear and cold, and knew that somewhere close the Void was being opened.

"Just because you're telling me this now," she said softly, "doesn't mean you're not Suraklin."

The muscles of his bare arms moved again as he twisted against the wires. "Joanna, I swear it," he said softly. "What can I say to make you believe me?"

"Nothing," she said. "Because if you are Suraklin, you would say anything. Even . . ." She shut her mouth on the words, *Even that you love me.* After a moment she went on, "Salteris said Suraklin had the gift of making others trust him."

"I see he was right," Antryg said bitterly.

Joanna felt herself grow red. "He didn't give me lies and half-truths and evasions."

"He told you a lie that was consistent from beginning to end," the mage retorted. His breath was fast and uneven. Like her, he could sense the movement in the darkness outside. "Joanna, I followed Suraklin's mark to this place, to the room where I first met you, upstairs here. Later, when I felt the Void opening again, I followed him back and found you in whatever hideout in the hills of Kymil he'd brought you to after his accomplice had kidnapped you from here. I didn't know what he'd done with you before, if anything. For all I knew, *you* could be his slave as well. And then," he said, "at Devilsgate . . ."

She thrust aside the memory of the cobalt dimness of the drawing room, her overwhelming need for him, and the softness of that velvet voice in the gloom. "I don't want to talk about Devilsgate," she said stonily. "I was a fool. . . ."

"As was I," he murmured. "I saw in the cards there that you would betray me. The sixteenth card, the Dead God—the sign they put on wizards to cripple their power when they lead them out to execution. In spite of that I wanted to trust you and found myself doing so, although I knew it was insane. I have always trusted too easily. I could not risk it."

"And I," Joanna said quietly in the darkness, "I can't risk this."

He lay silent then, the kitchen light shining on the sweat on his face and on the lenses of his specs. He stared at the ceiling. Gary, Joanna found herself thinking, would have been gazing accusingly at her; she pushed the comparison from her mind. The fact that Antryg had never shown her anything but caring, kindness, and, she suspected, love, the fact that he had risked his life to save her from the Regent and the Inquisition, and the fact that she loved him did not alter the fact that he was Suraklin, the Dark Mage. Or—was he?

It was not a case of two and two equaling four, but rather a hellish quadratic equation, in which there were two equally correct answers and no way to choose between them. Either everything Salteris had said was a lie or everything Antryg had said was. There must be some logical way to learn the truth, she thought, but she could not arrive at one. She wished desperately that she were better at understanding people or that she had more data.

In the darkness outside, she was aware of movement, and dread chilled her like the onset of fever.

"Joanna," Antryg said quietly, and under the forced calm of his deep voice she heard the tremor of his panic. "I can't prove any of this to you. I know I can't. And it is unfair to ask anyone to make a choice based only on the heart. But you are in danger, too." He shook aside the dampened ends of his hair, where they clung to his bony temples and the last bruised remnants of the Regent's whip marks.

"Suraklin left Salteris' body. He can only have taken over someone else's—at a guess, the accomplice in this world who's been doing his programming for him. The accomplice would have met him at the shed—the shed's marked with his sign as well, you know—when Suraklin guessed Salteris would be more good to him dead than alive, if I'd get the blame for his imbecility as well as the Emperor's. But Suraklin wanted you for something. He stalked you in San Serano—he had his accomplice kidnap you from here and came here to get you, to bring you to that hideout of his, wherever it was. And it's my guess he still wants you."

"Of course," Joanna said, fighting the fear his words brought and her anger at the thought of how easily her fears were manipulated. "He might want me enough to save me from the Regent, or break me out of the Inquisition's prison . . ."

His eyes met hers in the darkness. "You know perfectly well why I saved you."

She turned away. Her voice shook again. "I don't," she said. "That's the whole point. I don't know."

In the hot, gluey darkness outside, the patio gate creaked. Antryg's head came around quickly, and she saw the track of sweat along the high cheekbone. Low and very rapidly he said, "Let me go, Joanna. Please. When they're gone, he'll come back for you, whoever he is now. . . ."

"You're trying to scare me into releasing you. . . ."

"I'm trying to save you, dammit!" He wrenched his arms furiously against the binding wires. In the patio, Joanna could see nothing in the dark, but thought she heard the slur of homespun robes against the stiff leaves in the planters and the pat of quiet feet on cement. Desperately, he said, "Joanna, they'll kill me. . . ."

His eyes changed, looking past her to the doors. Joanna turned her head. Caris stood framed by the night, his face, for all its dust-covered exhaustion, set and queerly serene, but much older, a man's face, not a youth's. His naked sword blade flashed coldly in his hand. Behind him, nearly invisible in their dark robes against the darkness, she sensed others. From that shadowy assemblage, a woman stepped, tall and beautiful in her sable garments, the silver embroidery of the hyacinth stole she wore a pin-prick of reflected light beneath the loose curls of her dark hair.

"Joanna," she said softly. "I am Lady Rosamund Kentacre. In the name of the Council of Wizards, I thank you for what you have done."

Beside her, Joanna was aware of Antryg looking at the Council with the face of a man who knows that nothing he can say will save him.

"Caris told us what happened," the mage said, still in that low, sweet voice that, underneath its beauty, was colder than an assassin's knife. "On behalf of the Council, I can only ask your pardon for the fact that you were drawn into the affairs of wizards. I promise you, for whatever it is worth, that this man will be punished, not only for what he has done to you, but for what he has tried to do to both our worlds."

Caris stepped forward, his dark eyes remote, stern, and curiously peaceful for all their weariness. He was once more a weapon of the Council; he had fulfilled his mission and encompassed his revenge. He had returned to being what he was, something Joanna knew already that she would never do. Three other mages stepped forth from the darkness behind him—all young men, strong, and grim-looking. Two of them wore the blood-colored robes of the Church wizards, and Joanna guessed that peace had been made with the Bishop and the Witchfinders.

Her stomach felt cold at the thought that it would be Peelbone who presided over Antryg's questioning. With the Council and with Caris' account of Salteris' murder, the Regent would not protect him. She remembered the sudden iciness of those evil blue eyes and the shrill voice saying in the dimness of the attic, *You will long for the death my father ordered for you. . . .*

In a kind of daze, she stepped aside, and the mages untwisted the wire bonds from Antryg's booted ankles and pulled him to his feet. He looked deathly white. He knew as well as Joanna did what waited for him on the other side of the Void. *I want to be done with this,* Joanna desperately thought, sick and wretched, knowing that whatever the necessity for destroying Suraklin, this would always remain something she had done. *I want this to be over. . . .*

Lady Rosamund had turned back to the patio doors. Beyond them, Joanna could see forms moving, the stray glint of light on the pool, pale hands uplifting and with laborious concentration making the signs necessary to open one last time the gate in the darkness which separated world from world, time from time. Wind moved the gray draperies and lifted back the dark sleeves from Rosamund's arms. It touched Joanna's cheek and stirred in the graying mane of Antryg's hair. Queer and cold, the smell of the Void filled the room with the terror of the haunted abyss. She thought, but wasn't sure, she heard Antryg whisper despairingly, "No . . ."

Beyond the doors lay nothing, an empty gulf of blackness, as if, beyond the frame of curtain and glass, all the universe fell away.

Caris turned his head. For a moment his eyes met Joanna's. Through the wall of his grief, which was already transmuting into a desperate perfectionism of his warrior's vocation, she saw the last glimmer of his regret—regret at leaving her, perhaps his only nonsasennan friend, and at leaving the possibilities of the strange affairs of the world beyond the perfections of the killing arts. Joanna realized she would never see Caris again. When the Void closed up this final time, it would all be gone—the beauty of dawn on the marshes of Kymil, the twisting, cobbled streets of Angelshand, Magister Magus, and the poor, mad Regent. . . .

With a violent wrench, Antryg twisted free of his guards and made a last, desperate run for the room's other windows. He didn't make two strides. Caris and the mages fell upon him like dogs, bringing him to the floor. Caris' sword flashed as he raised it and brought the weighted pommel down on Antryg's skull with a crack Joanna felt in the roots of her teeth. Then they dragged him to his feet again, still struggling, though he couldn't have been more than half-conscious.

In a chill voice Lady Rosamund said, "Bring him." Caris and the Church mages half dragged, half carried him through that terrible door and out into the eternal darkness that lay beyond.

From where she stood in the doorway, it seemed to Joanna that she could see them for a long time, vanishing down the endless corridor to nothing. She saw a last glint of light on Antryg's spectacles—or perhaps it was only the glimmer of the water in the swimming pool. The air around her was warm again. The wound in the night was healed.

Only what they had been and what they had done remained, tracked indelibly like footprints across her soul.

She realized it was Wednesday. She'd have to go to work in the morning and unravel the hideous mess left by her disappearance.

It was only then that she shed tears.

She knew she could have lain there on the couch where Antryg had been bound and wept all night from weariness, self-hatred, and the stress of shock after shock. But the detached part of her mind told her it was God knew how late already, and Gary would be coming. Of all the people in the world, the last one she wanted to see, to deal with now, was Gary. The thought of listening to that whining self-pity nearly nauseated her.

If only she'd had some proof, she thought, weary at last to numbness. One clue, one way or the other . . .

Antryg could have figured it out. She recalled the blithe, Holmesian quickness of his deductions. *It has been my misfortune to be a good guesser. . . .* Except, of course, if Antryg were really Suraklin, he'd lie.

But the memory of Holmes' name triggered another thought.

She shook her head, telling herself that, for better or worse, it was over. What she wanted to do was useless. But in spite of that conviction, she felt the sudden lurch of her heart as she realized that there had, in fact, been a way to tell.

As she had felt on the island, with the pistol heavy in

her hand, she had the sensation of not wanting to know, of wanting to be powerless because then nothing would be expected of her. After a long time, she mounted the stairs to the computer room again.

Only the small orange lights of the surge suppressors and backup batteries illuminated the darkness, with the ruby gleam of power lights and the green luminosity of the clock. She stood for a long time, looking at the doorframe where Suraklin's mark was. When she had first seen Antryg at the party, she remembered, he had brushed his fingers along the wall, not making the mark, but calling it forth, as Salteris had done only a few hours ago. She'd seen Antryg do the same in the hot, smelly closeness of the rooms upstairs in the Imperial Palace—God, had that been only this morning?—and the Prince's rooms last night. The memory was very clear. All her memories of him were. Antryg in his long, black coat and shabby ruffles, passing his hands in wide sweeps over the lacquered paneling, until his fingers paused on one spot or another. . .

Except for one deliberately placed high up, the marks had all been at only slightly different heights. Hadn't Conan Doyle written in *A Study in Scarlet* that a man will mark a wall at his own eye level?

With terrible vividness, she saw Salteris in this room again, calling forth Suraklin's mark—at the level of his own eyes, six inches below the level of Antryg's.

It proves nothing, she thought desperately. *If he'd thought about it, Suraklin could have made his mark at the level of his chin. . . .*

But other memories crowded back of hands strong around her throat and the hot stir of breath against her temple at San Serano—and then of how, in the alleys near the St. Cyr fortress, panting and exhausted in the silence of the enclosing fog, she'd had to reach up even to put her arm around Antryg's neck so that their mouths could meet.

The man who'd attacked her at San Serano was a shorter man.

Through the open window, she heard the scrunch of tires on gravel. Headlights tracked across the drive, and the barred shadows of the iron fence chased each other over the flickering surface of the pool.

Gary, she thought, sickened with a bitter distaste. She could hear his voice now: *Hey, babe, you can stay here if you want, you know. . . .*

All she wanted was to be alone and to cry for hours, not knowing what it was that she'd done.

The Void was closed.

She would never know for sure if Antryg had told the truth or lied.

No, she thought. If Antryg told the truth—if he was not Suraklin—that uncaring deadness would return, to drain the life and hope from the world. And by that time, Antryg would be dead. She pushed aside the hideous details Caris had once given her. On the other hand, it might be that Antryg's—or Suraklin's—death would prevent that from ever happening.

She was back to the quadratic equation again, with positive and negative solutions, and no way of telling which was which.

He would have come back to this world, she thought, to find Suraklin's computer, and the teles relays which powered it.

Or, she thought, to find another dupe.

She hated to leave the darkened sanctum of the computer room. She felt safe in the fortress of those tiny, steady lights, as she always had. They were idiots savants, but in their inhuman way far more reliable than anyone she'd ever met . . .

. . . If it was inhuman reliability she wanted, that is. If all she wanted to get out was what she herself had put in.

She heard Gary moving around downstairs and knew she had to go.

Done is done, she thought. If Antryg was Suraklin, she had just saved the world.

If he wasn't . . .

There was nothing, literally nothing, that she could do.

Quietly, she descended the stairs.

Gary was sitting at the kitchen table, a glass of red wine before him, the glare of the electric light shining harsh and yellow on his soft brown hair and catching like blood in the highlights of the wine. His elbows were propped on the table, his hands folded before his chin, and his forefingers extended against his lips.

Joanna stopped in the doorway, her first thought only that Gary hated wine.

She wondered where she had seen that forefingers-- extended gesture before. Then he looked up at her with an ironic half-smile.

"Joanna, my dear," he said. "I see you've returned. You should probably telephone your friend Ruth. She's been pestering the police of three states to distraction."

She thought, *Oh, God.*

And for a moment it was just that.

The only answer to two and two seemed to be four, and she understood then why the Prince Regent had gone mad at the age of ten.

Praying she was wrong, knowing she was right, she was perfectly sure where she'd heard that alien, unGarylike speech pattern and seen that gesture. She knew then why she had been stalked and kidnapped, why Gary had insisted she come to his party, where Suraklin was getting his computer, who his accomplice had been, and what had happened to that accomplice when Suraklin had gained what he needed.

She said something—she didn't know what. She felt numb and half-drowned in implications that were pouring into her mind like the sea pouring over a cracked wall; her mind revolved back on itself in a single phrase: *Oh, God— oh God ohgod* . . .

And she knew that Antryg, beyond any ability of hers to find or save, had been right.

The same personality she had known as Salteris—the one who was, she understood now, the Dark Mage Suraklin—was looking at her out of Gary Fairchild's eyes.

EPILOGUE

A CAR SWEPT BY ON VICTORY BOULEVARD, WITH A RISING roar, then a soft swish of retreating tires. One of the pile of cats on Joanna's mangy fake-fur bedspread stretched a hind leg, shook its head, and settled back to sleep. Bright in the darkness of the room, the glowing green list on the monitor screen reached its end: ZYMOGEN ZYMOLOGY ZYMOSIS ZYMOTIC ZYMURGY OK>.

Joanna sipped her tea, and stared at the screen for some moments in silence.

She thought, *Scratch one*.

With the calm persistence of one who works with computers, Joanna hit the reset key and began again, opening the modem, dialing up the communications directory, hitting the S on the menu to call up the San Serano mainframe. When the carrier tone whined, she punched in, not her own user number, but Gary's, tracked down out of the membership directory.

PASSWORD? swam into the screen.

She hit the break key, and typed BABY.

It was a long shot, one of several breaker programs she'd devised to keep herself amused while waiting for the engineering department to bring in test results when she was working overtime at San Serano. In spite of the fact that the computer at San Serano contained classified information and was allegedly protected, breaking into it was relatively simple. Once into the computer itself, she had only to get into whatever files Gary was using to program Suraklin's mind, memories, and magic, preparing them for later transfer to whatever computer it was he'd stolen, piece by piece, by breaking shipping codes—the computer that would be fed by the teles relays.

She took a sip of her tea, scarcely noticing that the liquid, dark and strong as coffee, had long gone cold. The green glow of the clock proclaimed it to be 3:48 A.M. She'd have to be up at seven, if she were going into San Serano to report.

Gary said he'd covered for her with management, creating a tale of family emergency. His questions to her regarding her actual whereabouts and activities for the last two weeks hadn't been particularly convincing, but it had confirmed in her mind that he didn't suspect she knew. They were the questions she'd have expected him to ask, the questions she'd have wondered if he didn't. He'd even pestered her to stay with him—for the sake of appearances, she hoped, though it had taken all her self-control to conceal the loathing and terror she felt, looking into those ironic dark eyes.

I doubt one person in ten notices . . . Salteris—Suraklin —had said. *In time, they cease to remember and don't miss what they've forgotten they had.* . . .

She wondered why she hadn't realized then that there was something wrong or guessed it when Salteris had gotten them into the Summer Palace by terrifying the Prince's horses, injuring them and undoubtedly earning a flogging for the innocent grooms. Antryg would never have been that careless of the safety of others.

Around her, the bedroom of her little apartment was silent. The cats slept again across the foot of the bed like a carelessly dropped fur coat; the dark leaves of the plants glistened with the yellow reflections of the street lamps outside. No breeze fingered the curtain of the open windows. In the dimness, the flashing of the green cursor on the CRT seemed very bright.

Program Baby didn't take long to run. When it finished, the words PASSWORD INADMISSIBLE were still shining on the screen, the cursor flashing expectantly.

Joanna sipped her tea again and stared at the screen. She was beginning to have a bad feeling about this. Getting another user's number was easy enough—it was getting the password that went with the number that was the hard part. The files had to be there—there was no other computer large enough to which Gary would have access and on which he could devise programs for something as complicated as all of a wizard's mind, all of his knowledge, all of his personality, and his magic. It would also be child's play for Gary to write these programs so that they would lie about their own existence, assign larger numbers of bytes to other programs on the directory so that the discrepancy of available space would pass unnoticed. Joanna had similar files of her own in the mainframe. To get into them required a password of up to eight characters, and therein lay the hacker's problem.

Joanna's first hacker program consisted of all words in a standard directory of up to eight letters. In spite of the vast number of random combinations of 26 letters plus 10 digits available, most users selected some easily remembered English word as their password, and the program was written to try them all in succession, with the sublime, uncaring patience of a machine. In her spare hours at San Serano, it had gotten her into any number of classified defense files which the United States government and San Serano's management fondly believed to be secure.

That in itself took several hours. Her second program was the contents of a "What to Name the Baby" book, since most users had a tendency to select names as passwords—that of a wife, lover, child, or dog. She had a third, with those random proper nouns culled from popular culture: Tardis, Gandalf, dilithium, Yoda, Mycroft.

If not A, go to B.

She rubbed her eyes, dialed into San Serano, and punched through Gary's number. The green letters inquired, PASSWORD? and she hit the break key and ran in that third hacker program. As the pixels shimmered across the screen, she massaged the stiffened muscles of the back of her neck, praying this one would work. She'd calculated that trying all combinations of 36 to the eighth power, at the some ten tries per second of which her small desk computer was capable, could take, 3,265,173.5040 days, or roughly eight thousand years. Usually she'd hit pay dirt before that time, but even if it was weeks, she had no way of telling how many days Antryg had left to live.

When she thought about what she knew she had to do, she was perfectly well aware that she was terrified. Throughout the dark hours of the night, since her return from Gary's, intermittent rushes of adrenaline had coursed through her, making her shiver as only social encounters and conversations with her mother or Gary had done, up until two weeks ago.

Caris had told her once that for all his training in the killing arts, he had never, up until a few weeks before, used his skills to protect his own life. Joanna knew nothing about heroism or rescues, but she did know about the patient phlegmatism of computers. As with the problem of the abominations in the meadow, her mind was breaking her task into manageable subroutines.

First, she thought, get the contents of Suraklin's files.

Then stick close enough to Gary to follow him through the Void. Magic wouldn't work on this side of it. He had to go back through. She remembered Antryg's words about Gary's still needing her and shivered. Getting through the Void might be easier than she was prepared to think about at the moment.

Then—Caris? Scarcely likely. The Prince? She shuddered again, recalling the evil glint of those pale eyes. For all his paranoia, he had put his trust once, hesitantly, in Antryg. He would never forgive the violation of that trust.

She pushed the panic urge to hurry to the back of her mind. First things first. You can't get to C until you've gotten A and B out of the way. Part of her wailed, *But they'll torture him*, and the cool, semicomputerized portion of her brain retorted that there was nothing to do but what she was doing. Hurrying would only make it last at least fifty percent longer.

She hit the reset button, opened the modem, dialed, and selected the S for San Serano from the menu. When the carrier tone whined, she punched in Gary's user number and stared at PASSWORD? flicking into life at the center of the screen. Her finger touched the break key, to interrupt function so she could run the main hacker program through.

I can't do anything else, she told the sudden, anxious misery in the pit of her stomach. It could take days— breaking into the files of an employee at San Serano whom she'd idly suspected—correctly—of being a CIA employee had taken weeks.

Antryg was in the hands of the Witchfinders. He didn't have weeks.

Whether Antryg had killed Salteris or left him alive, imbecilic as the Emperor was, he'd been extremely lucky that Caris hadn't cut his throat on the spot. Perhaps that's what Suraklin had been angling for.

There's nothing else I can do, Joanna told herself again.

It will take the time it takes. There are other preparations I have to make in the meantime. If I'm too late . . .

With sinking heart, she knew she almost certainly would be. There were 2,821,109,907,456 possible combinations of eight letters and digits. Even subtracting the some 60,000 entries from the dictionary breaker program and the baby-name program combined, the number remained astronomical . . . and that was only the eight-letter combinations. It could conceivably be smaller. Eight was only the outside limit.

Then she thought, *Suraklin* has eight letters.

So does *Salteris*.

She hit the escape key, and typed, SURAKLIN.

PASSWORD INADMISSIBLE.

She muttered a word she'd picked up from Caris and tried again.

SALTERIS.

PASSWORD INADMISSIBLE.

It had been, she thought, too easy. But the ebb of the rush of hope was hurtful, more so than if she had simply put through the hacker program and gone to bed. Her throat aching, she thought, *I can't be too late to save him. I can't. . . .*

The cursor blinked at her in the gloom. Across the room, the window was no longer black, but a sickish gray, surrounded by a frame of inky shadow. The tepid air felt clammy and close. She was sorry she had hoped. She had been a fool—as Antryg was a fool. Magic was predicated upon hope, he had once said. And it was upon hope, upon life, that the Dark Mage's computer would feed, draining the life of the world.

Joanna frowned to herself, something snagging in the back of her mind. She looked back at the screen. She had one more try at manually breaking into the password, before turning it over to the hacker program, and it occurred to her there, was one other eight-letter combination someone connected with Suraklin might use.

She typed in, DARKMAGE.

The screen went blank, the green shadows of the letters fading sharply out. Then in the middle of the darkness blossomed the words:

WELCOME TO THE SAN SERANO COMPUTER

Her breath went out in a shaky sigh. Her hand a little unsteady with tiredness, she hit the printer switch. The machine hummed to life with a faint, preliminary whirr.

She glanced at the clock again. It was nearly six—time enough to start that long line of subroutines toward a goal too frightening to think about whole.

She typed, PRINT FILES, drained the remains of her cold tea, stood up achingly, and headed for the shower. Behind her, the printer chattered to itself in the darkness.

Watch for **The Silicon Mage**
from Del Rey Books,
Barbara Hambly's brilliant sequel
to **The Silent Tower.**

ABOUT THE AUTHOR

At various times in her life, Barbara Hambly has been a high-school teacher, a model, a waitress, a technical editor, a professional graduate student, an all-night clerk at a liquor store, and a karate instructor. Born in San Diego, she grew up in Southern California, with the exception of one high-school semester spent in New South Wales, Australia. Her interest in fantasy began with reading *The Wizard of Oz* at an early age and has continued ever since.

She attended the University of California, Riverside, specializing in medieval history. In connection with this, she spent a year at the University of Bordeaux in the south of France and worked as a teaching and research assistant at UC Riverside, eventually earning a Master's Degree in the subject. At the university, she also became involved in karate, making Black Belt in 1978 and competing in several national-level tournaments.

Her books include *Dragonsbane*; *The Ladies of Mandrigyn*; THE DARWATH TRILOGY: *Time of the Dark*, *The Walls of Air*, and *The Armies of Daylight*; and a historical whodunit, *The Quirinal Hill Affair*, set in ancient Rome.